ANN BENNETT

The

Orphan
House

Bookouture

Published by Bookouture in 2020

An imprint of Storyfire Ltd.
Carmelite House
50 Victoria Embankment
London EC4Y 0DZ

www.bookouture.com

ISBN: 978-1-83888-156-6
eBook ISBN: 978-1-83888-155-9

The
Orphan
House

To the memory of my great-aunts Georgie and Evie, daughters of Brice Bennett, Superintendent of the County School for Pauper Children in Wargrave, Berkshire. A photograph of the two aunts in the conservatory of the Homestead, Wargrave, taken in 1890 caught my imagination and inspired this story.

Prologue

Connie opens the back door of the orphanage and steps into the chilly passage. It is just after dawn. She stands still for a few moments as she always does, absorbing the atmosphere of the old place. There's the familiar clatter of pots and pans and the breakfast smells floating from the kitchen, the pounding of a hundred pairs of feet on the wooden stairs as the children come down from their dormitories to morning prayers, snatches of their whispered conversations, bursts of laughter. These are the things she hears every morning. But today, there's something else in the air. Something unusual.

She can feel it as she walks down the echoing passage towards the front of the building: a sense of excitement, of pent-up tension. Then she sees what it is and a chill goes right through her. Her father is speaking to Mrs Noakes, the housekeeper, beside the front door. She can only see his back, his silk smoking jacket, his flowing chestnut hair. He is bending forward, peering at something in the housekeeper's arms. Mother is there too, keeping herself to the shadows.

Mrs Noakes is staring up at Connie's father, hanging on his words, her mouth open, her eyes wide with excitement. As Connie walks closer, her heart stands still. The housekeeper is holding a bundle that wriggles and squirms in her arms.

'Yes, Mrs Noakes,' Connie can hear her father's words now, his voice smooth, reassuring, 'As I said, the baby was here when I arrived, a little before daybreak. It was just lying there, quite peacefully, on the step, the poor little mite. It must have been left in the night, just like the others. A gift from our dear Lord.'

'That poor, poor mother,' breathes the housekeeper, 'I can hardly bear to imagine...'

Connie is rooted to the spot. Into her mind's eye steps a young woman – a teenage girl; the picture is blurred because she has no idea what the girl's features might be like, but she is dressed in thin, cheap clothes, wrapped in a shawl, her face pinched and pale. She is walking along the High Street in the dead of night, cradling a bundle in her arms. The baby is crying; the girl's cheeks too are wet with tears. The little town is quiet and dark; the gas lamps would have gone off hours ago. The girl creeps along the front wall of the orphanage and hesitates near the front steps. There is a narrow porch in front of the entrance. She holds the baby to her for one last, agonising, precious moment before laying it down on the step inside the porch. Then, she walks slowly backwards down the steps, and turns to run back the way she came, tears streaming down her face.

The baby starts to cry, the high-pitched sound breaking into Connie's thoughts.

'Here, let me take the little one back for a moment, Mrs Noakes,' her father says.

'It's wonderful that God guides those poor unfortunates to our door, Ezra,' Mother whispers, her eyes nervous, flicking towards her husband for approval.

Connie steps forward. 'Can I see?'

She peers at the tiny face, swaddled in shawls, as her father rocks it to and fro in his arms. The baby is perfect in every way, with its little face crumpled, its chin dimpled. But as she looks into its eyes, a bolt of recognition goes through her and she takes a step back.

The baby quickly responds to the calming motions and its cries gradually slow and die down.

'You've got such a way with newborns, Reverend Burroughs,' says the housekeeper, admiration shining in her eyes. He smiles, and inclines his head in gracious acknowledgement.

'Here, take the baby up to the nursery, Mrs Noakes,' Ezra says gently, handing the baby back. 'I need to go and take prayers. The children are waiting for me.'

'Of course, Reverend.'

'Oh, and Mrs Noakes, I will take care of the paperwork myself this morning. I'll deal with this one personally, just as I have with the other foundling babies.'

Then he frowns and wheels round to face Connie.

'And you need to come along to prayers too, Constance. Right away. No need for you to be lingering here.' His voice is sharp now.

Connie starts at his change of tone and looks up at his face. She sees the look in his narrowed eyes, and suddenly, in that moment, everything falls into place.

Chapter One

Sarah

Present Day

Sarah pulls off the road and parks up on the High Street in front of the old house. She switches off the engine and sits in her car, listening to the steady drum of the rain on the roof, taking deep breaths. She needs to steady her nerves, to empty her mind of everything that has happened over the past two days. Of the stress and the anger, and of Alex.

She knows she's delaying things, not quite ready to face anyone yet. As she sits here, parked in this anonymous place, nothing is final. She's spoken to no one about it, at least not to anyone who matters to her. She isn't quite ready to drive on to her father's house yet, to tell him what has happened, to face his questions and his sympathy.

She fumbles in the glove compartment, groping for the comforting feel of the smooth cigarette packet. The one she keeps for emergencies. This surely must count as one of those.

'Shit.' She remembers, now, taking it out when the car went in for a service.

In the wing mirror she spots a newsagent's shop in a row opposite. She gets out of the car and, without stopping for her coat, rushes across the road and into the shop.

The middle-aged woman behind the counter eyes her curiously.

'I saw you parked up opposite. Have you come to look at the house, love?'

Sarah stares at the woman, trying to focus on what she's saying.

'The old house?' the woman probes. 'The one you're parked in front of. I just assumed… I saw them put up the sign this morning.'

Sarah slips the change into her purse and takes the cigarettes. 'I'm just passing through.'

'Oh.' The woman doesn't look convinced. 'Dreadful mess the place is. Good job it's being sold. That's what I say.'

Sarah lights up as soon as she's back on the pavement and takes a long grateful drag, savouring the sensation of nicotine creeping through her veins. She crosses the road and is about to get back into the car but something stops her. It would be good to stretch her legs, to get some fresh air and calm herself down. Dad won't be expecting her just yet.

She'd managed to hold her anger in check as she'd driven through London, around the North Circular, along the Westway and out onto the M4. Once on the motorway, though, she'd been so overwhelmed by the sheer physical force of her feelings that she'd turned the car stereo up to maximum volume and simply screamed. And as she screamed, she'd pushed her foot to the floor and watched the speed of the car rise through the seventies, eighties, nineties and beyond.

It was only when she'd realised the car in front was slowing down and had to slam on the brakes that she drew back, shaking and sobbing.

There must have been an accident up ahead. All three lanes were blocked, the traffic hardly moving. The next junction was signposted Weirfield, and something deep inside, curiosity, a niggling memory perhaps, compelled her to take it. She'd pulled off the motorway, but was still trembling as she'd swung onto a side road, not sure of the way.

She'd found herself driving through the outskirts of the little town of Weirfield-on-Thames and had hardly recognised the place at first, it had changed so much. As she drove through the town centre, she slowed down out of mild curiosity, trying to remember where the orphanage had been.

The site is now covered by an estate of neat modern houses. Anyone who doesn't know would be unaware of the austere red-brick building that once occupied a half-mile plot. But Sarah knows. She remembers driving past it as a child, before the motorway took the traffic away from the through road.

Now she stares at the rusting front gate of the old house. She doesn't remember noticing this house when the orphanage was here, but it must have always been its neighbour, tucked away behind those tall hedges, shaded by great cedar trees. She notices the For Sale sign, half-hidden in the unruly hedge.

She peers over the gate at the house, dark and brooding, its roof glistening in the rain. It looms over the garden. It's unmistakeably Edwardian; three storeys with twin bay windows either side of a solid front door with a stained-glass window. There are no lights on inside and judging by the state of the lawn, no one lives there.

The cigarette is burning down between her fingers and rain is seeping through her thin sweater. No one's going to notice if she pops into the garden and finishes smoking it on the porch.

She lifts the rusting latch. The wrought-iron gate has dropped on its hinges and as she eases it open, flakes of rust and green paint rub off on her jeans. She steps into the wet garden and pauses on the flagstone path beneath the dripping cedars. Mingled smells of damp grass and mouldy autumn leaves rise to meet her. She hesitates, taking in the shabby paintwork, the missing roof tiles, water spurting from broken guttering, then takes a few steps up the path.

Greying net curtains hang limply in the bay window. A sign on the front wall, half-obscured with moss, pronounces CEDAR HALL.

A sudden gust blows a shower of raindrops down from the trees. Sarah hurries onto the front porch and takes another drag on her cigarette. A note is fixed onto a plastic milk crate with a clothes peg. *One pint only from now on please* is scrawled on it in spidery writing.

'Can I help you?'

Sarah jumps and spins round. A man in a raincoat is approaching, holding an umbrella. She can't see his face in the gathering dusk. A pang of guilt makes the blood rush to her cheeks.

'I… I was just having a quick look,' she stammers. 'I saw the For Sale sign.'

'Excellent. It's doing its job then.'

He holds out a hand and comes closer. Sarah quickly drops the cigarette on the step and grinds it with the heel of her boot.

'I'm Jonathan Squires, of Country Squires, the estate agency in town. I just popped over to check if the sign had gone up, as a matter of fact. I can see we need to clip the hedge a bit.'

His handshake is warm and firm.

'I'm Sarah Jennings.'

'Would you like to have a look inside while I'm here?'

'Oh no, I was only passing through.' How can she explain that she's not interested in the house when here she is, standing on the front porch?

He flashes her a bright white smile.

'It would really be no trouble at all, Mrs Jennings, if you'd like to take a peek. I was going to have a check around inside anyway. You'll have to excuse the state of the place though.' He moves towards the front door, concentrating on a large bunch of keys.

'Old lady who owns it had to go into hospital suddenly. It's only just coming onto the market. No one's had a chance to have a proper clean-up yet.'

Before Sarah has time to find an excuse, they're standing inside the dark entrance hall. She shudders. It's as cold as the grave.

The man fumbles on the wall beside the door and clicks the light on. A single bulb spreads a sickly glow around the room. Sarah takes in the parquet floor and wooden panelling and the smell: mould and cat pee. She can see the man properly now. Close up, he looks older than she'd first thought. Fine lines score his face and she wonders if his luxuriant dark hair is quite natural.

'Do you have a place to sell yourself?' he asks, his voice casual. 'I take it you're on the move?'

She focuses on his face, concentrating on keeping her eyes steady and her mouth from contorting. She tells herself she must try to appear normal, even if she feels far from it.

'Yes, probably, quite soon,' she says, her voice unnaturally bright.

He smiles, a professional smile, still probing. 'Is it in the area?' He shakes his umbrella and slips it into an oak stand beside the door.

Her fists clench involuntarily. She's not going to tell this man that her life has imploded. That only a few hours ago she walked out on her husband with just three suitcases and a couple of tea chests to show for fifteen years of marriage. How can she talk about it to this stranger before Alex himself knows – even though she owes him nothing? Panic washes over her at the thought that she'll have to face this type of conversation soon. People will ask, and she'll have to tell them. How on earth will she deal with that?

'Mrs Jennings? Are you all right?' Jonathan Squires' eyes are on her face.

Her cheeks are hot now. She looks away. 'Of course.'

'You were saying… about your own property? I'd be very happy to come and look. Do a free, no-obligation valuation.'

'That's kind of you, but actually it's not in the area. It's in London. Primrose Hill.'

'I *see*.' He raises his eyebrows approvingly. 'I take it you have children?'

Sarah clears her throat. 'No, as a matter of fact we… I… don't.'

From the flicker of surprise in his eyes, she understands in that second he has reappraised her. He must be wondering if he's misjudged the situation, thinking she's a waste of his time after all. What would a childless, thirty-something woman want with a huge semi-derelict place like this?

He moves quickly towards a door and switches on another light.

'Here's the living room. The old place needs a bit of updating, of course. No central heating, I'm afraid. Try to ignore the décor… and the furniture.'

He gives a short, derisive laugh, nodding at two brown arm-chairs, shiny with age, either side of an enamel gas fire. A couple of faded portraits hang side by side on one wall. One is of a man with a square-set jaw and wild eyes, his white hair swept back from his face, and the other of a mousy-looking woman. On a veneer coffee table are some china cups and a plate covered in crumbs. It's as if someone has left in a hurry. Again, that smell of cats, this time mixed with stale food and town gas.

Mr Squires follows Sarah's gaze.

'They weren't coping very well, Miss Burroughs and her sister. When the older sister died, a few months ago, Miss Burroughs tried to carry on alone, but she's well into her nineties now. Of course, she couldn't manage. She had a fall, you see. That was the last straw.'

'Poor lady,' Sarah murmurs, her eyes resting on a large leather-bound Bible open on the sideboard.

'Well – let's move on,' Jonathan Squires says briskly. 'Come on through to the dining room.'

He strides in front of her across the hall and opens another panelled door. Sarah follows obediently. What a fraud she is, letting him think she might be interested in the house. Why didn't she just say she wanted to stand on the porch and smoke her fag out of the rain? It's too late now though, she's just got to go along with the pretence.

'Once again, needs a bit of work,' he goes on. 'The two Miss Burroughses lived here their whole lives. Their father, old Ezra, was superintendent of the orphanage next door. That got demolished back in the seventies or eighties, I believe. Look, there's a picture of it there. Grim-looking place, wasn't it? Started out life as a workhouse, apparently.'

A shiver runs through Sarah. Above the fireplace hangs a black and white photograph.

CEDAR HALL, WEIRFIELD, BERKSHIRE – ORPHANAGE AND COUNTY SCHOOL – 1910.

She stares at it. The building is just as she remembers, a forbidding edifice, acres of brick and square blank windows, but in the photograph it appears to be occupied, unlike the carcase of a building in her mind. In the photo, children in white pinafores sit on the front steps. A horse and cart trots past on the road.

A memory surfaces, of driving past it in her father's car on their way to London.

'There it is, Joan,' her father would say to her mother in a teasing voice, slowing the car so the building loomed above them, 'my alma mater.' And Mother would stiffen in the front seat and retort in a scandalised whisper, 'Don't talk like that, William. It's no joking matter.'

Sarah would press her face to the glass, staring up with wide eyes at the blind windows. 'Can't we stop and have a look round?'

'Don't be ridiculous, Sarah. It's far too upsetting for Dad. I don't know why you insist on coming this way, William,' her mother would snap, staring ahead rigidly.

One day though, when it was just Sarah and her father, he did stop, and they walked around the outside of the dilapidated building. There were padlocks and chains on the front door and some of the windows were shattered. He led her down an alley at the side and lifted her up to look through a high window. All she could see through the dusty glass was an empty room, as big as her school hall, with a pile of chairs and tables stacked in one corner. It looked neglected and dirty, with torn curtains at the windows and piles of bird droppings on the floor.

'Can you remember it here, Dad?' she'd asked as he let her down.

He laughed and took her hand. 'Not at all. I was only a baby when I left.'

She would often lie awake as a child, staring into the darkness, thinking about that empty hall, imagining it full of children. In her mind's eye, they looked exactly like the orphans in *Oliver Twist*, dressed in rags and pitifully thin. The thought that they had no homes to go to would bring tears to her eyes.

'It was quite a place, wasn't it?' says Jonathan Squires, breaking into her thoughts. 'Oh, and here's a photograph of Miss Burroughs and her sister.'

On the sideboard stands a framed sepia portrait of two fresh-faced teenage girls in floral pinafore dresses, their hair cut short. They are in a greenhouse, surrounded by plants. The shorter of the two holds a watering can and is smiling. The other is serious, staring straight at the camera, a garden fork in her hand. Sarah peers at the inscription:

CONNIE AND EVIE. CEDAR HALL, 1935

'That's the conservatory they're standing in – it's at the back of the house. I'll show you through there now, if you like. Of course, it's deteriorated quite a bit since that photo was taken.'

He ushers her through an old-fashioned kitchen, past a butler sink, an enamel gas cooker on legs and a dresser stacked with crockery. This room smells different: of cooking grease and mouse droppings.

The conservatory runs the length of the house; slatted wooden shelves line the walls, a few plants wilt in earthenware pots, and on the wall the withered remains of a vine. The pull of the past feels strong here, perhaps because of the photo of the two girls, the contrast between how it once was and what it looks like now.

'Just one more room downstairs. I forgot to show you the office.'

Squires shows her back through the kitchen into a large square room at the side of the house. Unlike the other rooms this one is carpeted, lined with bookshelves, and at one end stands an oak bureau. Sarah's eyes are drawn to the ornate marble fireplace and above it, a painting of an exotic landscape. Snow-capped mountains fade into a pale sky. In the foreground a small white church nestles incongruously among palm trees.

She peers at the title written in golden letters on the frame:
ST JOHN THE BAPTIST CHURCH, KANDAIPUR

She really wants to leave now, but feels obliged to follow the estate agent through the rest of the rooms, up the solid staircase to the first and then the second floor, into each of the bedrooms. Her eyes skate over each. They all look the same: lino on the floor, faded floral wallpaper, wooden bedsteads and heavy furniture. The bathroom contains an iron bathtub, corroded with age. Sarah nods and makes polite noises as he opens each door.

'I should be making a move,' she says as they head downstairs.

'You haven't seen outside. Let me show you the outbuildings.'

'No... no. Thank you, but it's quite all right. I must be getting on.'

'Of course, but don't hesitate to give me a call if you'd like to come back. There's an old coach house and stable in the backyard. There's a room above it too. The whole block could be done up. It would make a delightful annexe, should you need additional accommodation.'

He slips her a card. 'Do let me know if you'd like to take another look.'

Back in the car the stress of the last few days and the pain of the morning hits Sarah afresh and she has to take a calming breath to stop it from overwhelming her. She starts the engine and lets it run for a few minutes while the heater clears the windscreen.

Once she's on the road, driving through the outskirts of Weirfield, although Alex and the pain he has caused her are constantly in her thoughts, that crumbling old house, and its hidden memories, forces itself back repeatedly. A strange, tingling feeling creeps over her as she thinks about those dingy rooms frozen in time. She can't get the faces of those two girls in the photograph out of her mind, and soon she's thinking about them instead of Alex, wondering what their lives in that old place had been like.

It's dark as she drives along the main road towards Henley. Rain lashes the windscreen, twigs and leaves dance in the beam of the headlights. She senses the wide river nearby, knowing it is there between gaps in the houses and woods that line the road.

Dad will be waiting for her now, watching from his kitchen window for her headlights.

'I might need to stay for a couple of days, Dad. I hope that's OK?' She hadn't explained why she was coming when she'd phoned him earlier, and he didn't ask.

'Of course. Stay as long as you like. I'll make up the spare room.'

'Don't worry about that. I'll do it when I get there.'

'It's no trouble, Sarah. No trouble at all. I'll cook something nice for supper. One of my stews.'

He'd moved to the house when Sarah's mother had died five years ago. Sold up the old family home in Bristol and bought himself a bijou cottage with a river frontage beside the Thames. Sarah had been surprised; it wasn't an obvious place to retire. She'd worried that he might be lonely.

He seems busier now than ever before, though. He's made friends at the local pub, joined the history society and the chess club and started walking with the Ramblers. He tends his vegetable plot, and has a small rowing boat moored at the end of the garden. He often potters about on the river, fishing half-heartedly.

He appears on the drive in an old knitted sweater as Sarah pulls up. When she gets out of the car, he puts his arms around her and she can't hold back the tears. He says nothing, just hugs her and strokes her hair until the sobs subside.

'Come on inside, Sarah, darling. It's chilly out here. The kettle's on.'

She follows him into the bright kitchen and sits down at the familiar square table. He puts a mug of hot tea in front of her. She takes a deep breath.

'It's Alex, Dad. He's in some sort of trouble.'

'Trouble? What do you mean?'

'The police have been at the office going through the paperwork for the past two days.'

His face drops as she knew it would and he sits down opposite her.

'Good God. What on earth for?'

'I'm not sure. They questioned me too.'

'What did they ask you?'

'They were asking all about the new company Alex has set up. You know he did that recently to fund the expansion of the business. I told the police I don't know anything about it. I haven't had anything to do with it. They could see that once they'd checked through the paperwork. But until they'd done that they kept on questioning me. They were very thorough, Dad.'

Her father's face is drained of colour. He suddenly looks his age, his eyes puffy and sunken. She feels his hand on hers on the table.

'Poor you, darling. How stressful for you. Why didn't you call me? I could have driven up to help you, given you some moral support.'

'I didn't want to bother you with it, Dad. And anyway, they asked me not to contact anyone other than a solicitor.'

'Did you do that?'

She shakes her head. 'I knew I hadn't done anything wrong. It didn't seem worth it. I just wanted to get the whole thing over and done with.'

'Alex is in New York, isn't he? Does he know?'

'Not yet. He arrives home tonight.'

She glances at her watch. His flight will have landed by now. She pictures him strolling through the airport, his raincoat slung over one shoulder, a couple of duty-free bags in the other hand, oblivious to what awaits him.

'They're going to meet him in the arrivals hall and take him in for questioning.'

'Good God! I'm stunned, Sarah. I don't know what to say.'

They sit in silence. The nightmare of the past two days comes back to her; the humiliation of watching the team of strangers rifling through files in the office, removing boxes of papers into the Transit van parked behind the building, while she'd sat there helpless, her stomach clenched with nerves.

'Did the police mind you coming down here?' Dad asks, breaking the silence.

'They didn't need me there any more. I couldn't face staying, to tell you the truth.'

There's a long pause but from his expression she knows he wants to say something.

'Don't you think...' he says finally. 'Don't you think that perhaps... well, perhaps Alex might have wanted you to be there?'

'Oh, Dad.'

She can't answer him. At the moment, she can't voice her anger. She can't tell him that it's not just the police investigation that made her walk out. There's something else, something she's finding hard to believe herself.

Dad is shaking his head, puzzled. 'Are you sure there's not been a mistake? Alex seems so, well, so straight down the line.'

She shakes her head and stares at the table. 'What an absolute idiot I've been,' is all she can mutter.

'Don't say that, Sarah. It's not you who's to blame.'

They sit there without speaking for a while. 'What about the restaurant? Is someone looking after it?' he says eventually.

'No, I had to close up for a couple of days. Cancel all the bookings for the weekend. Tell the staff not to come in. I made up some story about a power failure…'

She thinks about how she'd phoned through the list of clients, smoothed things over, apologised and cancelled all the food orders from the suppliers. She'd done it all in her usual efficient way, in her professional voice, amazed that she was able to speak without betraying her feelings. It occurs to her now that perhaps that's what she's been doing in her own life too: smoothing everything over on the surface, refusing to accept anything is wrong. She's been doing it for a long time.

'I can't go back there, Dad,' she says suddenly.

'But it's your whole life, darling,' her father says gently. 'Think carefully.'

'I know it's my whole life, Dad, but I can't go back there, not after this. I can't work with him now.'

'It's *your* business too, Sarah. Surely something can be sorted out.'

'I can start again.'

Her father looks troubled and gets up to take the casserole out of the oven. He sets it on the side, lifts the lid and sniffs. The kitchen is filled with delicious smells of beef and garlic. When he turns back towards her, she sees tears in his eyes.

'Please don't worry about me, Dad. I'll be fine. I'm strong, you know.'

As if on cue, her phone buzzes. Alex's name flashes on the screen. She presses the button to cancel the call and slips it back into her bag.

Chapter Two

Connie

If Connie turns sideways in her chair and looks away from the television screen she can see the trees outside the window. Since she's been in the nursing home they've gradually turned from green to rainbow shades of russet, orange and brown. She has measured her days here by those changing colours. When the leaves started falling from them a few days ago, the sight filled her with dread. Winter will soon be here. Then the branches will become bare black bones against a white sky.

It will be the first winter she will have faced without Evie. The first winter in her whole life that she won't be at home at Cedar Hall.

She hadn't realised before they started falling, but the leaves seemed to shield her from something; to shelter her from the world and from the sky. She isn't quite sure why it troubles her that they'll soon all be gone. Her mind is hazy nowadays, especially since her fall, but in the back of it lurks the suspicion that he's out there watching her, and that once the leaves have gone, he'll be able to see in through the windows. He'll know without a shadow of a doubt that it really *is* her in that room in the nursing home. He'll be able to see that she has deserted Cedar Hall along with all his possessions and memories; abandoned them to fate when he would have expected her to stay there, his appointed guardian, until the day she dies.

She's still angry with herself for tripping over the cat on the kitchen step and breaking her leg. Poor old Felix. It wasn't his fault, but she had hurt him too when she fell on him. They'd told her, when she got a little better, that he'd been given away.

She looks down at her fragile body under the brown knitted jumper and grey woollen skirt, her frail legs with their knobbly veins, the left one bandaged to the knee and resting on a footstool. What a contrast to the agile, fit girl she once was. In those days, she could walk miles without tiring, work in the orphanage garden digging weeds or tending vegetables for hours without any aches and pains. Time has done strange things to her body.

The door squeaks and one of the carers comes into the room. It's Erica, the Ukrainian girl with the bleached frizzy hair and tight jeans under her overall.

'How are we today, Connie, my dear?'

Connie notices a streak of lipstick on Erica's teeth as she smiles. She purses her lips. Why do they always say 'we' and speak as if she's a child or an imbecile?

'Could you pull the curtains shut, please, Erica?'

The girl goes to the window. 'But it isn't getting dark yet,' she says. 'Don't you want to see the sunset? It's always very lovely from this window.'

Of course she doesn't want to see the sunset. That's why she asked for the curtains to be closed. Has the girl got no sense?

When Connie doesn't reply, Erica whips the beige curtains across the window and switches on a lamp.

'You want the TV up louder, Connie? It is very quiet.'

'You can switch it off if you like,' Connie huffs.

Erica's hand hovers over the button. She frowns, her blue eyes searching Connie's face. 'You are quite sure? Won't you be bored?'

Connie shakes her head emphatically. How can she be bored with all the things she must think about? All the past events she needs to go over, to fix in her mind. She has to get them straight now because for years she's buried them and not spoken about them, even though they've terrorised her thoughts and dreams.

At least she can think about them properly now that she's away from Cedar Hall. The past was such a force in that house that it used to frighten her to step over the brink and go back there to that terrible time.

'I'll put your tea down here,' Erica says.

'Thank you,' she murmurs, hardly noticing Erica move about the room, tidying quietly, moving magazines, clearing a dirty cup from beside the bed. Although Connie doesn't want to admit it, Erica's gentle movements are soothing, comforting even. Her eyelids are soon drooping. It's very hot in the room and, not meaning to sleep just now, she rests her eyes, letting them close for a few seconds.

Soon she is drifting off.

She needs to understand why she acted as she did. She needs to forgive herself for being weak when she knew she should have been strong. All those hours and days, years even, reading the Bible with Evie in the evenings in front of the gas fire, kneeling before bed to pray to God for deliverance, couldn't make up for her weakness. It was like putting a plaster on a dirty wound without cleaning it first. One day the plaster would peel off and the wound would be worse than ever; swollen and angry and oozing with pus.

Would Father be angry with her for leaving the house? For leaving all his things in the office? She's the only one left to guard his memories, to guard the past and all the secrets and lies. It's up to her now, she knows that. She twists her hands anxiously. She also knows that she's failing in her duty.

Connie senses that Erica has stopped tidying and is standing beside her. She can feel the girl's eyes on her face. Connie screws her own eyes tighter, fearing what's coming next.

'It will soon be supper time, Connie. Are you going to come down to the dining room tonight?'

Connie remains silent, but she knows Erica won't be fooled. Erica has leaned even closer now; Connie can feel her hot breath on her face, smell her stale perfume.

'Connie! You are not asleep, I know it,' the girl says, half teasing, half admonishing. 'Do you want me to help you along to the dining room when you've finished your tea?'

Connie opens her eyes. 'What did you say, dear?' she asks, trying to sound vague.

'I asked if you'd like help getting to the dining room. You did so well with the Zimmer frame yesterday.'

'Not tonight. I'm tired tonight.'

'Oh, but Connie! You had such a lovely time yesterday. You made so many friends.'

Connie's heart quickens. She can feel the tension in her body radiating out from her heart, reaching her limbs, making her arms quiver and her palms sweat. She shakes her head and meets Erica's gaze.

'I can't,' she whispers, her mouth dry. 'Please don't make me.'

She sees the concern in Erica's eyes. 'Oh, but they will be so disappointed, Connie. The other ladies… They love to see a new face.'

The tears start welling before Connie can stop them. She lets them fall.

'I'm so sorry, Connie, I didn't mean to upset you.' Erica hands her a tissue.

Connie shakes her head and screws the tissue into a ball in her fist. Why can't the girl just leave her alone?

'Well, if you really don't want to go today, I'll bring your supper in on a tray. But you looked as though you were having such a nice time yesterday.'

The panic begins to subside. It's true, she *had* been having a nice time, for a while at least. Erica and Matron had helped her along the passage to the dining hall. It had felt strange, being out of her room after so long. She hadn't wanted to go. It was a long time since she'd had to meet new people. She could barely remember having a proper conversation with anyone other than

Evie. It had just been the two of them together in that old house for years. They hardly went out in the end, only across the road to the shops to buy food.

But Matron had insisted, and Matron was a formidable force.

'It will do you good, Connie. Help you to get better. Now come on, I won't take no for an answer.'

Connie's bones and muscles had felt weak, and even though she'd had the walking frame to lean on, progress was very slow. It had taken an age to get all the way along the corridor.

Connie had wanted to turn round and go straight back to her room when she'd seen how many people were in there. The noise of conversation and the clatter of pots and pans had suddenly felt overwhelming.

She'd wished she was back at Cedar Hall, hidden away behind those tall hedges, guarding her silence and isolation. But Matron had given her no choice. She'd found her a place at the nearest table next to an old lady with white hair.

'Elsie? Elsie, dear, this is Connie. Could she sit with you? You'll look after her, won't you, dear?'

Elsie moved aside so Connie could sit down. She held out a frail hand.

'Pleased to meet you, Connie.'

Connie eased herself into the seat between Elsie and another woman, stouter and with steel-grey hair, who introduced herself as Marjory.

One of the kitchen staff brought Connie a plate of ham salad and a glass of water.

Elsie smiled, her false teeth even and white. 'Looks healthy, but a bit boring, doesn't it, my love? You're new to Fairlawns, aren't you?'

'I've been here a little while... but I haven't been well,' Connie muttered.

'Oh, I see. I didn't think I'd seen you before. I've been in this place far too long. I know everyone here.'

She introduced Connie to the others around the table. Connie smiled shyly at them as they either raised their glasses of water or gave her a wave and a smile. She tried her best to keep up, but as soon as Elsie had finished introducing everyone, she'd forgotten all the names apart from Elsie and Marjory and a pale woman on the opposite side of the table: Dorothy.

'It's nice to see a new face,' said Elsie. 'Some of us on this table were born and bred in Weirfield. The Weirfield lovelies, we call ourselves.' The other ladies chuckled.

'Marjory and I were at school together, back in the day.'

Marjory smiled. 'You were always the talkative one, even then, Elsie.'

'Dorothy over there is a newcomer,' Elsie said. 'She's only lived in Weirfield since the nineteen-thirties.'

'Yes. I come all the way from Henley originally. I was in service in one of them big houses in the market square,' said the third woman. 'I remember Weirfield when it was just a sleepy little place. A couple of streets of houses. Not like it is now, all built up. We were just talking about it when you came in, weren't we, Marjory?'

'Oh yes. I was just saying how I used to come into the market on Wednesdays with my dad on the front of his cart. We lived on a farm, you see. A couple of miles out of town. There were hardly any cars about in them days.'

'And what about you, Connie? You're not from round here, are you?' asked Elsie.

Connie hesitated, her early confidence deserting her. She hadn't had time to prepare herself for this. What would they remember from back then? What should she tell them? She couldn't lie about who she was, or where she came from. She swallowed and took a deep breath.

'I come from Weirfield too,' she said in a thin voice. The three others stared at her. They were waiting for her to go on.

'Cedar Hall. That's where I grew up,' she said, staring down at the tablecloth.

'Cedar Hall?' asked Marjory. 'The orphanage? Oh, Connie, you poor lamb. You must have lost your parents then?'

Words hovered on Connie's lips. But what words? What should she say? She looked up and her eyes darted nervously from face to face. Father's voice was inside her head now: *Go on, tell them, Connie. There's nothing to fear. As long as you're careful what you say.*

'No, no. I wasn't an orphan,' she explained. 'My father was the superintendent there. We lived in the house in the grounds.'

She looked round anxiously at the others, at their puzzled frowns. She watched their expressions changing as thoughts came to them down the years, as their recollections gradually surfaced.

Elsie was the first to speak. 'So, you must be Miss Burroughs!'

Connie nodded, her cheeks flaming now.

'Your father was the Reverend Ezra Burroughs?'

'Yes,' Connie said in a whisper.

'Really?' said Elsie. 'Well, I *do* remember Reverend Burroughs. He was quite someone about town, wasn't he?'

Connie remained silent. Where was this going? What would they remember? Her heart was beating so fast that she didn't trust herself to speak.

'Oh yes,' chimed Marjory, 'I remember the Reverend Burroughs too. I remember him giving prizes away at the summer fete once. He was quite dashing in those days, wasn't he? Tall. Lovely hair. Always dressed pukka. A real gentleman.'

Connie permitted herself a smile this time. Perhaps it was going to be all right after all.

'Didn't he have *two* daughters? You've got a sister, haven't you?' asked Dorothy.

'My sister Evie, yes. She died a few months ago.'

'Oh, I'm so sorry, my dear,' said Elsie, reaching out and squeezing her hand. So unaccustomed was she to kindness and sympathy, Connie had to focus all her efforts into suppressing tears.

'Well, I remember Cedar Hall too,' piped up Dorothy. 'Huge place it was. Went to rack and ruin before they knocked it down. But I remember when it was full of children. They always looked so well turned out, didn't they? I used to see them on Sundays, in their white pinafores, walking in a great long crocodile down the High Street towards the Baptist church.'

'So they did!' said Marjory. 'And your father was a saint to them, wasn't he? So popular. Do you know, it sounds a bit strange, but when I was small, I remember thinking how nice it would be to live at the orphanage. To have so many friends. I was an only child, you see.'

'Your father had a beautiful car, didn't he, in those days?' remembered Elsie. 'Like Dorothy said, there weren't many cars about in Weirfield then. We used to stand on the pavement and watch it pass. What a wonderful childhood you must have had, my dear!'

Connie nodded, relaxing a little. Perhaps there was nothing to fear from these ladies after all. All they seemed to know about were the good things. Father's secrets were still where they should be; where he had told her to keep them, sealed away in Cedar Hall.

'We didn't have a car on the farm until 1955. But Dad did buy a tractor just after the war,' said Marjory.

The conversation moved on. Soon Connie felt relaxed enough to start eating her salad. She chewed the ham with care, careful not to let the bits slip between her teeth.

Elsie, Dorothy and Marjory chatted away. When they'd exhausted the subject of the first car they'd owned, or been driven in, they began telling Connie about the other residents. They gave her a snippet of their life history, an interesting titbit about each one. They didn't seem to expect her to reply, and Connie was glad of that. She didn't have anything much to say, she was so out of the habit of conversation. But as she listened to their harmless anecdotes she gradually realised that Matron had been right: for a full ten minutes she had forgotten all about the pain in her leg. She had even stopped worrying about home and about Father.

When she'd finished her food, she pushed her plate aside and dusted the crumbs from her lap. The tables were being cleared now.

'Would you like to come and play cards with us, Connie? We usually play a round of rummy before bed.'

Connie's heart fluttered. She had no idea how to play rummy. What would Evie have said? Or Mother for that matter? She could feel their scandalised eyes on her face.

'That's very kind of you,' she replied, 'but I think I'll go back to my room now.' She hoped her new friends weren't offended.

'I expect you're tired,' Elsie said with an understanding smile. 'Do you need help getting back to your room? I'll go and find Matron.'

Elsie pushed back her chair and got up from the table. Connie watched her move between the tables towards the door.

Other residents were getting up too and making their way out of the dining room. Connie watched them leave in pairs and small groups. Everyone here seemed to have made friends. It struck her that none of them looked as she felt: solitary and awkward. A wave of panic washed through her. Would it be possible to learn how to be sociable at her age? After a lifetime of living within the constraints that she had? Did she even want to? It was much easier just to be alone.

Her eyes followed a group of old gentlemen passing her table, laughing and joking as they went. One of them, a tall man in the centre of the group, walked with a stick. He was almost bald, with the remnants of white wispy hair floating on top of his head. She couldn't see his face but something about the set of his shoulders and the way he moved, even with his stick, stirred something deep inside Connie's subconscious. Her heart stood still. She was aware of the whole room blurring out of focus, the clatter of plates and the voices of the residents becoming distorted. She gripped the edge of the table.

'Connie, are you all right?' Marjory asked. 'You've gone a bit pale.'

Connie couldn't tear her eyes away from the man. It couldn't it possibly be *him*, could it? Surely not. It was definitely someone else. Someone who moved a bit like him. But on the other hand, if it was him, *how on God's earth* could it be?

Connie shudders now as she thinks about it. She looks up at Erica, who is still waiting for a reply.

'I'll have supper in my room tonight, Erica,' she says weakly.

She hardly hears Erica leave. She's drifting off again, her mind wandering as it always does, back to that time she tried for years to bury. Tonight, against her will, it takes her to a place that she has trained herself never to visit. But there is no stopping it now. The memories rush to the surface like bubbles in a bottle of champagne when the cork is popped.

It is spring. The hedgerows are coming into bloom, dusted with powdery white hawthorn flowers. Drifts of yellow primroses sprinkle the bank. She's not alone. Her arm is tucked inside his. She can feel the smooth cotton of his shirt against her skin. His body is strong and warm next to her, a comforting shield between her and the river. She knows she should feel guilty, she should feel bad about this, but she doesn't. She can imagine the shock and recriminations that would follow if Mother or Evie were to find out; their wide eyes, their outraged faces, their wagging fingers.

She shakes her head, trying to banish the memory. She can feel the tears welling again, aware that they're tears of self-pity and of mourning for what might have been. She rubs them away with the tissue Erica gave her. This must stop. *There's no use crying over spilt milk.* It's Mother's voice inside her head this time.

With difficulty, she heaves herself out of the chair and, holding onto the furniture, hobbles across the room to her sewing box, the exquisite walnut cabinet on legs that Father had given her on her fourteenth birthday.

Her hand hovers over the lid. She needs courage for this, but seeing that old man with the white hair and the stick has given her a jolt. She needs to confront the past. She's running out of time. She pulls the lid open, takes out the trays of thread, boxes of buttons, folded squares of material. With trembling fingers, she reaches deep into the box and pulls up the velvet lining. She fumbles in the bottom for a few seconds and then her hand closes over it.

The diary is still there. Still there after all these years. She has guarded it, unread, down the decades. She can still see the tear-stained face of the girl with the long dark hair who gave it to her, as clearly as if it were yesterday.

Connie starts as the door opens and Erica comes in with the tea tray. She shoves the book back under the lining of the box and turns back to her chair.

'Wait while I put the tray down and I'll help you,' says Erica. 'What were you doing? Do you want to do some sewing after you've eaten? I could help you get started if you like.'

Connie shakes her head and lets Erica guide her back to her armchair, and set the tray of food over her lap. Is it relief she's feeling; that she's been saved, at least for the moment, from stepping into the unknown?

'Do you want me to shut your box up?'

'Yes, please,' Connie whispers, staring down at the pie in glutinous gravy on her plate. Perhaps God was telling her something when he sent Erica back into the room to interrupt her. Perhaps it isn't the right time after all to start reading the diary. Best not to think about it now. Perhaps tomorrow.

Chapter Three

Sarah

'Sarah! Thank God you've finally answered. I've been trying your mobile all night. It's just been going to voicemail. Where on earth are you? Why aren't you at home?'

She swallows. His voice is just the same, and the sound of it tweaks her emotions in a thousand different ways. Did she expect it to sound different?

'I'm at my dad's.' Her throat feels croaky. 'I've only just woken up. My phone was switched off.'

She props herself up on the pillows. She had a troubled night. Disturbing images in her mind: the police, the restaurant, Alex, a strange old house with musty rooms. She'd twisted and turned for hours, and even after she had finally got off to sleep she'd woken numerous times, sweating, her heart beating fast. She glances at her watch now. Eight fifteen.

'What are you doing down there, Sarah? I thought you were coming to the airport,' Alex goes on. 'And what have you been playing at? Why did you shut the restaurant?'

'Well, isn't that obvious? Haven't the police spoken to you?'

'Sure they have. They met me at Heathrow. I didn't know what was going on, Sarah. You could have warned me! They surrounded me and ushered me into a bloody police van. It was like something out of *The Sweeney*. It was a hell of a shock, I can tell you. They've been questioning me all night.'

'Well, *that's* why I shut the restaurant. I didn't want customers finding out.'

'Why not? I've got nothing to hide. Surely you know that? Bring it on. That's what I said to the guy in charge. Surely *you* didn't think I'd done anything wrong?'

She doesn't answer. How can he be so brazen, so cool? The police had rattled *her* with their questions, and she *knew* she hadn't anything to hide. But Alex has always been the sort of guy who could come out of a bad situation smelling of roses. As if to confirm that, he goes on, his voice bubbling over with ideas, full of optimism.

'I've been thinking. I'm going to open up at lunchtime. I've already been on the blower to Carlo and the rest of the staff. They're on their way in now.'

'What?' Her mouth drops open.

'I'm not going to let them beat me. I'm going to tough it out.'

'I can't believe it,' she murmurs. 'You're not even taking this seriously.'

'Why would I? It's all rubbish. They've got nothing on me.'

'Look, Alex… what are they looking for? Why did they take away the computers and all the accounts and files for the new business?'

'Didn't they tell you? They're looking into how I'm financing the expansion of the restaurant chain.'

'But why would they look into that, Alex? What are they looking for?'

'Search me. Everything's completely above board. All documented, completely legal. They won't find anything wrong.'

'Are they still there?'

'They're coming back later on, but they've gone off to interview Jack at his office in Cheapside.'

A shudder goes through her. Jack Chalmers, a regular at Taste, always coming in with different people for long expensive lunches.

Unsavoury types, who look as though they'd be happier wielding illegal firearms than wearing a suit and sitting in business meetings.

'OK. I know what you're going to say. You've never liked Jack.'

'That would be an understatement.'

She resists the urge to remind Alex that she'd warned him against trusting Jack. It seems irrelevant compared to the other thing, the real reason she can't go back. Anger surfaces again as she remembers.

'When are you coming home, kitten?' he says, his voice softening. 'I need you here. Can you be back for the lunchtime shift?'

'No, I can't, Alex. I'm not coming back.'

There's silence at the other end of the line. Then he laughs, a short punchy laugh of incredulity.

'You're joking, right?'

'No, I'm not joking,' she says in a cracked voice. She mustn't cry now.

'Well, thanks for that. What the hell do you think you're doing, walking out now when I need you most?'

She clamps her teeth together. She's not going to tell him what she knows. Not just yet. Let him sweat for a while.

'Well?'

'You'll manage,' she says finally, keeping a grip on her anger.

'But you're part of the reason people come here, Sarah. You know that. It's you and me. Always has been you and me.'

'Give me a break, Alex. I'm not the reason people come to Taste and you know that. You'll do just fine without me. Carlo knows what to do.'

'I can't believe I'm hearing this! We *are* married, Sarah. Have you forgotten that bit?'

'No, but—'

She stops herself.

'Well? What were you going to say?'

'I'm sure you know why I'm doing this. I don't need to embarrass both of us by spelling it out, Alex.'

'Well, you do, actually—'

She cuts him off and throws the phone on the bed. Within seconds it's buzzing again, Alex's name flashing on the screen. She snatches the phone up and switches it off.

She gets out of bed, pulls a dressing gown on and catches sight of herself in the bedroom mirror. Beads of sweat stand out on her forehead and she's breathing fast. Her long dark hair, usually glossy and carefully styled, is unbrushed and wild-looking. Her face is flushed. Then she sees in the mirror that the door is open and Dad is behind her. He's standing awkwardly in the doorway, carrying a tea tray.

'Are you OK, darling? I couldn't help overhearing some of that.'

She wheels round, about to tell him not to eavesdrop, but there is such concern in his face, and his eyes look bloodshot, with bags of yellowing skin under them.

She stops herself. 'I'm sorry, Dad. I don't want to drag you into this.'

He sits down beside her on the bed and takes her hand. They sit in silence for a few minutes.

'I suppose I should see a solicitor,' she says at last.

'Is that really a good idea? Wouldn't it be better to let things settle for a while?'

She shakes her head.

'I need to move on. Get away from all that. It hasn't been right for a long time, Dad.'

'What do you mean?'

'It's not just the police thing, although that's enough in itself.'

'Really?'

'Yes. There's more. I can't talk about it right now. I can't...' The tears threaten and she takes a deep breath.

'You don't need to tell me anything you don't want to. But I'm always here. You know that.'

'I know, Dad. I appreciate that. Really I do.'

He eases himself up. 'Why don't you have a shower and get dressed and I'll go down and put some toast on? I take it you'd like some breakfast?'

Later, they sit at the kitchen table, sipping coffee and eating toast.

'So, do you know anyone, Dad? A lawyer, I mean, who might be able to help me?'

'Well, if you're sure that's the right thing to do, there's a firm over in Weirfield. Cartwrights. I've been to them a few times. In fact, they did the conveyancing when I bought this house. I'm sure they deal with family matters too.'

'I didn't know you had a local firm to do the conveyancing. I thought it was someone in Bristol.'

'The estate agent put me in touch with them. They were very good. As I said, I've been there for a few things. They've got my will, by the way, when the time comes.'

'Oh, Dad.' She reaches for his hand across the table. 'Don't talk like that, please.'

He's silent for a moment. He opens his mouth to say something, but seems to stop himself. He smiles apologetically and changes the subject. 'I've spent quite a lot of time over in Weirfield lately, actually,' he says. 'I joined the local history society. Pop over there most Wednesday mornings for meetings and the occasional talk.'

'Really? I thought that was in Henley.'

'No. It's a bit more of a drive, I know, but I'm more interested in Weirfield. It's where I started out, after all.'

'Of course. Silly of me, I should have thought of that. Have you found anything interesting?'

'Not very much, I'm afraid. Keep drawing a blank. But I've made a few friends. They're all very interested in my story.'

'What have you been looking for, Dad? Information about the orphanage?'

'I've been trying to find out about my mother, actually.'

Sarah pictures Granny King, a formidable white-haired old lady who always brought chocolate pennies when she came to visit. She'd died when Sarah was about five. Sarah frowns at her father, puzzled momentarily, but then with a sharp intake of breath she realises that he doesn't mean Granny King.

'Your mother? You mean… you mean, your real mother?'

He nods and looks down, avoiding her gaze. 'It's one of the main reasons I came to live in the area actually.'

'Really, Dad? Why didn't you say?'

'Oh, I don't know. Your mum was so anti all that. She hated the whole idea that I was an abandoned baby. Tried to bury it, didn't want to know. After she died I suppose I felt it would be betraying her memory to go digging up the past. But time has moved on and now I feel differently. I feel as though it's the right thing to do. I need to find out before… well, before long, Sarah. I need to find out as much as I can.'

'Of course,' she murmurs. 'I had no idea. It must have been so hard for you, growing up, not knowing who your real mother and father were.'

He smiles. 'It wasn't that hard. I was very lucky in lots of ways. Granny and Grandpa King were wonderful parents. I had an idyllic childhood in many ways.'

'Were you very young when you found out you were adopted?'

'Nine or ten.' He nods. 'At school we were doing something in history about family trees. It got me wondering, for some reason. When I got home for the holidays I did something I'd never done before. I went into Father's study when he was at work and I rifled through his drawers. I found my birth certificate. I was so shaken that it took me a while to confront Mother with it.'

'I can't imagine having that kind of strength at that age,' says Sarah. She's never really considered her father's childhood before, the emptiness he must have felt discovering that his birth was shrouded in mystery.

'It took some courage, I'll admit. Mother was a formidable character as you know. She was a bit angry at first, and that didn't help. But she was a woman of steel, not one to be swayed off course for long. She was quite straight with me. She told me that she and Father hadn't been able to have children, but they'd longed for a son. They'd adopted me from an orphanage when I was a few months old.'

'That must have been a dreadful shock for you, Dad,' she says. Her heart goes out to him, imagining the pain he must have felt as a child, discovering this distressing news.

'I was glad that she'd had the courage to tell me, but I was a little hurt. I felt very disorientated for a while. It was if my foundations had shifted, as if everything I'd ever taken for granted wasn't quite what I'd thought. But children are resilient, and after a while I accepted the situation. I went back to school in the autumn and told everyone I'd found out I was adopted. They all looked at me in a new light. It lent me an air of mystery. Little Orphan Will, they used to call me. Some were unkind, of course, but for the most part it gave me a strange sort of kudos. It seems odd, looking back.' He smiles ruefully.

'When I left school and started working with Father in the business, he wanted to send me over to the States. He gave me my birth certificate to take to the Passport Office. It was then that I noticed that my birth had been registered in Weirfield. Father admitted that I'd been in an orphanage there.'

'Is that when you first visited the orphanage?'

'Not at the time, no. I was back and forth to America, establishing contacts out there. Life was busy. I met your mother, and it wasn't until the mid-seventies that I finally got round to making the trip to Weirfield. By which time the orphanage had closed down, as you know.'

Sarah thinks of the picture of the orphanage hanging in the dining room at Cedar Hall, the silent rooms where the past seemed to lurk in the shadows, the faded portraits and the musty smells.

'I meant to tell you before, Dad. I should have said yesterday but because of everything else... well, I stopped in Weirfield on the way over here yesterday. I needed to buy some cigarettes and I parked outside a house that's for sale. It looked empty and I wandered into the garden to have a smoke. The estate agent turned up out of the blue. There was a bit of a misunderstanding and he insisted on showing me round. It was a spooky old place. It was the house beside the orphanage.'

'Cedar Hall? How extraordinary. That's where the old ladies lived. The Burroughs sisters. Their father was the superintendent of the orphanage. They both taught there themselves until it closed.'

'But they don't live there any more. One of them died recently and the other is in a nursing home.'

'Really? How very sad. You know I tried to speak to them once, a couple of years ago. I wanted to find out what I could about the orphanage. See if they had any old records that might help me with my search.'

'And?'

'I wrote them a letter first, telling them what I wanted, so as not to surprise them. I knew they were very old. I waited a month or so and they hadn't replied, so I went to the house. I got short shrift, I can tell you. One of them came to the door after I'd rung the bell three times. Tall and stately she was, with grey hair piled on her head like an Edwardian lady. She wouldn't open the door fully, kept it on the chain and peered at me for a long time as if I was a burglar. I explained who I was and that I was interested in finding out about the orphanage. When she heard that she got quite frosty. She basically sent me packing, saying there were no records in the house and that I wasn't to bother them again. She did suggest I tried the church, though. It was very odd, getting that sort of reception. She struck me as a terribly cold customer. I've wondered about her ever since.'

'How strange.' Sarah shudders. She thinks of that photograph again, of the two young women in the conservatory, so fresh-faced, so full of life.

'I could hear the other one in the background calling from another room, asking who was at the door.'

'How very unsettling. Did you try the church records in the end?' Sarah asks.

He shakes his head. 'I did try, but didn't find anything very much. The church warden showed me the parish records for the year I was born, 1934. There were dozens of single women living in Weirfield then. It's impossible to know who my mother might have been. It could have been someone from another parish altogether.'

Sarah watches him for a moment. This sudden interest in his birth mother is all so new and strange. It's good that he has found something he's passionate about, but all the same, what if it ultimately leads nowhere? How will he feel then? She doesn't want his hopes to be dashed. He's getting on now, and beginning to look a little frail. What effect could that sort of disappointment have on his health, she wonders.

'What does your birth certificate say again?' she asks carefully, after a pause.

'Wait a minute. I'll go and fetch it.'

He leaves the room and Sarah listens to him opening drawers in his desk in his little office across the hallway. In a moment, he's back.

'Here it is. Doesn't say much.'

Sarah stares at the fading, yellowing parchment.

Baby boy, born approximately September 5th 1934. Place of birth, unknown; father, unknown; mother unknown.

*

She looks up at him. The pain in his eyes makes her start. She has never thought before how it must have felt over the years, knowing that your real mother gave you up, wondering what dreadful events or circumstances would have led her to abandon her precious baby. She feels a rush of sympathy for him and once again she reaches across the table. He takes her hand and squeezes it.

She glances back at the certificate and looks at the signatures at the bottom of the page. Although she should have known it would be there, the name written with a confident flourish still sends shivers down her spine. She's not quite sure why.

Signed the Reverend Ezra Burroughs, before the Registrar of Weirfield District, R. Hunter, this 30th day of September 1934.

Chapter Four

Connie

Connie shrinks down in her armchair, listening to the other residents making their way along the corridor for lunch. Her nerves are taut, her ears alert for the sound of someone approaching her door. She is dreading Elsie, Dorothy or Marjory knocking on it and asking her to come along to the dining room. Matron might even put them up to it. Connie has her answer ready, though, in case they do call. She's feeling poorly; her leg is worse today. She strains to hear their voices among the others. There's another voice she's listening out for too, although she barely acknowledges the thought.

How will she ever be able to face another trip to the dining room? He'll be there again, for sure. Along with those bittersweet memories. She doesn't want to remember those times. It's too painful. Even more painful than remembering the other things she's been burying all these years.

Despite herself though, she allows her mind to pause for a second and wonder how different her life might have been if he'd stayed. Would she be here now, lonely still among all these strangers? How would she have spent those decades? Not studying the Bible and praying with Evie in that chilly old house, she's sure of that. Tears of self-pity prick at her eyes and she tries to stifle those thoughts.

Instead she allows her mind to wander back to what Elsie and the others had said at lunch yesterday about Father in his glory days. The father who would cut a dash about town.

She remembers how much he cared for fashion, dressing like a gentleman in silk shirts and coloured waistcoats. He would spend days away in London getting fitted for new suits, and come home in his beautiful Jaguar, the back seat and boot laden with boxes of new clothes and shoes. Connie smiles as she pictures the ripple of excitement in the orphanage when he strode in to take prayers each morning; his mane of thick chestnut hair flowing behind him, the sleeves of his silk shirt billowing, and his fine chiselled face held high. His intense black eyes would scan the room, taking in everything and everybody.

Elsie had remembered Father's motor car too. The Jaguar was his pride and joy. He kept it in the old coach house, and at first, he would pay some of the older boys in the orphanage a few pennies to polish it every week. When he brought it home for the first time Connie must have been nine or ten. She and Evie were allowed to sit on the slippery back seat that smelled of new leather while Father drove them out of town and along the river to Henley. They had dressed up in their best for the occasion. How proud she'd felt as they swept along Weirfield High Street, where people stopped to stare. Perhaps Elsie and the others were among the bystanders that day?

Father had taken her and Evie for afternoon tea in the Red Lion Hotel at Henley, where they sat at a table in the window overlooking the River Thames. She remembers how Father drank beer out of a tankard at the bar, chatting to the barman.

She sighs. It was the Jaguar that had brought Tommy into her life years later. Soon she is back to thinking those forbidden thoughts again. There's no escaping them.

'Would you take a cup of tea out to the coach house, Constance?' Father had said after breakfast one morning. She remembers that day clearly. It was the spring of 1937.

*

'Tommy's out there working on the car.'

'Tommy?'

'Tommy Braithwaite. You must remember him. He was one of our dear orphan boys. Went to work on a farm near Wokingham when he was fourteen or fifteen. He must be twenty-one now. Old Farmer Webb has sadly passed away and Tommy came to see me last week, saying he was out of work. I've given him a job as my driver.'

Mother raised her eyebrows and Connie sensed her disapproval. But Mother said nothing. She always did. And in any case, Father's generosity in giving a young man a chance in life outweighed any negative thoughts it might engender. He had a habit of making grand gestures like that.

As Connie carried the cup of tea out to the garage that morning, she tried to remember Tommy's face. There had been so many boys passing through the orphanage, it was difficult to distinguish him in her memory from the others.

She remembers now how she paused with the cup, seeing him squatting in front of the car, polishing the chrome radiator, as she approached. Even in that position she could tell that he was tall and lithe. He was wearing a white shirt with the sleeves rolled up. She noticed his hard, muscular arms, sunburnt from his outdoor life. He turned when he heard her approach and she instantly remembered his face from the old days. Lively brown eyes, full of mischief, unruly dark hair flopping over his forehead.

He leapt up, smiling, thanking her for the tea. The way he looked straight into her eyes with his frank honest gaze sent the blood rushing to Connie's cheeks. There was something about that look that made her feel so self-conscious she couldn't wait to get away.

They hardly spoke on that first occasion. Connie hurried back into the house, confusing emotions flooding her mind.

But as she took her class in the orphanage schoolroom that day, he was all she was able to think about.

She'd felt compelled to go back the next morning with another cup of tea, and this time they'd exchanged a few words. She can't remember what was said but she knows that he insisted on calling her 'Miss Burroughs', and that she gently corrected him each time he said it.

But it wasn't the words that mattered. She was drawn to his honesty and his simplicity.

Tommy had a twinkle in his dark eyes. She stayed longer each morning when she brought him his tea, letting him pay her compliments, even though they made her blush. She had the feeling that it was wrong, that Father and Mother and Evie would disapprove, but that didn't stop her. In any case, all three of them were occupied from morning until night, looking after the hundred or so orphans at Cedar Hall; taking prayers with them, teaching them, tending to their needs. They didn't have time to notice Connie's new interest in Tommy.

She whittles nervously at the filigree chain she wears around her neck. The tiny key is smooth between her fingers; her eyes stray to the sewing box. She stares at it for a long moment as she wonders whether she has the strength to begin reading the diary today.

A trolley rattles along the corridor, the sound of plates and glasses chinking together. Erica or Mairead, the young Irish girl, will be here with her lunch soon. She closes her eyes and takes a deep breath. After lunch she will force herself to do it, in the dead hours of the long afternoon.

In the meantime, she needs to put Tommy out of her thoughts. She remembers the promise she made to herself to go back to the beginning and face up to the past. Her eyes still screwed shut, she scans back down the years, back to well before the time that Tommy came to work for her father, trying to pinpoint exactly when things had started to go wrong. Or at least when she started

to question some of the things that happened around her, things
that she and Evie and Mother never spoke about.

Some workmen came to paint the room above the coach house
where once a stable lad would have lived. She remembers how
Father took to spending time up there alone. He forbade Connie
or Evie to go into the room.

Evie and she used to play hide-and-seek there, and it irked her
that it would be out of bounds. Once, they plucked up enough
courage to ask their mother about it. She sat them down in the
parlour and told them that it was Father's private room, and that
they were not to go up there or ask questions about it or he would
get very angry.

'But Father already has a private room,' Connie protested. 'He
has his office.'

Evie shot her a warning look. Connie knew it was wrong to
challenge her mother and already a flush was creeping up Mother's
neck.

Mother leaned forward. 'Your father is a very busy and important
man, Connie,' she said quickly, in a low voice that trembled ever
so slightly. 'Running the orphanage is a big responsibility for him,
and we and all the poor orphan children all depend on him. I don't
want to hear you questioning what he does, or mentioning that
room ever again.'

Connie hung her head.

'Now go and fetch your prayer book and we will pray for Father's
health and give our thanks to God for Father's love and protection.'

Connie never spoke about Father's room again, but she couldn't stop
thinking about it, and glancing up at the curtained window whenever
she was out in the yard. It fascinated her, and she would have loved
to go up the stone steps at the side of the building to peep through
the window, but even the thought of doing that made her tremble.

Evie didn't seem to have the same sort of curiosity as Connie
did about the room. Perhaps it was the difference in their ages, or

perhaps it was just because they were so different generally. Connie couldn't help thinking, although she felt dreadfully disloyal when the thought came into her head, that Evie lacked imagination. In comparison to Connie, she was remarkably accepting of the world around them; the world Father mapped out for them. Evie seemed to accept what Father said without question and took it as her mantra, never deviating from the narrow path he wanted them to tread. Connie, on the other hand, was naturally imaginative and curious, and it took all her effort not to ask the questions that were burning on her lips.

Evie was particularly tight-lipped about the room above the coach house. She would give Connie a severe look if the subject ever came up. It was almost as if she'd been sworn to silence about it, as if she knew something Connie didn't.

Sometimes Father would not go up there for weeks at a time, but at other times he would spend long hours in there, even sleeping in the room overnight. On those occasions, when he finally emerged he would look dishevelled, his face grey with exhaustion. And his eyes would be preoccupied and brooding. Connie and Evie would know that they must take care not to disturb him or do anything to upset him.

It was years later, when Evie was sixteen and had made the transition from pupil to teacher, taking over a class of orphans, that Connie first noticed something new and strange about Father's room.

She was walking back through the orphanage gardens towards the house alone. It was winter and a storm was whipping up. A wooden gate in the high brick wall separated Cedar Hall from the orphanage. She had struggled to close the gate against the wind and dropped her exercise book. The wind had snatched the book up and carried it, pages fluttering, across the lawn and flower beds. She'd cried out and ran after it, knowing the ink would be running in the rain and imagining the schoolmistress's cane on her knuckles the next morning. The book blew across the yard and came to rest in front of Father's car, parked in the garage inside the coach house. It was dark inside the garage, but she didn't have to see it to know the book was ruined. She stood there catching her breath, wondering what words she could use the next morning to tell the teacher what had happened.

But as she stood there beside the gleaming car, she heard a strange sound. It was coming from the room above the coach house, directly above where she stood. The sound was muffled, but she was almost sure it was the sound of someone crying. Chills ran through her body. Whoever could that be? Was she imagining it? Perhaps it was the wind? She was still wondering what to do when she heard the outside door above her slam and the sound of someone walking down the steps. She flattened herself against the wall and held her breath. As she watched the doorway, she saw her father silhouetted against the wall by the lights from the house as he crossed the yard.

Chapter Five

Sarah

Sarah parks in a quiet backstreet. The town is bustling. There has been a market today and stallholders are starting to pack up, stacking crates into vans, sweeping rubbish into piles. She crosses the market square and walks past the shops that line the High Street.

The solicitors' office is in an imposing red-brick Georgian townhouse, set back from the road with black railings separating it from the pavement. She walks up the front path, hovers on the flagstone step and glances at the brass plaque beside the door:

CARTWRIGHTS, SOLICITORS AND COMMISSIONERS FOR OATHS, FOUNDED 1925

The receptionist shows her into the waiting room and she sits on the edge of a button-back leather armchair and bites her nails, wishing she'd had time to have a cigarette before coming in. Perhaps Dad was right. Perhaps it was too soon to be taking this step, but she had felt the need to do something.

'Mrs Marshall is the partner who deals with family matters,' the receptionist had said when she called. 'She's had a cancellation this afternoon, so we can fit you in. It's lucky you called when you did.'

Sarah looks around the room. It's fitted out like a cross between a country club and a library in a stately home. It's furnished with heavy antiques and leather armchairs and smells of polish and cigars. Bookcases housing copies of law reports line the walls, and above the fireplace hangs an oil painting of a Victorian hunting scene. A grandfather clock ticks away in the corner.

How Alex would laugh at all this. He loathes anything he considers to smack of small-town snobbery and his taste is reflected in the décor of the restaurant where she's spent so much of the last few years. Ultra-modern and minimalist with clean lines and no clutter. Her mind wanders back there. It is three thirty. Normally, at this time, the lunch guests are drifting away, back to their offices. Carlo will be ushering them to the door, finding their coats. The waiters will be clearing the tables, preparing for the evening. The kitchen staff will be winding down, putting equipment away, scrubbing the surfaces, cleaning the floor.

It feels odd not to be there, in charge, looking after the staff, chatting to the diners, making sure things run smoothly. Dad was right, it has been her whole life. All she has ever really known since she left college.

'Mrs Marshall will see you now.' The young, blonde receptionist is standing in the doorway, a sympathetic smile on her face. *She must know what I'm here for. She feels sorry for me*, Sarah realises. Feeling defiant, she raises her chin and smiles brightly as she walks past.

Judith Marshall is a large woman dressed in a tweed suit and flat practical shoes. She looks to be in her mid-fifties, with wispy grey hair caught up in a straggly bun. She reminds Sarah of an eccentric schoolteacher. She gives Sarah's hand a firm shake and offers her tea.

'Do take a seat.' She pours the tea and hands Sarah a cup. 'Now, how can I help you, Mrs Jennings?'

'I need some advice,' Sarah says, settling herself into a chair opposite the desk. 'I've left my husband and I need to know my position.'

'Of course. I understand.' A reassuring, almost motherly smile. 'That's what I'm here for. Now, fire away. Tell me all about it. When exactly did you leave?'

'Yesterday.'

'And was it a sudden decision? Did something particular happen?'

'It felt sudden, but in actual fact, it has been building up for some time. What happened this week brought it all to a head.'

Sarah hesitates. This feels odd, telling it all to a stranger when she hasn't told anyone else the full story, not even Dad. Judith Marshall is looking at her with kindness and sympathy in her soft grey eyes. Her pen is poised above her notepad and her attention is completely focused on Sarah. It's good that she isn't intimidating, but will she understand? She must have heard different versions of the same story a thousand times. How on earth can she stand it, seeing nothing but the rotten side of life, the underbelly of people's relationships, like turning over a stone in the garden and seeing all the worms and insects crawling underneath.

'I don't quite know where to start.'

'Well, why don't you start by telling me why you left? We can work back from there.'

Sarah takes a deep breath and tells her about the early-morning visit from the fraud squad. Was it really only two days ago? She tells her everything. All about how the police had gone through the files in the office, through the computers, all the accounts, how they had questioned her and how they had removed all the files and paperwork that related to Alex's new business.

'I went back home, packed a few things and left.'

'Was it the shock of the investigation? Do you think your husband *has* done something wrong?'

She shrugs. 'I'm not sure, but perhaps. He can get very carried away with his ideas. Sometimes he doesn't have the best judgement. He cut me out of the expansion of the business completely and set up a new company with people I don't trust. I wasn't happy about it, but he went ahead without me anyway.'

'I see. Do go on.'

'We'd always done everything together. I met him when I was at university, in the holidays. I was working as a waitress in a restaurant in Bristol. He was the head chef there. He was so charismatic, so inspiring. He had all these ideas about setting up his own place. He persuaded me to leave university and go and live with him, work with him. It all happened very quickly.'

'We bought a shabby old Victorian place in the city centre and did it up ourselves. Worked all hours, put everything into it. Alex took the lead in setting up the restaurant business and I organised the renovations. It seemed to work out well, and the restaurant really took off. After a few years we moved to London and bought premises there, the same formula on a grander scale. We were a good team. It was going really well in just two places, but Alex wanted more. He'd got a bit of a name for himself as a chef by then, written a few cookbooks.'

'Yes. I'm sure I've heard of him.'

'He could have capitalised on that. He was offered a TV series, but he didn't want to go down that route. He was happier in the restaurant, cooking for customers, doing what he loved. Things were fine for a few years, but after a while he got restless. He got this idea that he would open up branches all over the country, in foreign capitals too. But he needed an investor. I didn't want to go into business with the people he chose. That's when things started to go wrong, really. We argued about it a lot. But in the end, he didn't care about what I felt. He went ahead anyway.'

'I can see why that would cause difficulties. So, when the police came calling, that was the last straw? I need to understand why you've left your husband, you see, so that I can advise you of the best way to proceed.'

Sarah nods. She hesitates but she knows she has to say it now. Tell this woman the truth. The trouble is, she has not spoken the words to anyone, not even herself. How will it feel when she says them out loud? She digs her nails into the palms of her hands and takes a deep breath.

'It was, but…' She looks down, trying to summon the strength to say it. 'But there was something else. I might have been able to withstand all that business with the police, but…' She screws her mouth up in an effort not to cry.

'Take your time, Mrs Jennings, please. If there's something else, I'll need to know about it.'

'Well… when the police were going through the accounts, they showed me some of the entries, to see if I knew anything about the new business. They thought I was in on it too at first, though what they're trying to prove I still have no idea.'

'And?'

'And… there were two bank accounts set up in the name of the new business, and I'd never seen one of them before. It was a personal account in Alex's name, meant to be used for expenses when he went on trips. Regular sums were coming into it from our main business account and regular sums were going out too, to a name I didn't recognise. Well, not at first anyway. A Miss Jemima Brown. I stared at it for a long time, and then I realised. Jemma. She was one of the part-time waitresses in the restaurant. She only worked there for a few months. She was a lot of trouble from the start, always flirting with the customers, causing problems among the staff. I had to fire her in the end. That was two years ago. This account was opened around that time, and payments had been made to her every month since then. Thousands and thousands of pounds…

'I was stunned. I couldn't believe it. I felt sick. When I finally managed to get away from the police, I went home and the whole thing went round and round in my mind. He must have been seeing her all this time. Over the past few months he's been away a lot on trips to look at new premises… I'd never even given it a second thought. Never considered he might be seeing someone else. I couldn't bear to think about it. So that's why I left him. It wasn't just the police investigation.'

Judith Marshall is looking at her with a furrowed brow. 'I'm so sorry…' she says, shaking her head and scribbling something on her notepad.

There's a silence. Sarah's eyes wander around the room. High-ceilinged, furnished in the same style as the waiting room, only here there's a homely feeling of comfort and organised chaos. Papers and files are piled on a side table, there are pot plants everywhere, a comfortable-looking settee with worn upholstery is under the window that looks out over a small park. A mother is pushing a toddler on a swing, to and fro, to and fro. The child is wearing a red anorak. For a moment Sarah is drawn into the scene, but she checks herself quickly and looks back into the room. Judith Marshall is still busy making notes, head down, hair falling out of its pins.

On the wall behind her is a black-and-white framed photograph of a man. He wears round pebble glasses and a three-piece suit with a waistcoat and watch-chain. His skin has the smooth appearance of a plump man's and his hair is receding. He has an elaborate moustache. Under it he is smiling. As she looks at him, it feels as though he's looking right through her.

She tears her eyes away. Mrs Marshall has finished writing.

'Thank you for going through all that for me, Mrs Jennings,' she says, looking up. 'It must be very painful for you, but as I said, I needed to have all that information to advise you on your best grounds for divorce. Now, without further ado, let's get to the nub of the financial side of things as far as we can today. I need to know all about the business and about your home. What you think they might be worth, who put what in when. All your assets, in other words. Then we can work out what you might be entitled to.'

There's a knock at the door and a man puts his head round.

'So sorry to disturb you, Judith,' he says, 'but do you have those papers we were discussing this morning? I'm about to go to a meeting about that matter, and think I left the file in here. Many apologies,' he says in Sarah's direction. She looks at him and almost starts. It could be the same man she's just been looking at in the photograph.

'Mrs Jennings,' says Judith Marshall, 'this is Peter Cartwright, our senior partner. Peter, Sarah Jennings, a new client.'

He strides into the room and shakes Sarah's hand.

'Please don't get up.' He waves her back into the chair. 'Delighted to meet you. I'm so sorry to butt in.'

Sarah can't help staring at him. The resemblance is uncanny. Only his blond hair flops over his forehead untidily.

Judith hands him a file and he is soon gone.

'Peter's the grandson of Joshua Cartwright. The man who set up the firm in the thirties. He resembles Joshua's portrait quite a bit.' Her eyes move to where Sarah's had been just moments ago.

'Yes. I was quite shocked.'

'It takes everyone by surprise. Apologies for the interruption.' Judith pauses, looking back at her notes. 'Now, where were we?'

Later, Sarah wanders back along the street, glad to be out in the fresh air, released from the tension of the discussion with Judith Marshall. Her head throbs from the effort of exposing and discussing her pain. She stops in a shop doorway and lights a cigarette, feeling as though she needs to walk for a long time. Walk until her legs ache and her head is clear. If only she'd worn flat shoes instead of these uncomfortable high-heeled boots.

She walks along the High Street glancing absently into the shop windows. There's nothing much here. It's a small town. A florist, a couple of bakers, a butcher's, a gift shop and a coffee shop. She carries on past them, past a Victorian pub – The Boatman's Arms – and a French bistro – Le Gastronome. With the eye of a professional she glances through the window and fleetingly takes in the gloomy interior, the worn Moulin Rouge-style décor and the fact that only three tables are occupied. After that the shops peter out, so she crosses the main road and heads down a side road. She has no idea where she's going, but it feels as if it's in the direction of the river.

Her mind is occupied with what Judith Marshall has said. She should be entitled to half the value of the business and the proceeds of the sale of the house. But it hasn't meant much to her. The money is secondary to the hurt and confusion she feels. Before today, she'd hardly considered what her share of the business might be worth. The whole thing had been indivisible, like she and Alex had been when they first started out. And even though Alex has hurt her deeply, it seems a betrayal to think like that, a betrayal of all those years they spent as partners, building it up together.

'Of course, we'll have to find out more about this police investigation. They might well try to freeze the assets of the whole concern while they look into this new business, but we can try to prevent that,' Judith had said.

Sarah's head reels with information. She hadn't expected things to move forward at this speed – she'd gone there to try to stop feeling powerless, to find out her rights. But now she feels as though she's put something in motion that she has no control over. Her head is spinning as she walks along the tree-lined street with its red-brick villas and lush, well-kept gardens.

At the end of the road stands a small stone-built chapel with plain arched windows either side of a wooden door. She stops outside. ST JOHN THE BAPTIST, WEIRFIELD is written in faded lettering at the top of a noticeboard. Pinned to the board is a torn poster proclaiming, 'God is the Answer'.

She stubs out her cigarette on the pavement and wanders into the little graveyard behind the building. She sits down on an old wooden bench and stares at the gravestones nestling in the uncut, yellowing grass. They look grey and forlorn and the sight of them brings home her sadness. A painful lump forms in her throat and finally, she lets the tears come. Sobs shake her body and the ache in her chest and head becomes intense, but letting the tears flow doesn't dull the pain.

Finally, she dries her eyes and gets up to go. She knows she needs to put her sadness behind her and move on. Talking to Judith, it has come home to her that her life in London is over. She realises now that it makes sense to spend some time around here, be near her father. There's a niggling feeling in the back of her mind that she hasn't seen enough of him over the years. It would be good to do something to redress the balance, especially as he seems rather vulnerable now. All that talk of his birth mother last night had shocked Sarah. She doesn't want him to be hurt by what he finds. Perhaps, by staying in the area, she will be able to support him in his search; to protect him if what he finds is unexpected or unwelcome in some way.

Opposite the bench are three graves in a row, close together. The gravestones of two of them are weathered and worn, but the third one is new. The grass on that grave itself is young and sparse. She peers at the names on them and draws back quickly.

EZRA BURROUGHS, BORN IN THE YEAR OF OUR LORD 1890, LONDON, DIED 1985, BELOVED FATHER OF EVELYN AND CONSTANCE AND HUSBAND OF EDITH.

The second gravestone belongs to Edith Burroughs, BORN 1900, DIED 1982, and the third grave belongs to Evelyn Burroughs, BELOVED SISTER OF CONSTANCE. A chill runs through Sarah from her scalp to her toes. How strange that she should be confronted by the graves of the Burroughses, when they've been so much on her mind since she went inside Cedar Hall. Suddenly she doesn't want to be in here any more. She picks up her bag and leaves quickly.

Chapter Six

Sarah

This time she doesn't cross the main road back to the market square but turns left and walks along the pavement closest to her. There are a few shops and businesses on this side. The pavement is narrow and each time a vehicle thunders past, the draught blows her sideways, but it soon widens out and the shops give way to the estate of modern houses where the orphanage once was. This isn't the way back to the car, but seeing the names of the Burroughs family on those gravestones has made her want to have another look. As she gets nearer to the shabby evergreen hedge she sees the For Sale sign and her heart gives a little leap. It's more prominent now. The hedge has been clipped around the sign so it can be seen from cars passing by.

When she reaches the front gate, she stops and looks at the garden. She realises that she doesn't want to go inside. Instead, she stands for a few minutes and stares at the silent building, at the overgrown garden and at the blank, dirty windows with their peeling frames. People have thrown litter over the gate; a dented Coke can bobs in a puddle on the front path and sweet wrappers blow about on the lawn. She pictures her father walking up the path full of hope, ringing the doorbell and waiting on that step. Poor old Dad.

She crosses the road and goes back into the newsagent's. The woman's eyes light up in recognition.

'Back again already, love?'

'Yes. It's a very bad habit, I know,' Sarah says, wondering what business is it of this woman anyway how much she smokes. 'I've managed to smoke my way through nearly a whole packet already,' she adds with a smile.

'Oh, I didn't mean the fags, dear. Good God, you should see how much I smoke! No, I meant that old house. I saw you going in there after you'd been in here yesterday afternoon. You were in there for quite a long time with the estate agent, weren't you? You must be keen if you're back to have another look.'

Sarah's breath is taken away by the cheek of the woman and she opens her mouth to tell her to mind her own business, but her ingrained politeness kicks in. A lifetime working in restaurants has trained her not to react to needling comments.

'I'm not, actually,' she says in an even voice. 'I wasn't even meant to be looking round yesterday. It just happened on the spur of the moment.'

'Well, between you and me, a fair few people have been to see it today. It's been one after another. One or two couples, but mostly blokes in suits. Business types. Probably property developers. That Jonathan Squires fella has been back and forth all day showing them around. I've seen him driving in and out of the side entrance in that Range Rover of his.'

'Well, the house has got a lot of potential. It could be beautiful. Someone will buy it soon, I'm sure.' Sarah takes the packet of cigarettes and turns to go.

'I just hope they don't knock it down and build on the land. So many of them big houses round here have gone that way.'

As Sarah leaves the shop, a black Range Rover passes her and she recognises Jonathan Squires in the driving seat. She turns and watches it. Sure enough, the car turns into the driveway of Cedar Hall.

With a pang of regret, she begins to walk back to where her own car is parked. As she walks, she tries to understand her own feelings.

What is it about that old house that seems to draw her to it? Is it the connection to Dad's past that is exerting this pull on her? Is it the story he told her about the two old sisters who'd lived there? She recalls how vulnerable he'd appeared when he spoke about it. How it had come as a real blow to him that one of the sisters had virtually shut the door on him. Perhaps it's the desire to lessen his pain, the wish to help him in his quest that keeps calling her back there? She thinks again of the photograph of the two sisters in the conservatory. There was something about that picture, about the expressions of the two girls staring out of the frame, that had intrigued her; made her curious about what their lives might have been like in that great echoing house full of memories.

The red-brick edifice of Cartwrights comes into view and she walks quickly past, head down. Judith Marshall will be tapping away on her computer even now, drafting a letter to Alex, dropping the bombshell, asking for his financial details.

Blanking that from her mind, Sarah walks on past the row of shops, turns left off the road and starts to cross the market square again. On one side is a row of offices and businesses, in the middle of which is a white-painted shop with bow-fronted windows: 'Country Squires'. She strides over to it and stares in the window. There it is in pole position in the middle of the display:

CEDAR HALL. FIRST TIME TO MARKET FOR GENERATIONS, THIS IMPOS-ING EDWARDIAN GENTLEMAN'S RESIDENCE HAS GREAT POTENTIAL FOR RENOVATION OR, SUBJECT TO PLANNING PERMISSION, FOR DEVELOPMENT. FURTHER DETAILS ON APPLICATION.

There's a huge flattering picture of the front of the house, taken on a sunny day.

Sarah puts a hand on the door handle and is about to push it open when she stops herself. The office is full of people. A woman is showing brochures to a young couple at one desk; at the other, a young man in a sharp suit is chatting to two men with their backs to the door. Other people are standing around, waiting to be served. Suddenly this doesn't feel right. All she'd wanted to do was to find out a bit more about the house, but to go inside the office and pose as a potential purchaser doesn't seem to be the right way to go about that. She turns away and walks back to her car.

Dad is in the kitchen peeling potatoes when Sarah gets back.

'I thought I'd make a roast,' he says. 'There's a chicken in the fridge. How did it all go, darling?'

'Oh, pretty grim, really,' she says, pulling off her boots and coat. 'It was quite difficult, having to talk it through with a stranger.'

'What did she say?'

Sarah sits down with a heavy sigh. 'She said I've got grounds for divorce. We went through some of the financial stuff too. That bit gave me a bit of a shock. There's so much tied up in the business and because of this investigation it's not clear when it could be released. Quite worrying, really.'

'You don't have to worry about money, Sarah. I can support you until you get things sorted out. You know that. In fact, it would make sense if I transferred some of my savings to you right away. I was going to say that to you anyway, even if this hadn't happened.'

'Oh, Dad,' she says, turning to him. Tears threaten at this act of generosity. 'That's really kind of you. I know you'd help me, but I've never asked you for money and I wouldn't now, unless things got really desperate. You know that.'

'You shouldn't be so proud, Sarah. Sometimes we all need to accept a helping hand,' he says quietly.

'I know. It's really kind of you, but I'll be fine. I've got enough in my savings account to keep me going until I decide what I want to do next.'

He leaves the sink and sits down opposite her, drying his hands on a tea towel. His birth certificate is still on the table, together with a notebook filled with his familiar scrawling writing. He must have been looking through his research notes while she was out. He closes the notebook and draws it towards him.

'But seriously, Sarah. I've been meaning to discuss this with you and now is as good a time as any. When I sold some of my shares in the company when I retired, I didn't do too badly, as you know. The shares I did keep have gone up quite a lot since then. You know I tried to persuade you to take something at the time. You could have had some of those shares back then.'

'And I said that I didn't need anything. The restaurants were just picking up. We could manage.'

'But things are different now, aren't they?'

'I suppose they are... but I can still manage, if you don't mind me staying here for a little while.'

'You're welcome to stay here for as long as you like. As long as you don't mind me and my bumbling ways. It's a bit different to Primrose Hill though, stuck out here in the sticks. Won't you be bored?'

She shakes her head. 'I couldn't stay there with this going on. And like I said, I need to get away from it all. I'll miss the restaurant, of course, and all the people, but I can't think like that. I need to move on. Get out from under Alex's shadow. You know he was the life and soul of that place. It was his baby really, not mine. People came to see him, to be cooked for by him. Sometimes I felt a bit sidelined by that, to tell you the truth.'

'Well,' Dad smiles, 'it will be lovely to have you here. To spend some time together.'

She looks into his eyes. 'I'm so sorry, Dad. I feel as though I've neglected you all these years. I've been so wrapped up in the business. Time has just flown by. I've been so selfish.'

'Nonsense. Now, like I said, you can stay here as long as you like, until you decide what to do. You might even decide to go back to Alex, you never know.'

'I don't think that will happen,' she says.

'You say that now, but you might think differently in a few weeks' time.'

She shakes her head. 'Well, either way I want to be close to you, Dad. Make up for lost time.'

She thinks again about Cedar Hall. It's odd the way that old house keeps calling her back. It might be a crazy thing to do, she reasons, but if she were to buy the house it might address a few issues. It might provide a window into history for Dad. The old place must be harbouring some secrets from the past, so owning it could provide a means of unlocking them, helping Dad in his quest for answers.

'What about your friends, though? Your life in London?'

She laughs. 'My life was the restaurant. It was all-consuming. I hardly had any time for real friends. I lost touch with most people I knew from school and college over the years. They were all settling down, having families. We drifted apart.'

He gets up and switches on the oven.

'Well,' he says, 'if you need me to advance you some money you only have to say the word. I'm sure it will take time to sort things out with Alex on the finance front. I'd be only too happy to help. It's all yours anyway. Well, it will be one day at least.'

Chapter Seven

Sarah

Sarah falls into her father's undemanding routine, welcoming the change of pace. Each day begins with them sharing breakfast in the kitchen. After that, Dad usually has somewhere to go for the morning. It might be to the garden centre or shopping for groceries, or to a meeting of one of his clubs or societies. She's aware that he spends a lot of time in his study, obsessing over local history on the internet, or poring over records. It worries her that he is investing so much time and emotion on something that could well lead nowhere, or worse, to some unwelcome revelations.

While he's out, she potters around the house, listening to the radio, tidying or cleaning, preparing lunch, sometimes just sitting in Dad's sunroom at the back in a basket chair, soaking up the weak rays of winter sun and reading through his collection of detective novels. Except that she can't really ever relax. All the time she thinks of Alex, imagining him embracing Jemma, the girl with the thick mascara, the bottle-blonde hair. Picturing them together makes her shudder, but she can't stop herself.

Jemma must have been laughing at her for such a long time. They both must have been. Sarah tries to shut it out of her mind but the images keep forcing their way back. When she thinks of him paying the girl every month for the past two years out of their own money, it makes her seethe with anger.

She tries to visualise times she'd seen Alex and Jemma together, trying to pinpoint when it had started between them. How could he have lost his judgement to such an extent? It goes round so much in her head that she begins to think she's going crazy. In the end she tries to blot it all out, to empty her mind of the pain.

The trouble is, her mind can never be empty for long. Whenever she makes a conscious effort not to think of Alex and the restaurant and that girl, she worries instead about the police investigation. The stress and humiliation of watching them rifle through all the files and papers. Why wouldn't they say what they were looking for? What had Alex got himself mixed up in? He had always been so impulsive.

These thoughts and worries harry her so much she often feels near to breaking point. Then she buries her head in her hands, screws her eyes up in frustration. In those moments it's the old house that appears in her mind. It seems to beckon her. She tours it again and again in her imagination; a welcome distraction. She is always alone walking round those musty rooms, staring at the pictures, at the old furniture, at the decay. She also dreams of it at night. It won't leave her in peace.

Those first few days Alex tries to call her many times. At first, she doesn't answer the calls, and doesn't listen to the messages he leaves either. He must have had Judith Marshall's letter by now, setting out that she wants a divorce on the grounds of his adultery. She can imagine his reaction to that. Nothing she can say will change anything and she really can't face a showdown with him until things have calmed down. She goes outside into the garden and lights a cigarette. She stands on the step, drawing on it gratefully, letting the nicotine creep through her veins, calm her jangling nerves. She stares down at the river at the bottom of the garden, brown and wide and fast-flowing, at the bare winter trees blowing in the breeze.

Finishing the cigarette, she drops the butt end onto the patio and grinds it in. She needs to get out of the house for a few hours, a change of scenery. There's no point in hanging around the house feeling sorry for herself. She needs something to focus on other than Alex. She knows just the thing.

She goes upstairs, and pulls on her jeans and a sweater. Staring in the mirror, she notices her face has filled out a little over the past few days. It must be the rest she's been getting away from the relentless routine of the restaurant, and Dad's cooking. She puts on her make-up carefully, layering on the blusher. She scribbles a note for her father on the kitchen table and locks the house up.

Pulling out of the drive onto the main road, she turns right, in the direction of Weirfield. She drives along parallel to the river. She needs to go back there to look at the old house again, to see if the For Sale sign is still up, or if it's been replaced by another one saying Under Offer. It surely won't have sold yet, but why not check anyway?

As she drives through the outskirts of Weirfield, a tingle of anticipation runs through her. As she approaches Cedar Hall, she slows down and stares. A white removal van is parked in the yard behind the house. She pulls up on the other side of the road and winds the window down to get a better look, but from this angle it's difficult to see what's happening; the house is in the way. She gets out of the car and crosses the road, noting that the For Sale sign is still up beside the gate. She walks along the pavement beside the overgrown hedge and stops by the entrance to the stable yard. The gates to the drive are open. She can see very little except the open double doors at the back of the van. There are thumps and bangs coming from inside, and the sound of men's voices. The words *JAMIESON HOUSE CLEARANCE, NO JOB TOO SMALL* are painted on the side. They must be moving everything out. Does this mean someone has bought it already?

She's about to turn to go when two men in suits appear from behind the van and start walking across the stable yard, deep in conversation. Now she spots the black Range Rover tucked in the corner of the yard next to the coach house. She realises that one of the men is Jonathan Squires, and with a jolt of recognition she sees that she knows who the other man is too, although his back is to her. She recognises his unruly blond hair. It's Peter Cartwright, the solicitor she met briefly in Judith Marshall's office.

As she gets back into the car she realises she's parked directly in front of the newsagent's. She glances through the window. The woman is staring straight at her, smiling a knowing smile, her pencilled eyebrows raised in expectation. Sarah raises a hand in an awkward wave.

She parks on the market square. It's quiet today; there are no stalls. She crosses the square quickly to Country Squires and, without pausing, goes inside. The woman behind the desk looks up.

'I'd like the particulars for Cedar Hall, please.'

The woman smiles politely. 'Please take a seat, madam. Would you like to register with us? We have a number of very desirable properties in the same price bracket.'

'No, thank you. I'm just curious about this particular house. Is it still for sale?'

'I'm afraid not. It's now under offer and the vendors have instructed us to take it off the market.'

'That's a surprise. The sign in the window says nothing about that.'

'No, I'm afraid we haven't had time to change the display. It was only confirmed this morning.'

Sarah swallows, taking in this new information. Disappointment washes through her.

'Could I take particulars of the house anyway in case the sale falls through?'

'I suppose so,' the woman says reluctantly, handing her a glossy brochure from the pile on her desk. 'But I very much doubt that will happen. The purchasers are regular clients of ours.'

Sarah thinks for a few minutes, absently fingering the brochure.

'Can you tell me how much it went for?' she asks eventually.

A flush appears on the woman's neck and travels up to her cheeks. She shuffles the papers on her desk.

'I'm sorry, I can't do that. If you'd like to speak to Mr Squires, he'll be back later. In the meantime, would you like to look at any other properties? As I said, we have several on our books in the same price range.'

'No, I'm only interested in Cedar Hall. Mr Squires showed me around a few days ago.'

The woman frowns. 'Really? What's your name, please? I don't think you're on our books. Perhaps you'd like to register?'

'It's OK,' says Sarah, getting up. 'Thank you. I might call to speak to Mr Squires.'

She crosses the market square deep in thought, aware that she must acknowledge now what she's been afraid to acknowledge before: how much she wants to own that old house. She's wanted to ever since she first looked over the rusty gate and inside the garden. She needs to own it for a reason that she can't quite fathom. Perhaps it's because she needs to start something new, put her imprint on somewhere without Alex in the background? Or perhaps it might be in order to establish some sort of connection with her father's past?

By now Sarah has walked the length of the High Street, barely noticing her surroundings. She pauses outside Le Gastronome. There's a sign in the window: *WAITING AND KITCHEN STAFF WANTED, ASK INSIDE.* She sighs and smiles sadly, thinking that the perennial problem that besets restaurant owners is no longer her worry. Inside, an awkward young man shows her to a table in the window. Only two other tables are occupied, one by an elderly couple and the other by two middle-aged women deep in conversation.

She glances at the menu, noting the tired, obvious choices: the steak tartare, the boeuf bourguignon. Alex would have a field day here. He'd turn this place around in a few months: change the menu, revamp the décor, energise the staff. She sighs and suppresses the thought.

The waiter is hovering over her, waiting for her order. He has pimply skin and looks very young, unsure of himself. 'I'll just have the French onion soup, please. Oh, and could I have some French bread with that too, please?'

While she's waiting for her soup she glances through the brochure for Cedar Hall. The photographer has done a good job. The rooms are transformed. They don't look dirty and neglected in these pictures. The furniture appears shiny and the rooms elegant, light and cavernous, with the aid of a wide-angle lens. She bites her nail. Perhaps if she could find out how much it had gone for, she could make a higher offer. Perhaps she *could* accept an advance from Dad until things are sorted out with Alex. But how would he feel about her buying somewhere that has such poignant connotations for him? He might not like it at all.

'Interested in the old Burroughs house?'

She looks up. A man is standing beside the table. He holds out his hand.

'I'm Matt Drayton by the way. I own this place, for my sins…'

She shakes his hand. 'Hello, I'm Sarah Jennings. And yes, I *am* interested in the house.'

'I've lived in the town all my life. It's a beautiful old place. Very neglected, though. The Burroughs sisters lived like church mice there for years. Hardly went out. It will be great if someone buys it and restores it to its former glory.'

Sarah puts the brochure down with a sigh. 'It will. That someone won't be me though. I'm probably too late. I've just come from the estate agents. It's already under offer.'

'Already? It only went on the market the other day.'

She shrugs. 'Bad timing on my part, I suppose.'

He smiles sympathetically. 'Are you from round here? I don't recognise you.'

'No, but my dad is,' she replies without pausing for thought. 'I'm staying with him for a while.'

'Really? What's his name? I might know him.'

'Oh no, I don't think so… he left when he was still a baby…'
She looks down. There's a short silence.

'Here's your soup,' he says, taking it from the waiter and putting it on the table in front of her. 'I hope you enjoy it.'

'Thank you.'

She looks up at him, noticing him properly for the first time. He must be in his early forties. His dark hair is streaked with grey, there's a film of stubble on his chin and although his eyes are smiling, there are fatigue lines under them. She recognises the familiar exhaustion and desperation of the restaurateur who is working harder and harder only to find their business losing money and customers each day. It had often felt like that when she and Alex started out, all those years ago, but somehow they had brought it round.

She tucks into the soup, noticing with surprise that it is actually rather good. Home-made, and probably with excellent-quality beef stock. The bread is fresh and warm too. She hadn't realised how hungry she was.

When she's finished she sits back and stares out of the window. The restaurant is not in a good position: right at the end of the town with a narrow pavement, a long walk from the car park.

Across the road is a row of businesses in red-brick buildings that must once have been houses. There's an accountant's office, a dentist's and a doctor's surgery. As she looks at the surgery, housed in one of the few modern buildings in the row, the front door opens and someone steps out. An old man with a shock of white hair, dressed in an oversized anorak. He stands on the step for a moment and it's a few seconds before it registers with Sarah.

'Dad,' she breathes. She begins to push back her chair, intending to rush out to him, but something stops her. He's walking slowly away from the surgery towards the town now, hunched in the cold air. He has a defeated look about him and her instinct tells her he needs to be alone.

Chapter Eight

Connie

Connie wakes with a start. She's alone in her room, although she didn't notice Erica leave. There's no light seeping from behind the curtains, and she senses it's dark outside. Remembering that Erica had brought her some tea, she gropes on the coffee table and with a shaking hand lifts the cup to her lips. When she takes a sip, it is unpleasantly cold and she puts it back on the saucer, spilling some as she does so.

She is shivering, although the room is warm and fuggy as usual. She gathers her knitted shawl about her shoulders. It must be that recurring dream that has made her feel so chilled. The one that makes the past more real than the present. It always makes her shiver. That, and all the other episodes from back then that come to her, day and night. Especially now she's here, away from home, away from where it all happened. It's as if the memories have become more vivid, released from their surroundings.

Outside in the passage, the sounds of supper being prepared float along the corridor from the kitchen. The voices of the kitchen staff, the clatter of pots and pans, pop music blaring on the radio. So different from home, where the only sounds were the ticking of the grandfather clock and the cat mewing for his food.

Even before Evie died the place had been quiet. Evie wouldn't have a radio or a television in the house. They had an old gramophone, though. Sometimes, when Evie was in a good mood, she would say after supper, with a glint in her eye, 'Shall we treat ourselves to some music, Connie?' and she would select one of the albums of organ music or hymns, and place it carefully on the ancient turntable, and sit back down with a blissful smile on her face, her head thrown back, her eyes closed as the music crackled out from the machine.

Connie's mind wanders back to her sister. She remembers how Evie had always loved music. It had always puzzled Connie how musical Evie actually was. How different the two of them were. Connie had never had a musical bone in her body and she often wondered where Evie's ear for music might have come from. Neither Father nor Mother could sing anything like Evie.

'It's a gift from our dear Lord,' Father would say, beaming, when Evie sang to them sometimes after supper.

Connie can still picture Evie seated at the old organ in the Baptist chapel, swaying from side to side at the keyboard as she belted out hymns with skill and gusto, encouraging the congregation to sing at the tops of their voices.

Father would sometimes ask Evie to sing solos of hymns at the orphanage at morning prayers. She would stand up there on the low stage at one end of the hall and perform to the packed room, accompanied by one of the teachers on the jangly piano. Her voice had the sweetest tone and a huge range. She would clasp her hands together as she sang; almost in a reverie, while the children watched in rapt attention, not moving a muscle, a hundred pairs of unblinking eyes trained on her face. When she'd finished, she would always look surprised and flustered, as if she'd woken from a dream, and she would hurry off the stage and back to her seat almost apologetically.

Connie lets her mind wander back to the past, trying to pinpoint when she'd started to question some of the things that happened around her as she was growing up; things that Evie and Mother and she never spoke about.

Cedar Hall and the orphanage were all she'd ever known. Evie and she were born there a year apart and grew up there together. It felt quite natural to live alongside a hundred or so other babies and children in that huge building next door to the house. To Connie, it felt like being part of an enormous family.

As schoolmistress their mother taught the younger children in the big schoolroom in the orphanage every day. Connie remembers how she and Evie spent their early years in the nursery with the orphan babies. As they grew older, they took breakfast and lunch in the cavernous dining room with the other children, and sat side by side with them in the schoolroom for lessons.

Mother was a patient teacher, gentle and kind. But she was shy. She always spoke in a timid voice, as if she was ready to change her mind if someone disagreed with her. She used to blink a lot too, like a startled rabbit. To Connie, Mother seemed never to change all through those years. She remembers her wearing a plain dark dress down to her ankles, with a starched white collar. Her hair was always pinned up in a severe bun. She despised adornment and never wore jewellery or lipstick, or even put cream on her face.

Despite that, Connie had always thought that Mother had a sort of understated beauty. It had never been allowed to blossom. Looking back, it feels strange to her that she has no memory of Mother's hair being anything other than grey. In fact, Mother herself has almost disappeared from Connie's memory, like a photograph that has faded in the sunlight.

Father was quite the opposite, though. Thinking about him always brings a confusing mixture of emotions to the fore in Connie's heart: love and admiration mixed with fear. Father was what people might call a 'larger than life' character. All the children had loved and revered him. Evie and Connie had been taught that these poor children had no families and that they looked on their father as their own.

Connie remembers sometimes, although she knew it was wrong of her, feeling a pang of jealousy when she saw other children running after Father in the yard, clinging to his coat-tails as he swept through the corridors, or when they looked up at him with shining eyes as he led prayers before breakfast every weekday morning, or gave his sermon in the Baptist church on Sundays.

Father had once been out in India, spreading the word of God. He ran a mission and a church near a military station, Kandaipur. From an early age Connie had been fascinated by his stories about India. He would sometimes take her on his knee and tell her about his time out there. They were impossibly exciting, romantic stories; stories she still carries with her all these years later.

'You know, Connie, I often had to trek all the way up into the mountains to help villagers when there was an outbreak of disease,' he told her once, and she imagined him striking out alone, along a rocky mountain path, in a billowing white shirt, his hair flowing behind him. She imagined the villagers flocking to greet him as he arrived, grateful that at last help was at hand.

'Once a tiger had been stalking a village. The villagers were terrified. So, I hid out in the bushes one night with my rifle, and when I caught sight of it prowling around, I clapped my hands to attract its attention. As it bounded towards me I took a shot, got it right between the eyes, and it fell to the ground.' Connie stared at him then, wide-eyed, marvelling at his bravery.

A knock on the door breaks into Connie's memories. Matron puts her head round and says in her gratingly cheery voice, 'How are we, Miss Burroughs? Feeling all right? There's a visitor to see you. There's just enough time for a quick chat before supper.'

Connie draws the shawl even closer around her, sits up straight and pats her hair.

'Hello, Peter,' she says as her visitor walks in. 'This is very late. Is everything all right?'

He strides towards her and shakes her hand. 'Good evening, Miss Burroughs. No need for alarm. Could we speak for a few moments?' He takes a seat beside the television and crosses his gangly legs, pushing his hair out of his eyes. Connie purses her lips. Why does he let it grow so long? It looks so untidy. He doesn't look like a professional should. Not like his grandfather, that's for sure. Old Joshua was always beautifully turned out. Just like dear Father.

'We moved everything out of the house today,' he begins and Connie draws in a sharp breath and holds it, imagining the scene. All Father's beloved furniture, his pictures, the great oak wardrobe where he used to hang his clothes. His clothes even! How will she bear it? She feels her hands shaking and she can't let out that breath. It won't leave her. It must be Father, punishing her for letting this happen.

'You quite all right, Miss Burroughs?'

Peter is leaning forward and peering at her, an anxious frown on his face. 'Would you like some water?'

She nods quickly, clutching her throat, and he brings some from the jug on the sideboard. The breath leaves her with a choking sob as she takes a gulp of the water.

'We talked about this last week, didn't we?' He's speaking gently, leaning forward, looking into her eyes.

'Yes, I know.'

'The things you agreed to sell have gone to the second-hand shop in Wokingham. The other things are in storage. When you're well enough to go out, I'll take you along there and you can decide what you want to keep for your room here. There'll only be room for a few things, of course,' he says looking round at the small space that is now her home. 'I've just had a word with Matron. She said they'll move out anything that you don't want of theirs to make room.'

She nods. 'What about the papers? Father's... I mean all the papers in the office.'

'Well, as we agreed, I've boxed them up and taken everything down to my office. We keep a lot of old deeds and records in the basement. We'll keep them there until you're strong enough to come and go through them with me.'

Perhaps that's not so bad. Father had always used Cartwrights. Old Joshua Cartwright was in his inner circle. But still, her stomach churns with nerves and upset at the thought of the house, empty of everything.

'There *was* just one hitch, though, I'm afraid.'

'Hitch?' She looks at him sharply.

'There was one piece of furniture we couldn't actually remove.'

'What was that?' Alarm rushes through her.

'It was the old bureau actually. Just wouldn't go through the door of the office. The men tried every angle, but in the end, they had to give up.'

Father's bureau. She recalls him sitting there night and day writing letters, working on the paperwork for the orphanage. Sometimes when she was small she would tiptoe in to watch him work and he would look up and hold his arms out to her, taking her onto his knee. She loved those moments when she could be his special one, even if it was only for a short while. She can still smell the pomade on his hair as she snuggled against his smooth shirt.

'Miss Burroughs?'

'Yes?'

'The bureau?'

'Oh, yes. That bureau belonged to my father. It was very special. He had a local carpenter in to make it to order. It was built inside his study. The carpenter bought the wood specially. The finest oak. I don't remember where from now, perhaps the New Forest… no, maybe not…' She frowns, trying to remember.

'If it was made inside the room, that must explain why the men can't get it out of the door.'

Connie nods. 'Yes, I suppose so. I remember it quite clearly now. I must have been very small. The excitement of watching it grow, bit by bit. I would creep in and watch the carpenter at work… now what on earth was that man's name?'

'Miss Burroughs, I'm wondering what to do about it. We agreed that the house would be sold empty. The buyers won't be expecting to have to dispose of a large piece of furniture.'

'Dispose of?' she gasps, her hand flying to her mouth. She sits forward in the chair, glaring at him. Father's precious desk! It's bad enough all the furniture having to go into storage, some of it being sold. Father's wonderful wardrobe, Mother's dressing table, where she used to sit brushing out her long hair before winding it up on her head.

'I'm sorry. Please don't be alarmed. Unfortunate turn of phrase. I meant that they would have to make arrangements for the desk. They would find that a bother.'

'Well, I'll have to think about it. It's not going to happen yet though, is it?'

Peter's face is flushed now. His eyes flick sideways. He clears his throat.

'Well, actually, Miss Burroughs, a buyer has been found already. Mr Squires has been very efficient.'

'Already? But I thought… you said it might take months.'

'Hmm… Well, it's a company who've got great plans for the place. They've offered a very decent price. Certainly enough to pay your bills here and ensure your future comfort. I think it would be wise to take the offer while it's on the table.'

Her scalp tingles in alarm.

'Plans for the place? What do you mean?' Her hands are shaking again.

He pauses for a second, frowning.

'I wanted to break it to you a little more gently,' he goes on, 'but since you ask, they're planning to build some beautiful new homes on the plot. That's their business. Pinsent Homes. A very reputable company.'

Connie is breathing quickly now, her mind running over the implications. Father's voice comes into her head again, *You'll look after things for me at the house, won't you, Constance?*

'They can't do that,' she manages to blurt out. 'They'll need permission, won't they? Permission from the council?'

'Oh, I don't think there'll be any difficulty about that,' Peter Cartwright says, giving her a smooth smile. 'They're professionals, after all. They don't foresee any difficulties with the planning team. Bearing in mind that Cedar Hall is already surrounded by other modern houses.'

Connie is shaking all over. Thoughts are swirling around in her mind. One hand fingers the filigree pendant at her throat for comfort, the other plucks at her skirt. She takes a deep breath and holds it as if she's under water.

'There's a document,' she says finally. It's like the first gasp of a drowning person coming up for air. 'A document to stop that. Father signed it when he bought the house from the County Council, when the orphanage was closed, forty-odd years ago. I remember it quite clearly.'

She stares at Peter. He's staring back at her, the flush even deeper now, his mouth wide open.

'You must be mistaken,' he says. 'I've been through all the deeds myself and the title is quite clear.'

Again, she has that drowning feeling. She struggles for breath. She must make her voice heard.

'That's not right, Peter. There is something that Father signed to say that there would only ever be one house on that plot. Your grandfather knew all about that. Or perhaps it was your father...'

He's sitting up straight now. His mouth is twitching as if he's about to shout at her. He loosens his tie.

'It seems that your memory is playing tricks on you, Miss Burroughs. Please don't worry. I'll double-check, but I can assure you that I've been very thorough.'

'You *must* check please, Peter. It's very important.'

'Of course. Everything will be taken care of.' He's recovering his composure now, his face returning to its normal colour.

'We were saying a moment ago. About the desk. We'll need to work out what to do about it. If the house is to… to be demolished, I'm afraid they will just take it away with the debris.'

Connie swallows but her throat is dry. No words will come because of the images dancing around in her head. Yellow diggers and cranes in the stable yard, crashing through the masonry, splintering the beams, smashing the glass in the conservatory.

'No!' she says, her throat hoarse. 'I won't let it happen. It *can't* happen.'

Peter's eyes flicker, a mixture of irritation and something else she can't quite fathom. Desperation perhaps?

'Now please, Miss Burroughs. We went through all this last week. There is very little money left in your bank account to sustain you here. As your trustee and legal adviser, I told you that we need to liquidate your assets. Your only asset, actually. We must do that as soon as we can, otherwise… well, otherwise we'll have to look for somewhere else for you to live. That might not be so pleasant, and it might be very far away from Weirfield.'

'Yes. You explained all that. But… but surely you can't sell the house to a developer if that deed—'

'There is no deed, as I said. The developer is offering a very good price and we need to make a decision in the next few days otherwise they'll pull out and invest elsewhere. Now, please could you have a think about the desk?'

'Have you cleared out all the papers from it?' she asks in a thin voice, near to tears.

'Of course. As I mentioned' – there is impatience in his voice now – 'they are all safe and sound in our archives downstairs in the basement at the offices. When you're better, you can come along and we can go through them together.'

There's a pause. Connie is still thinking about those machines, knocking down the coach house, now churning up the lawn where she and Evie used to play croquet in the old days.

'Well, Miss Burroughs. Do you have any suggestions regarding the bureau?'

She stares at him for a few moments, then shakes her head slowly.

'I really can't think *what* to do about it.'

'You don't think that it might be best to dismantle it and take it out?'

She shakes her head vehemently. 'No, that might ruin it. It must stay where it is.'

Peter Cartwright gives a deep sigh and sits forward in the chair.

'That might not be possible if... well, if the house itself isn't going to be there, I'm afraid.'

As Connie tries to digest his words, he glances at his watch and gets up.

'Look, I must get off home now. It's very late. We can talk about this another time.'

He crosses the room and his hand is on the door handle when she remembers something. 'What about the carpet in that room?'

He turns, his shoulders sagging. 'The carpet is fine. You mean the fitted carpet, of course?'

'They didn't damage it, did they, when they took out the rest of the furniture?' she asks in a whisper, dreading the response.

'No, no. Of course not. But as I said, the carpet might not be staying for much longer anyway.'

'Evie and I had that carpet put down,' she goes on, ignoring what he's just said. 'It isn't old. But the floorboards were...' She looks away and swallows.

'Well, I'll be off then. I'll come again soon and let you know how matters are progressing.'

He's gone and as his footsteps echo away down the passage, Connie sits staring at the thick beige curtains, breathing quickly, imagining again those machines razing the old house to the ground. Eventually though, her breathing slows down and her mind returns to Father's office. She remembers how she would watch him bent over the bureau, scribbling away at the ledgers, savouring the fact that for one precious moment it was just the two of them. No Evie, no Mother, none of the orphan children running after him, shouting his name, grabbing his coat-tails.

'Tell me about India, Father,' she would say if he was in a good mood.

He would laugh and say, 'What do you want to know, Constance my dear?'

'All about when you were a missionary there, Father. Everything,' and her eyes would wander to the fireplace, where a hollowed-out elephant's foot stood filled with coal in the hearth, to the mantelpiece where carved statues of Hindu gods and goddesses would dance mysteriously together, and to the picture above it of the little church surrounded by palm trees, nestled among the great mountains. Those things gave her a queer feeling in the pit of her stomach. Especially the gods. Her mind would soar as she tried to imagine that land, far, far away.

'Well, my little one, I could tell you about the time I had to walk to a village that was miles along a mountain trail to help the people during an outbreak of cholera. I've told you that before, haven't I?'

'I think so, Father. Is the village in the picture?'

'No, no. You can't see it. It's behind that great big mountain.'

'Did you see any tigers on the way?'

'Of course not. Not there, anyway.'

'Did the people get better, Father?'

'Most of them. But God didn't see fit to spare them all.'

Connie would pause, picturing her father tending the sick, mopping the brows of suffering people lying on mats inside wooden huts, bringing them water and prayers.

'Why did you come home to England?'

His face would cloud over whenever she asked this question. She knew it troubled him, but he had never answered it properly, and she needed an answer. Wouldn't it be so much better, if she, Evie and Mother could have lived in India among all that beauty, helping the poor village people to come to God, rather than here in the cold, in this mundane place, sharing Father with a hundred other children? One day, he gave her an answer of sorts: 'I had to, my dear. They needed me here to do God's work, running this orphanage.'

She knew this wasn't the whole truth, but details about those years were very vague.

Sometimes, though, he wouldn't smile and take her on his knee when she brought his tea from the kitchen, or his letters from the postman. Sometimes he would scowl at her and turn away, and sometimes he would speak roughly, snatching the post or pointing to where she should put his cup down and turning straight back to his work. She and Evie learned to keep away from him at those times, and Mother would behave even more like a ghost than usual, tiptoeing around the house so as not to disturb Father. Connie would notice nervous perspiration on Mother's top lip at supper time when they sat in silence in the dining room.

'Supper time, Connie, my darling,' a voice says, breaking into her thoughts. She stiffens in alarm. Will they try to make her go to the dining room again? It's Mairead, the plump Irish girl, this time. She has kind misty-grey eyes.

'Erica told me that you weren't so keen on going along to the dining room yesterday, so I've brought your supper to you instead.'

Mairead is carrying a tray with plates with tin covers. Why is there someone different all the time? So many people to get used to. The girl looks harassed. There are dark patches of sweat under her arms.

'Is it all right to put it down on your lap?' she asks, the tray rattling in her shaky hands.

'I'm not hungry.'

'You weren't hungry yesterday, Connie, my darling. You must eat.'

She sighs. What difference will it make? Who will care if she never eats another morsel? Then she stops herself. God will care. It is very wrong to think like that.

Matron appears in the doorway again. 'Oh good. I see your visitor has gone. I hope he didn't tire you out?'

Connie shakes her head. 'Of course not. But Matron, I really must go out tomorrow. I need to go back home before the house is sold. There are some things I need to check.'

'Miss Burroughs, my dear lady, you're in no fit state to go anywhere. Especially if you can't even go along to the dining room.'

Connie begins to shake, and her fingers fly once again to the filigree chain at her throat. She holds it to try to soothe her nerves. 'I must, Matron. I really must.'

'But Mr Cartwright is taking care of it all, isn't he? You can ask him to check things. I'll bring you the telephone tomorrow and you can call him if you're worried.'

'I need to go there myself. It isn't something I want to ask of Mr Cartwright. Please, Matron.'

Matron looks curiously at Connie, then her eyes soften. 'Perhaps we can find a way to get you back there before too long. But it won't be tomorrow, end of the week perhaps. Now eat up. You must keep your strength up, my dear.'

Connie picks at her food, but she can't concentrate on it. Now she has started thinking about the past, all those memories come rushing back to her, as fresh as if they happened yesterday. The thought that Cedar Hall will soon be sold, along with the ghosts of the past, brings them back with fresh intensity.

Suddenly she knows she can't put the moment off any longer. She has been putting it off for seventy-five years. But now she forces herself to remember Anna, with her long dark hair and her brown eyes.

Connie thinks back to that night in 1934. The night when her curiosity about what was going on in the room above the coach house finally became too much for her. Over the preceding few days, her father had been spending time up there again. Connie had watched the window, convinced there was someone in there. From her bedroom window, very late one night, she was certain she could see movement in the room through a crack in the curtains. She knew that her father was asleep in the house. She couldn't contain her need to know any longer. Silently, she got dressed, taking care not to wake Evie, crept downstairs and out through the back door, her heart beating furiously.

It was raining heavily, even though it was springtime. Connie stood at the bottom of the coach house steps, staring up at the door, trying to pluck up the courage to go up there. She wondered whether to go into the garage and see if she could hear anything through the ceiling. As she watched, she was astonished to see the side door to the upstairs room open slowly. Chills ran through her as she saw someone emerge and stand on the top step. She froze to the spot. Perhaps it was Father after all. But as she looked closely, she realised that it wasn't him at all. It was a slight figure. A young woman with long dark hair. She was dressed in a nightgown. For a split second, Connie wondered if it was a ghost.

Connie waited at the bottom of the steps as the young woman started to come down. She hesitated when she caught sight of Connie, but then she carried on walking slowly down the steps towards her. As she got close, Connie could see that her face was deathly pale, and her hair lank and wet. Rain was soaking through her nightie and she was shivering.

Connie spoke to her then. The young woman said her name was Anna. Connie recalls the girl's distress and her tears as she handed her the little hardback book with its blue cover. She remembers Anna's pinched expression, the rain streaming down her face, plastering her hair to her head.

'Could you pass this on when the time is right,' she'd whispered, handing Connie the book. 'It might help explain why I've done what I've done.'

Connie knows that Anna didn't intend anyone to read it, not even Connie herself. Connie was just meant to pass it on, but she'd even failed in that task. What does it matter now, though, after all this time? But reading the diary might help her understand what happened back then. Help her come to terms with her guilt.

With difficulty, she eases her stiff body out of her chair and, holding onto the furniture, crosses the room to her sewing box. She pulls it open, and again takes out the trays of thread, boxes of buttons, folded squares of material. There it is, right at the bottom.

She draws the diary out and feels for the tiny key on her filigree chain. Will it still fit? Miraculously, the key slides into the minute lock. She turns it, and after a slight resistance, the leather clasp falls open.

Connie carries the book back to her chair and settles down. She needs a magnifying glass to read nowadays. She takes it off the table beside her. Poor eyesight isn't going to stop her. Not now she's decided. She opens the book, holds the magnifying glass above the opening page and begins to read.

Chapter Nine

Connie

Anna's Diary
February 7th, 1932

It has all passed me by in a blur. I feel as though I've been standing outside myself, watching it all happen, like a newsreel in the cinema. The smiles, the chit-chat, the congratulations. Was that really me standing there in front of the vicar at Mount Mary Church in Bombay, Uncle John on one side and the Colonel on the other, saying 'I do', all clad in startling white?

It had to be quick like that, Donald said so. He insisted. Very politely, but insisted all the same. He said he had no more leave from the regiment, and that he had to be back at the station in Kandaipur in a couple of days. Aunt Nora explained to me that India is like that. Sometimes people marry straight off the boat from England, by special licence. As she was telling me I could see her eager expression, her keenness to get it over with; to dispatch me with the Colonel to his station so she could relieve herself of the embarrassment of having me around.

When I first arrived in Bombay, after all those weeks on P&O it felt quite strange to be on dry land again and no longer rubbing shoulders with that little troupe of shipmates with whom I became quite intimate. A little part of me wonders if they'd have been quite so friendly if they'd known about Father? Perhaps they would. Perhaps they knew all about it anyway and were too kind and polite to say anything. I did think I noticed a hush fall over the restaurant a couple of times when I went down to dinner. But maybe I was just imagining it.

I'll never forget the excitement at seeing India for the first time as we crowded against the ship's rail and made out the thickening of the horizon and the faint blue-grey line of the mountains. When I sniffed the air, I caught that exotic smell drifting on the warm breeze. Spices and woodsmoke mingling with sea salt and the bitter smell of drains. As we got closer to the hills, I could just about make out the glint of the white buildings of Bombay lining the bay, and then as we finally drew alongside the Apollo Bunder, I saw the majestic Gateway of India dominating the quayside, just as it does in all the picture books.

The clamour of the docks was overwhelming. Porters rushing to and fro with luggage, beggars calling for backsheesh, street vendors shouting for trade. A great seething mass of humanity. Then miraculously in all that hue and cry as I leaned over the rail I spotted Aunt Nora in the crowd, cool and serene in a white suit and solar topee, shading her eyes and searching the decks for me.

She met me with a horse-drawn cart (a tonga, she called it) for my luggage and as we jolted through the city, she pointed out some of the landmarks.

I was worried for the poor horse, with its ribs sticking out and its bare haunches. But Aunt Nora said, 'You'll soon get used to it. Just look around you. Poverty everywhere. There's no room for concern about animals here.'

And indeed, as I looked about me, all I could see were poor, downtrodden people going about their business, under *the glare of the fierce, relentless sun. Whole families squatted under tarpaulins on the pavements, children begging at every crossing. Everywhere, people swarming, and traffic crawling, the odd cow moving among the vehicles. And so much noise. Horns blowing, bells ringing, people shouting. It was deafening.*

After so long on board ship, it seemed odd to be in one place. And life in Aunt Nora's ordered, beautiful house didn't feel quite as I imagined India might be. It seemed oddly cosseted and insulated – a bit too much like home.

February 8th, 1932

After the ceremony and a short reception at Aunt Nora's house, indistinguishable from all the other parties I'd attended there, with identical faces and identical conversation, Donald and I were driven to Victoria Terminus to catch the night train to Kandaipur.

We had a carriage all to ourselves, fitted out like a regular sitting room with carpets and wooden chests and armchairs. At the end of the carriage was a sleeping compartment. As Donald showed me around and I stared at the wide bunk, made up by the stewards with linen sheets and pillows, it finally came home to me what this meant. Donald was right beside me, the stiff cloth of his uniform brushing my bare arm and I couldn't raise my eyes to meet his. I felt my cheeks burning.

But there were a couple of awkward hours to fill yet. A uniformed bearer came in and pulled the blinds down as the train pulled out of Bombay, and after a light supper of chicken pie and salad accompanied by champagne, I knew there was no putting it off any longer.

Donald cleared his throat. 'Time for bed, I suppose, Anna my dear.'

I nodded, my eyes on the table. He got up from the chair. 'I'll pop through and get things ready.'

Get things ready? When I followed him into the sleeping car, I saw what he meant. I was unnerved by the clinical way he'd set about it. He had it all planned out. He'd spread a large white towel on top of the sheets. It made the whole thing feel very real and very sordid. Still avoiding his eyes, I slipped through to the cubicle to change. It felt cold in there, despite the steamy heat of the evening, and I was soon covered in goosebumps. The train kept swaying and rocking and more than once I fell over as I got out of my clothes. I kept thinking about that thing that I was about to do, and that there was no getting out of it now. No escape. There he was, sitting on the bunk, probably in his socks and suspenders, waiting for me, getting impatient. I kept thinking that it shouldn't have been like this, that I shouldn't feel like this on my wedding night. I took the cold cream out of my vanity bag to remove my make-up and as I peered into the rusting mirror I saw that my face was as pale as death.

When I stumbled back into the carriage, Donald had turned the gas lamps down very low. He was already in bed smoking a cigar. His eyes were on me as I crossed over to him, and I could see from the high colour in his cheeks that he was as embarrassed and nervous as I was. I sat down beside him, not knowing what to do or say, but he immediately pulled me down beside him and started kissing me, hard painful kisses tasting of whisky and cigars. At the same time, he started yanking off my nightie with rough hands.

I wanted to push him off, but there was no point in that. It was his right, and there was no going back now. I felt no *flicker of desire as he pawed at me, kissed my breasts and finally moved on top of me. I felt marooned, and dreadfully lonely. And moments later, the pain.*

He turned over and lit another cigar and said, 'I thought you'd probably be a virgin.'

The words sounded so blunt I could hardly reply. 'Didn't you expect that?' I asked finally.

'One never knows nowadays,' he said.

I lapsed into silence, allowing the rattle of the wheels on the tracks and the swaying of the carriage to numb my mind. Finally, he stubbed out his cigar and pecked my cheek.

'Well, goodnight then, Anna my love,' he said and turned over.

After a few minutes he began snoring. I lay down and shut my eyes, but I couldn't sleep. There was so little room and his body was hot beside mine. I slid out of bed and crept to the open window. I lifted the blind and through a slit in the shutters I could make out the sweep of the great plain stretching for miles beneath the soft blanket of the night sky. Here and there were pinpricks of light that must have been villages. It made me feel so small and insignificant in this great alien continent. Here, in this tiny moving capsule of cosseted comfort, snaking its way across the dry, barren land. A sense of desolation descended on me as I wondered what on earth I'd done.

I keep thinking back over how I got to this point, how I ended up being married to the Colonel. I realise now that it was almost an act of desperation.

When I first arrived in Bombay, I felt stifled by the life I was forced to lead in Aunt Nora's house; mixing only with Europeans, going only to places the British go. I asked her a few times if she could take me to the bazaar, or to see a temple, but each time she rolled her eyes and made some excuse. Finally, she said, 'It's just not done, Anna my dear. The communities don't mix. We keep ourselves to ourselves. You need to understand India in order to survive here, my dear, and it's clear to me that you don't yet. Otherwise you simply wouldn't have asked to go to those places.'

I could hardly protest. After all, she invited me here to get me away from all the trouble at home. But it was frustrating all the same. Stuck up there in a house that could be in Surbiton or Tunbridge Wells on the hill above that fantastic, vibrant, tantalising city.

Aunt Nora entertained three or four nights every week. As the wife of a senior civil servant, she explained to me, it was expected of her. It felt as though every eligible bachelor in the vicinity of Bombay together with a good many more who were simply passing through were paraded for dinner at Aunt Nora's house. I tried to get out of these embarrassing occasions, but Aunt Nora was always insistent; she was on a mission.

'I promised your mother I would look after you and look after you, I will. And looking after a young woman your age in India means finding her a husband.'

'I don't want a husband, Aunt Nora,' I would say.

'Don't be ridiculous, every young woman wants a husband. Someone like you, especially. You need a new start, my dear,' she'd say, raising her eyebrows meaningfully. 'There are so many eligible young men earning good money out here just waiting to be snapped up. You'll be spoilt for choice. Then you can settle down out here, far away from your past.'

But none of the young men showed any interest in me at all. Aunt Nora must have been aware that I wasn't what they were looking for: a companionable, jolly-hockey-sticks sort of girl who would cheerfully join in with life on the cantonment, socialising at the club, whist drives, amateur dramatics and tennis. I knew I didn't fit the bill. I liked books and painting and walks in the country.

Conversations at those stultifying dinner parties centred on army gossip and sport. I used to find myself drifting off, while the rest spoke of polo or cricket or shooting tigers. I would end up staring out of the window at the lights of the bay twinkling on the water, dreaming of what was going on in the city far below.

And, of course, my age was against me too. At twenty-eight I was older than many of the young officers and civil servants who came to the house. I often wonder if Aunt Nora told any of those empty-headed young men the real reason why I came out to India. It didn't really bother me if they knew. But I did know that I was tainted by the scandal surrounding Father.

One evening, though, there was someone quite different for dinner. He was older than the others, and had a calm assurance about him that made him mildly interesting.

Uncle John introduced him as Lieutenant Colonel Donald Foster and he sat next to me and asked me all about myself. Soon we were talking about writers and artists and the plays he'd seen in London when he had last taken home leave. By coincidence we'd both seen Private Lives by Noël Coward at the Phoenix Theatre.

When he left, he took my hand and said gallantly, 'It was delightful to meet you, Miss Baker. I would be honoured if you would consent to accompany me tomorrow evening for a drive.'

It was a rather stilted way to ask and I nearly laughed, but stopped myself just in time as that would have been unkind.

I accepted his invitation without any reflection. But later, alone in my room, watching the ceiling fan turn above my head, I tried to work out why I'd agreed to go out with him. I wasn't in the least bit attracted to him. He seemed to be nearer to Father in age than me. I could hardly remember his first name, thinking of him only as 'the Colonel'. There was something that drew me to him, though, despite those things; I think that in him I sensed an echo of my own loneliness.

He collected me in a shiny black army car, driven by an Indian chauffeur. I sat back on the leather seats and watched from the window as we glided down Marine Drive, along Apollo Bunder and through the darkening city. There was something magical about the twilight in Bombay. Office workers were rushing home along the crowded pavements, white Brahman cows wandered the roads and held up the traffic or slept in the middle of busy junctions. We drove past street hawkers, beggars, rickshaw-wallahs struggling with their loads, sweating in the heat of the steamy evening, past the red-brick Gothic facade of Victoria Terminus. As we drove, the Colonel pointed out places of interest, temples and street markets, hotels and government buildings. He seemed to know the city intimately; such a contrast to Aunt Nora and Uncle John.

I was surprised and impressed that the Colonel spoke to the driver in fluent Hindi. As we drove, he told me he'd been born in Kandaipur, and that his own father had once commanded the regiment he was now in. He was sent back 'home' to school, but after military training at Sandhurst and a spell in the trenches during the Great War, he had returned to Kandaipur and the regiment as a junior officer.

'So, India is your home?' I asked.

'Of course. We all call England home, but that's just a word. I could never live there.'

We strolled along the waterfront and watched the stars dancing on the water of the bay, and the lights from the ships moored up, from which snatches of conversation floated on the steamy air.

I was glad to be alone with someone who seemed content to accept me just as I am. He was stiff and formal, but even the long silences between us didn't feel awkward. As we turned and walked back to the car, he held out his arm, and after a moment's hesitation I slipped mine into the crook of his.

When the Colonel called for me the next day, Aunt Nora was sure I'd found the one.

I felt myself blushing. 'It's not like that, Auntie.'

'Oh, but I think it is, Anna, darling,' she'd said. 'Donald Foster's been a mystery to us all for years. We couldn't understand why he never married. He's had plenty of opportunities. He must just have been waiting for the right person. He's quite smitten with you. It was obvious from the moment he set eyes on you.'

'Don't, please…' I'd muttered, tingling with shame.

He had hired a private launch from Victoria Dock that day, and we sailed across the calm waters of the bay to Elephanta Island. The sea air was balmy and there was a fine mist over the bay. It was wonderful to be out of the British quarter and finally seeing something of the place.

We landed on the island and strolled through a line of hawkers and beggars and into a cave temple with sculpted pillars at the entrance. I stood there and closed my eyes, breathing in the incense and taking in the exotic mystery I could feel all around me. I clasped my hands together and turned to smile at the Colonel: 'It's wonderful. I've *never been anywhere like this before.' But he didn't seem to understand how I felt. He ushered me round the caves, telling me the detailed history of the place as if he were a tour guide.*

When we sat in the shade of a banyan tree on the little beach afterwards, and ate egg and cucumber sandwiches and drank lemonade, looking out over the misty bay, the Colonel fell silent as he ate his food methodically. I was relieved for that, but at the same time I was besieged by doubts.

Had I misjudged him the previous evening, or was his behaviour a symptom of his nervousness? What was I doing coming out with him anyway? I knew I was there partly through curiosity and partly through boredom at being cooped up in Aunt Nora's house. It troubled me, though, that the Colonel might think I was complicit in my aunt's matchmaking plans. As I finished eating, I vowed that I wouldn't mislead him any more, but the reason for his quietness took me by surprise.

'I only have until the end of the week in Bombay, Miss Baker. Then I must return to my regiment in Kandaipur. You haven't said how long you're planning to remain in India. I sincerely hope it will be a long stay. It would be a great honour if you would agree to come up to Matheran with me before I go back.'

'Matheran?'

'It's a little hill station, only a few hours' drive from the city. There's a toy train that goes up to the town and there are wonderful walks and rides around the hilltops. The views are marvellous. Do you ride, by the way?'

I shook my head, remembering how I'd pleaded with Mother and Father for a pony when I was little.

'No, I never learned. And it's very kind of you, Colonel— I mean Donald, but I don't think I should come. I'm afraid

Aunt Nora's going to keep me rather busy over the next few days.'

I felt guilty about rejecting him like that. He looked so crestfallen. When he dropped me off at Aunt Nora's he handed me his card and told me to call him if I changed my mind. But once inside the house everything changed. I slipped silently through the hallway and started up the stairs. I could hear the hubbub of voices and the chink of glasses from the drawing room. The door was slightly ajar, and I paused halfway up the stairs. I could hear Aunt Nora's penetrating voice.

'It's simply awful for the poor girl back home, you know. The family had to move countless times over the years. All the businesses that dreadful man dabbled in turned out to be dismal failures. And now! Well, now that he's in the clink, she can hardly show her face in her home town. He's diddled that many people out of their life savings she'd probably be lynched on the street. She got some very unpleasant letters, death threats some of them.

'Her mother left him several years ago now, of course. She's got someone else in tow. A much younger man. Now she's a selfish one, my little sister. She's got no time for the girl either.'

'I'd never have guessed, Nora, darling! She seems such a quiet little thing. How long will she be staying with you?'

'As short a time as possible, to tell you the truth, Martha. It's a dreadful bind having her here. She's not much company. I put it down to her frightful childhood. It's made her very withdrawn. Always has her nose in a book, not interested in socialising at all. Not really one of us. But I do feel an obligation towards her, all the same.'

I felt tears springing to my eyes as I dashed up to my room and threw myself on the bed. Humiliation swept over me in *waves as I buried my face in the pillow and sobbed. What Auntie said was all true, of course, but hearing the words spoken out loud like that hit me like a physical blow. And alongside the humiliation, that dreadful hollow loneliness I'd often experienced descended on me with renewed vigour. I had thought that Aunt Nora, for all her matchmaking and gossiping tendencies, was at least caring and kind. I had not suspected that I was here on sufferance and that she was desperate to get rid of me.*

Panic started to set in. Aunt Nora was right: life was untenable for me at home. Mother was so wrapped up in her drinking and her new relationship with that dreadful foppish boy Cedric (hardly older than I am) that she had no time for me. And it was true that because of the collapse of Father's latest business venture we had to sell the house in Buckinghamshire to pay the debts. My friends all drifted away, one by one. Coming out to India had been my last and only option.

The only thing that might have kept me in England was the thought of poor Father. We'd always been close. I felt shivers of horror remembering the day he was convicted of fraud and sent to Pentonville Prison. Poor Father. I knew he wasn't guilty of anything other than naivety, allowing dishonest men he shouldn't have trusted to lead him into a carefully constructed trap while they walked away unscathed.

When I heard Aunt Nora's shrill voice calling me downstairs for supper, I stared at my tear-stained face in the dressing table mirror, wondering how I'd get through another evening with her insufferable friends. Especially now I knew what she really felt about me.

Mechanically, I reapplied my powder and lipstick, but the dread of the evening to come descended on me. I could feel it in my drooping shoulders and as a dull ache in my chest.

Something made me feel for the Colonel's card in the pocket of my dress. I pulled it out and stared at it.

Lt. Colonel Donald Foster.
1st Battalion Kandaipur Rifles, Indian Army.
c/o the Royal Majestic Hotel, Victoria Crescent, Bombay.

I thought about his crestfallen expression as he said goodbye and felt a fresh pang of guilt.

I don't know how I endured that painful dinner with another of Aunt Nora's eligible bachelors sitting next to me, his bulging eyes fixed on the neckline of my blouse. He asked me question after question about Mother and Father, all of them insinuating, all of them designed to humiliate me. But I made a decision during that dinner: I realised that I simply could not bear it there any longer. Especially knowing how Aunt Nora felt about me. I needed to do something to get away from her and her matchmaking. There was only one choice. I decided to write to the Colonel and accept his invitation to Matheran.

It was an enchanting place. A range of round red-earth hilltops covered in pine trees among which nestled a community of quaint English-style bungalows. We stayed in adjoining suites in a little wooden building, one of the bungalows in the grounds of a guesthouse, which was run by a stout English lady called Mabel Stokes. She greeted Donald like a long-lost friend. Then she noticed me, lingering behind him in the lobby.

'Well, goodness me, Donald,' she said with astonishment in her voice. 'You've finally brought a lady friend to meet us. What a turn of events!'

'Yes. This is Miss Baker, Mabel,' he said awkwardly, and I felt a rush of sympathy for him, thinking the woman very rude and tactless.

Our bungalow was perched on the side of a great precipice. The whole of the valley was spread out beneath it, thousands of feet below. You could see for miles in this vast landscape, and if you stretched your eyes and looked far enough, the brown Indian plain eventually melded into the smoky, hazy sky. It was so beautiful.

We caught the tiny toy train that puffed and strained its way up the mountain for an hour or two, whistling at every bend. The views of the valley below as we climbed were breathtaking, but I was afraid to lean out to look at the view in case the tiny train tipped sideways.

Once we'd checked into the guesthouse, Donald suggested we rode around the ridge to a lookout point, where the land dropped down steeply to the valley floor. I rode behind him, a little nervously, only having been on a horse a couple of times before. There were those views of the endless dusty plain again, this time even more stunning as the mist had cleared and the sky was blue and cloudless. It wasn't just riding that was making me nervous, it was the thought that he was about to ask me to marry him. I knew it was on the cards. It was what I had tacitly acknowledged when I'd written to him. But when it came down to it, I felt dread stealing over me. Could I really tie myself to this stiff, awkward, buttoned-up man for the rest of my life? There were times when he'd surprised me during our brief acquaintance: his knowledge of the language, his feel for India, the fact that he was so different from Aunt Nora and her narrow-minded circle. But still… He was a good twenty years older than me. Did I really want to give up my youth so soon?

But then I thought about home, about Father in disgrace in prison and how the whole town and all our 'friends' had turned against us, about Mother, making a fool of herself with a much younger man. Life had become impossible for me there. But I couldn't bear the thought of living with Aunt Nora, even if she had actually wanted me there.

As it turned out, he didn't ask me when we were out on the ride. I think he might have done, but one of the horses was spooked by an animal that ran out of the undergrowth and we returned to the guesthouse earlier than planned.

I went out onto the terrace and got my sketchbook out. I tried to capture the beauty of the landscape, but it is elusive. I realised then that India's beauty is not just visual, everything about it is captivating. The smell of woodsmoke on the evening air, the huge burnished sun shimmering above the milky landscape as it slips lower and lower in the sky, the cries of the wildlife in the scrub, the chatter of crickets, and the lizards on the wall of my bathroom. Donald had at least shown me a different India from the one Aunt Nora and Uncle John occupied. He had opened my eyes to its wonders. As I sat there sketching, I realised that I was grateful to him for that.

So, when later, after dinner, he suggested a nightcap on the terrace, and we sat in the cool night air watching the stars twinkling in the clear sky and the pinpricks of light from a thousand tiny villages in the vast dark valley below, I was ready for what he was about to say. I tried to look him in the eye as he stumbled over his words, but his formality made it difficult to do that. His awkwardness was such that I just wanted him to get it over and done with. I hung my head while he spoke.

'It would be a great honour if you'd consent to marry me, Anna. I have a very comfortable bungalow on the

*cantonment at Kandaipur, being a Lt. Colonel in the
First Kandaipur Rifles. Of course, I have been living in
the officers' mess and not using it, but I am entitled to it
through my rank, particularly if I marry. You would have
a very high status among the memsahibs, the only higher
wife being Mrs Smethurst, the Colonel's wife. Of course,
one day, I hope…'*

*I put my hand out to take his and found his fist clenched.
'Donald,' I said, 'Please. There's no need to go on. The
answer is yes.'*

Connie puts the diary down and rubs her aching eyes. She thinks
again about Anna, about how she stood on the steps distraught,
that miserable night so long ago, unaware in her distress of the
rain soaking through her nightdress.

How on earth had Anna ended up at Cedar Hall? It's something
Connie had often wondered about. She pictures again Anna's tear-
stained face, her desperate eyes. Reading the diary now is helping to
explain to Connie something of Anna's loneliness and isolation. It's
making her realise that she has experienced those feelings herself in
so many ways down the years, and that her connection with Anna
that started that fateful night in 1934 is as strong now as it ever
was. But can it explain why Anna travelled five thousand miles to
seek help from Father?

Connie shakes her head, still puzzled after all this time, but even
more certain that she needs to protect the house, and its precious
memories. She understands too that the secrets her father asked
her to keep no longer belong to him alone.

Chapter Ten

Connie

Connie's never been in a wheelchair before. It's strange being pushed across the stable yard and towards the back door of Cedar Hall. She feels out of control and vulnerable, a bit like when she and Evie went on a fairground ride in Henley all those years ago.

Mr Squires collected her from the nursing home in his Range Rover this morning after Matron had lent the wheelchair, following a lot of discussion. Over the last few days she's been taking hesitant steps with the help of the Zimmer frame, and yesterday managed to walk all the way down the passage to the day room by herself. Even so, it took a long time for Mr Squires and Alfie, one of the carers, to manoeuvre her out of her chair, onto the wheelchair, and finally into the front seat of the vehicle. Longer even than it had taken Jonathan to drive the short distance across the town to Cedar Hall. She'd felt helpless, like a baby. On the short journey, she'd tried to talk to him about the house.

'I don't want it to be pulled down, Mr Squires,' she'd said. 'I couldn't bear it.'

Jonathan had carried on staring straight ahead. 'There isn't much choice as I understand the situation, Miss Burroughs,' he'd said in a hard, even voice. 'The developers have offered a very good price and we need a quick sale. We're just going there so you can say goodbye to the house.'

'But there's a deed. A deed my father signed. Didn't Peter tell you?'

He was driving through the gates at that point, making a show of concentrating on getting the wide car through unscathed.

'Did you not hear me, Mr Squires? About the deed.'

'Peter didn't mention anything about that to me, Miss Burroughs. You're in safe hands with him. I'm sure he's done all the necessary checks. Now, here we are. Let's get you out of the car...'

Jonathan has left her now and is standing at the back door, fumbling with the bunch of keys. The icy wind whips around her, blowing litter and papers about the yard, stinging her cheeks. Such a contrast to the fuggy warmth of her room. She tucks the tartan blanket around her lap and does up her top button with trembling fingers.

'It's the one with the red fob,' she says, watching him take his time with the lock, but her thin voice carries away on the wind and he keeps on trying the different keys, one by one.

By the time he has opened the door and manoeuvred Connie up the steps and inside the house her teeth are chattering. The house feels different now, echoing and bare, not at all like the home she remembers. It smells strange too; of bleach and disinfectant. He pushes her along the passage into the front hall. Her eyes flit around the room. The fireplace has been swept clean and the furniture has gone; there are faded rectangles on the walls where the pictures used to hang.

'Please could you get the walking frame from the car and help me out of this wheelchair, Mr Squires? I would like to walk around downstairs.'

'Of course. I'll pop back to the car. One moment.'

The back door bangs behind him and Connie is alone in the house. The past closes around her. The air is heavy with the weight of so many memories. From her wheelchair she can see her younger self sitting impatiently on the bottom step, waiting for Father to come in through the front door at the end of the day. Then there's Mother stooping at the tiled grate to build the fire, the sun streaming through the stained glass, colouring her hair red and yellow. Evie, old and thin, comes in from chapel on a winter's day, hanging her threadbare grey coat carefully on the coat-stand, rubbing her dry hands together to warm her fingers.

Connie puts her head on one side and listens carefully, expecting to hear voices, but all she can hear is the rumble of traffic passing on the road. She had expected – no, dreaded – to hear Father's voice coming to her here, the quiet one he used when he was beyond rage. The fear of it had made her sweat and tremble all week; it had almost put her off coming back to the house. She'd gone over and over it in her mind. *Constance,* the voice in her head had said, *what have you done with the house? Where is the furniture? All my precious belongings? My clothes? My papers? I trusted you to look after them, Constance, and you have disappointed me more than I can say.* The thought of his being here, concealed in the shadows, waiting for her, watching her, made her shiver, but she knew she had to come back to the house somehow. She had to make sure.

The back door creaks and Jonathan's footsteps approach along the tiled passage. The images of Mother, Evie and her former self dissolve into nothing. It strikes her that she will never be alone here again.

'I've brought your Zimmer frame, Miss Burroughs. Shall I help you out of the chair now?'

His hands are on her arms, pulling her to her feet. He's not used to this and nor is she. She hardly knows Jonathan. What she does know, though, is that he's only doing this for his commission on the sale of the house. She has no one else to help her.

Clutching the Zimmer frame, she inches it forward towards the door to Father's office.

'Could you open the door for me, Mr Squires?'

He darts ahead of her and pushes the door open. With tottering steps, she inches towards the opening. Her bad leg throbs and the good one feels weak. She stops in the doorway and stares into the room. It's empty apart from the bureau at the far end.

She has a vision of the room as it was when Father entertained. Three or four men would be sitting around in their shirtsleeves, smoking, talking. Father would ring for the housemaid to bring glasses for his whisky and brandy. Connie would wait in the hallway when the girl took the tray of glasses inside. Smoke and alcohol fumes would engulf her from the open door.

Mother would purse her lips and draw herself up tall during these visits, but she would say nothing. Male voices would rumble on in the office for hours, sometimes raised in anger, sometimes laughing. Angry or amused, those voices always frightened Connie. She knew they frightened Evie too, by the way she would grow pale and take her hand silently. They would creep upstairs to their bedroom under the eaves and snuggle in their beds, hiding from the voices. Sometimes they would look out of the front window when they heard the visitors leaving and see men in dark coats and hats striding away from the house towards the station with their briefcases and umbrellas, but they would never see their faces.

With a shudder she moves forward onto the carpet. It's more difficult to push the frame here than on the parquet flooring of the hallway. She moves with great effort across the room, breathing heavily. Sweat trickles down her forehead and into her eyes. She blinks it away. She notices deep depressions in the carpet where Father's bookcases have been taken away, and although someone must have vacuumed the room, the carpet is still grey with ingrained dust where furniture once stood.

Above the marble fireplace is a huge patch of faded wallpaper where the picture of Kandaipur church hung for decades. She pauses and thinks again of Anna, her journey to India, and the loneliness and isolation she'd expressed in the diary. Those emotions had spoken to Connie so clearly from the pages. She feels a fresh tug of guilt that she let the diary lie unread for so long.

Now she manoeuvres herself across the room and stops beside the far wall. She stares at the patterned wallpaper. She takes her hand off the Zimmer frame, now slippery with sweat, and fingers her filigree necklace, glancing back at Jonathan. He's standing in the doorway, tapping on his mobile phone. She moves closer to the wall and runs a hand over the surface. It feels perfectly smooth at first, but then her fingers touch the telltale ridge under the wallpaper. She sighs. If she'd had a chance to sort things out before the house was put on the market she would have had time to do something about it. But she can't do anything about it now. She will just have to put her faith in the Lord. She moves slowly and painfully across the room and stares down at the carpet beside the grate. If only she could get down on her knees and run her hand over that too.

Tearing her eyes away, she edges towards the bureau. Peter said he had emptied it out, but she still needs to check. She positions herself beside it, runs her palm over the tooled black leather top, then with her hands shaking awkwardly, she lifts the lid. She gasps as the smell of Father's spicy pomade wafts towards her from the interior. She hooks the lid up and peers inside. There's nothing there except an ink stain and a couple of paperclips. One by one, she opens the drawers on either side of the lid. Nothing in them either. Peter was right: he had been thorough. Anything Father had left is now in the vault in Peter's office.

Of course, she and Evie had never disturbed Father's papers. They'd been too fearful to do that, even after his death. Even when, after Evie had gone, Connie had had the room decorated, she'd watched the men move the bureau from one side of the room to the other, but never once had she had the temerity to look inside it. She's glad it was Peter and not she who'd had the task of emptying it. She wonders fleetingly if there might have been something in the desk to explain Anna's connection to Father.

She reaches up to unhook the lid from its catch. It slips from her trembling fingers, falling shut with a slam.

'Are you all right, Miss Burroughs?' Jonathan hurries over. He's peering at her face. She feels flustered and she knows she is shaking. Her heart is hammering so hard. She should have left well alone. Father would have hated her peering into the interior of his desk, checking through the drawers, even if it was empty, and he himself had been lying in his cold grave in the chapel graveyard for twenty-five years.

His voice comes to her now; the thin, stretched, painful voice, the one she remembers from his deathbed. She and Evie had sat with him for hours, days even, as he wasted away. They had hardly dared to leave him for a moment, even to prepare food, even to sleep. But once when Evie had slipped away to visit the bathroom, he'd grabbed Connie's hand. He held it in an unnaturally strong grip for a dying man, so strong that she'd been afraid he would crush the bones. She'd stared at his bloodshot eyes, terrified.

When I'm gone, Constance, you must look after my belongings as if I was still here. Make sure that no meddling hands get hold of my papers. Don't let anyone into the office. It will remain private, just as it has been for all these years. You will remember that, won't you? Constance? Constance? I'm relying on you.

She'd nodded. Her mouth had been so dry that she couldn't reply.

'Are you done here, Miss Burroughs?' Jonathan Squires is glancing at his watch, tapping his foot in the doorway. 'I really need to get back to the office, if you don't mind.'

She nods mutely and turns away from the desk.

'Come on then. I'll help you into your wheelchair and get you back to the nursing home in time for lunch.'

The wind has dropped as he pushes her outside into the stable yard. She hears the back door slam behind her and feels a sudden rush of regret that she's leaving here forever. Leaving the old place to be destroyed. As Jonathan pushes her across the yard towards his car, she looks up at the blank coach house windows. It could be a trick of the light, but she could swear she sees a shadow move behind the glass. Or perhaps it's her memory playing tricks on her? Perhaps she's expecting to see something there, some reminder of what happened to the orphans, or to Anna, back in the past she has tried so hard to forget.

Chapter Eleven

Sarah

'You sure you're OK, Dad?' Sarah asks for the umpteenth time, glancing across at him as she drives along the main road towards Weirfield. He sits in the passenger seat with a rug tucked around his knees. She can't help thinking that his face looks pale and drawn.

'Of course. I'm quite all right, darling. There's no need to keep asking.' He flashes her a benign smile.

Now she knows she feels guilty. Thinking back to the first few days of her stay with him, she *had* registered vaguely that he looked rather pale, that he occasionally crept off quietly to lie down for the odd half-hour. She'd been so preoccupied with her own worries, though, that she'd hardly given it a second thought. He hadn't mentioned the crippling headaches once, and she knows now that he'd been trying hard to hide it from her; sneaking off for tests and medical appointments without a word.

She'd come home from Le Gastronome to find him sitting quietly in his sunroom watching the blood-red sun dip beyond the trees on the hills opposite. She'd questioned him gently, hinting that she'd seen him in town. He'd been reticent at first, but she could tell from the haggard look on his face that the news was going to be bad.

'A brain tumour?' she'd repeated, when he finally told her, shock rolling through her.

'It's slow-growing, they tell me. And I didn't want to worry you,' he said weakly. 'You had a hell of a lot on your mind, I would have told you when the time was right.'

'You should have told me before, Dad,' she'd said through tears. 'It's such a serious thing to bear all by yourself.'

'What difference would it have made?' he'd said, shrugging.

'I could have looked after you, taken you to your appointments.'

'I've been coping. I'm not quite helpless yet.'

'Oh, Dad. I wasn't saying that... I'd just like to help.' She'd paused for a moment, unsure of what to say, how to bring them back together. 'You know, I could help with your search,' she says finally. 'That could be something we could do together.' She looks at his moist, bloodshot eyes. She's so desperate to ease his burden. He's become obsessed with his quest, spending long hours poring over websites, agonising over records. She understands now that the search for his birth mother is directly connected to his deteriorating health.

He'd slid his hand on top of hers. 'I'd really appreciate that, Sarah.'

For a few days she didn't think about the old house. She hardly thought about Alex either. She needed time to adjust to the knowledge that her father was seriously ill and had kept it from her. Why had she taken him so much for granted over the years? Why hadn't she spent more time with him, made the effort to take time off from the restaurant to come and see him more often? What if there wasn't enough time to make amends? She'd followed him around the house, trying to relieve him of tasks, trying to make his life easier in any small way she could.

A few days after he'd broken the news about his illness, he'd been reading the local paper over breakfast. 'Did you know Cedar Hall is under offer?' he'd said.

She'd turned from the sink and wiped her hands on her apron. He was holding the paper up, showing her an advert, a picture of the house with a diagonal banner across it. 'You told me it was for sale, but I didn't realise it was going to happen so quickly.'

She'd told him then about how she'd seen the furniture being moved out of the old house, about how she'd been to the estate agents to ask about it. He looked up at her and smiled.

'I could tell you wanted to buy it, Sarah, when you spoke about it before.'

'Could you?' she said, smiling down at him. 'I probably didn't even know myself then. But I have been thinking...'

'Go on?'

'You know that old house could have been a project I could really get my teeth into. And it might have helped with your research too. It could hold some clues about what happened at the orphanage,' she said. 'But it's too late. Someone else is buying it now.'

'Well, we could see if they would take a higher offer?'

'I doubt they would. I tried to find out how much it was going for, but I didn't get very far. The woman in Country Squires was very cagey.'

'If you think about it, it seems the perfect solution,' he went on, not acknowledging what she'd said. 'I could use some of my savings to buy the place. That would give you somewhere of your own near here, completely independent of Alex. If and when you do manage to get your share of the business from him, you could buy the place back from me. In the meantime, you could do it up. You've got a real gift for that sort of thing. Remember what the old place in Bristol was like when you bought it?'

'But, Dad, even if they would take a higher offer, wouldn't you prefer me to stay here with you? You're not well. I could cook for you, clean the house.'

'I don't want you tied to me, Sarah. You've got your own life to lead. And besides, you wouldn't be far away, would you?'

'I suppose not.'

'Look, if you won't take a gift, it could be a business arrangement. I could fund the purchase and the renovation, and we could share the profits when it's sold. How about that?'

She left the washing-up and came to sit down opposite him. She knew he was only humouring her, that it could take years to do up the house, and by then... She bit her lip to stop the thought.

'Are you sure? It's a very generous offer.'

'Quite sure.'

'That's so kind of you, Dad,' she said, taking his hand. 'You know if we do manage to buy it, we could look into its associations with the orphanage. It could help in your search for your birth mother.'

'Let's hope so. I think it would be rather interesting to own that old place, whatever happens. Far better for us to buy it than for it to be knocked down, don't you think? It's probably going to developers. Lots of old houses in the town have been demolished or turned into flats. The history society is up in arms about it, but there's nothing they can do. None of the houses are listed.'

So, she'd agreed to speak to Mr Squires about making a higher offer. Over the next few days she'd called his office several times, left numerous messages, but he'd never called back.

'If he's not going to return your calls, why not go in there and speak to him in person?' Dad had said eventually. 'I'll come with you, if you like. Moral support. And I can be on hand to back you up, to confirm the funds are available straight away.'

As she drives through the outskirts of Weirfield, the creeping anticipation she feels at the thought that she might soon be able to buy Cedar Hall is gradually replacing the pain of the conversation she'd had with Alex that morning.

'I need to see you,' was the first thing he'd said when she answered his call. 'I need you to come here and meet me in the restaurant.'

She'd held the phone away from her ear, speechless for a moment.

'It's all about what *you* need, isn't it, Alex?' she'd said finally.

'I'm sorry, Sarah. It's just that I need to talk to you about the business.'

'I'd rather you dealt with Judith Marshall,' she said stiffly. 'She told me you'd sent her some financial details. I'm going in next week to discuss it with her.'

'It's not about that. It's not about our spilt, Sarah, it's about the other business. About the investigation.'

His voice sounded weary. Her heart started to twist with pity before she took a deep breath and stopped herself.

'What about the investigation?' she said. 'I told the police everything I could. What else is there to say?'

'It's complicated. Look, it's hard to talk about it over the phone. Won't you come up here and talk to me? Or maybe I could drive down to you. Could I come down this afternoon?'

'No, not this afternoon. I'm busy.'

'Busy?' He gave a short laugh. 'What's there to do in deepest Berkshire? I'm sorry, Sarah, but this is important. More important than whatever you're amusing yourself with down there.'

'I think it would be far better for you to deal with Judith,' she said tersely.

'This doesn't concern her. Look, I need you to tell them. I need you to tell the police something for me.'

'Well, maybe they could get in touch with me, they know where I am. But anyway, as I said, I've told them everything I know.'

'I can't believe this! You're saying you won't help?'

'It's difficult for me, Alex. And I really don't know how you've got the cheek to ask me to help you, after what's happened.'

Cedar Hall looms up on the right. She slows down and glances through the gate, spotting Mr Squires in a dark overcoat, pushing someone in a wheelchair across the yard.

She wonders briefly if she should drive on to his office and speak to one of his assistants but instead, acting on impulse, she pulls off the road and parks beside the newsagent's.

'Look, there he is, Dad. Why don't I go and talk to him here and now? He's obviously been avoiding me. He won't be able to do that if I go up and speak to him.'

'Hmm… Maybe it's not such a good idea, Sarah. It looks like old Miss Burroughs in the wheelchair. It might be a bit awkward.'

'Well, if it is, she needs to know too, surely? I won't be a moment. You wait here.'

And without a further word she's out of the car and hurrying across the road.

'Mr Squires!'

She walks quickly towards him. He stops pushing the wheelchair and his face drops. Sarah draws closer. The old lady in the wheelchair stares at her. Her hair is wispy and grey and her face is scored with lines, but it's the eyes that Sarah notices first. Those bright eyes. She's unmistakeably the girl in the photograph that she'd seen in the old house. The younger one, the one who was smiling.

'I'm sorry to bother you, Mr Squires, but I've been trying to reach you for several days now.'

'Ah, Mrs Jennings, isn't it?' His voice sounds measured, but she can see from his eyes that he's irritated at her for approaching him like this. 'Mrs Jennings, let me introduce Miss Burroughs. Miss Burroughs is the owner of Cedar Hall.'

Sarah holds out her hand and the old lady lifts a trembling hand from under a tartan blanket. Sarah takes it and holds it in hers.

'I'm pleased to meet you, Miss Burroughs.'

The old lady's hand feels cold and skeletal, as if the bones are very light under stretched skin.

'Mr Squires,' Sarah says, 'I hope you don't mind me coming straight to the point, but I'd very much like to make an offer for the house.'

'I'm afraid it's sold, Mrs Jennings. It isn't on the market any longer.'

'Well, that's a pity because I have funds available. I won't have to arrange finance and I would be able to complete very quickly. Could you let me know what the sale price is, please? I might be able to offer something more.'

'I'm afraid not, Mrs Jennings. The place is sold, as I said. It's a confidential matter. Look, if you'll excuse me, I have to get Miss

Burroughs back to her nursing home. She's been out long enough, she needs her lunch.'

He begins to push the wheelchair away and Sarah walks beside him.

'I'm sure I could better the current offer,' she repeats. 'If you could just let me know what it is, please.'

'That would be most unethical of me, Mrs Jennings.'

'Two hundred and fifty thousand.' It's the old lady's voice. She's looking straight at Sarah. 'Two hundred and fifty thousand pounds. To knock this beautiful old place down and build a lot of ugly little houses here, on my father's land.'

'Now, Miss Burroughs, please—'

'Would you take two hundred and sixty from me?' Sarah says, seizing the opportunity.

'I'm afraid she can't, Mrs Jennings,' says Jonathan Squires. 'You see, I've given my word.'

'Of course we will take it,' the old lady's shrill voice chips in. 'I told Peter, I told him there was a document. Some sort of deed stopping the land from being built on, and he wouldn't listen to me. He tried to force me to sell it to those builders. I know my money is running out, so I agreed to it. But I didn't want to do it. If this young lady is prepared to offer more then I'd much prefer to sell it to her. *You* won't be wanting to knock the place down, will you, my dear?'

She looks up at Sarah with anxious eyes. 'Of course not—' Sarah begins, but Jonathan Squires cuts in.

'Now, now, Miss Burroughs. Slow down. Please. It's not as simple as that.'

'Of course it is, Mr Squires. This lady has offered more. And Peter told me he must take the best price he can. It is his duty as my trustee to do that. He told me so yesterday.'

Jonathan Squires opens the car door, a sickly smile on his face. 'Now, come on, Miss Burroughs. Let's get you in the car. We can talk about all that later.'

He bends down and puts his arms around the old lady. As he lifts her into the passenger seat, her pleading eyes are fixed on Sarah's.

'Mr Squires, will you please speak to Peter about this lady's offer?' the old lady says. 'Please tell him that I want to accept it. I won't make a fuss, I won't say any more about that old deed if you see to it that this young lady gets the house.'

He's fumbling with the seat belt. 'Mr Squires, please…'

'All right, I'll speak to Peter,' he mutters. 'I'll see what can be done.' He glances towards Sarah. 'Perhaps you'd kindly drop into my office after lunch, Mrs Jennings. I can take your details down and we'll take it from there.'

Chapter Twelve

Sarah

Miss Burroughs is true to her word, and after Sarah's initial visit to Jonathan Squires' office that day, everything moves very quickly. Sarah passes the next three weeks in a frenzy of preparation, dealing with the paperwork from the solicitors', looking after her father, and ensuring everything is ready for the day when she's able to collect the keys from Country Squires and the old house is really hers.

At last, she stands in the hallway of Cedar Hall, looking around her in amazement that she's finally achieved it. She's actually the new owner of this wonderful old house.

'Hey, look at this, Sarah,' her father's voice echoes from the other end of the hall. 'They've left a piece of furniture in here. An old desk.'

Sarah walks down the passage and through the panelled hallway towards the study. She stops in the doorway. Her father is standing in the middle of the room, staring at a huge oak bureau that fills the entire wall at the far end. The sight of it gives her heart an odd turn. She hovers on the threshold. Her father turns and smiles.

'I wonder why they left it?' he says.

'I'm not sure,' she says. 'Cartwrights didn't say anything about it to me. Nor did Mr Squires.'

'It's a beautiful piece of furniture,' muses her father, running a hand over the tooled leather top.

'Hmm, maybe…' she says dubiously.

It's true, it is beautifully made, but it's also old-fashioned, dark, and heavy. And it has a sort of brooding presence about it that feels vaguely unnerving to Sarah. The sight of the old desk stirs the memory of the first and only time she was inside this house before, and of how the strange atmosphere of the place, so redolent of a forgotten era, had stayed with her for days afterwards.

'Perhaps they couldn't get it out of the room?' ventures her father. 'Perhaps that's why they left it.'

'Perhaps,' she says, trying to ignore the chill running through her. 'I wish they'd told us.'

Her father smiles at her mischievously. 'I don't think we were flavour of the month with Jonathan Squires, Sarah, coming in with that offer, gazumping their developer chums at the eleventh hour.'

She laughs. 'Yes, I'm sure they're furious with us. It's all a bit cosy around here, isn't it? At least old Miss Burroughs was on our side, though.'

'Perhaps their noses were out of joint and they thought that leaving this old desk here would make things a bit difficult for us.'

'I suppose I could give Cartwrights a call and insist they come and take it away.'

'No, don't do that, darling. It suits the house. And it must be quite valuable.'

'Maybe,' she says, turning back into the hallway. 'I'll see how I feel about it when my furniture arrives this afternoon.'

At Sarah's request, Judith Marshall had sent Alex a list of furniture and other items she wanted from their house in Primrose Hill. She'd visited the restaurant and her old home three weeks ago now. It had left her feeling so low that she'd decided not to go back there for a long time, at least not until she felt stronger. She'd also made herself a promise that she wouldn't contact Alex directly again.

She'd gone back to her old home in London to collect some clothes too. The house felt strange as she let herself in through the front door. It smelled of stale cooking, of neglect. She stood in the kitchen doorway and ran her eyes over the mess inside: dirty crockery piled beside the sink, takeaway food cartons on the table, the bin overflowing with litter. Then she went upstairs to their bedroom and filled a suitcase with clothes. She couldn't wait to finish. She needed to get out of there as quickly as she could, but she was halfway down the stairs with one large suitcase and a holdall slung over her shoulder when the phone in the hall started to ring. She tried to ignore it, but as she moved towards the front door it stopped and the answerphone kicked in. A voice sounded from the machine that made Sarah's blood run cold.

'Alex? Are you there?' It was a young woman's voice, bright and clear. Sarah instantly recognised it. She dropped the bags down in the narrow hallway and stood there in shock.

'Alex, can you pick up the phone, please? I need to talk to you. Please, Alex. Call me as soon as you get this. It's important.'

Sarah was tempted to snatch up the phone and yell abuse at the girl, but with a huge effort of will she stopped herself. Instead, trembling and feeling sick with rage, she rushed through the door with her bags and slammed it behind her. She ran towards her car, not looking back.

The voice of that girl on the answerphone had rung in her ears all the way back to her father's house, and the painful conversation she'd had with Alex in his office had gone round and round in her mind until she was exhausted with the turmoil it provoked. How could he have had the cheek to ask for her help with the police investigation when all the time he was lying to her about seeing Jemma? Why couldn't he show her enough respect to admit his sordid little affair? She knew she would never be able to trust anything he said again. It reinforced the feeling she'd had that day at the restaurant, that she really knew nothing about him at all.

Without any protest, Alex had agreed to send the furniture. He also agreed to the condition she'd insisted upon: that the things would be brought to Weirfield by a removal company, and not by Alex himself.

That morning, she'd been so thrilled to receive the call from Cartwrights that the sale had gone through that the painful situation with Alex had temporarily been displaced in her mind. It had felt like a new beginning as she'd set off to Country Squires to collect the keys. She'd driven Dad into Weirfield tingling with excitement, the back of her car loaded with boxes of her belongings. The weather had fitted her mood too; a crisp winter morning, bright and clear, the great River Thames sparkling in the sunlit valley below.

As she'd pulled up in the empty courtyard and parked in front of the old coach house she'd turned to her father with shining eyes.

'It's actually ours, Dad, this fantastic place. I can hardly believe it!'

Her hands were trembling as she'd opened the back door with that bunch of ancient keys. When she stepped into the back hallway, any trepidation she felt that the house might seem forlorn and forbidding had lifted instantly.

The house had been cleaned from top to bottom. It was light and airy, the walls bare and the floorboards clean. It smelled of lavender and lemon. There had been no trace of the former occupants. Sun streamed through the clean windows and without the clutter and detritus of the Burroughs' lives, and their heavy, shabby furniture, the rooms felt far more spacious and welcoming than she remembered them.

But the sight of that enormous oak desk has given her a strange sense of unease. She goes back through to the kitchen and unpacks the kettle from the box she brought from her father's house. She fills it from the gurgling tap in the butler sink and plugs it into a dangerous-looking plug on the windowsill. She hears her father's footsteps in the hall.

'Are you all right, Sarah? You looked a bit upset in the study.'

'I'm fine, Dad.'

'Sure?'

'Quite sure. Why don't you get the teapot and teabags out of the box and I'll make a cuppa.'

He peers at her with curiosity, but says nothing.

They stroll around the rooms while the kettle boils. Each time she opens a door she wonders whether some other reminder of the Burroughs family will have been left behind, some piece of history for her father to add to his papers. But there is nothing else here. Each room is bare and the only traces of the former occupants are the pale patches on the walls where pictures have been taken down.

'It's lovely, Sarah,' her father says as she shows him around. 'I thought it would be gloomy, but it's not like that at all. It's got so much potential.'

They walk into every room, admiring the space and the symmetry of the house, the big windows, the views of the garden.

Last of all she shows him the conservatory behind the kitchen. In the back of her mind lurks the picture. The photograph of the two young Burroughs girls standing in there all those decades ago. She's thought about it so much over the past few weeks that she half expects the two of them to be standing there as she goes down the steps into the conservatory. It's empty, of course, the flagstone tiles on the floor swept clean. The withering vine has been removed and there are no plants at all left on the slatted shelves.

Her father stands with his hands on his hips and looks around admiringly.

'This is all so elegant. Look at the workmanship in those window frames. Wonderful floor tiles too,' he says. 'You know you could really make something of this. You could knock out that back wall and incorporate it into the kitchen. It would make a huge, light room that opens straight out onto the garden.'

'That's not a bad idea,' says Sarah.' I'd have to raise the floor up to the level of the kitchen, though.'

They stroll into the overgrown garden and her father walks across the grass towards the garden wall.

'Where are you going, Dad?' she asks as she walks beside him, keeping pace with him. His expression is determined, his jaw set, but when he speaks, his voice betrays deep emotion.

'I just wanted to have a quick peep over at where the orphanage was. Just curious.'

Sarah joins him and they peer over the wall and straight into the back garden of one of the modern houses on the neighbouring estate. There's a climbing frame and slide on a neat lawn. A sandy-coloured Terrier runs towards them yapping, and they draw back.

'It's amazing to think that enormous building was once right there,' her father says, 'just where that garden wall is. In fact, that wall might even be the end wall of the orphanage itself… Do you remember when we stopped and looked around it that time, Sarah?'

'Of course I do. I'll never forget it,' she says, smiling.

'You know, if I ever did that journey on my own I would always stop in front of the old place and have a walk around.'

'Really, Dad?'

'I don't know what I was looking for. Mad, really.'

'Not mad at all. It's quite natural.'

'Trying to find some sort of connection to the past, I suppose,' he muses.

They are back in the courtyard again now. 'Shall we go back inside and make the tea?' Sarah asks, anxious not to tire him.

'Why don't we take a look in the coach house first? Do you have the keys?'

'Yes, they're here in my pocket. Are you sure you're up to it?'

'Of course. I want to see it all.'

'I haven't been in there myself yet either, Dad. There are a couple of stables behind there too.'

She takes out the great bunch of keys and finds the one labelled 'Garage'. The key is rusty and the lock stiff, but she persists, and is soon pushing back the rickety wooden doors. They step inside. Sunlight filters in from a dusty window, but there's nothing to see, only oil stains on the brick floor and a few rusting paint cans in one corner.

'Why don't we take a look in the room above while we're here?' her father says.

'I'm not sure I have the key for that...' Sarah examines the bunch of keys. Each of them is labelled with a coloured plastic fob, except one. That has an old-fashioned leather keyring attached to a handwritten label. She peers at it and recognises the elaborate handwriting that she'd first seen on her father's birth certificate:

Strictly Private.

'Got it? Come on then.'

Feeling strangely reluctant, Sarah follows her father back outside and up the crumbling steps at the side of the building. Weeds are growing in the cracks where the cement has worn away between the bricks. The door at the top, with its peeling black paint, is stiff like the door to the coach house below. As she struggles with the lock, Sarah gets the feeling that it hasn't been opened for decades. But it finally yields, and as they step inside a shower of powdery dust falls on them from the top of the door.

'I don't think they've bothered to clean at all in here,' says Dad, dusting down his jacket.

Sarah stares around her. Bird droppings and black dirt cover the floorboards. Cobwebs hang in shrouds from the filthy ceiling, which in one corner has come away from the wall. Beneath that there's a huge streak of green mould where rainwater has leaked through.

'God, it's filthy,' she says, but it isn't the dirt that troubles her as much as the remnants of the past. On one wall a metal bedframe stands rusting and sagging. Beside it, a chipped enamel bucket. Beneath the leaking ceiling is a chaise longue, its springs protruding, sawdust and stuffing spilling out of the upholstery. It's so blemished and filthy that it's impossible to guess the original colour. In one corner is a wooden washstand with a marble top, a cracked jug and bowl. Under the window stands a small writing table, a cup and saucer on it, as if the previous occupant has just left.

Sarah takes a couple of steps into the room. There's a sudden fluttering of feathers from the gap in the roof and a clump of dirt falls down from there. At the same time a tiny mouse jumps out of the cup on the table and scuttles along the wainscot, disappearing through the floorboards. Sarah lets out a stifled gasp.

'Let's get out of here, Dad,' she says, then she sees his face. 'Don't laugh! You know I hate mice.'

'They're more afraid of you, you know. You seem very jumpy, Sarah.'

'I just didn't expect this place to be like this. They were meant to have cleared everything out. I could call them…'

'Is it really worth it? Like we said before, they're probably annoyed with us, and with Miss Burroughs too, that they didn't manage to flog the place to those developers. They probably want to put you to some trouble. Don't worry about it. It would only take one trip to the tip to get rid of all this. And we don't want to get poor old Miss Burroughs into any more trouble, do we? It was wonderful, and very brave of her, to stand up to her advisers and insist on selling you the house.'

'I suppose you're right.'

She glances out of the window. The bonnet of a lorry is edging through the double gates and into the courtyard.

'Let's go down, shall we? The furniture has arrived. We can grab that cup of tea while they're unloading. I could do with a cigarette as well.'

She glances round at the room again, drawn in by it but repelled by it at the same time. All this dilapidated furniture and equipment and the air of abandonment gives her a strange, shivery feeling, a strong impression that the past still has a firm hold over this place. What happened here? Who stayed in this strange, inhospitable room all those years ago? A chill runs down her spine as she tries to imagine its faceless previous inhabitants, now long gone. She follows her father out of the door and down the outside steps.

Chapter Thirteen

Sarah

Sarah wakes at first light to winter sunshine streaming in through the bay window opposite her bed. For a few seconds she's in a confused fog, wondering where she is. Gradually through the fog emerges the half-memory of unsettling dreams that disturbed her sleep and made her wake sweating in the dead of night. It had taken her a long time to go back to sleep. Each creak of the boards, each stirring of breeze in the cedar trees outside the window had made her sit up, her scalp tingling, her ears straining for the sound of footsteps on the stairs, a voice in the corridor.

When eventually sleep did come again, the dream returned as if she'd never awoken; a shadowy figure paced around downstairs, walking through each room in turn, moving nearer all the time, up the stairs along the corridor and finally into Sarah's room. She lay paralysed on the bed, unable to move or to speak. The figure leaned over her bed and stretched out an icy finger to move a lock of hair out of her eyes. She tried to sit up but the figure pushed her back. She sensed its great strength.

But now, in the morning sunlight, everything looks different. She laughs to herself, remembering how terrified she'd been in the night. She glances at her watch. Seven o'clock. There are no curtains at the window so the light of dawn must have woken her.

She gets out of bed, pulls on her dressing gown and walks along the bare boards to the bathroom at the end of the corridor. The huge cast-iron bathtub is rusty and stained. She sighs, knowing she'll have to make the most of it. The exertions of yesterday, humping boxes into the house, unpacking, moving the furniture into place, have left her bones aching and her body grimy. Not to mention the sweating in the night. She turns on the tap and after a few minutes of empty gurgling, a trickle of water emerges reluctantly from the hot tap. The ancient gas heater above the bath whoofs into life, blue flames flickering through the window in the front.

She finds a sponge and sluices a couple of dead flies out of the bath. While it fills, she goes back to the bedroom and decides to put a few things away. It's likely to be a long wait. She opens the top drawer of the small chest that Alex sent from Primrose Hill. She looks down in surprise at what's in there: a white envelope addressed to her in his handwriting.

She rips it open. It's a card with a sketch of a tumbledown cottage on the front. Inside he has scrawled a few words:

> *To my dearest Sarah. Welcome to your new home and good luck with your renovations. Watch out for spiders!*

She smiles in spite of herself, recalling her fear of any recess in the old house they had done up together, terrified that spiders might be hiding in them. How well he knows her! Her heartstrings twist momentarily, but then she pulls herself up, reminding herself how she'd felt when she'd heard the girl's voice on the answerphone.

'What am I doing?' she says out loud.

She shoves the card back in the envelope and pushes it to the back of the drawer.

She bathes in the few inches of water the boiler has yielded and dresses quickly. There is no central heating; the only heat upstairs comes from a small fan heater in the bedroom that her father lent her. As she pulls her hair into a rubber band she crosses to the window and peers out. Through gaps in the tall hedge she can see the row of modern shops opposite. She recognises the woman from the newsagent's standing at the door, opening the shop up. She wears a headscarf and is carrying a bundle of newspapers under one arm. As the woman pushes the door open, she grinds a cigarette into the pavement with her heel. Sarah begins to crave one herself. She takes a deep breath and checks herself. Not before breakfast, that's a rule.

Downstairs in the kitchen she switches on the electric fire – another donation from her father – and while the kettle boils, she clears the pile of fish and chip papers into a bin bag. She and Dad had sat at the table and eaten them before she'd driven him home yesterday evening. She coaxes the gas grill into action on the ancient stove and toasts a couple of slices of bread, which she eats quickly while gulping her tea. Then, reasoning that it is now after breakfast time, she reaches for her handbag.

She looks around her at the kitchen with its ancient sink and fittings, through the dusty window and into the bare conservatory. She remembers the photograph of the Burroughs sisters that had so intrigued her that first time she'd seen the house. Why had the older sister been so prickly when Dad had come calling? The thought of him desperately seeking answers to his family history really pulls at her heartstrings. She's sure that this house must hold some clues and she's determined to help him find out as much as she can.

'Damn.' She realises that she smoked her last cigarette on the way home from dropping her father last night. She pulls on her coat, lets herself out of the back door and hurries down the drive.

The woman looks up and smiles as she enters the shop.

'Hello, my dear!' she says, her voice full of warmth and curiosity. 'I heard that a young lady had bought the house. I thought it might be you. It *is* you, isn't it? You did buy it, didn't you?'

'Yes, I did.' Sarah smiles.

'Well, I'm jolly glad it's you and not some bloody builders. I thought Pinsents were buying it. At least that's what I heard.'

Sarah decides not to be drawn into discussing the details.

'No, it was me,' she says simply. She takes a wire basket and collects a few essentials from the shelves: milk, butter, bread, cheese, eggs, bacon. Then she returns to the counter, where the woman is busy setting out the morning papers.

Sarah's eyes scan the front pages: a story about the royal family, a celebrity marriage is in trouble, a minister resigns, a possible interest rate rise. Then she sees it and her heart stops.

Top chef Alex Jennings connected to
international money laundering operation.

She stares at the paper, colour draining from her face.

'You all right, my love?'

The woman is watching her through her false lashes, her eyes all-seeing. Sarah makes an effort to regain her composure. She looks up and smiles brightly.

'Yes, quite all right, thanks. Could I have twenty Marlboro, please? And I'll take a copy of the *Daily Mail* too.'

Someone else comes into the shop and crosses to the fridge.

'Morning, Simon,' says the woman.

'Hello. Have you got any more eggs, please? We need three dozen.' The voice is young, boyish. Sarah knows it from somewhere.

'I think so. I'll check out the back. Let me just serve this lady.'

'No, don't worry,' says Sarah. 'I'm not in a hurry.'

The woman bustles away, and the sound of doors banging comes from the room behind the shop. Sarah glances at the newcomer. It's the young waiter with the pimply skin from the bistro. She smiles at him. A flush rises on his pale cheeks and he looks away.

The woman returns and as she rings up the till she says, 'Did your dad forget to order eggs again, Simon?'

'Yes, he did,' mumbles the boy. 'And there's a group of businesspeople in for breakfast.'

'Well, tell him not to worry. I'll put it on his tab.'

'Thank you.' The boy shuffles out of the shop, his head down, and the woman smiles at Sarah conspiratorially.

'Nice lad,' she says. 'His dad runs the bistro along the road. The place isn't doing too well, between you and me.'

'I went in there for lunch recently. The food was very good.'

'Oh, it is. It is, but I do worry about them. It's been very difficult for the pair of them since poor Rosie went. That's the boy's mother, you know.' She lowers her voice and leans forward to whisper, 'Passed away a couple of years back.'

'Oh, I'm sorry,' says Sarah, fleetingly remembering the owner, how he'd seemed anxious and a little lost. She picks up the paper and cigarettes.

'I could deliver the *Mail* to your house every day if you like.'

'That's kind of you. I'll think about it, but I probably don't need a delivery,' Sarah says. 'I can always pop over to get a paper.'

'What's your name, my dear?'

'Sarah,' she replies, leaving out the surname for now. The woman holds out a hand with painted red nails. Sarah takes it.

'Pleased to meet you,' says the woman. 'I'm Jacqui Tennant. Now if there's anything you need, you only have to shout. I live in Treehill Close just round the corner, but I'm in here every day. Come rain, come shine. We're neighbours now. I'll do anything for me neighbours, you'll see.'

'Thank you. That's very kind of you.'

Sarah starts for the door. She can't wait to read the article. But then she pauses, a thought occurring to her.

'Well, there *is* something you might be able to help with, actually. I'll be needing a builder soon. Someone local, I hope. I'm planning a few alterations to the house. Nothing too drastic, just updating and decorating mostly.'

Jacqui nods knowingly. 'I'm not surprised, love. I thought you would be. That old place is in a hell of a state, isn't it? Well, you're in luck. I do happen to know someone. A local chap, Terry. Very good and very trustworthy. It's an old family firm, Applebys. I've got his card in here somewhere.' She rummages in a drawer under the counter.

'Here you are.'

Taking the card, Sarah thanks her and leaves the shop hurriedly, anxious to get back to the house and look at the newspaper.

In the cold kitchen she makes a pot of coffee and sits down at the table with the paper. The article is short and doesn't give much away but even so, as she puts the paper down, her hands are shaking. She goes out into the courtyard and lights up a cigarette. She thinks of Alex and how he'd pleaded with her to help him convince the police he wasn't involved. Anger and bitterness have been clouding her mind, but now some time has passed, she's beginning to soften. She thinks of the card he sent her and how his message had pulled at her heartstrings. She takes another long drag on her cigarette and mulls it over, staring up at the dark windows of the coach house.

She grinds the cigarette end into the step and as she turns to go back inside, she glances up at the coach house. Something seems to move behind the glass. She stops and peers up at the window, her scalp tingling. She remembers the feeling she'd had stepping into that room yesterday, the air of neglect, the strange atmosphere. Her mind turns to Miss Burroughs. What might the old lady remember about the room and what happened there? And if she did remember anything, would she be prepared to tell Sarah what she knows?

Back in the kitchen she calls her father to ask him how he slept. She'd felt a sudden sense of loss as she dropped him home last night. He'd looked very frail as he went inside the house and turned to wave. These past few weeks have brought them closer than they've been for years. At least she's going to be nearby to help him now, but she can hardly bear to think of the doctor's words; his memory might start to fade soon, he could start to become more forgetful. As she dials his number, it occurs to her that there is a pressing need to find out about his birth mother before these changes start to happen and while he is still well enough to help her in the quest.

His voice sounds upbeat this morning, though. He assures her that all is well. He's going to spend the day on his computer doing some more research.

'Do you want me to pop over later? I could come and cook for you.'

'That would be lovely, Sarah, darling. But if you don't mind, I think I'll have an early night. I expect you've got lots to do in the house.'

'Nonsense. I'll come over early. Six-ish? I promise I'll be gone before nine, though, so you can go to bed.'

After they've rung off, she dials the number on the card Jacqui gave her. It rings for a long time, but just as she's about to ring off, a gruff male voice answers. She explains that she needs an estimate for some renovation works. He asks about the house and for her address. When she says the name of the house there's a long silence. She begins to think he has ended the call.

'All right,' he says finally in a grudging voice, 'I'll pop over tomorrow if you like. Late afternoon, see what's what. But I'm fully booked for the next couple of months, mind. Won't be able to start until well after Christmas.'

'That's fine. I can be getting on with decorating the rooms that don't need any structural work. I'll see you tomorrow then.'

He rings off without saying goodbye. Sarah frowns, puzzled at his reaction, but quickly puts it out of her mind.

She gets up from the table. Having mentioned the decorating to the builder has made her think that there's no time like the present. She needs to get on and at least paint some of the rooms, get rid of that dirty old wallpaper that seems to harbour the past in the layers of filth that have accumulated over the years. But where to start?

The house is so cold outside the kitchen that she pulls on her coat, but still shivers as she lets herself into the passage. She wanders around the ground floor. The living room and dining room are papered with a floral pattern in varying shades of sepia. If she half closes her eyes the colour doesn't seem too bad, even approaching neutral. Maybe she could live with it for a while? She opens the study door and ventures inside, averting her eyes from the bureau on the far wall. The wallpaper on three of the walls is dark brown, covered in a diamond trellis pattern of dull pink roses. The paintwork is brown too, chipped and scuffed, clashing with the black marble of the fireplace. One wall is papered in plain dark brown, though. That looks newer, as if it's been decorated more recently. Even that wall though is scratched and scuffed in places where furniture has been moved. Perhaps this is the place to start? It would be good to get rid of this dreadful gloomy colour. Then perhaps the room won't feel so full of ghosts. She glances again at the old desk. It will be difficult to decorate around it. She might be able to move it into the middle of the room herself, or perhaps she'll be able to persuade the builder to help her.

She quickly scribbles a note, listing what she'll need. She'd noticed a builders' merchant on the small business park on the edge of town. She switches off the electric fire in the kitchen, lets herself out of the back door and crosses to her car. Glancing nervously up at the coach house, she pauses. There's that movement again in the window.

She takes the coach house steps two at a time, turns the key and gives the door a great shove, aware that her heart is hammering. She steps inside. All is silent and still for a few seconds, then from nowhere a pigeon flies straight at her, beating its wings in panic, squawking.

She lets out a cry as the bird flaps towards her, narrowly misses her and hits the wall behind her with a dull thud. It falls to the ground at her feet.

'My God.' She stands there shaking, taking deep breaths, trying to make her heart slow down.

'You poor thing,' she breathes, bending down and picking the
bird up. It's surprisingly heavy. Its head flops to one side, eyes
half-closed, its neck broken. Its body feels warm as she carries it
outside and across the courtyard. She doesn't know what to do
with it. She sets it down on the lawn, feeling shaken. She'll bury
it later, when she comes back.

It's almost noon when Sarah returns to the house, the car boot full
of decorating materials, a spade wrapped in brown paper lying on
the back seat. It's starting to drizzle as she unwraps the spade, eases
the dead pigeon onto it and carries it carefully to the overgrown
border beside the garden wall. She buries the bird quickly and
efficiently, determined not to let it cast a shadow over the day.

She's impatient to get on with the decorating and she unloads
the car and takes her portable radio through to the study. She
tunes it to a station playing West Coast rock, needing something
as far away from what would be playing on the sound system at
Taste as possible.

She fills her new bucket with warm water, spreads a plastic
groundsheet over the carpet and, standing precariously on a
chair, begins to soak the wall above the fireplace with water, then
to scrape the paper off methodically. It isn't easy – the paper is
practically welded to the wall – but Sarah persists. She gets into her
stride, scraping away vigorously in time to the rhythm of 'Hotel
California'. It feels good, doing something practical at last, like the
start of a long journey to restore the house to its original glory.
After half an hour, though, her arm is aching and her shoulder is
begging for a rest.

She gets down from the chair and runs a hand across her brow.
Perhaps the other walls aren't quite so unyielding? She runs a hand
across the wall opposite the fireplace to test it, and as an experiment
scrapes a little of the wallpaper away. It comes away more easily

here and, encouraged, she attacks it with renewed energy. There's no need to even soak it. Soon, about a square metre of plaster is exposed. She stands back to admire it.

Even in the dim light she can see something is protruding, a horizontal line along the wall, raised, about a metre wide. Curious, she takes the scraper and chips away at the plaster. A few millimetres below the surface, a ridge of wood emerges. She carries on chipping, revealing the top of a door frame. The plaster comes away in chunks, falling on the groundsheet in dusty piles. She works methodically, and the outline of a door quickly appears. It must be a cupboard, it isn't high enough to be a proper door.

It's dark outside by the time she's chipped away enough plaster to attempt to open the door. There is no handle, so she slides the scraper between the frame and the door. She has to run the scraper up and down repeatedly to remove the dust and plaster before there's some movement.

At last the door comes open with a splintering, cracking sound. Plaster and dust fall from the crack as she manages to get her hands inside and tugs it open, revealing the inside of a good-sized cupboard. Sarah peers tentatively inside, afraid that spiders might crawl out at her. There are dusty cobwebs in there but, as far as she can see, no live occupants. There are two shelves, a few objects on each, covered in black dust.

The largest object is round and heavy. At first Sarah can't make out what it is. She sets it down on the floor and dusts it off with a cloth – and gasps when she realises. It is an elephant's foot, complete with toenails, hollowed out, a brass dish inside, stained black by the stubbings of cigars.

Then there are around a dozen models of gods and goddesses. Some look to be made of ebony, others jade. Sarah can't remember their names, but she knows they're all Hindu gods. There's a set of whisky glasses and a cut-glass decanter too, all full of dust and cobwebs. At the back of one of the shelves is a gentleman's cane.

Sarah turns it over in her hands. The handle is made of tortoiseshell and the cane itself bound with plaited leather. In a small square box sit two sparkling cufflinks, and beside that an old-fashioned gold watch and chain, with an engraved lid. It is dull with age. She dusts it off and peers at the inscription:

To Ezra, with heartfelt thanks, your devoted friend, Charles Perry.

Chapter Fourteen

Connie

'Dear God,' breathes Connie, bowing her head, closing her eyes, 'who passeth all understanding. Forgive me, dear Lord, for my weaknesses when I was young. Forgive me for not acting when I should have done, for passing by on the other side, for having let others suffer through my own inaction. It is I who suffers now. But you know that, don't you, dear Lord in your infinite wisdom. Please God, hear my prayers.'

It is impossible for Connie to kneel down to pray nowadays. It feels odd, sitting here in the nursing home, in her cramped and cluttered room in the reclining chair, her leg propped up in front of her, closing her eyes and praying to God twice a day.

It doesn't feel right. It doesn't feel like proper prayer. Throughout her whole life she has knelt to pray. She can't remember a time, until her fall a few months ago, a single morning or evening, when she didn't get down on her knees on one of the little embroidered prayer cushions at home, bow her head, close her eyes and pray to the Lord. Sometimes, in recent years, when things had been preying on her mind, when she couldn't rid herself of the guilt or shame of how she'd acted when she was young, she'd spent whole evenings in prayer or Bible study. Evie had never asked her why, but deep down inside Connie knows she must have guessed. Evie seemed to approve of Connie's piety at those times. She'd join her during those long sessions, a comforting, steady presence by her side, intoning the prayers they'd learned as children.

Evie was always the strong one, the one who knew what to do in any situation, the one who took charge in difficult times, who organised everything in the house after Father died, who paid the bills, dealt with builders and tradesmen. How lost Connie feels without her guiding presence. It had always been that way. Connie remembers Evie's iron will and her rigid sense of discipline. Evie had always been the one to insist that they knelt down to pray before bedtime, even if neither of them felt like it or when Connie's instinct had been to pull on her nightdress and flop into bed, exhausted. Evie had always been the first one up in the mornings when they worked in the school room. Even when in their unheated attic room they could see their breath in the air and there was ice on the insides of the windows.

'A bit of fresh, cold air won't kill you, Connie. Come on, we need to get up. God's work beckons in the orphanage.'

Evie loved hard work, relished it. On cold days in their youth when Connie would have preferred to sit inside by the fire, Evie would be out there, digging the vegetable patch with vigour, bringing in coal, chopping wood for the orphanage stoves.

'God makes work for idle hands to do,' she would say when Connie balked at a task.

How different the two of them were, Connie muses. In looks as well as temperament. Evie was tall and angular, with thin dark hair she always scraped back in a bun. Her energetic nature ensured there was not a spare ounce of fat on her body. Connie herself was short and slight, with thick fair hair that refused to be tamed, and a languid temperament.

Evie kept on going right to the end. She'd been a powerhouse of energy. Right into old age she'd kept Cedar Hall pristine without any help. Each morning she'd risen before dawn, washed in cold water and got down on her knees to pray.

She remembers how she used to envy Evie her certainty, her drive and purpose, her unshakeable faith. She could never tell anyone, least of all Evie, how uncertain this made her feel. She didn't share this love of the place, of the work; she wasn't certain, like Evie was, that this was what she was born to do. As she grew older, this uncertainty grew into a sort of yearning for something different, to be free to be herself, to make her own choices. It was this yearning feeling that had first drawn her to Tommy.

Now, in her room at the nursing home, Connie worries that sitting upright in the chair to pray, God might not be able to hear her properly. And then there's that other nagging worry: what would Father think? Would he disapprove? She picks at her cardigan nervously as she tries to imagine what he might say. She can hardly bear to contemplate how angry he'd be if he knew what she was trying to tell God now. She's not sure whose wrath she fears most: that of God, or that of Father.

Nobody in the home seems to bother much about God.

She squeezes her eyes shut, fearing deeply for them. 'Dear Lord, forgive them. For they know not what they do.' Of course, some of the younger, more mobile residents go in the minibus on Sunday mornings along to St Mary's church in the centre of town. St Mary's is Church of England, but that can't be helped. The Baptist church closed down years ago, not long after Father died.

As she watches them discreetly from the front window on Sunday mornings, making their slow and painful progress out to the vehicle to be helped on board by the staff and driven away, she catches sight of Elsie and Marjory in the group and wonders if she should go too. Now she can walk quite well with the Zimmer frame, it would be possible. But would Father mind if she went along with the others to that church that she's never before set foot in? Surely he couldn't object? It's still a house of God, after all, even if it isn't the one reflecting the true Holy Path. But still, she's not sure. She chews on a nail nervously. Oh, if only Evie were here to advise her. To remind her of the right thing to do.

She opens her eyes. It's useless. She can't pray properly with all these unsettling thoughts buzzing around in her head. And anyway, she hasn't got to face that dilemma today. Today isn't a Sunday, it's a normal weekday. A Thursday, in fact. Sometimes she loses track of the days, they're all so similar, but this week is different. The day before yesterday was an important day. It was the day that Cedar Hall was finally sold. Connie had clutched at her shawl when she'd heard those words. She'd known they were coming, but it was still a shock.

Peter was still angry with her when he came to see her that morning. But it was hardly fair for him to reprimand her about it, was it? She'd caught him out and outwitted him, old and befuddled as he might think her. He should feel ashamed of the way he'd behaved. She sighs heavily. If Peter's grandfather was around, if Father was around, Peter would have a lot of explaining to do.

It is some comfort at least that Father's papers are safe in the basement at Cartwrights. Soon, when she's strong enough, she will ask Matron to arrange for her to go down there to check through them. Make sure there's nothing left that Father wouldn't want anyone to see. She begins to breathe heavily again, thinking about those papers. They are such a worry. She knows she must face those demons before it's too late but the thought fills her with dread.

She tightens her grip around the necklace, holding it in her fist now. How different things would have been if she'd been strong all those years ago. If she'd at least tried to make a stand. Her own life would have taken such a different course. And what about all those others whose lives Father had power over back then? Poor Anna, and the ones whose names she'd never known. They were the ones who were never spoken about. The ones she'd let down.

It's true, she'd tried to do it more than once. She'd practised what she planned to say in front of the mirror upstairs, mouthing the words silently so that Evie and Mother wouldn't hear. But her courage had always failed her at the last minute. She would get to the door of his study, her heart beating fast, and hover there on the threshold. The very sight of his back, the great intimidating bulk of his presence, would make her knees turn to jelly. She would stand there wondering, trying to glean from the way he sat what sort of mood he was in. Would he be in his charming mood, the one he was in when he preached on Sundays, or led assembly in the orphanage, when she would gaze around at the adoring looks on the children's faces as they listened, their eyes shining. Or would he be in one of his brooding moods, liable to bursts of anger? Both were equally frightening. Each time she tried to muster the courage to challenge him, she failed. The words would freeze on her tongue. They sounded so… so outrageous that she could never bring herself to utter them.

She'd tried too, with Mother and Evie, but Mother would not brook any challenge to Father. Not one question, not even a curious look. Evie was similar. Even after Father died, when Connie had tried to show her the box of letters. Even then, with the truth staring her in the face, Evie didn't want to know.

'Put them back, Connie,' she'd said, her eyes wide with outrage and disapproval. 'They are Father's private papers. He would be very angry indeed if he knew you'd looked at them. I don't want to know what they say. Put them back where you found them and we'll never speak of the matter again. I mean it, Connie.'

There was no one else to talk to. At least not at that time. No one in the whole wide world. She'd had to bear the knowledge and the suspicions alone. But God knew, in His infinite wisdom. God must have known what went on. How would Father have dealt with God when he met Him face to face? The thought makes sweat break out on her brow.

There's a gentle knock at Connie's door. Matron appears.

'Connie, my dear, I have a visitor for you.'

Connie looks up, confused, her mind taking its time to swim to the present. Not Peter again, surely? What does he want this time?

Connie can't face him today. She draws herself up in the chair and pulls her shawl tightly around her.

'I'm not feeling very well, Matron.'

'Really, Connie? You were fine at breakfast.'

'Yes, I'm sure.'

'All right. I'll ask the lady to come back another time.'

'Lady?'

'Yes. It's a Mrs Jennings to see you. She's in reception, waiting.'

'Oh!'

'Are you feeling well enough to see her, Connie?' Matron asks, smiling.

'Yes. Yes, Matron, I think I am. Please show her through.'

The young woman appears, carrying a huge bunch of flowers.

'Lily of the valley,' Connie says, surprised. 'My favourites! How did you know?'

The young woman smiles, a row of even white teeth. She's dressed casually in jeans and a navy sweater, but she somehow manages to look smart. How old would she be? Connie wonders. It's hard to say, everyone looks so young now. Thirty? Thirty-five perhaps? She has beautiful dark hair with a natural bounce that tumbles around her shoulders, and smiling brown eyes. Her skin glows as if she has just come into the warmth from the freezing cold. She seems to fill the drab room with energy and vitality, and for the first time in a very long while, Connie's spirits lift.

'I asked Matron what you might like and I popped back to the flower shop on the corner. I brought them to say thank you. I really should have come to see you before, but I've been so busy with the move.'

'You shouldn't have brought flowers,' Connie protests, but she is pleased all the same. No one has brought her flowers before. Well, not since...

'What's there to thank me for?'

'For letting me buy your house, of course. It can't have been an easy decision.'

'It had to be sold. I didn't have a choice. Besides, I'm very glad it went to you and not to those dreadful developers.'

'You lived in Cedar Hall a very long time, didn't you?'

'All my life.'

It seems such an enormous thing when she says it out loud. Her whole life was spent back there within those walls, and it isn't hers any more. Suddenly she feels it deeply, a great emptiness in the pit of her stomach. The young woman is waiting politely, still smiling.

'Do you have a vase?' the woman finally asks.

'Yes… of course. Forgive me, my mind wanders. I think there's one in the cupboard under the washbasin. Over there in the corner.'

The woman crosses the room and as she passes, Connie catches a hint of lemon-scented perfume. Connie watches as she busies herself with the flowers. She works quickly, with deft hands, arranging them in the vase.

'Here we go – where shall I put them?'

She turns towards Connie and holds them up.

'You've done them beautifully! You have a real gift.'

'Oh, not really. Just practice. I do… I used to do the flowers at our restaurant.'

'Restaurant?'

'Yes. It's in London. I don't work there any more, though.'

'London?'

Connie mouths the word as if it's an exotic, far-off place. How long is it since she went there? She tries to think back. It must be a very long time ago now. She went with Evie a few times after Father's death, on the train to listen to concerts in the Albert Hall, but she can't pinpoint the last occasion. When she was younger, they hardly ever went. Hardly ever left Weirfield. The furthest they ever usually went was Henley in the back of Father's motor car. She fingers her necklace to try to focus her mind but then she remembers that she isn't alone. She must stop her thoughts wandering back to the past. She has a visitor, after all.

'I'm sorry,' she says. 'You were saying?'

The young woman is still smiling. There's something about her steady gaze that's appealing – and strangely familiar. Connie looks back into her eyes and smiles, and it feels almost as though they met in another life. She banishes that blasphemous thought quickly. There is no other life. Not until after this one, not until God sees fit to ask her to come to be with Him and with Mother and Father, and Evie too.

'Nothing. It wasn't important. You have some beautiful furniture in here,' she says, glancing around the cluttered room.

'Thank you. Yes, it all came from the house. I could only keep a few things. That armchair in the corner belonged to my mother. She used to sit in it to do mending or embroidery in the evenings. That bookcase belonged to Father. I wanted to keep his Bibles and prayer books. He wouldn't like…' Her words trail off. The young woman is looking at her with a quizzical expression, waiting for her to go on.

'I mean, Father was fond of his books. I didn't want to throw them away.'

'What about the picture? I remember seeing it in the house when I first looked round.'

'Oh, that's the church in India where Father was a missionary. Before he came here to run the orphanage.'

'What a wonderful life he must have led!' The woman is looking at her with shining eyes.

'Perhaps,' Connie answers stiffly. She has gone too far. What would Father say about her discussing his life like this?

'Why don't you sit down, my dear?' she says to change the subject. 'Would you like me to ring for some tea?'

'Oh, I can't stay long. Please don't bother about the tea.' But she sits down in Mother's armchair and leans forward, looking at Connie closely.

'I came here because there's something I wanted to ask you.'

'Really?' Alarm bells start ringing. What could there possibly be to ask? At this stage? The girl's only been in the house a couple of days.

Sarah clears her throat. 'I decided to start decorating. I know it's early, but I couldn't wait to get on with it.' Connie's scalp is already tingling with dread. She holds her breath and clenches her fist around the filigree so hard it might break. She stares at the young woman intently. What is she going to say?

'I took the wallpaper off one of the walls in the study, and… well, perhaps you know about it?'

Connie's mouth drops open but she can't answer.

'I found a cupboard under the plaster. There were some wonderful things inside. Valuable things. Some ornaments. They look as though they are made of ebony, some of them, others jade. They look Indian, so I'm thinking they were your father's. There was also an elephant's…'

The young woman pauses. She must have noticed Connie's expression. Connie knows she must look very odd. Stock-still, her eyes blazing, her mouth wide open. But she can't help it. The young woman goes on slowly, gently, 'An elephant's foot, I think.'

'I know… I know. You don't need to say.' Connie's voice comes out in a strangulated gasp, but she has to blurt it out, to stop the woman speaking. She can't bear to hear it.

'I'm sorry. I mean… I didn't mean to upset you. I thought perhaps you'd forgotten about it. That there'd been some mistake.'

Connie shakes her head emphatically. 'No. There's no mistake. None at all. They were my father's things.'

'Well, perhaps you'd like them back? I can bring them over in the car.'

'No. I don't want them back.'

There's a silence. The young woman is looking at her with that curious look again. She must think it all very strange. Well, it can't be helped. What does it matter what she thinks anyway?

'Are you quite sure? Some of the things look valuable. There's also a gold watch…'

Connie stiffens again. Isn't she going to get the hint?

'I'm quite sure. You keep them, I have no need of them now.'

'Well, that's very kind of you.'

There's another awkward silence. The sound of daytime television echoes down the corridor. Someone walks past the room, laughing.

'Do you know why your father sealed the valuables away in the cupboard?' Sarah asks at last.

Connie looks at her sharply. She can feel her breath coming quickly, her chest going up and down under the shawl and the grey cardigan. She knows she must calm down, but the young woman carries on looking at her, waiting for an answer.

'It wasn't Father who sealed up those things,' Connie snaps.

The young woman stares at her, frowning now, 'Really? Well, if—'

Before Connie can stop herself, the words are out of her mouth. Her hand flies up to stop them, but it's too late. 'Father didn't seal those things away in that cupboard,' she says with ferocity. 'It was me. I did it.'

Chapter Fifteen

Connie

Connie feels unsettled for a long time after Sarah's departure. She couldn't help noticing that Sarah had left a bit abruptly. She must have noticed how startled Connie had been by her own admission about boarding up the cupboard. Thoughts buzz around in Connie's head now. What she'd dreaded might happen *is* actually happening. And it is happening so quickly, too. She hadn't expected that. The girl has only been in the house a few days. What if she finds out more? It is inevitable really, and Connie knows she did her best to make sure that house went to someone who looked kind and honest, who might understand her feelings about the place. But if only Connie hadn't had that fall. If only Peter hadn't insisted on selling the house so quickly. She could have sorted things out. Got the builders in. Someone she could trust, to open up that cupboard and remove everything. She should have done that in the first place, when she'd had the chance after Evie died. She needs to face the truth, though: even after Evie was gone she hadn't had the courage to go that far.

What a dreadful mistake she'd made, getting Trevor to seal the cupboard up. What had she been thinking? She hadn't been acting rationally, of course, but she'd felt at the time it was the right thing to do. It was shortly after Evie died. She'd left the bath running by mistake and the water had overflowed, flooded the bathroom and seeped through the floor and down the walls of the study. The wallpaper had bulged and started peeling off the wall. She'd had to get Trevor in to sort things out, and when he said he'd need to replaster, sealing the cupboard seemed the perfect solution. The things would still be where Father had left them, she wouldn't be throwing them away, but at the same time they would be hidden from view. She wouldn't have to think about them ever again.

She'd needed to put the things in that cupboard out of her mind. Put that part of Father out of her mind too. Concentrate on the good things. The Bible, the prayer books, the pictures of the church at Kandaipur from his missionary days. Those were the wonderful things about Father. The things she needed to remember and to preserve, and to make sure everyone else knew and remembered too.

Trevor had looked at her curiously when she'd asked him to do it.

'There's nothing wrong with the cupboard. It's a useful space, Miss B,' he'd protested in his mild-mannered way. 'I could rub it down and put some fresh gloss paint on, make it look smart again.'

'No. No, thank you, Trevor,' she'd said stiffly, drawing herself up in an attempt to appear authoritative. 'I would prefer it if you just plastered over it. I'd like to put some furniture against that wall there, and the cupboard sticks out into the room.'

'Is there anything in there?'

'Only old junk,' she'd heard herself saying, her heart in her mouth. Was that a lie? *Dear Lord forgive me*, she'd thought. 'Just leave it in there, please.' She'd had to use her imperious voice on Trevor, the one that made her sound like Evie.

He'd looked at her even more curiously then.

'There's no need for you to open it, is there?' she'd said sharply.

'Not if you don't want me to,' he'd said with a shrug and turned back to his work.

She stood there in the study all morning, standing over him as he worked. Just to make sure. To make sure he didn't open the cupboard to see what was in there.

She thinks of those things now. The dreaded elephant's foot, Father's whisky glasses and decanter. His leather-bound cane with the tortoiseshell handle, his diamond cufflinks, that beautiful gold watch with the engraving, and all those terrifying Hindu gods.

She remembers the first time she'd spotted them on the mantle-piece in Father's study. When she'd seen them dancing there, so lifelike, but at the same time otherworldly, a thrill had gone right through her. She'd been fascinated by them for years. Fascinated but repelled at the same time. To Connie there was something terrifying about the gods of a mysterious religion practised in a far-off land, so very different to her own dear God. When Father was out, she would stand and stare at them for a long time, trying to picture the place where they'd come from, the sounds and smells of the temple in that exotic land, the chanting of the faithful, the boom of gongs and the tinkling of bells.

She pictures him taking his cane and slipping the gold watch into the top pocket of his jacket before striding over to the orphanage to take prayers. She thinks about the words engraved on the back: TO EZRA, WITH HEARTFELT THANKS, YOUR DEVOTED FRIEND, CHARLES PERRY. Then her mind goes back to that fateful night in 1934.

She had woken suddenly. The moonlight was playing on the sloping ceiling as the wind disturbed the branches outside her bedroom. Gentle snoring came from her sister's bed. Evie was sleeping soundly. As well as the creaking of the trees, the usual night-time sounds from the orphanage next door floated on the breeze. The whispered breaths of a hundred children sleeping in long dormitories, side by side on truckle beds.

That night she'd been woken by a strange sound. It had come from somewhere behind the house. She'd propped herself on her elbows and listened carefully. Had she dreamed it? No, there it was again, an odd strangled cry, like a trapped animal. Long and pitiful, almost a howl. Shivers coursed through her body and she stayed there motionless, hardly breathing, straining her ears to catch any sound. Could it be foxes in the woods, or cats fighting? No, this was different.

She sat like that for a long time, until her shoulders and elbows ached. As the minutes passed and she didn't hear the sound again, she began to wonder if she'd imagined it. She pushed the blankets back and slipped out of bed. Shivering in her thin nightdress, she crept across the wooden boards to the window. Kneeling, she gripped the windowsill and stared out. Light from the moon flooded the gardens, lighting up the rows of potatoes and runner beans in the plots behind the orphanage. Directly behind the house, the bushes cast distorted shadows on the lawn.

Then a different sound came from the direction of the coach house. It was the creak of a door opening. Her heart was suddenly hammering as a figure emerged from the side door on the first floor and started slowly down the outside steps. She knew instantly that it was Father. He was carrying something in his arms; at this distance she couldn't make out what it was. It looked like a bundle of rags.

She drew back behind the curtain and watched him cross the yard and make for the back door of the house. Seconds later his footsteps were inside, walking steadily up the stairs. She held her breath, listening.

The footsteps stopped on the first-floor landing.

Connie lost her nerve. She tiptoed back into bed between the stiff, cold sheets, her heart thumping. Would he come upstairs? She thought of all the times she and Evie had heard his boots on the attic stairs as he came up to check on them. They would pretend to be asleep as he opened the door. Sometimes Connie would open her eyes a little, just enough to see his outline silhouetted in the doorway. In the silence she would hear his breathing, smell the pipe smoke on his clothes, the pomade on his hair.

'Connie? Evie? Are you awake?' he would whisper.

Sure enough, after a few moments' pause, his footsteps did carry on, getting louder as he walked up the wooden staircase towards their room. The door handle squeaked and then came the sound of the door being pulled back slowly. Then silence. She sensed him standing there in the doorway, watching them, checking that they were sound asleep. She hardly dared breathe.

After what seemed an age, she heard him moving, heard the door creak on its hinges, and then he was gone. She listened to his footsteps going steadily down the stairs. For several minutes there was silence.

Finally, she began to relax a little. Perhaps she might be able to get some sleep after all. But within minutes she was startled again by new, different sounds. This time the noises seemed to be coming from somewhere beneath her, perhaps from inside the house. At first, she couldn't make out what they were. Once again, she slid out of bed, crept over to the window and opened it. She leaned out and peered down. A dim light flickered in the conservatory behind the kitchen.

Then came a scraping sound, the sound of something heavy being dragged. And shortly after that the thud of metal on earth. *Chop, chop, chop.* Striking it again and again.

Connie ran back to bed and pulled the pillow over her head, over her ears. She pressed her face into the mattress and screwed her eyes shut tight. A sob escaped her as she tried to block out the sounds. The sounds and the memories.

She finds herself breathing heavily, thinking about it now.

She's tempted to let herself off today, to spare herself the pain of going back there. But with a deep sigh she takes the diary from the top drawer of her bedside cabinet and unlocks it again with the tiny key. She turns to the page where she'd left the silk ribbon in place last time.

She holds it up to her failing eyes.

Chapter Sixteen

Connie

Anna's Diary
February 21st, 1932

*I realise that it is quite a while since my last entry, but
I have been getting used to my new surroundings. Here
I am on the cantonment at Kandaipur in my bungalow.
The one befitting the rank of Lieutenant Colonel. It
is called Connaught Lodge and is situated at the end
of Dalhousie Road, a neat little road on the edge of a
well-laid-out estate of similar dwellings, all with perfect
gardens and clipped hedges. It is slightly larger but also
shabbier than the rest. Donald told me proudly that it
has two more bedrooms, larger reception rooms and more
space for servants than the other homes along the road.
It also has a bigger garden.*

*I have been alone a lot of the time since my arrival. The
wedding was only two weeks ago, but it feels like a lifetime.*

*When we arrived on the train that first day, there was a
little welcoming party waiting on the platform at Kandaipur
station. Colonel Smethurst, Donald's commanding officer,
and several other officers and their wives were there. We
were presented with garlands of chrysanthemums to put
round our necks and had to walk under a tunnel of crossed
swords while people threw rice at us. I found it excruciating*

to be the centre of attention, and I'm sure I blushed flame red, but Donald seemed to take it in his stride. In fact, he looked rather proud as he held my arm and ushered me through to the station building.

We were whisked off in a pony cart straight to the club, a low building with a huge veranda that looks out over immaculate croquet lawns and tennis courts. It is all a bit musty and old-fashioned inside, though, with threadbare carpets and worn leather sofas, the moth-eaten heads of stags mounted on the walls. Donald took me into the bar, where a cold buffet supper was laid out in our honour. He introduced me to some of the officers' wives. It was all a bit of a blur and after what seemed an age of nodding, shaking hands and making small talk, my jaw ached with the effort of smiling that fixed smile. And although I tried, I found it hard to remember any of their names. The women all looked the same to me, with floral dresses, elaborately coiffed hair and a lot of powder and lipstick. I couldn't help noticing that they all looked at me in the same way as they took my hand. They peered into my eyes meaningfully, not even trying to hide their curiosity. I stared back at them with a puzzled frown, wondering if they already knew about Father, although I don't know how they possibly could. I haven't even told Donald yet.

I was very tired, having got virtually no sleep on the train, but each time I glanced over at Donald, I saw that he was surrounded by other men. He stood a little awkwardly among them as they laughed and talked, but he looked intent on appearing sociable. It wasn't until ten o'clock that someone encouraged him to take me home.

'I'll have to be up before dawn. I'll sleep next door so as not to disturb you,' he'd said, closing the door. I was so

exhausted, it was a relief to be able to sink into the soft, saggy bed alone and let sleep overcome my senses.

The next morning when I woke up, Donald had already left for the parade ground, so I was left to get up and explore our new home alone. I opened the shutters to let the sunlight in, hoping it would cheer things up, but it only made the bare shabby furniture look worse. I was just getting dressed when I heard footsteps in the hall and a penetrating female voice calling me from upstairs.

With my heart sinking, I smoothed down my hair and went out into the living room. Donald's bearer, Ali, had already shown the visitors in. It was Mrs Smethurst, the Colonel's wife, and Mrs Napier, one of the other women I recognised from the previous evening in the club.

I took them out onto the veranda. Ali brought tea on a tray and we made small talk for a while. Mrs Smethurst seemed very disapproving of the state of the house and garden. She more or less told me it was my duty as Donald's wife to make it more homely. I couldn't help wondering what business it was of hers anyway. Before she went though, she said something a bit strange.

'Donald is a very lucky man to have found you. I hope he appreciates it.'

I didn't know how to respond and found her comment disconcerting. I glanced over at Mrs Napier, who had hardly said a word so far, but she was examining the pattern on her cup, her cheeks a little flushed.

'I'm sure he does,' I said in the end, hoping she wouldn't pursue this line.

'Well, as I said, you've got your work cut out. Donald has let this place go, it needs a woman's touch.'

'I expect he spent a lot of time out and about,' I said, feeling the need to defend him.

There was an uncomfortable silence. Mrs Smethurst drained her tea and put her cup down on the table, and Mrs Napier appeared lost for words. I wondered what I'd said.

'I expect a lot of bachelors end up doing that,' I went on, feeling the need to fill the silence.

'Yes, he certainly did spend a lot of time out and about, as you put it,' she said, fixing me with her piercing gaze. 'I hope you'll be able address that, my dear. We're counting on you.'

This time it was me who was lost for words. Whatever could she mean? I wanted to ask her outright to explain herself, but I didn't feel brave enough. It will have to wait until I know her a little better. I stood on the veranda and watched them rattle away in their rickshaw. And I felt just as I had on the train from Bombay, looking out over the barren plain, alone and terribly homesick. The feeling swept over me like a wave, almost knocking me sideways.

Since that first day, I've spent a lot of time alone. When Donald leaves in the mornings, I sit on the veranda and have breakfast. There is no breathtaking vista like at Aunt Nora's, just a view over the garden, which unlike the others in the road is parched and empty. I'm sure it would be overgrown but for the army lawnmower (two boys, a bullock and an antiquated grass cutter) that comes round once a week. There are no pretty bushes or flower beds, no pots of geraniums or canna lilies. Although there is a gardener, who clips the bushes and attempts to water the lawn each day, he doesn't seem to be very effective. Once again, I suppose it is my job to make the garden look pretty too. But that feels even more daunting than the house.

There are five servants: Ali, an old man who has looked after Donald for years. He shuffles about and tries to ignore me. He probably resents my presence after all that time with just the two of them. There's also a cook, the gardener and a punkah-wallah, whose job it is to keep the air moving by pulling the punkah to and fro, and a sweet-faced young girl, Manju, who is to be my own 'ayah' or maid. She arrived on my second day, and as soon as I saw her, I liked her instantly and felt a little comforted. She has beautiful dark, liquid eyes and a calm, soothing presence.

February 23rd, 1932

Today, I went to a coffee morning at Mrs Napier's house. It was just like similar stultifying gatherings in Bombay. There were ten or so women there, who all looked me up and down with that sympathetic-curious look that I'm getting used to. The talk was of army gossip and trouble with servants, and how hot and unpleasant the weather is. They didn't hold back discussing their Indian servants in the most derogatory of terms, even though Mrs Napier's bearer was in the room waiting on us. I felt for the poor man and kept glancing at him in embarrassment. But his face showed not a flicker of concern. He stood there impassively, rocking back and forth on his heels, waiting for orders.

Mrs Smethurst taught me the rudiments of bridge and promised to teach me again the next time I'm at the club.

'You're a quick learner,' she said grudgingly. 'We'll make an ace player of you yet, my girl.'

I came home feeling empty and lonely. Even lonelier than I feel on the days I actually spend alone. In the afternoon I decided to go out on my own. On the way to the club I'd noticed the place where the rickshaw-wallahs wait for trade, at the end of the maidan in the shade of a huge banyan tree. I left the house after lunch and walked the half-mile

*or so along the road into town to the place where they were.
They were all asleep on their vehicles, their feet up on the
shafts, resting through the hottest part of the day.*

*I coughed politely and one of them stirred. He jumped
down, rubbing his eyes and bowing.*

'Where to, Memsahib?'

'Could you take me to the bazaar, please?'

*'Bazaar, Memsahib?' He looked as surprised as if I'd
asked him to take me to the moon.*

*'Yes, please. The bazaar. You do know where it is, don't
you?'*

'Oh yes, Memsahib. Right away, Memsahib.'

*As I sat behind him as he pulled me through the main
street, under the full glare of the afternoon sun, past the
palatial courthouse, the white stuccoed post office, the
government buildings with their grand portico, I felt my
mood lift. I suddenly felt buoyed by a delicious sense of
freedom. Something I hadn't experienced since arriving in
Bombay. It felt wonderful after the cloistered existence I'd
led at Aunt Nora's house. I suddenly realised that perhaps
it wasn't so bad that Donald was out for long hours each
day and I was left to my own devices. It finally gave me
the opportunity to discover the real India. The one that I'd
wanted to experience ever since I arrived.*

*The rickshaw came to a halt in front of a large brown
and white building, with a clock tower and Gothic arches.
The rickshaw-wallah nodded towards it.*

'Bazaar inside, Memsahib,' he said. 'I wait here for you.'

*I picked my way carefully up the front steps, between the
hawkers selling fruit there, and in through one of the arches.
Inside was a huge covered market. The noise under the
high glass roof was deafening. People chattering, shouting,
bargaining, the cries of hawkers advertising their wares, pipe*

music playing on a tinny wireless. I was instantly engulfed in the crowd, but I pushed my way through the press of people between the cluttered stalls. They were overloaded with colourful displays of tropical fruit, or overflowing with brightly coloured spices: red, vermillion and all shades of orange and brown. Others were loaded with meat, buzzing with flies that I had to cover my face and turn away from, yet others were selling bolts of cotton and silk for sarees, all colours of the rainbow. I was stunned and overwhelmed by the constantly moving throng of people, the colours and the smells; of spices, Indian cooking, exotic incense and the all-pervasive smell of drains.

I had brought a large silk scarf with me, and covered my head and part of my face, but still people turned to stare, not unkindly, but with open curiosity. There were no other Europeans in the bazaar, and somehow that fact enhanced my sense of freedom, my desire to lose myself in the crowd.

I walked the length of the building, just looking and marvelling, wishing I had brought my sketchbook, but I knew it would be impossible to sketch here; I would have to do it from memory when I got home. When I had reached the end, I took a side aisle and worked my way along that. Here were stalls of jewellery, of cheap shoes, of household goods, of incense and candles.

I made my way down every aisle, soaking up the sights, the smells, the atmosphere. After an hour or so I had completed my tour and was about ready to leave. By now my blouse was clinging to my body in the clammy heat and I felt in need of some air and water. As I peered through the press of bodies and tried to work out which archway I should make for to find my rickshaw, I noticed a white man emerge from one of the side doors in the wall of the building. Instinctively, I stopped and moved behind a rack *of sarees. I didn't want to be seen. I watched him as he made his way through the crowd. I didn't recognise him. He was tall and dark, wearing a pristine white linen suit, and a solar topee. He moved with easy confidence, and the crowd seemed to part to let him pass. I hardly saw his face. I was a little disconcerted that I wasn't the only European in the bazaar that afternoon after all.*

But as he approached the stall where I stood, a crowd of ragged children emerged from nowhere, shouting, running, pushing each other. They tumbled into me and I was jostled out into the aisle, right into the path of the man. He stepped aside, appeared to be about to move on, but then as his eyes rested on me, he stopped and raised his topee.

'Well, good afternoon!' he said, looking straight at me. He had brown eyes, dark hair and his well-made face was deeply tanned.

'Hello,' I said, colour rising in my hot cheeks. I'm not sure why, but I felt like a truanting schoolgirl being discovered on the run. I looked down, hoping he would move on quickly, but he didn't. I could feel his eyes on me, appraising me.

'It's very rare to find an Englishwoman in a place like this,' he said. 'And who might you be?'

It occurred to me that he was being impertinent, but I raised my eyes to meet his and replied, 'My name is Anna Foster.'

'Ah...' he said, contemplating for a moment. 'Donald's young bride. I heard he'd got married. I've been in Delhi for the last week or two or I'd have been at your homecoming.'

He held out a hand. 'I'm Charles Perry, by the way. People generally call me Charlie. I'm the District Officer for the Kandaipur area.'

I took his hand, aware that my own was very clammy.

'Can I drop you anywhere, Mrs Foster? My motor car is outside.'

'Oh, no, thank you. I have a rickshaw waiting.'

'Quite the independent young woman! Donald's a very lucky man. I hope he realises that.'

I smiled, not knowing what to say. His words echoed those of Mrs Smethurst and I got that uncomfortable feeling again, that everyone here knew something that I didn't.

'Oh well, I expect we'll bump into one another at the club before long,' he said when I didn't reply. 'Good afternoon to you, Mrs Foster.'

He bowed his head slightly, raised his topee and disappeared into the crowd.

June 15th, 1932

I've been in Kandaipur for several months now and have spent most of that time on my own. Each day, I wake alone in my bed to the sound of Donald getting up in the room next door. He rises before dawn and I hear him go down to the bathroom, and splashing in the bathtub. Then he returns to his room, where Ali helps him dress in his uniform. I can hear them talking in low voices through the wall. He then goes into the dining room, eats the breakfast that Ali brings him, and leaves for the military station in his chauffeured army car.

Since that first and only time on the train, he's not even tried to touch me. There's certainly been no suggestion that he might want to share my bed. Each night, he simply says goodnight, pecks me on the cheek and retires to his own room. I'm half relieved about this turn of events, because all I can remember about that night is embarrassment, awkwardness and pain. However, I do find it odd. He is my husband after all, and in Bombay and in Matheran too, he seemed to be attracted to me, to show real affection for me. I can't say he isn't kind and caring when we are together, it's just that he seems to be quite happy to spend each and every day, from early in the morning until late at night, out of the house and away from me.

It's plain to me that he is devoted to the regiment. I once asked him why he needed to work such long hours and he spoke of his training and the riots in the district he is responsible for preventing.

Occasionally I leave the house and wander down to the club in the mornings. If Mrs Smethurst is there, she always beckons me over to join her and calls for a pack of cards. Otherwise I sit on the veranda and drink tea. The other women are polite to me and ask me to join them at their tables, but I can't escape that feeling that they're all holding something back, that they're watching me, and that they know something that I don't. It makes me feel shy about speaking to them, and reticent about telling them anything about myself other than mundane details. All in all, it makes me feel lonelier than ever.

Once or twice Charles Perry has been in the club when I've been there. I've noticed how the other women react to him, blushing and simpering. If he talks to any of them, they always flutter their eyelids and lean in close to him. I suppose he is tall and good-looking but to me, his looks are slightly forbidding. He holds himself with an air of arrogance, as if he's aware of his attraction and that the attention he receives is his of right.

When I've glanced over at him at the bar, I've noticed that he's been looking at me, with a steady, calculating, slightly sardonic gaze. I've looked away quickly, but not before a chill has gone right through my body. I'm not sure where that has come from, or what it signifies, it only leaves me confused and disconcerted.

As well as my occasional visits to the club, each day I take the opportunity to explore the neighbourhood. I often wander down to the maidan after lunch, where my rickshaw-wallah is already awake and looking out for me. We have an understanding now. After that first time he always greets me with a broad smile, his teeth heavily stained with betel nut. I know his name now: Rajiv.

'Where to today, madam?' Rajiv asks, and I tell him where I want to go. I have visited all the Hindu temples dotted about the town, where I have removed my shoes and crept inside to watch people praying to their gods, to absorb the atmosphere and to breathe in the heady incense.

One day, he took me out of town to an abandoned temple, overgrown with bamboo and creepers, where I sat and sketched for an hour, drawing the crumbling ruins, the rampant undergrowth and the broken statues. Another day, he took me to a lake nestled in a valley. The water was perfectly still and reflected the hills around like a mirror. I sat on a rock and sketched the view. I have kept these sketches from Donald. Somehow, I don't think he would approve of me travelling the area in a rickshaw, sightseeing and sketching alone as I do, my only company a rickshaw-wallah.

One day, I was at a loss as to where to go.

'Take me somewhere new, Rajiv,' I said. 'Somewhere interesting.'

He pedalled me out of town and along a straight dusty road in the direction of the distant snow-capped mountains. We left the cantonment and the British quarter far behind.

*We passed villages of native houses and shacks, where people
lay in the shade of banyan trees, or herded their goats or
buffalos on the dusty plain. The only vehicles we saw along
the way were bullock carts, carrying vegetables towards the
bazaar in Kandaipur or hauling loads of hay to farms.*

*After a few miles Rajiv turned off the road and onto
a rutted side road. A little way along, we passed a couple
of derelict houses. Their walls and roofs were green with
mould, and they were almost buried in creepers. There
were bushes growing out of broken windows, and rampant
bougainvillea covered the front wall. I stared at them as we
passed and a chill went through me. They looked as though
they had been built for British people, who had planted that
bougainvillea in their front garden once upon a time. How
strange that those homes had been left to be reclaimed by
the jungle. Beyond the houses, around another bend in the
road, a church tower suddenly rose between the trees and
bushes. I gasped – it was such a surprise to see it there, and
so incongruous to see a church here at all. It was just like
one you might find in an English village, but so strange to
stumble across it out in the country on the Indian plain.
It had once been whitewashed, but the paint was flaking
off the walls, and several of its arched mullioned windows
were broken.*

*'Old church,' said Rajiv, gesticulating towards it and
beaming broadly. 'Madam want to look?'*

*'Of course,' I said, getting down from the rickshaw with
my sketchbook and pencils.*

*I found a place in the shade, sat down on a tumbledown
wall, opened my sketchpad and began to draw the old
church. Rajiv pulled the rickshaw off the road into some
bushes and settled down for a rest.*

I was completely absorbed in my task and the time flew past. I worked quickly and cleanly. It came together easily and I was pleased with the result. I thought I'd managed to convey the atmosphere of the old place with its air of forlorn loneliness quite well. I was just holding up my work to assess it when I heard the sound of an engine. A motor car appeared around the bend in the road. I shaded my eyes and peered at it, and my heart gave a strange twist when I saw Charles Perry peering back at me from the rear window.

'Mrs Foster! Whatever are you doing here so far from town? First, I find you in a native bazaar and now in the middle of nowhere in front of a derelict church. Wherever next?'

I tried to look nonchalant and calm, but probably appeared anything but.

'Oh, I like to get out and see the neighbourhood,' was all I could manage. I could feel my cheeks flaming under his gaze.

'Club not good enough for you?' he asked, with an amused smile. Then his eyes wandered to my sketchbook.

'Oh my! So, you're an artist too, are you? Let's take a gander.'

Unwillingly, I passed it to him, and cast my eyes down, my cheeks burning. I find it so difficult to show anyone my work, especially when I haven't had time to perfect it. He looked at it for a moment, raised his eyebrows. Then he looked into my eyes.

'It's really beautiful! You've got quite a talent there.'

'Oh, I don't know about that,' I muttered.

'Well, I do! It's astonishingly accurate. Now look, would you like a lift home? I've just been visiting one of the villages along the road. I'm heading back to the office for tiffin now.'

'No. Thank you all the same but it's fine. I have my rickshaw waiting.' I pointed across to Rajiv, who bowed shyly.

'Well, if you're sure. You must take care, you know.'

'It seems very peaceful. And I'm glad I've seen the old church. Why is it derelict? Do you know?'

'Ah, long story. It used to be a Baptist church. Thriving place a few years back. But the Baptist missionary here wasn't well liked by the establishment, though the villagers seemed devoted to him and he had a strong following. He fell out with the Baptist authorities in Delhi too, I understand, and was called back to England under a bit of a cloud. They stopped funding the place after that. It fell into disrepair.'

'How very sad. What on earth did he do that was so bad?'

'Oh… as I said, long story. I'll tell you all about it one day. I'll tell you now if you'll ride back to town with me.'

'No. It's kind of you, but as I said, I've already paid for the rickshaw.'

'It will have to wait then.' He stood silently for a few seconds, his eyes on my face. Then he smiled. 'I wonder… what would old Donald say about you being out here all alone?'

Panic rose in me. He'd pinpointed my weak spot with astonishing accuracy. I really didn't want Donald to find out about these jaunts. He might try to stop me, and I couldn't bear that.

'Look,' I stammered, blushing again in my confusion. 'I'd really prefer it if you didn't mention it to Donald, if it's all the same to you?'

His eyes were still on me, assessing me. Just as they did in the club. He smiled as I raised my eyes to meet his.

'Of course,' he said evenly. 'And as a matter of fact, I'd prefer it if you didn't mention that you met me here. Or that time in the bazaar, for that matter.'

I looked at him, confused. I was about to ask why when he went on, 'So, let's keep it between ourselves, shall we? Just you and me. It will be our little secret.'

He got into his car, the engine roared into life and it rumbled away in a cloud of dust.

I sat on the wall going hot and cold at the thought of what I'd asked him to do. I was still mystified as to why he wanted my silence, but I'd asked him to hide something from my husband. It wasn't just that, it was what it meant. It meant that this man now had some sort of hold over me.

Connie peers at the page, trying to make out the flowing lines, which have started to blur in front of her eyes. She looks up and realises that the light is fading. She hears the clatter of pots and pans in the kitchen along the corridor. It only feels like five minutes since she ate her lunch, but it must be hours and approaching supper time.

The image in the diary of the decaying church has unsettled her, and Charles Perry's words echo in her mind: *'the Baptist missionary here wasn't well liked by the establishment… He fell out with the Baptist authorities… and was called back to England under a bit of a cloud.'* Connie can hardly bear to entertain the possibility that the Baptist minister in question could possibly have been Father. It just doesn't make sense. How could it have been the Father who told her fantastic stories of helping poor families back in India, of trekking miles through the mountains to nurse them back to health when they were sick? The Father who would passionately preach the word of God each morning in the orphanage and on Sundays in church, to enraptured congregations who stared up into his blazing eyes, awestruck by his eloquence, hanging on his every word. How could that possibly be the same person? She chews her lip, contemplating the possibility.

Father had definitely been in Kandaipur, and the description of the church in the diary meets the one she knows so well. Her eyes wander to the painting hanging on her wall of the tiny church, nestling there among the exotic trees, under the shelter of the great mountains. Tears of sadness suddenly flood her eyes at the thought that that very same church had gone to ruin in a matter of a few years, that creepers and weeds had penetrated its walls, wild shrubs had grown through its broken roof tiles. Could it really be the same place? She hopes with all her heart that it is not. Had Anna some connection to Father in India? Connie had never imagined that it could possibly have gone that far back.

At the same time she cannot prevent her long-suppressed memories of the other side of Father from surfacing briefly. The side she'd prefer to forget. She recalls his thunderous expression and words of rage as he reprimanded some of the orphan boys who'd been caught scrumping apples from the orchard. And the time she'd witnessed him caning a boy for stealing money from the church collection. The whole orphanage had been made to stand in the hall and watch as the boy was forced to bend over a table while Father ran at him with a cane and slammed it down on his backside a dozen times. Connie, standing near the front, had glimpsed Father's expression as he brought the cane down. His face was red with effort and thunderous with rage, but there was a glint of something else in his eyes that sent a chill right through her.

Shaking her head now, to rid herself of the memory, she puts the silk ribbon from the diary down the middle of the page and closes the book. Her eyes are weary and watery. She shuts her eyes and drifts off to sleep, and as she does so, she is transported to a land far away, to a long-forgotten time. She is walking through a temple. Gongs are clanging, monks are chanting, and she is breathing in the exotic smells of incense and woodsmoke.

Chapter Seventeen

Sarah

Sarah leaves the nursing home and wanders back through the town. She has decided to walk the mile or so from Cedar Hall to get some exercise. She knows she's been spending far too much time in the car since she left London.

As she walks home, she thinks about Miss Burroughs. The old lady's reaction to the news about the valuables in the cupboard has taken her by surprise. In fact, the whole encounter had felt very odd. Miss Burroughs seemed to veer from befuddled confusion to sharp perceptiveness. It was disconcerting and very sad too. How frustrating and humiliating it must be to be in her situation, confused and frustrated, having lost your entire family, dependent on strangers for care, so alone in the world.

When Sarah had walked into the room with the flowers, she'd been shocked at Miss Burroughs' appearance. The old lady appeared frail, bundled up in a colourless shawl and grey skirt, her white hair unbrushed. She seemed lonely and confused at first. But Sarah had quickly realised that there was more to her than that. Behind the befuddled exterior lay a sharp defiance, and a brooding pent-up energy. Sarah had noticed it the first time she'd seen Miss Burroughs, when Mr Squires was pushing her across the yard in the wheelchair. The old lady had been sharp and decisive then, as she had been at points during their conversation this afternoon. Especially when Sarah had asked if she knew why her father might have sealed up those things in the cupboard.

Connie's words echo in Sarah's mind now: 'Father didn't seal those things away… It was me. I did it.' She'd looked almost triumphant as she said it, and Sarah had had another glimpse of the girl in the photograph; that defiant spirit in her piercing blue eyes was unmistakeable. But why? Why had she done that, and why was she so fierce about it? Sarah hadn't liked to probe her, because as soon as she'd said it, Miss Burroughs stopped herself. She began to shake and to fiddle with a chain around her neck, to pick at her shawl, and for a while she became quite withdrawn. She was silent for several minutes, and when she finally did speak, she reverted to being vague and muddled.

Sarah had wondered about asking Miss Burroughs if she knew anything about Dad's birth, but she'd decided against it. Yesterday evening, when she and Dad had been eating supper, she'd told him that she intended to visit Connie Burroughs in the morning.

'Do you want me to ask if she remembers?' she'd asked tentatively. 'About… well, about when you were a baby.'

He'd put down his fork.

'I'd love that, Sarah. That would be wonderful. All the things she must have seen over the years. Everything she must know. But on the other hand, she's very old. Perhaps it wouldn't be kind to trouble her about the distant past.'

'But she might remember something. It could be your chance to find out.'

He'd lapsed into silence then, and Sarah had begun to worry.

'Are you all right, Dad?'

'Yes. Quite all right,' he said, coming out of his reverie and smiling at her. 'Why not wait for a little while? It might be best not to spring too many things on her at once. She'll be surprised enough about the things you found in the cupboard. It might all be too much for her in one day. You could always go back another time, she might appreciate an occasional visit.'

When Sarah had left, she'd asked if Miss Burroughs minded if she returned one day. The old lady had stared at her, blinking, as if trying to understand her words.

'You want to come back and see me?' she'd asked finally.

'Only if you'd like me to.'

'Of course. That would be very nice. I don't get many… well, *any* visitors actually.'

Sarah thinks again about the pieces in the cupboard. The ornaments are beautifully crafted out of exquisite materials. She resolves to polish them up and put them away somewhere for a while. There is something about those Hindu gods, and the fact that Connie herself had hidden them away, that troubles her. Then there is also the cane, the watch and the cufflinks. They must have belonged to Ezra Burroughs. She pictures him wearing them, tucking the watch inside a breast pocket, the cane under his arm. A shiver goes through her. The elephant's foot must have been a coal scuttle. There's something deeply disturbing about that, too – that it was once part of a majestic live animal, roaming the jungle.

She's wandering along the High Street now, approaching the town from the other direction. She finds herself opposite the bistro. Why not stop off for a bite to eat? She hasn't done a proper supermarket shop yet and it would be good to have some hot food.

The young waiter greets her shyly, showing no signs of having met her in the newsagent's the day before. He shows her to a window seat. This time she orders boeuf bourguignon. It takes a while, but when it does come, it is the owner who brings it.

'So, you did buy the house after all,' he says, smiling broadly, setting the food down in front of her on the table.

She looks up at him and returns the smile. He looks less careworn and preoccupied than on the previous occasion.

'I did. How did you know?'

'Oh, word gets around. It's a small town.'

'I moved in a few days ago. But I suppose you know that too,' she says, laughing.

'Of course. Well, welcome to Weirfield.'

'Thank you.'

'Oh, and apologies for the wait, we're short-staffed at the moment.'

'That's no problem. I know what it's like.'

She'd said it without thinking and immediately regrets it. She feels the heat in her cheeks as the man looks at her with raised eyebrows, waiting for her to go on. When she doesn't, he says, 'Really? Are you in the trade too?'

'I was. Until recently.'

She waits for him to put two and two together. Has he remembered her name? She probably told him her surname the last time she came in. She holds her breath. How stupid of her to blurt it out like that. She really doesn't want to discuss Alex. Not here, not now. She feels relief when the man simply says, 'Well, if you're interested, I'm looking for someone I can trust for the role of front of house: to look after the customers in the restaurant, so I can keep a better eye on the kitchen. It's not really working out doing both.'

'That must be tough. It's very kind of you but I need to concentrate on the house for the next few months.'

'Well, if you change your mind, do let me know.'

Back at Cedar Hall, Sarah continues stripping wallpaper in the study. She makes quick progress, singing along to the radio. She thinks about her father, worrying about his health, his obsession with his birth mother, wondering how she can find a way to help him with his search. The paper falls in great sodden curls onto the groundsheet. She's surprised how quickly the time passes. Darkness falls, and she gets down from the chair and switches on the light so she can see to carry on. When the doorbell rings, she realises with surprise that it's after four o' clock.

'Mrs Jennings?' The builder stands on the porch. A balding man in his fifties. She invites him in. He steps inside the hall and looks around him warily. He seems nervous. Perhaps he's shy, Sarah thinks.

'Come through to the kitchen. Would you like tea?'

'Don't mind if I do. Two sugars, if that's all right. Miss B didn't ever used to have sugar in. Didn't approve of it.'

Sarah looks up from putting the kettle on. 'So, you know the house?'

'Oh yes. I used to come and do odd jobs from time to time. Needs a proper going-over, though. I used to tell Miss B that, but I don't think she wanted to spend anything on the place.'

'No. It looks as though the roof and gutters need attention. And of course the windows all need painting and renovating outside. Is that something you could quote for?'

He nods. 'I'll have to look in daylight, but I don't think you need a new roof. We should be able to patch it up. Replace some of the tiles.'

'That's good news. I've also got some ideas for a few changes inside. Shall I show you round? We can bring our tea.'

He follows her around the ground floor as she explains her plans.

'It's mostly decorating, as you'll see. The only structural thing I'd like to do is to open the kitchen out into the conservatory. Make it all one big room.'

He nods approvingly. 'Yep. We can take down the back kitchen wall, put an RSJ in there to hold it up. There'll be a step down, of course. Floor levels are different. But I can deal with all that, no problem.'

They pass the study door. Sarah follows his gaze as he glances inside.

'I've made a start on the decorating myself, actually,' she says. Then she sees he's staring at the exposed wall cupboard.

'It was very odd. I found that cupboard completely sealed up under the plaster when I took the paper off.'

He laughs. 'Sealed it up myself. Only last year, as a matter of fact. Couldn't fathom why the old girl wanted that done, but she insisted.'

'It was very strange. There were some interesting things in there too.'

'Really? She said there was only old junk in there.' He laughs again. 'Well, she always was a strange one, Miss B. Probably lost her marbles. She must have been well on the way before.'

'Why do you say that?' Sarah asks.

'Very strange family, the Burroughs. Her and the sister, Miss Evie. Lived like church mice they did, in their old age. This old place falling down around their ears. They must have had cash though, at some point. They used to be rich in their father's heyday. At least that's what me old dad used to say.'

'Did your father know them?'

'Oh yes. Dad started the family business. He was a carpenter. He built that old desk over there in the corner,' he says, nodding in the direction of the bureau.

'Well, it's a beautiful piece of furniture. He must have been very skilful.'

'Oh yes, he was skilful all right.'

'I'm sure Miss Burroughs would have kept it, only they couldn't get it out of the room.'

'There'll be a way of dismantling it and putting it back together again. Dad always built them like that. Don't suppose the removal men realised.'

'Really? It might be good to move it out of the room, so I can decorate properly. Perhaps you could help me one day?'

'All right. If you show me what else you'd like doing, I'll send you an estimate. When I start work, I'll help you move the desk.'

She smiles. 'It's a deal. When would you be able to start?'

'Next week. I've hit a few problems on another job. Waiting for some materials, so I've got some free time.'

As she shows him out, he turns back and says, 'I'm glad you're doing the old place up finally. Used to give me the creeps when I was a kid. It was rotting away even then. I've been dying to get my hands on it for years.'

Chapter Eighteen

Sarah

Sarah's life falls into a regular routine. Each morning, she gets up early, crosses the road for the newspaper and a few groceries and to pass the time of day with Jacqui in the newsagent's. She spends the rest of the day decorating the study. She still feels unsettled, though; she can't help thinking that Connie is harbouring a lifetime of secrets that she would love to unlock. Perhaps they are connected to her father's past?

Terry starts work as he'd promised the following Monday. He brings his workmate Rodney, a diminutive man with a ruddy face and a shock of white hair. Their first task is to renovate the living room, to take out the old gas fire and restore the marble fireplace. Every few hours, Sarah takes the men tea or coffee and stops for a chat.

It's good to be distracted by their banter and to hear the local gossip. Through them and through her daily conversations with Jacqui, she gradually begins to feel part of Weirfield. Alex and her life in London start to fade into the background. But not completely. Every week or so she gets an email from Judith Marshall, updating her on the progress of her divorce and the financial negotiations with Alex. She tries not to dwell on it; throws herself into renovating the house. Over time she thinks about it less, and after a while is able to put Alex out of her mind for several hours at a time.

He hasn't been in touch since she moved in, but sometimes, in spite of her resolutions, in moments of weakness she takes the card he sent her out of the bedside drawer, and lets her mind wander back there to the restaurant, to their home. She finds herself wondering what she would be doing now if the police hadn't knocked on the door before dawn that morning; it seems so long ago now.

After Terry and Rodney have gone home each day, Sarah drives over to her father's house to spend the evening with him. They take it in turns to cook, and after they've eaten they play chess, go through his research or play cards until it's time for Sarah to go home. She relishes these moments; it feels as if she's at least doing something to make up for lost time.

Each day, she enters his house anxiously, wondering how he'll be. Sometimes he'll be lying down in the sunroom, under a blanket, his face drawn and grey with pain.

'Bad day?' she'll say, and he'll nod with a rueful smile and heave himself up on his elbows, grasping for his pills.

'Not so bad now *you're* here,' he'll say, then insist on getting up and moving to the kitchen, where he'll want to know how the house is coming on.

On other days he'll already be in the kitchen when she arrives, chopping onions and garlic, his apron on, humming to the radio. He'll turn and kiss her and she'll know it's been a better day. But she also knows it will only be a matter of months that they will have like this before his condition gets worse and he'll have to go into hospital for treatment. They both know that the treatment might not work. They don't speak of that directly, but it's present in their looks and their gestures, and implicit in the plans they make.

Then one day she finds him virtually asleep at his desk. He's been poring over records on his computer. There is also a pile of papers, accumulated during his search, that he has been working through. She gently suggests he should stop and get some rest.

'But I need to do this, Sarah,' he says, looking at her with strained, bloodshot eyes. 'Time is short. It's running out, in fact. If I want to find answers, I need to spend as much time on this as I can.'

So, Sarah resolves to go and see Connie Burroughs again as soon as she can. She is sure that she must know something about him, one of the foundling babies from the orphanage. If only Sarah can persuade her to tell her what she knows.

But this time Miss Burroughs seems more confused than before. She's preoccupied, fiddling with her necklace and drifting off, her blue eyes far away in another place, another time. She has a small blue hardback book on her lap. It looks like a diary and it's firmly locked with a small metal clasp.

'Miss Burroughs, there's something I'd like to ask you,' Sarah says carefully.

Connie turns her eyes towards her, but they're not focusing.

'It's about the orphanage. I hope you don't mind me asking you this, it's just that my father was actually there when he was a baby.'

The blue eyes come to life and Miss Burroughs sits up straight. She turns her gaze on Sarah and it's as if a beam from a lighthouse has suddenly swung round to point at her.

'Perhaps I remember him. What's his name, my dear?'

'His name is William… William King.'

Miss Burroughs relaxes slightly and frowns. 'I don't remember anyone of that name, I'm afraid. And I used to know all the children by name. I grew up among them, and when I was old enough, I became a teacher there too. I'm afraid you must be mistaken.'

'Well, he wasn't there for long. He was just a baby. A foundling, in fact. He was only there for a few months, I believe. He was adopted, you see, by Mr and Mrs King. They took him to live with them in Bristol. That's where he grew up.'

'A foundling?' Miss Burroughs dabs her lips with a screwed-up handkerchief. Sarah sees that she's started shaking, just as she had when Sarah mentioned the artefacts in the cupboard. Her right hand makes its way to her throat and her fingers fiddle with the chain there, working their way up and down, up and down.

'I could bring you his birth certificate—' Sarah begins, but stops, seeing something in Miss Burroughs' widened eyes that looks almost like terror. 'No, no. Don't worry, I won't do that. Perhaps that's not a good idea. Please don't distress yourself. I'm sorry I mentioned it. It's just that my father's always wanted to find out more about his birth. He knows nothing about it.'

The old woman closes her eyes and Sarah can see that she is trying to compose herself.

'Are you all right?' Sarah asks. 'Is there anything I can get you?'

Miss Burroughs shakes her head vehemently. 'No. No, it's quite all right. It's just all so long ago. I'm not sure I can remember that far back. When is your father's birthday?'

'September 1934. His birth certificate describes his parents as "unknown".'

Miss Burroughs' eyes snap open again and now she is looking intently at Sarah. Leaning forward and peering at her as if she's searching for something.

'September, you say? September 1934? Are you quite sure it was September, not earlier in the year?'

Sarah shakes her head. 'Quite sure. His birthday is in September.' Miss Burroughs slumps back in her chair and her face seems to collapse. She whispers something under her breath that Sarah barely catches, then she seems to switch off completely.

'Miss Burroughs?' Sarah asks. 'Miss Burroughs, can you hear me?'

But she doesn't respond. Slowly, her eyes close and Sarah realises from her regular breathing that she's fallen asleep. Sighing, Sarah lets herself out of the room. She vows to come back and try again soon, frustrated that she didn't get further with her questions. It seemed to her that at one point there was some spark of recognition. But she doesn't want to read too much into what Miss Burroughs has said for fear of being disappointed later.

Chapter Nineteen

Sarah

Sarah crosses the road to the newsagent's. Jacqui looks up from her magazine and greets her warmly. As usual, she is eager to impart some local gossip: a couple along the High Street have gone their separate ways after thirty years of marriage. Sarah half-listens as she wanders round the shop with her basket, absent-mindedly collecting groceries. Her thoughts are on the difficult conversation she'd had with her father earlier. She'd driven over to his house after her visit to Fairlawns. She hadn't had the heart to tell him that her questions about his connection to the orphanage had all come to nothing, and that Miss Burroughs had reacted strangely and didn't remember him as a baby. She'd tried to let him down gently, telling him that she couldn't remember anything immediately, but was going to have a think about it. She'd seen the pain and disappointment on his face immediately, although he'd tried to hide it.

'Are you all right, dear?' Jacqui's voice breaks into her thoughts. 'You're a bit quiet today.'

'I'm sorry,' Sarah smiles, 'I was miles away.' She brings her basket to the counter and is about to go on when the door opens and in bursts Simon, the young waiter from the bistro. Sarah smiles briefly and steps aside. The boy's face is full of panic.

'Dad sent me to ask you a favour, Mrs Tennant. Do you think you could come and help out with the evening shift?' he asks Jacqui.

Jacqui sighs. 'I suppose I could. I was going to do the stock-taking, but I'm sure that can wait if it's an emergency. What's happened?'

'Chef's ill. Got flu or something. Dad's got to man the kitchen by himself this evening. He needs someone to greet the guests, deal with the money. I can't really cope on my own.'

'OK,' says Jacqui, reluctance in her voice. 'I suppose I could shut up the shop. Just give me five minutes.'

'I could come,' Sarah blurts out, not quite understanding why even as she's saying it.

Simon looks at her in surprise, and recognition dawns on his face.

'Are you sure?' he asks.

'Of course. What time do you need me?'

'About six, if that's OK. Thank you.' He dashes out of the shop.

'Well, thank you,' says Jacqui. 'That's a load off my mind. I would have gone, but I can't say I was looking forward to it.'

Sarah dresses carefully for the evening, in her little black dress and strappy shoes. She puts her make-up on, and her onyx earrings. She feels the thrill of anticipation that she'll spend the evening doing what she loves.

When she arrives at Le Gastronome, Matt Drayton emerges in his chef's whites from the kitchen, a relieved smile spreading across his face.

'Sarah! How kind of you to help out. I can't thank you enough.' He takes her coat.

'Thank me after the evening.' She laughs. 'Let's see how it goes.'

He laughs too. 'Come on, let me show you how things work.'

He quickly demonstrates how the till and online booking system work and then with further profuse thanks, he dashes back to the kitchen.

Within minutes the first guests arrive. She greets them smoothly, showing them to their table, making sure they're comfortable, taking their drinks orders. Soon, more people come and she does the same. She fetches their drinks and helps Simon bring their food from the kitchen. She begins to relax and realises she's in her element. Catching sight of herself in the mirror behind the bar as she passes, her eyes glowing, she sees someone cool and self-assured, perfectly in control. She realises just how much she's missed this.

At the end of the evening, when the last guest has gone home, Matt offers her a nightcap and they sit down at the table in the window with a coffee and a brandy each.

'You're so good at this,' he says, holding his brandy glass up to hers. 'Where did you train?'

'Oh, I didn't train really, just picked it up as I went along. I've worked in restaurants in Bristol and in London.'

'Well, you're a natural.'

She notices that he looks a little nervous, avoiding her gaze and no longer as relaxed and friendly as he'd seemed in the kitchen, taking everything in his stride.

'Is everything OK?' she asks.

'Yes, yes. Everything's fine. In fact, very much improved, thanks to you.'

'That's nice of you to say so, but I haven't really done anything.'

'That's not true. Things were going from bad to worse this evening before you walked through the door. I'm really very grateful.'

'I enjoyed it. There's no need to thank me,' she says and smiles at him, noticing, not for the first time this evening, the deep blue of his eyes and the fine lines around them. There's a long pause as they hold each other's gaze, and in those moments it feels to Sarah as if they've known each other for years, or at least that there's already a deep connection between them, forged in just the space of a few hours.

She thinks back over the evening and realises that the two of them worked like clockwork together, instinctively knowing, without having to speak, what needed to be done at any given moment to make sure the customers were happy, the food was served in perfect condition and that everything was running smoothly. And each time she'd been into the kitchen and glimpsed him cooking, she'd noticed what a natural he was; how his skill and enthusiasm for creating the food radiated from him and spread to everyone around him. It was a long time since she'd observed that raw, untainted passion and it really struck a chord with her.

He clears his throat now, breaking the silence and drops his gaze to the table, avoiding her eyes.

'It's been a bit of a struggle since Rosie died,' he says. 'You might have heard…'

Sarah hesitates before saying, 'Yes, I did hear that your wife passed away. I'm so sorry, Matt.'

'Thank you.'

There's an awkward silence as they both sip their drinks. Sarah tries to think of something to say, but finally, Matt clears his throat and says something that takes her breath away: 'Actually, I was wondering if you'd like to go out for dinner sometime.'

Again, Sarah's mind skates back over the evening and she realises that he must have felt what she felt. She feels colour creeping into her cheeks, suddenly exposed and confused, recalling a couple of occasions during the evening when they'd exchanged glances, their eyes lingering together a little longer than necessary. She's surprised that he's brought it into the open so quickly, but flattered too. She realises that she's gripping the handle of the coffee mug hard, her knuckles are white. She makes an effort to relax.

'Of course I quite understand if you don't want to,' he goes on. 'It's just that… it's just that I've enjoyed your company, Sarah, this evening, and when we've chatted before…'

'Look, Matt…' she begins, but falters. She isn't sure what to say. This is all so sudden, but all the same, not unwelcome.

'I'm so sorry,' he says, looking at her earnestly. 'This is probably far too soon, I know. It's just that I thought… well, I suppose I must have misread the situation.' He laughs self-consciously.

She makes an effort to look into his eyes. 'I'm so sorry, Matt. I'm really flattered that you've asked me, but just at the moment I'm not great company.'

'Don't worry, I understand,' he says.

'Look, you might have gathered that I recently split up from my husband. It's been really difficult. And with everything going on at the moment, just buying the house, my father's very ill… I'm just not sure where I am right now.'

'I understand. Look, no hard feelings. We can pretend this didn't happen. We can be friends, right?'

'Of course, Matt. I'm sorry. It's just that—'

'Please. There's no need to explain.'

In the morning, Sarah can't get the evening at the restaurant and the awkward conversation with Matt out of her mind. She thinks about it continually as she gets up, takes a bath in the rusting bathtub and as she sits at the kitchen table, sipping her morning coffee and eating breakfast. What if she'd accepted his offer to go out? How would she be feeling this morning? Matt is an attractive man and part of her is flattered. Again, she recalls the way he looked at her as they'd worked together; the connection she'd felt with him. She sighs, putting it out of her mind as she washes up at the butler sink and forces herself to focus on what the next task will be in the house.

Ezra Burroughs' oak bureau needs to be moved out before she can paint the back wall of the study. She's now reached the point where she can't make further progress with the bureau still there.

Terry and Rodney are already at work sanding the floorboards in the living room. She goes through and reminds Terry of his promise to help her move it. He puts down the sander and straightens up.

'Of course. Sorry, I'd forgotten. Rodney, come on, mate. Help me move me old dad's desk, will you?'

Sarah watches as Terry crawls under the bureau with a screwdriver and begins to work on the frame. After a few minutes she hears him exclaim, 'Oooohhh, it's one of these!'

She moves forward. 'What do you mean?'

'I knew Dad could do this, but I hadn't realised this was one of them.'

'One of what?'

'There's a false bottom to the desk. A hidden compartment.'

Sarah's heart begins to race. 'Really? Can you open it?'

'I'll try.' Terry grunts as he works the screwdriver. After a few minutes there's a scraping sound, like a warped door catching. Then more banging and grunting, and finally, he crawls out, red-faced. He kneels down in front of the bureau and pulls out a slim drawer at the front, revealed by a board that he has removed from underneath.

'What's in there?' She leans forward, eager to see. Terry steps back.

'You look. It's nothing to do with me,' he says.

She looks in the drawer. A sheaf of papers and a hardback ledger thick with dust. She takes the ledger out and it falls open. There are three columns of numbers written in flowing handwriting. The first column contains single numbers, the second and third contain blocks of six numbers. She stares at them, wondering what they might mean. Then she puts it back, momentarily disappointed. She's not quite sure what she was expecting, but it doesn't seem to mean anything.

Then she picks up the pile of papers. They are yellowing, but thick, of good quality, almost like parchment. They seem to be certificates of some sort. She looks at them closely, puzzled. There's a crest of arms at the top, and the words *Certificate of an Entry in the Register of Births in the County District of Weirfield, Berkshire.* She stares at the documents for a moment. Then the realisation of what they are hits her and she gasps in surprise: they are blank birth certificates.

Chapter Twenty

Connie

Erica is leaning over her as Connie opens her eyes.

'Are you awake? You must have taken a morning nap, Miss Burroughs.'

Connie stares at her. Erica's face is so close, Connie can see the lumps in her mascara, the foundation applied unevenly on the skin under her eyes. Her breath smells of cigarettes.

'What time is it?'

'It's nearly lunchtime, Miss Burroughs. Come along to the dining room.'

'I've only just woken up. I'm not really hungry.'

She resists because she knows Erica is expecting her to, but deep down, she feels a thrill of anticipation at the thought of going along to the dining room again, of seeing the old man who reminds her so much of Tommy and brings back so many memories. It's true, she'd been shocked when Sarah had revealed that she'd found Father's things sealed up in that cupboard; it had made Connie cast her mind back to those times when she lived in fear of Father, when he'd tried to control her every move. In fact, she's thought of little else since. And reading Anna's diary has brought back those times too; making those unwelcome thoughts of what Father really was resurface. How he'd struck terror into Connie's heart. Perhaps it is also the feeling that Cedar Hall is now in safe hands with Sarah Jennings. Whatever it is, she feels it deeply. Something inside tells her she is ready to face those ghosts now.

'It will do you good to get out of your room.'

Connie shrugs. 'All right. I'll come, I suppose,' she says, drawing her shawl close to her.

Erica's smile is triumphant. 'Good! I knew you would.'

Erica helps her out of her chair and holds Connie's elbow as she makes her way between the pieces of cluttered furniture to the door. Erica opens it to reveal Matron standing there in the corridor, holding the Zimmer frame. She's wearing her encouraging expression, nodding and beckoning Connie forward. *I'm not at nursery school,* Connie thinks. She takes the frame from Matron. She can walk quite well with the frame now, and resists their attempts to help her along the corridor, but when they reach the double doors to the dining room, Erica darts ahead of her and pushes them open so she can pass through.

Connie hesitates. The air in the room is hot and fuggy, just as she remembers from before. The noise of conversation and the clatter of pots and pans feels overwhelming. Again, she wishes she was back at Cedar Hall, hidden away behind those tall hedges, guarding her silence and isolation.

'Come along,' says Erica, smiling encouragement. 'There are your friends from the other day. Look, there's even a space at their table.'

Elsie, Marjory and Dorothy are waving to her, beckoning her over.

Connie eases herself into the seat between Elsie and Marjory.

'How are you, my dear?' asks Elsie. 'We've been worried about you. I wanted to come to your room to see you but Matron said you wanted to be on your own. I hope everything is all right.'

Connie nods, lost for words, just like the first time.

'I've just been feeling a bit under the weather,' she finally says.

'You had a visitor though, didn't you? Young woman. Is she a relative? I saw her coming through reception with some beautiful flowers.'

Connie looks at the other ladies. They're waiting for her reply, just like the first time she was here. She doesn't want to talk about

Cedar Hall and get them reminiscing about the old days again. Why did she let Erica force her to come? It would have been far better to have stayed in her room.

'Well?' asks Elsie.

'She's the young lady who bought our house,' Connie says at last.

The others exchange looks. She gets the feeling that they have discussed her in her absence.

'How nice of her to come and see you,' Marjory says. 'Hardly anyone comes to see me any more. My daughter lives in America. My son's busy with his family.'

The others murmur their agreement and the conversation moves on. There are no questions this time about Father or about the orphanage. It makes Connie uneasy. They must have talked about those days and decided not to mention them to her again. What had they remembered? What was there for them to remember? The people in the town had known nothing about Father's secrets. Or had they?

Elsie and Marjory are gossiping among themselves about a new resident. Connie listens with half an ear, concentrating on the pasta she's eating, trying to make sure the slippery twirls don't skid off her fork and fall onto her lap. All the time she's conscious that the old man who reminds her of Tommy is at a nearby table. Her eyes keep straying over that way. She can't help it, even though she doesn't want to be rude.

'We should really introduce you to the other new people,' Marjory finally says, clearly noticing that Connie is distracted. 'There's an old boy who's quite new too. That one over there in the corner, far end of that red table. Not been here long at all. Now, what's his name? For the life of me I can't remember. I know he said he used to run a garage or some such thing.'

Connie doesn't want to turn round and stare, but a thrill goes through her at those words, and she suddenly feels tongue-tied.

'What's his name, Marjory?' Marjory cups a hand to her ear, so Elsie leans forward and has to repeat her words.

'That one in the corner, new one. Says he ran a garage in south London somewhere.'

'Oh, that's old Tommy. Tommy Braithwaite.'

Connie freezes. Her heart stands still.

So, it is him after all. The room takes on a blurred appearance, as if time has slowed down almost to a stop and is doing strange things with her vision.

But how can that possibly be?

Her heart begins to pump fast and heat floods into her face. She puts up her hand to loosen her blouse. It's so hot in here. She must get some air somehow. She tries fanning herself with her hand, but it's no good. She's getting hotter and hotter. She gulps for air.

'Are you all right, Connie?' Elsie's face looms over hers. 'Matron! Matron! Could we have some help here, please? This lady is going to faint!'

Connie is dimly aware of hands holding her arms, lifting her body, but the black dots in front of her eyes are getting bigger. She can hardly see now. A glass is held to her lips. She sips a little water, then dribbles the rest down her chin. Now she is sitting in a chair and the chair is moving forward. Someone is propelling her. But the black dots grow bigger, blobs obscuring her vision until she can't see anything at all.

She's walking by the Thames again. That summer's day in 1940. Her heart is bursting with joy, feeling him next to her. Just the touch of his arm against hers sends currents of pleasure coursing through her body.

She doesn't want to even imagine Father's face if he were to discover their secret. She shies away from the thought. But she knows it's worth risking the terror of his wrath just to feel the way she does now. She has never felt this before. It's like a fever, an addiction. This boy fills her mind from the moment she wakes until the moment she drops off to sleep at night. She's distracted constantly and can't concentrate on anything else. In the schoolroom she finds herself drifting off, thinking about him, dreaming of the next time they'll be together. She wonders if anyone has noticed. When she looks in the mirror she can see it as plain as daylight in her own eyes. That mysterious secret, that glow, that fever. Is it normal? Does it have a name?

They walk away from the river and back through the town until the orphanage looms up in front of them and Cedar Hall beyond it. By now, Connie has stopped holding Tommy's arm, conscious of the dozens of orphanage windows looking out onto the street. She spots a couple of children in one of the upper windows staring out at the street and her heart lurches. What if they tell Father they've seen her and Tommy together? She quickly dismisses the thought. But still in the back of her mind is the worry that Father himself could be looking out of any one of those windows right at this moment. She stares down at the road as they pass, hoping against hope that no one will notice them.

They walk around the back of Cedar Hall and into the driveway, their boots scrunching on the gravel. Over the wall that separates the house from the orphanage float the voices of the children at play. Connie glances nervously over, checking that none of them are peeping over the wall or sitting on it, chatting, as they sometimes do.

She and Tommy aren't talking now. They don't need to. Tommy opens the garage door and beckons her inside. Her heart in her mouth, she follows him. There is Father's cherished car in all its shining splendour! Father's pride and joy. Tommy opens the back door, jumps inside and beckons her to follow. Their eyes meet as she steps up into the car and sits down on the leather seat beside him. She feels the blood rush to her cheeks. Has he realised from the look in her eyes? Does he know how much she cares for him?

The light is dim inside the garage, but shafts of sunlight filter through the windows in the door. Again comes the dread of Father finding them there. She knows this must be wrong and he would be right to be angry. But then she feels Tommy's arms encircling her. He's pulling her close, his lips on her mouth. She yields and is soon kissing him back, her doubts and fears evaporating.

When she opens her eyes and looks around she realises she is propped up against pillows on her bed and Matron is sitting beside her, reading a newspaper. It's quiet. All she can hear is the echo of the TV from the day room. After a few moments Matron turns and peers at her.

'Oh, you're awake. Are you all right, Connie? You gave us all quite a fright.'

It all comes flooding back now. The shock of hearing Tommy's name after all these years.

Matron is watching her anxiously.

'I'm quite all right, Matron, thank you.'

Matron gets up from the chair. 'Do you need anything? Would you like some tea?'

Connie shakes her head and lets out a sigh of relief as Matron leaves. She wants to be alone to gather her thoughts, to work out what to do. Will Tommy remember her? Will she be able to ask him what happened to make him leave so suddenly without saying goodbye? What happened to him during the war? She'd always assumed he'd been killed. That she would never see him again.

Chapter Twenty-One

Sarah

Sarah heaves a box of china off the kitchen table and, straining with the effort, carries it along the passage and into the dining room. It's Saturday morning and Terry and Rodney are due to start work on the kitchen on Monday, so she's moving everything out. They've already knocked down the wall between the kitchen and the conservatory and installed a joist in the opening.

She glances out through the gap in the kitchen wall into the conservatory. Already she can picture what the room will look like when it's finished. Huge and light, opening out onto the garden and making the most of the beautiful ornate windows. After much debate with Terry and her father, she'd decided to have the conservatory floor raised to the level of the kitchen to avoid having steps in the middle of the room. Terry and Rodney have taken up most of the tiles in the conservatory and stacked them in a pile outside. There are just a few in front of the door left to remove on Monday.

Sarah has helped out at the bistro on a few occasions since that first evening. Each time, Matt was friendly and grateful for her help, but has kept a polite distance. She'd felt the chemistry between them each time, but to her slight regret, he hasn't asked her out again. She sighs now, thinking about it. Matt had asked her to work this lunchtime, but she'd explained that she needed time to clear out the kitchen. It was the first time she'd refused when he'd asked and she feels a tingle of regret, thinking about it now.

She sighs again as she looks inside the old cupboards, amazed at how much stuff she's managed to accumulate over the few weeks she's been in Cedar Hall. She makes herself a coffee, turns on the radio and hums to the music as she works. Her aim is to clear the room and to have set up somewhere to cook and eat in the dining room by the time she needs to head over to her father's.

As she works, she worries about him. He's looking thinner and weaker by the day. More often than not when she arrives in the evenings he's still lying on the sofa in the sunroom, looking drained and exhausted. The last time she took him to the hospital for a check-up the doctor had taken her aside and said, 'Your father is doing really well, Mrs Jennings, but I'm afraid the illness is beginning to progress more quickly now. It will only be another month or so before he'll need to come in for some aggressive treatment.'

She is angry that his life is slipping away so quickly that she is powerless to stop it. She's still frustrated that she's made so little progress in the search for clues about his real mother.

She'd told her father as gently as she could that Connie Burroughs didn't remember his name. He'd shrugged and smiled, but she could tell from the downcast expression in his eyes that he was disappointed.

'Oh well. It was only to be expected. It's a very long time ago.'

'I'm sure there's still hope though, Dad. A foundling. It must have been something people would have remarked upon. Perhaps Miss Burroughs will remember something, in time.'

She'd held back from telling him about the old lady's strange, hostile reaction to her questions. Neither had she told him about finding the blank birth certificates in Ezra Burroughs' bureau. She's still puzzling over that herself, wondering what it could possibly mean. Why on earth would there be a stash of them in the desk? Did Ezra act as the registrar of births for the district? She has tried to do some online searching, but that hasn't given her any answers yet.

It's after midday by the time she's moved all the boxes of kitchen stuff through. She's just puzzling over how to move the table by herself when the back doorbell rings.

Matt is standing on the doorstep, holding a tray with a cloche-covered plate. Her mouth drops open.

'I guessed you might not have time to make any lunch so I brought this over. Courtesy of Chef,' he says.

She feels her cheeks heating up.

'Really, Matt! I don't know what to say. You shouldn't have done that.' She holds the door aside. 'Come on in.'

She realises he's never actually been inside the house, despite her talking about it. She's been intending to show him round for some time now, but he always seems so busy with the restaurant.

'I'm just moving stuff out of here,' she says, showing him into the kitchen. 'Why don't you sit down and I'll make you a drink. Or I could show you around the house first?'

'I'd love to see round. I've never been inside here before. I used to peep over the wall with my mates when the orphanage was still there.'

'Did you?'

'Yes. We'd play in the grounds behind it where those modern houses are now. Sometimes we'd creep along the alley at the side and spy on old Ezra, sitting out on a deckchair in the garden, puffing on his pipe.'

'Really? What was he like?'

'Scary. You wouldn't want to meet him on a dark night.'

'Really, Matt…' she begins with a shudder, then sees the twinkle in his eye.

'Not really, no. He was just a frail old guy. For some reason we kids were terrified of him, though.'

'Come on, I'll show you round the house.'

She leads him from room to room. The house is beginning to shape up, and suddenly she's glad that he's here and she can share her pride in the place with him. Terry and Rodney have installed the central heating and finished decorating the living room. She has invested in two white sofas, a teak coffee table and an Indian rug. The room looks stylish and comfortable now. She shows him the study, now elegant with pale walls. The bureau is newly polished and still in pride of place at the end of the room. The wooden floor and panelling in the hallway have been stripped and restored. The whole house smells of fresh paint.

'There's not much to see upstairs yet, but I'll show you anyway.'

He follows her up. Two of the bedrooms have been decorated, including her own. Cream linen curtains hang at the bay window. She's glad she made the bed and picked up her dirty clothes this morning.

'It's beautiful, Sarah. I can't believe how much you've done already.'

'Well, I'm not doing it alone. Terry and Rodney are amazing.'

Back in the kitchen she explains how she's hoping it will look once the builders have finished. They step out into the conservatory as she talks.

'They've nearly finished taking up the old tiles in here. They're going to raise the floor and put pale marble tiles down.'

'What are you going to do with those old flagstones?'

'Nothing. Terry will take them away. He'll find a use for them somewhere, I expect.'

'They're probably worth something.'

'Maybe. I'll ask Terry. He's very good like that. If he gets anything for them he'll knock it off my bill.'

'Would you mind very much if I took them off your hands? I'd pay you, of course. Do you remember I mentioned it would be good to put some tables outside in the courtyard in the summer? It's just a concrete yard out there at the moment. These would look great instead and there seem to be loads of them.'

'Of course. Yes, take them. That's a great idea. And I don't want any payment. I should have thought of it myself. Why don't you take some of them now? You've got the van, haven't you?'

'Yes. But don't you want to eat your lunch?'

'I can always heat it up in the microwave.'

'Whatever would Chef say?' he says and they both laugh, thinking of Gaston the French chef with his flashes of unpredictable temper.

'It won't take long to load up the flagstones. Come on, I'll help you if you like.'

They go outside and one by one, stash the flagstones in the back of Matt's van. Sarah fetches some cardboard boxes from the garage to pad them out so they don't move around in transit, and when they're done they sit at the kitchen table, Matt with a cup of tea and Sarah tucking into her lunch: Normandy chicken with apples and thyme.

'This is wonderful,' she says between mouthfuls. 'We used to serve this sometimes at our place, but it wasn't nearly as good as this.'

'I would have thought this dish was a bit traditional for Taste,' says Matt, his eyes steady on hers. She feels the heat in her cheeks again. She swallows and puts down her fork. She's never told him any details about Alex or the restaurant, preferring to keep matters vague, but it's somehow a relief that it's out in the open.

'How did you know?' she says.

'I wasn't sure. It's just a couple of things you said. You mentioned that you had places in Bristol and London. That, and the snippets I've read in the papers.'

She looks down at the table. She can't think of what to say.

'You must have been going through a really tough time, Sarah,' Matt says softly.

'It hasn't been easy,' she says, taking another mouthful as a distraction, still avoiding his gaze.

'If you ever want to talk about it, I'm always here, you know.'

She pulls a face that's intended to be a smile, but it doesn't feel like that. *Don't cry, Sarah, for God's sake*, she tells herself.

'That's kind of you,' she says, trying to keep her voice steady. 'You know, I haven't really talked to anyone about it much. Not even to my dad. He's very ill and I don't want to upset him. I've got so used to bottling it all up that I'm not sure I'd know where to start.'

'Well, the offer's there. I know what it's like to suddenly be on your own, believe me.'

Now she forces herself to look into his eyes. She owes him that much. He's hardly ever mentioned his wife and it must be hard for him to do that.

'I'm so sorry, Matt. It must have been dreadful for you, losing the person you love like that.'

'It was really tough at first. It's taken a long time and I still find myself spiralling back there occasionally. Just odd things will remind me. But you know, I feel as though I'm finally beginning to turn a corner.'

'I can't begin to imagine how it must have been,' says Sarah, looking into his eyes. He holds her gaze for a moment before he goes on.

'Things have been very difficult at times, but I've had to keep going for Simon. I couldn't just give up and hide away, which I wanted to do on occasion.'

There is a silence. Sarah gets the feeling that she's asked enough. She doesn't want to cause him any more pain by probing further. After a few moments, Matt changes the subject.

'And how are you coping on your own?'

'Of course it's not anything comparable to what you've been through,' she says. 'I admit that things have been a bit tough sometimes. I try to distract myself, I suppose, but sometimes I have to face reality. I had an email from the solicitor this morning.'

'Oh dear. Good news or bad news?'

'None of it is good news, really. Alex isn't playing ball. He's refusing to deal with my solicitor's letters. I wish he'd just accept that it's over as I have. It's all very tricky because everything is frozen because of the police investigation into the financing of the new business. You've probably read about it in the papers. It's such a mess, Matt. I wish I didn't have to think about the financial side. It gets in the way. I just want to focus on getting over what Alex did to me.'

Matt's eyes are on her face. They are kind, patient. She senses he's waiting for her to go on. She opens her mouth to say more, but can't find the words. The shame of what has happened overwhelms her, even though she knows it shouldn't be her shame.

'Look, I'd prefer not to talk about it at the moment,' she says, trying to keep her voice from cracking. She takes a sip of tea, her hand unsteady.

'Well, as I said, any time you need a friendly ear.' His eyes linger on hers for another moment and a tingling feeling goes right through her. Then he gets up. 'I'd best be getting back, I suppose.'

Sarah jumps up from the table, feeling somehow that she's said the wrong thing. She doesn't want him to leave just yet, with the conversation unfinished, unresolved. How can she avoid him leaving so soon?

'Hey, would you like the rest of the flagstones while you're here?' she asks as he reaches the back door.

'Terry was going to finish taking them up on Monday, but it would be easy to lift them ourselves. He left his crowbar. We might as well do it now so you can take them all at once. There are only a few left and it would be good to get rid of them.'

Matt stops and turns.

'Why not? If you don't mind, that is.'

Sarah smiles, a strange sense of relief stealing over her.

They go out into the conservatory and Matt takes Terry's crowbar that's leaning in a corner. He prises the first two flagstones up from the floor. The ancient cement holding them in place crumbles to dust. He leans them up against the door.

Sarah stands in the doorway, watching him work. He's rolled up the sleeves of his sweater and she can see the muscles in his arms flexing under his skin as he works.

'I'm glad you came round, Matt,' she says. He stands up, pushes his fringe out of his dark blue eyes and smiles at her.

She smiles into his eyes, and again she feels that connection; that spark of recognition between them.

There's one flagstone left. The one that serves as a step. It's hollowed out from a century of feet stepping in and out of the door. Already slightly out of place, it's chipped at the edges. There are no remnants of concrete left around the edges of this one.

The flagstone sits alone on the rubbly surface. Matt slides the crowbar under it and prises it up. Then he bends down to lift it, and drags it forward. As he does so the flagstone scrapes the surface of the sand below, making a hollow sound.

'What was that?' Sarah bends forward, frowning.

'I'm not sure.'

Matt lays the flagstone aside and scrapes at the rubbly floor with the crowbar. The sand and earth are soft and he has soon cleared away a small hole.

'What on earth is that?' says Sarah, a chill running through her. 'Wait there a minute. I'll go and get my shovel.'

She hurries to the coach house and fetches it. She hands the shovel to Matt and he clears the sand away, quickly and efficiently. They don't speak while he works, and neither do they look at each other. After a few minutes, he has cleared a big enough patch to reveal what looks like the lid of a black painted box about an inch under the surface. He slides the shovel down one side of the box and prises it upwards, grunting with effort. Finally, after much agitating and pulling, the box begins to come upwards towards the surface. Sarah looks on, transfixed.

There's a metal handle on the top of the lid, covered in black soil. She puts her fingers around it and pulls. Matt is still lifting with the spade. Between them they ease the box to the surface. Finally, they heave it out and lay it on the floor.

'What do you think it is?' asks Sarah, her heart giving a sickening beat.

'It looks like an old toolbox.' Matt bends down and dusts the surface with his hand, revealing tarnished gold initials: E.J.B. They exchange a glance.

The lid is locked down with a rusty padlock caked in soil.

'Shall I try to prise it open?'

She nods. Matt puts the tip of the crowbar in the crack between the lid and the box. He puts his foot on the top of the box and pushes the crowbar down. With a splintering sound, the rusting padlock comes adrift, with its plate and screws, and drops on the ground. Matt lifts the lid. Sarah peers in. Inside the box is what looks like a bundle of rags, yellowed with age, streaked with brown stains. She looks at Matt. His face is drained of colour.

He kneels in front of it and stares at her, and their eyes meet in mutual horror.

Chapter Twenty-Two

Connie

Connie slides out of bed and tests her feet on the floor. They are stiff but seem to be working. She stands up warily and reaches for the Zimmer frame. Matron hasn't come back yet, but that isn't going to stop her. She takes another gulp of water and glances at the bedside clock. Three o'clock. People will be drinking tea in the day room and watching the afternoon film on TV.

She's never even been to the day room, but she needs to go now. She takes a step. Her head swims a little, but she takes a deep breath and ignores it. She pulls her shawl around her shoulders and glances in the bedside mirror. For a second, she doesn't recognise the face that stares back at her, wreathed in wrinkles. She's been dwelling so much in the past, in her thoughts and dreams, it's a shock to see what the years have done to her. She tucks a strand of white hair behind her ear and pinches her cheeks. *Silly girl, Connie. It doesn't matter what you look like now*, she tells herself.

She fizzes with anticipation as she makes her lumbering progress along the passage. It doesn't matter that she hasn't prepared what she's going to say. Nor does the gap of seventy-odd years since they last spoke.

She reaches the threshold of the day room and looks inside. There are a dozen or so people there, sitting in high-backed chairs. Some are dozing, others staring at the TV, their mouths lolling open, eyes glazed. One of the kitchen staff is wheeling a trolley round, handing out mugs of tea.

Connie narrows her eyes and scans the room, beginning to feel foolish. He doesn't seem to be here, should she just turn around and go back to her room? Then her heart does a strange lurch as she spots him in the far corner, sat reading a book by the light from the window.

She sets off towards him, the effort making her breathe heavily. She tries to suppress her nerves. She just needs to get over there and God will help her find the right words.

She reaches his chair. He has his back to her and all she can see of him is the top of a bald head with the occasional wisp of white hair that trembles as he breathes, like reeds in a breeze. She gradually manoeuvres herself around so she is standing in front of him. He's still reading, his head bowed to the book, a bony finger tracing the words. He's deep in concentration; she can't see his face.

As she watches him and waits, her whole life seems to contract into this moment. Once again, she is back there, walking along the river path beside him, that day in 1940. She's on the point of telling him the dreadful secret that has been troubling her for years. Her heart is singing because she knows she has finally found someone who will listen, someone she can trust to help her.

She holds back though, waiting for precisely the right moment. But they walk on. He's talking, animated, telling her an anecdote, and she doesn't want to interrupt him.

When he squeezes her arm and says, 'Let's go into the woods,' she nods, and the words on her tongue evaporate. The moment passes. She knows now that everything turned on that moment. It was then she had her chance. She could have chosen to run away, to release herself from her suffering, there and then, but she didn't.

She waits for him silently now and after a few breathless seconds he looks up. There is no longer any doubt in her mind that it's him. She can tell too, from the way his old eyes widen, that he knows who she is. The years fall away.

'Tommy?'

'Connie?' The book slides between his legs and drops from his lap.

'They told me someone called Tommy Braithwaite was here, but I wasn't sure it would be you,' is all she can think of to say.

She swallows, gripping the Zimmer frame tightly to stop her hands from shaking.

'I had no idea. No one told me you were here,' he says, smiling into her eyes.

She stares at him, examining his face. She can still trace the shape of his square jaw beneath his pale chin, and his brown eyes are still defined by those long dark lashes. He is looking at her too, probably trying to find in her lined face some trace of the girl he once knew.

'Why don't you sit down?' he asks at last.

She manages to manoeuvre herself into the chair beside him.

'I had a fall,' she explains. 'I'm not quite better yet.' She feels the need to tell him that, to reassure him that she's not as decrepit as she might look.

'I'm very sorry to hear that,' he says.

'So, what brings you here?' she ventures after an awkward silence.

'Oh, my daughter found the place. She went to all the old folks' homes in the area. She lives nearby, it means she can visit.'

'Your daughter?' Connie repeats. Despite the distance in time, the meaning behind the word hits her hard. She admonishes herself. Did she really expect that he'd have lived a hermit's life like she had?

'That's nice,' she forces herself to say. 'Where have you been living?'

'In south London. That's where I ended up after the war. That's where I stayed.'

'I thought—'

She stops herself. She mustn't say that she thought he'd died in the war. It sounds so brutal. But what *can* she say? How can she ask him all the things she wants to ask? She lapses into silence, staring out at the darkening sky, remembering that evening in 1941.

She'd slipped out of the house after bedtime and, keeping close to the wall, out of sight of the windows, she'd walked to their usual meeting spot in the shed on the far side of the orphanage building, next to the chicken coop.

She'd waited there, as usual, sitting on an old deckchair in the dark, listening for the slam of the side gate, his footsteps on the path, her nerves leaping at the slightest sound. The hens shifted on their roosts in the coop. An owl hooted somewhere far away by the river. She'd waited for over an hour that night, until she was sure there was no chance of him coming. Then she'd retraced her steps, mystified, thinking about the last time he'd held her, covered her face in kisses and sworn his love. There had to be some explanation. Perhaps he was ill? Worse still, perhaps he'd had an accident?

She'd lain awake all night fretting, imagining the worst, while Evie snored away in the next bed. But in the morning at breakfast, Father had looked up from the paper and said casually, 'Oh, by the way, Tommy Braithwaite won't be working for me any longer.'

Shock had washed through Connie. She couldn't look at Father, she couldn't look at anyone. She concentrated hard on buttering her toast, spreading it again and again, back and forth, back and forth.

Mother said, frowning, 'Really, Ezra, my dear? That's very sudden. He hasn't mentioned that he would be leaving.'

Father cleared his throat. 'It was a surprise to me too. He told me yesterday. He's decided to enlist. Quite a sudden decision, in fact. Set off for London this morning. Good luck to him, I say. The army needs all the strong young men it can get to fight this evil enemy.'

Connie couldn't swallow her toast. Feeling faint with shock, she excused herself and got up from the table. But as she hurried from the room she caught Father's eyes upon hers, and the expression in them shocked her. They were sharp, accusing, but there was something else in them – did he know?

But what is there left to say to Tommy now? After seventy years? How can she begin to ask him why he didn't come that night, why he left without telling her, why he never wrote to say why he'd gone, not even once?

'How long have you been in Fairlawns, Connie?' he asks, breaking into her thoughts.

'Oh, not long. A couple of months. It was because of my fall.'

'Oh... I see,' he says, assessing her words. Then he says, 'Family? Do you not have any family now?'

She shakes her head and shifts her eyes away from his, picking at her shawl, her fingers working their way up to clasp the filigree necklace.

'No... no. Not now. Evie passed away last year.'

'Oh, I see.' He nods slowly. 'I'm so sorry to hear that, Connie.'

He must know from that that I've never married, that I had nobody else. That after him there was nobody else, she thinks.

She's bursting to say, 'You didn't come that night. I waited for you,' but she knows that she can't say that. Not yet. Perhaps not ever.

'Would you like some tea?' Jenny, the amiable kitchen assistant, is hovering in front of them.

'Connie?' he asks. She nods. 'Two mugs, please. Oh, and two sugars for me,' he says.

Two sugars! That's how it had all started. She remembers again the cups of tea she used to take out to him in the garage when he was polishing Father's car. She thinks again about how he would engage her in conversation. She doesn't remember what they talked about, just that he would tease her and flatter her, and she would blush and stammer, but she wouldn't want to leave. Jenny pushes the trolley away and they are alone again.

'So, Connie, tell me... What are the people like in here? Everyone seems very friendly,' he says.

'Oh yes. Everyone is very nice.'

She tells him what she knows about the other people in the home, which isn't much. And all the time she's thinking, *why are we talking about these trivial things when there's so much else to talk about?* But she carries on. Telling him about Elsie, Marjory and Dorothy. She talks about Matron and Erica and the other staff, about the routines in the home, about the food. Distracting herself, distracting them both.

'Do you still go to church?' he asks suddenly.

She looks away.

'Not any more. The Baptist church in Weirfield closed down. Evie and I used to go on the bus to Henley every Sunday. But after Evie died, well, it was difficult… What about you?'

He shakes his head.

'No, not me. I haven't been to church since… well, not since I left Weirfield, to tell you the truth.'

She looks at him, blinking with incomprehension. Worship had been so much part of life in the orphanage that it was unthinkable that anyone who had grown up there could have abandoned the Lord.

'But why not?' she asks at last.

He isn't meeting her eyes. He's staring down at his lap, his head bowed. Finally, he looks up. His expression is grave, deadly serious for the first time.

'You mean you don't know?'

She frowns, shakes her head. Whatever can he mean? He's silent for a long time, his eyes distant. She waits. Finally, he speaks.

'I started to lose my faith before I left here, actually. Things happened then that made me doubt God and everything that the Church stood for. It had a lot to do with your father, Connie.'

'Father?' she asks, alarmed. 'What things, Tommy?' She frowns, trying to think back. What could Father possibly have done to make Tommy lose his faith? Father, that most pious of men, who loved

God with a fierce passion. She remembers that Tommy used to go to church during the time he worked for her father. He would sit in the pews at the back, several rows behind the family. She remembers that she used to have to resist the temptation to turn around to look at him; she could feel his eyes on her back, burning her neck and shoulders.

But he shakes his head and doesn't answer that. Instead he goes on, 'You know in the war we were posted to Malaya. Captured by the Japanese in Singapore. I was sent to work on that railway in the jungle in Thailand. The things I saw…' He bows his head again.

'I'm so sorry, Tommy. I had no idea,' she whispers.

'It's all in the past now,' he says with an air of finality. 'A long time ago.'

Connie takes a sip of her tea, feeling at a loss as to what to say now. What's the use of raking up the past? She hears Mother's voice in her head again: *There's no use crying over spilt milk, Connie, my girl.* It's true. There is no use crying over it, but looking across at Tommy now, the shell of the man she had loved, she can't help wondering again how different life might have been if he hadn't left, and whether his leaving was somehow connected to his loss of faith.

They sit in silence watching the light fade outside the window. Connie knows that there will be plenty of afternoons to come, plenty of opportunities to speak. One day, the time might be right to ask him why he left. But that day isn't today. All the same, talking to Tommy has brought home afresh to her that she needs to face up to the past, to remember everything she's been suppressing for so long. Not just for her own sake, for Sarah's too and for Sarah's father.

The silence isn't awkward between them as it would be between two strangers. It feels almost as it used to when they sat on the riverbank together, watching the sun play on the water, the boats passing, the swans gathering on the little island in the middle of the river.

Chapter Twenty-Three

Connie

Back in her room, Connie takes up the diary again and turns to the place she left off. She has a couple of hours before supper time to read. Tommy had gone to make a phone call to his daughter, but there was no awkwardness as they parted; they both knew they would speak again soon.

Talking to Tommy and having all those old memories flood back into her mind has made her keen to finish the diary as quickly as she can. There is so much about that time that unsettles her that she needs to understand before it is too late. She is almost sure that Anna's diary might hold some of the answers to those long-unanswered questions.

November 1st, 1932

The months wear on, and despite my freedom, and the pleasure I'm taking in getting to know the real India, I feel lonelier than ever. Each afternoon now, Rajiv either takes me out into the countryside to see a village, to some remote beauty spot, or to one of the temples or bazaars in town so I can sketch. And the more I learn about Charles, the more unsettled I feel that I've been alone with him. When I saw his wife drinking alone in the club I was shocked by what I heard.

'That's Isobel Perry,' Mrs Napier had told me. 'Charlie boy's wife. Rumour has it they're not happy, though. You

*can tell that by the way she drinks. He only married her
to get a leg-up on the career ladder.'*

'What is it that he does, exactly?'

*'You really don't know anything, do you? You must
know that he's the D.O. That's the District Officer? Most
important official around these parts. But that's not all.
Rumour has it that he's got some other role too. He's involved
in some sort of secret diplomacy with Congress. That's the
Indian independence movement, in case you didn't know
that either. He's the Viceroy's man on the ground round here
apparently. But that's all meant to be hush-hush. Look, I
told you. She's got whisky and soda in that glass.'*

*I was silent, digesting this new information. Charles
Perry's request to me not to tell anyone I had seen him in
those out-of-the-way places was beginning to make sense.*

'Hadn't we better invite her to join us?' I asked.

'No, she doesn't mix with the likes of us. Let her be.'

*That evening, I got ready for supper and waited for
Donald. I'd made a special effort to dress up because I
had made up my mind to tell him about Father and I
wanted to be feeling my best to give me confidence, but
when I finally had the courage to explain, it seemed I
was too late.*

*After we'd finished eating, I took a deep breath. 'It's about
my father,' I began. 'I'm afraid there are things I need to tell
you about him. He got into trouble with his business a few
years ago. Made several silly investments. A lot of people lost
money because of him, and well… I'm afraid to say that he's
in prison in England. He's been there for two years now.'*

*I said it quickly, so he wouldn't be able to stop me. All
the time I stared at the floor, at the red-and-gold-patterned
Indian rug beneath my feet. I looked up, searching his face,
terrified of his reaction.*

He was taking another swig from his glass, so I couldn't see his expression.

'I know all about that,' he said casually, and the words struck me like a hammer blow. My mouth dropped open.

'You knew? Who told you? Why ever didn't you say?'

'Probably for the same reason you didn't. It's a pretty unpleasant business. Not one that one would perhaps want to dwell over.'

'But how did you know?' I repeated.

'Your Aunt Nora told me, of course. That first time I came to have dinner at her house. Said you needed a husband, but that the business with your father would probably put most people off. If I needed a wife, which I did, then that was the reason that you were available, but that I'd have to accept it and live with it.'

I stared at him, open-mouthed. I knew Aunt Nora was desperate to get rid of me, but I hadn't realised how duplicitous she'd been.

'But why didn't you mention it?'

'Like I told you, not something I wanted to dwell on overly much. It was part of the bargain.'

'Bargain? Bargain? Donald, whatever do you mean?'

My voice was shaking. I felt panicky. I stared at him, but he looked quite unperturbed. As if this sort of conversation between man and wife was nothing out of the ordinary at all.

'What do you mean?' I repeated.

He took another gulp of brandy. His eyes were looking glazed now.

'I'd been told in no uncertain terms that there was no chance of promotion, of getting to the rank of colonel, if I wasn't married. Simple as that.'

'So that's why you came to Bombay?' I said in a low voice. He nodded.

'I can't say I wasn't charmed by you, Anna. You're a very beautiful and accomplished young lady. You fitted the bill perfectly.'

'And I walked straight into your trap,' I murmured.

'Don't look at it that way. It's a mutually beneficial arrangement. Unlike a lot of marriages, I'm sure it will be very successful.'

'There's one more thing I want to know,' I said, my voice still shaking. 'Mrs Smethurst said something very odd to me when I first arrived. She said they were counting on me to address something. The fact that you spend a lot of time out and about. Do you know what she might have been talking about?'

A red flush crept up his cheeks.

'Meddling old cow,' he muttered.

'Well? What was she talking about?'

'It's nothing, Anna. Nothing at all. And if I were you I wouldn't spend my time indulging in malicious gossip like those empty-headed bitches at the club. It will only lead to trouble.'

With that, he turned and stomped into his bedroom, slamming the door. I could hear him bashing about in there. After a few minutes, Ali crept through to help him and I could hear them talking in low voices.

I felt so alone at that moment, so full of anger at Aunt Nora, at Donald too. I felt like smashing my glass against the wall. Instead I took a great glug of the drink and went out onto the veranda. It was a beautiful warm night, the cicadas were chattering in the bushes, dogs were barking in distant villages. I had the urge to walk. To walk and walk for miles until I had worked out my feelings and purged myself of my anger.

I fetched my wrap from the living room and left the house. I walked along the road, past the neat bungalows that were lit up for the evening, and out onto the wider road that led through the cantonment and into the centre of town. I had no idea where I was going. I had a vague notion that I would go and find Rajiv at the maidan and ask him to take me somewhere.

I walked quickly, my head down, going over and over the conversation I'd just had with Donald. I went back over the times we'd met in Bombay, the way the courtship had progressed so quickly, the pressure from him and Aunt Nora. As these thoughts swirled round in my head, the streets began to narrow and become more built up. Soon I was in the centre of town.

I had not realised how busy the place would be at this time of the evening. The streets were filled with people, and the roadside stalls and shops were open for business. Hawkers were frying on makeshift stoves, and people were sitting at little tables eating food from which delicious smells of herbs, garlic and spices wafted. No one seemed to notice me as I walked. I felt comforted by the presence of so many people and the anonymity of the place.

There were no rickshaws waiting when I reached the maidan. I felt foolish to have thought that Rajiv might be there waiting for me at this time of night. I turned to go, feeling a little calmer now, and I retraced my steps towards the cantonment.

I was about halfway home when I heard the roar of an engine and a motor car drew up beside me. I looked up and stopped walking. The window was pulled back and Charles Perry put his head out.

'We meet again,' he said, an amused smile spreading over his face. 'Wherever have you been, Mrs Foster, out all alone at this time?'

'I just needed a walk,' I said.

He opened the door. 'Why don't you hop in? I'll drop you back home.'

Wearily, I got inside the motor car. It was pointless protesting, and anyway, a blister was developing on my heel that I'd been trying to ignore.

'You look very beautiful tonight. Have you been somewhere?'

I shook my head and stared down at my lap. I couldn't reply, because I knew that if I started to speak, I would probably burst into tears.

'Is something wrong, Mrs Foster?'

'I'm fine, thank you.'

'Drive on, please. To Foster Sahib's house, Connaught Lodge.' He tapped the partition with his cane and the car began to move.

'Are you quite sure you're all right? You look as if you've been crying.'

I looked up at his face and he was looking at me intently, his eyes full of genuine concern.

'If there's anything I can do to help you. You seem very... well, very alone and lost, if you don't mind me saying so.'

'Please don't,' I said, but the tears were already falling. My shoulders were shuddering and I couldn't hold back the sobs.

I felt his arm slip around my shoulders and he was holding me tight against his body. It was wrong, I knew, but it felt wonderful to be held close by another human being, to feel the warmth of his body and the beating of his heart. I felt his strength and the power in his touch.

But still the tears came.

'Hush, Anna. Things will be all right. I will take care of you,' he whispered, and he was kissing my hair and the back of my neck and his lips were moving around my throat. A thrill went through me but I knew it must stop. I edged away from him.

'Anna, please don't fight it. Don't you feel the attraction between us? Why can't you admit it to yourself?'

I was thrown into fresh turmoil at these words. Was it true? Was that confusion and discomfort I felt in his presence actually desire?

We sat in silence on the back seat of the car and when we arrived outside my bungalow a few minutes later, he helped me out.

'Until next time, Mrs Foster,' he said, kissing my hand and looking into my eyes. 'And please, do take care of yourself.'

Connie closes the diary. Her heart goes out to Anna and she thinks again of the girl's desperate face that evening in May 1934. She was beginning to understand the reason for her sadness. She let her thoughts wander to the past again. Who were these people Anna mentions? Did they have some connection to Father? Some of the names seemed vaguely familiar.

'Charles Perry,' Connie whispers into the silence. Where has she heard that name before? She thinks for a long time, frowning in concentration, but can't remember.

If Father had been Baptist minister in Kandaipur at that time perhaps he had known some of these people? But he would never have gone to the club to socialise and drink at the bar. Then the image of his study during one of his drink-fuelled evenings comes into her mind. She remembers glimpsing through the open door Father and a group of men sitting around, drinking and smoking, their faces red and bloated. She purses her lips and a little whimper escapes her. Once, she'd happened to go into the room the following morning when Father had left for the orphanage and the maid hadn't yet been in to clean up. She'd been shocked by the state of it; repelled by the smell of alcohol that lingered on the stale air, the sight of the overflowing ashtrays, the half-finished drinks, some of them with the butt ends of cigars stubbed out in them.

Chapter Twenty-Four

Sarah

Sarah and Matt sit opposite each other at the kitchen table, waiting for the police to arrive. They are drinking strong sugary tea. Matt had insisted it would help with the shock. They sit in silence. There had been no need for a debate about what to do when he unwrapped the blanket and revealed that tiny skeleton, with its skull as small as a rabbit's.

'We'll have to call the police, won't we?' Matt had said. Sarah had nodded, her heart sinking.

'Do you want me to do it?' he'd asked, but barely waited for her response, seeing how quiet she was.

Now, sitting waiting at the table, Sarah's experience of the police during her last days at Taste comes back to her: the intrusive questions, the strange hands rifling through the files, opening private drawers, searching the premises.

The sound of a vehicle pulling into the drive breaks the silence. Car doors slam.

'That must be them now. Do you want me to answer the door?'

He must realise what I'm feeling, she thinks, getting up from the table.

'No, it's fine. Let's speak to them together.'

'You sure? You looked really shaken for a while. I thought you were going to faint.'

She nods. 'Of course. But thank you, Matt,' she says, looking into his eyes. 'I really appreciate your support.'

'Don't thank me! I feel responsible for all this. If I hadn't suggested taking those tiles…'

'It was me who suggested taking up the last one. And anyway, if it hadn't been you then it would have been Terry on Monday.'

The doorbell rings and Sarah goes to open it. She can feel Matt behind her in the passage. Two uniformed policemen stand on the doorstep. They have walkie-talkies clipped to their uniforms. They are holding their caps.

'Mrs Jennings?' says the taller one, who looks the more senior of the two. 'Is Mr Drayton here? I understand you've reported a suspicious finding.'

She nods.

'It's out in the back. We left it where we found it. I'll show you through to the conservatory.'

'Why don't you sit down here in the kitchen? We'll take it from here. If you're feeling up to it later, I'd like to take a statement from you. Now, when exactly was it that you moved in to Cedar Hall?'

Later, she and Matt watch from the conservatory window as two new policemen patrol the garden with sniffer dogs. They have already been through the house with the dogs, encouraging them to sniff in the cupboards, along the floorboards, up the stairs, but they found nothing. A little earlier, after they had both given their statements, Sarah and Matt had watched the first policemen remove the box and the remains of the baby into a police van.

'We'll be doing an autopsy,' the senior one had explained. 'That should give us a rough date to work from.'

Sarah shudders and thinks again of Miss Burroughs. Does Connie know about this? She lived in the house her whole life, surely she must know? The police had asked Sarah who had owned the house previously and she'd told them. Now she thinks of Connie, alone in her room in Fairlawns, and her heart goes out to her. She's so old and frail. And alone. However will she cope when the police come calling?

'I can't believe this is happening,' Sarah says now.

Matt shakes his head. 'It's bloody bad luck.'

'What will Dad say?' she says suddenly. 'He'll be so shocked by this news. It's so gruesome. I'll have to go to him. I don't want him to find out from someone else. He's not strong.'

'Are you sure you're OK to drive?'

'Of course. I'm fine.' She glances at her watch. It is four thirty now. 'It will be getting dark soon. I said I'd go over at six, but I might go a bit earlier.'

'I could always drive you over, if you like.'

'It's fine, Matt. Really. Won't they be missing you at the restaurant?'

'Yes, you're right. I suppose I'd better get back there.'

After the police have finally left, she watches Matt go, then locks the house, gets into the car and sets off towards her father's house on the darkening roads. As she drives, images of the gruesome remains of the baby keep dancing in front of her eyes. She remembers the strange feeling of dread and despair she got in the coach house, and the sense of unease that had descended on discovering the bureau was still there. She thinks about the strange hold the past had seemed to have over the house when she'd looked round it that first time. She remembers too her restless first night there, how the dream that someone was pinning her down to her bed had felt so real. She shudders, realising she is not looking forward to spending the night alone.

She's suddenly filled with anger and disappointment. Buying Cedar Hall was meant to be a new start, something positive and exciting in the midst of her troubles, a way of finding answers for her father. But finding those remains in the box today has changed everything. At this moment, the place feels like a millstone around her neck, a burden rather than a pleasure. She's beginning to wish she hadn't ever set eyes on it, let alone taken the foolhardy step of buying it.

She swings into her father's drive and parks the car. The front door is locked and she fumbles for her key, beginning to panic. Has he gone out, forgetting that she was coming over? Has he had a fall? She lets herself into the hallway and switches on a light.

'Dad?'

She waits, and after a few seconds her heart starts beating again when she hears his voice; thin and weak, coming from the back of the house.

'Is that you, Sarah, love?'

'Are you OK?'

She finds him lying in darkness on the settee in the sunroom.

'I must have dropped off,' he says, blinking, as she switches on the light.

'Are you all right, Dad?' She notices with alarm his pale, sweaty face, his bloodshot eyes full of pain.

'Blinding headache, that's all. Could you get my pills?'

'Of course.' She goes through to the kitchen and finds his prescription painkillers in the cabinet. She fills a glass of water from the tap and takes it to him. She kneels down beside him and watches him take the pills and raise the glass to his lips with trembling hands.

'Bad day, Dad?'

'Not so good, I'm afraid,' he replies with a weak smile. 'What about you?'

As she smiles at him and squeezes his hand, she knows that she can't tell him what happened today. It will have to wait, and she will just have to pretend that her day was a good one. She also knows that it won't be long now, a matter of days perhaps, before the doctors insist on him being admitted to hospital for some heavy-duty treatment. A lump rises in her throat at the thought, but not wanting to alarm him, she chatters away, telling him about her day, about how Matt brought lunch round, and how he was taking the tiles to the restaurant to put in the courtyard.

Her father can't eat much supper, and can hardly keep his eyes open. There are no card games or chess this evening, he hasn't even the energy to watch television. She helps him upstairs to bed at around nine o'clock. As she does so, she has a fleeting memory of all the nights that he sat on her own bed, patiently reading bedtime stories when she was small. How things have come full circle.

A feeling of trepidation steals over Sarah as she heads back along the river road towards Weirfield. She keeps going over in her mind how ill and tired Dad looked today. If only she'd been able to find out something about his birth mother, that would surely have helped him to bear his illness? Discovering the bones in the conservatory has made her worry that whatever she finds out might cause him more pain.

She realises her palms are sweating at the thought of spending the night alone in the house. She even thinks about turning back and staying the night at her father's instead. But she doesn't want to wake him, and she doesn't want him to suspect anything is wrong.

'You'll just have to tough it out,' she says aloud, her knuckles white on the steering wheel, but the feeling of dread only gets worse as she gets closer to the house. How will she sleep? How will she last the night? She even thinks fleetingly about checking into a hotel.

She swings into the drive and pulls up beside the back door. Then she sees the other vehicle parked beside the coach house, and her heart leaps.

'Matt.'

He's sitting on the back doorstep with a small backpack by his side.

'I thought you might appreciate some company tonight,' he says, getting up.

'I'm so pleased to see you!' she says, unlocking the back door. 'I was dreading being alone, I have to admit.'

'Is the sofa the best place?' he asks, making his way through the passage. She watches him go and pauses.

'Yes, if you don't mind. None of the spare bedrooms are furnished yet. I'll bring you some bedding.'

She smiles to herself as she goes upstairs, a warm feeling stealing over her. For a moment there, she'd been on the point of inviting him to spend the night upstairs with her, but something had stopped her. It wouldn't be quite right, somehow, not after the events of the day. She was too overwrought to make proper decisions. She might find herself regretting it afterwards. If something is meant to happen, it will happen when the time is right. And the time isn't quite right yet.

Chapter Twenty-Five

Connie

Anna's Diary

I got down from Charles Perry's car, my nerves a-jangle, my emotions in turmoil. The driver shut the door, returned to the cab and started the engine. I could sense Charles watching me from the back window as the car pulled away, but I didn't look back. Instead I went on up the steps of the bungalow and let myself in. I could still feel his arm around my shoulders, the touch of his thigh against mine. It had stirred something deep inside, something I didn't fully understand. I was being disloyal to Donald. I knew I should suppress these thoughts and feelings, but they were so strong, I wanted to scream out loud for them to stop.

It was dark in the living room, and I expected it to be stifling hot, but strangely, the punkah-wallah was still sitting on the veranda pulling the punkah, or fan, back and forth across the ceiling, so there was at least a faint breeze wafting over the room. I began to make my way across the room towards my bedroom door.

'You're back then?' Donald's voice made me freeze. There was a lamp on a table near where I stood, so I switched it on.

Donald was slumped in one of the armchairs, in his shirtsleeves. His face was red and he glistened with sweat. He held a glass unsteadily in his hand and the decanter was on the table beside him. It was nearly empty and I could have sworn that it had been nearly full earlier in the day. He must have downed almost half of it while I'd been out of the house.

I stared at him. I'd never seen him drunk before.

'Where have you been?' he asked now, his voice slurred.

'I just went out for a walk, I needed some air.'

'You shouldn't walk around alone in the dark out here. You should have taken one of the servants.'

'It seemed perfectly safe.'

'I heard a car. Did someone bring you back?'

'Yes. It was Charles Perry.' I cast my eyes down and could feel my cheeks grow hot.

'You should watch that one,' said Donald. 'He's a ladies' man.'

I didn't reply; I didn't want to pursue the matter. I'd seen Charles at the club enough times surrounded by simpering women to understand where that reputation might have come from. But Donald's tone made me uncomfortable.

'I think I'll go to bed now, Donald,' I said.

'No. Come and sit down for a moment, I want to talk to you.'

I went and sat in the chair opposite him, dread in my heart. He reached for another glass on the table and poured me a drink. He held it out.

'Here, have a drink.' I didn't feel like it, but took it anyway. I didn't want to argue with him.

'I might as well tell you now. You might as well know,' he said.

'Know?' I asked, my feeling of trepidation increasing.

He took another swig. 'That question you asked me earlier. About why I needed a wife.'

'Oh. Yes,' I whispered.

'Someone will tell you eventually, if I don't.'

I stared at him. I'd been desperate to find out, but now it came down to it, I dreaded hearing whatever he had to say.

'Well, don't you want to know now?'

'Of course I do, Donald. Please go on,' I said, but still I couldn't meet his eye.

'Well, it's this.' He held his glass up. 'I can't take my drink, you see.'

'Oh, Donald…'

'It got so bad that I was missing parade. I couldn't think straight, I was a liability. And when I did make it, I wasn't fit to appear in front of my men.'

'But… but how did it start?'

He shrugged. 'The army is everything to me. I was brought up expecting to get to the top. But the trouble is, I'm not like other men. I'm not sociable. I like my own company. I don't like all the hearty, back-slapping socialising that goes on. I didn't find it easy to live the life of an officer in the mess. I found social occasions difficult. And when you live in the mess as I did, every single evening is a social occasion.'

'Go on.'

'But I found that the booze would help me cope with all that. With a few shots of spirits inside me, the bonhomie didn't seem so difficult any more. At first it was fine, it was under control. No one noticed and I didn't drink more than any of the other officers. But as time went on, I needed more. I needed that Dutch courage to face the world. Without it, I was nothing.'

I stared at him, trying to take in what he was saying.

'So what happened?'

'I used to go on regular benders. Sometimes I would get into arguments. Once I got into a fight with one of the *other officers, and there was a lot of damage done in the club. Colonel Smethurst had a stern word with me then. Said if I didn't go on the wagon he would transfer me to another regiment.'*

He paused and I sensed the pain he felt remembering. He went on, staring at the floor.

'I couldn't bear the thought of that. I went on the wagon, but of course it didn't last. That happened three or four times. The last time, Smethurst got the General involved. The General came up to Kandaipur to talk to me. Said I needed a wife to settle me down. That I must go down to Bombay on my next leave and find someone. If I didn't, I'd be on permanent desk duty. And that would mean I'd never get the chance to command the regiment.'

There was a long silence while I tried to digest what he was saying. Finally, I said, 'But why ever didn't you tell me, Donald? You led me into a trap.'

'I was desperate, Anna. When I met you, I genuinely liked you. I had respect for you. I couldn't believe you might consider me. But your Aunt Nora took me aside and told me all about your difficult situation at home. We struck a sort of bargain.'

'You must think me so naive,' I said bitterly.

'Of course not. You're a beautiful, intelligent woman. I have a lot of affection for you, Anna. I'm glad it's out in the open now. I wouldn't blame you if you wanted to leave, though, now you know the truth. In fact, if you want to go now, get on the train back to Bombay tomorrow, I'll pay your passage back to England.'

I almost jumped at the chance, but then I thought again. What was there left for me in England? I had nowhere to live, no money of my own. I had been driven out of my own community by the hate campaign against Father. India had felt like a new start and I had loved it from the first day. It had certainly got under my skin. I loved the landscapes, the dusty skies, the constant chatter of insects and the cries of the hyenas at night. I loved the chaos of the bazaar and the noisy colourful streets, the smells of incense and spices cooking on the air, the evening fires at sunset. However unsatisfactory my situation, I was in a place I loved, I had a roof over my head, which was more than could be said for back in England.

March 3rd, 1933

Several months have passed. Life has gone on much as before. Donald and I live more or less separate lives now. His confession to me seems to have triggered his drinking habit afresh. Sometimes he doesn't come back to the bungalow at night and I know he's been drinking at the club.

I try to content myself with my drawing and my trips out in the rickshaw, getting to know the neighbourhood. I sometimes go to the club and chat to Mrs Smethurst, Mrs Napier and the other wives, but although they are kind to me, I still don't feel I know them or that we have much in common.

Charles Perry hasn't been around much lately. In fact, I haven't seen him since the night he gave me a lift. Someone mentioned that he's at a conference in Delhi as part of the Viceroy's delegation. Sometimes his wife comes to the club. When I see her there alone, drinking, I realise what he meant by the words, 'You and I have a great deal in common, Anna. More than you know.'

May 15th, 1933

Yesterday, Donald came home earlier than usual and looking as pleased as punch. We sat down to eat together in the dining room for once.

'You look as though you've had some good news,' I said as I helped myself to chicken curry and rice.

'I have, as a matter of fact. Heard today that the regiment is to be posted to the North West Frontier.'

'The North West Frontier? That sounds a very long way away.'

'Oh yes, it is. On the border with Afghanistan, hell of a way away.'

'So when are we setting off?'

'Ah. I'm afraid wives and families have to stay behind on the station at Kandaipur, Anna.'

'Oh, really?' That was a disappointment. I had already started imagining a journey through a windswept pass into the snow-capped mountains where only yaks and the hardiest sheep can survive.

'Yes, I'm afraid so. Some regiments have wives up there, but there isn't enough accommodation for wives and children from every regiment. And in any case, it's dangerous. They're expecting trouble from the Pashtuns imminently so they need extra forces.'

'How long will the posting be?'

'Not sure. Probably several months.' He helped himself to more rice, heaping chillies on top. The idea of the North West Frontier seemed to have put a spring in his step.

Once I had digested the news, I decided it wasn't such a bad thing after all. It would be good to be on my own for a few months, to be free from the fear that Donald might come home rolling drunk as he had done for so many nights.

July 31st, 1933

So now Donald is gone; all the men are gone. They went last week by special train from Kandaipur junction. All the wives and families turned out to wave goodbye.

For days beforehand, I could see in Donald's face that he was impatient to leave. In the build-up to the departure, he had a gleam in his eye and an energy in his manner that was quite new. When it came to saying goodbye, he brushed my cheek with his lips and I felt the prickle of his moustache on my skin.

'Goodbye, my dear. Take good care of yourself. And do write to me often.'

My days have continued much as they did before, except for last night, when I heard some news that shocked me to the core. My cheeks are wet with tears and I'm finding it difficult to process what Mrs Smethurst told me. Although it was shocking to hear, it does have the horrible ring of truth about it. When she made her revelation I almost collapsed with shock. She had to get the bearer to bring brandy to revive me and they took me to lie down in an anteroom.

She took me by the arm and walked me through the whole length of the club to the front door. I could feel the eyes of every member on me as I walked through the bar to reach the front door.

'Chin up, girl,' said Mrs Smethurst in my ear. Did they all know? Did they all know the facts that she had just revealed to me? If they did, it would perhaps explain the pitying looks I got every time I entered the club, and

the way everyone tries to subtly avoid getting close to me. No wonder I have failed to make any true friends among the army wives.

As Mrs Smethurst helped me down the steps and into her car, another car drew up on the drive; one that I recognised. Charles Perry and his wife Isobel got out. I had never seen them together before. I could tell straight away that they were arguing. She walked ahead of him with her head held high, and swept up the steps past me and into the club without a backward glance. He followed more slowly and I felt his eyes on me as he passed. He raised his solar topee and looked at me with concern. I know I must have looked a sight, with blotchy skin and red eyes from crying, but at that moment my appearance was the last thing on my mind.

I keep going over and over Mrs Smethurst's words. It was my own fault. I had pressed her and pressed her until she told me.

We'd been playing bridge and when the game was over and the other players had drifted over to the bar, I plucked up my courage and said to her, 'You mentioned something about Donald not having changed his ways the other day. There seems to be something about him that people are hiding from me. Now we're alone, perhaps you'd tell me what you meant.'

She looked flustered. Her leathery cheeks went pink and she began fussing with the cards.

'Oh, I'm really not sure I should tell you, my dear. Not if Donald hasn't told you himself.'

'Well, he has told me about his drinking. I've tried to help him with that, but I haven't been very successful these past few months, as you know. But I get the sense there is something else. That he hasn't told me the whole truth.'

She cleared her throat and took a sip of her gin fizz.

'Only a very few people on the station, including Toby and myself, know about the other matter. I was sworn to secrecy by Toby.'

'But I'm his wife, Mrs Smethurst. Surely I have a right to know something that serious.'

She pursed her lips and looked coyly into her glass.

'I don't need to tell you twice that what I'm about to tell you must remain a secret. That Donald's whole career, his place in the regiment, his reputation among the men depends upon your silence and discretion.'

'Of course,' I whispered, looking down, dreading what her words would reveal. She took a deep breath.

'Well, my dear, it started some years ago, when Donald was a major and the Rifles were stationed near Simla. Donald took to frequenting the native bazaar in the evenings. Toby knew about these trips, he mentioned it to me, and he thought it strange, but said nothing. Then, after a few weeks, Toby got his servant to follow Donald. He was worried that Donald might be gambling, getting into debt. But it wasn't gambling that was the problem, Anna.'

She took another swig of gin and I could see her hands were shaking.

'What was it?'

'It was young men.'

My hand flew to my mouth.

'Extremely young men, as it turned out. Young men from the brothels hanging round the bazaar. Donald had been picking them up, going home with them and paying them for… well, shall I say, for their services.

'Toby read the riot act to him. Said that by rights he should be court-martialled and discharged from the army, but Donald pleaded with him to give him another chance. Soon after that, the regiment came back to Kandaipur.

Donald seemed to have put it behind him and a few months went by. Then the drinking started and that became a problem too. It went on like that for years. It got worse and worse. He got into a fight in the club once.

'After that, Toby told him he must get off the drink. He said he was drinking to forget what he was and who he was. A few months after that, he was in trouble again. He came to Toby because some young man had been trying to blackmail him. He said he would reveal everything to the Kandaipur Gazette if Donald didn't pay him a thousand rupees. Toby had the man arrested, but it was then that he got the General up here and he laid down an ultimatum to Donald. He said he must stop drinking and he must stop this life otherwise he would be out of the army. The army was his first love, you know that, Anna. The General told him to go to Bombay and find someone to marry. People were beginning to gossip about him because he was still a bachelor, and the gossip was beginning to take root and spread. It could damage the reputation of the whole regiment. So that's why Donald came down to Bombay when he did.'

'And met me.'

'Yes. And met you.' She held out a leathery hand and clasped mine. Tears sprang to my eyes and I felt the shock of her words begin to hit me. My mouth flooded with nausea and my vision began to blur. Mrs Smethurst was leaning towards me, peering into my eyes.

'Oh, my dear, you're not going to faint, are you? Bearer? Brandy, please. Quickly. The memsahib isn't feeling well.'

Chapter Twenty-Six

Connie

Connie shuts the diary and rubs her eyes. Anna's desperate face swims once more before her. Connie is beginning to understand that desperation now – how Anna had been manipulated and used by those around her; those who should have loved and protected her from harm – her husband and her aunt. Connie's mind automatically drifts to Father. She tries not to entertain unflattering thoughts about him but she knows there is no hiding from it now; she must face the truth. Father had been like Donald in many ways. A similarly powerful man with a secret life who brought his influence and pressure to bear on all those around him, in pursuit of his own interests. The similarities are quite striking.

She locks the clasp with the key on her chain and slips the diary into her bedside drawer. She doesn't want Matron's or Erica's prying eyes spotting it.

It's dark outside now, and from the clatter of crockery and pots and pans, Connie knows it must be nearly supper time.

There's a knock at the door. She hesitates.

There's another knock and Matron puts her head round the door. She isn't wearing her usual smile. In fact, she looks positively flustered. There are high spots of colour on her cheeks, and anxiety in her eyes.

'Connie, there are some people here to see you,' she says.

Connie starts in surprise.

'People?' she says.

She has never had visitors in the plural. Could Peter Cartwright and Sarah Jennings, her only regulars, have possibly arrived at the same time? What a coincidence if so. It might be a touch awkward, she muses, given the business over the sale of Cedar Hall.

'Yes, I'm afraid so.' Matron comes into the room, closes the door firmly, and stands in front of it.

'Matron, whatever is wrong?'

'Connie, I don't quite know how to tell you this. There's no easy way, I'm afraid. The fact is, Mrs Jennings is in reception, and she's with three police officers. I've shown them into the waiting room so the other guests don't start asking questions.'

'Police officers?'

'Yes. They need to talk to you about Cedar Hall. That's why Mrs Jennings is here too.'

Connie pauses as the words sink in. What could it mean?

'Well, they must know that I don't own it any more,' she replies. 'Mrs Jennings should be able to answer any questions about the house.'

'No, they need to speak to you, Connie. It's about something they've found there.'

Connie's scalp tingles and goosebumps prickle her arms.

'Found?' she whispers. 'What is it?'

'They wouldn't tell me, I'm afraid. Do you want me to help you through to the waiting room, or do you want to see them here?'

'Show them through here please, Matron,' she whispers, a sick feeling in the pit of her stomach.

Sarah, looking flustered, comes into the room first, followed by two men and a young woman. They seem to fill the room with their blue uniforms, their radios and their air of authority. Sarah sits down beside Connie. The young woman sits in the armchair, and Matron brings chairs from the dining room for the others and sits on Connie's other chair herself.

One of the men looks very young; so young in fact that Connie wonders if he is old enough to have left school. The other, the more senior of the two, begins to speak.

'Miss Burroughs, thank you for seeing us this evening. I'm Sergeant Coxon, this is PC Redmund and this is WPC Kirk. We're from Weirfield Police station. Now, Miss Burroughs, something has been found at Cedar Hall that requires us to investigate. I understand that Cedar Hall used to be your home?'

Connie stares at him blankly and blinks. She isn't going to give anything away.

He clears his throat.

'I'm sorry, Miss Burroughs. This isn't easy for any of us. Please prepare yourself for a shock. What has been found under the flagstones in the conservatory is very disturbing.'

She closes her eyes, waiting for the inevitable.

'When Mrs Jennings here and her friend, Matthew Drayton, took up the flagstones in the conservatory, they found an old wooden box buried in the floor in there. It looks like a toolbox. It had initials engraved on the top: E.J.B. They were your father's initials, weren't they?'

Her hands begin to shake and she feels for the filigree necklace for reassurance. What would Father say if she told them anything? Is he listening to her? Can he see her now? She inclines her head and closes her eyes. Tears ooze from between the lids and roll down her cheeks.

'What we found inside that box was very upsetting.' He pauses. She screws her eyes even tighter and waits for the blow.

'It was the skeleton of a baby.'

Her eyes snap open and she stares at him. It is what she expected, what she has known for over seventy-five years, but hearing it spoken out loud is still a shock. She feels Sarah's hand take her own.

'Are you all right, Connie?' Sarah asks, concern on her face. 'It must be a dreadful shock.'

She nods and swallows.

'Do you want some water?'

Connie reaches out a hand and Matron hands her a glass. She takes a couple of sips.

'Miss Burroughs, do you know anything about that? Anything at all?' asks the officer.

It is wrong to lie. It is against all the teachings of Christ and all her beliefs, but she knows above all that, she must protect Father. His last words come to her, *Don't let anyone meddle in my business, Constance. I'm counting on you.*

'I know nothing about it,' she says quietly, her voice trembling. She carries on looking down in her lap at her shaking hands.

'We have run some tests and have found that the remains are likely to date from the early 1930s. You and your family were living in the house at that time, weren't you?'

'I'm not sure. I can't remember,' she says, vaguely, giving him another vacant stare.

The policemen exchange glances.

'Now, we know that your father ran the orphanage next door. There must have been many babies there. Do you remember any of those babies dying, Miss Burroughs?'

Again, Connie shakes her head. This time she isn't lying. 'All the babies in our care were very healthy. There were no deaths in the orphanage. Not one.'

'Well, we'd like to check the orphanage records if there are any remaining. We've asked the County Council, and they have nothing. I wonder… did your father have his own records?'

Connie swallows and doesn't reply. She thinks about the papers in his desk. The ones she had never dared to look at, not even after Father died. The ones Peter had taken away and stored in his basement. Would they reveal anything Father wouldn't have wanted known? She doesn't know, but she doesn't think she can take that risk.

'I don't think so. I believe they were all destroyed when the orphanage closed,' she says, still staring down at her hands. Will they suspect? Will they take her at her word?

'You're quite sure about that, Miss Burroughs?'

Again, she nods, staring at her hands. She can't look up.

The senior policeman gets up and sighs.

'I thought as much. Well, Miss Burroughs, thank you for your time. We'll continue our investigations, and if in the meantime anything occurs to you, anything at all about that time, please do get in touch with the station.'

They troop out of the room, the young policewoman giving her a sympathetic look and squeeze of her arm on the way out. Sarah stays behind and closes the door firmly. She moves towards Connie and looks into her eyes.

'Connie, why didn't you tell them what you know?'

Connie frowns and purses her lips, but doesn't respond.

'I got confused,' she says finally. 'I couldn't remember anything.'

Sarah carries on watching her, looking straight into her eyes.

'You know I don't think that you're quite the confused, forgetful old lady you sometimes pretend to be. The police have probably gone away thinking you don't know anything. That you're a bit dotty. They're all ready to close their files. But I'm sure that you know more than you're letting on.'

Connie looks at Sarah with a vacant stare.

'I don't know what you're talking about.'

'It's not a good idea to keep secrets. My husband kept secrets from me and it's caused a lot of damage, you know. I'm not religious, but I thought that truthfulness was one of the Commandments.'

Connie remains silent, but what Sarah said has struck a chord with her. Sarah is right: it's not good to tell lies or to keep secrets, particularly ones like this. She twists her hands in anguish.

Connie puts her face in her hands. She's trembling all over. She wants to cry properly but the tears won't come. All she can feel in her throat is a dull, dry ache.

'I have to go now and talk to the police again, but I'll come back very soon to see you. Perhaps you'll think about what I've said.'

The door clicks behind Sarah and Connie stays where she is, her face in her hands. She hardly notices Erica arriving with the tray. She's thinking about Sarah's words; she's thinking too about her memories. The ones she has buried for years. The ones she has hardly been able to acknowledge. All this time she has been trying to preserve the good side of Father in her memory. His religion, his preaching, his energy, his kindness to the orphans. She's tried to keep those things in aspic and to put aside the other things, to forget the dark side of him: the long alcohol-fuelled meetings in his office with strange men, the cries from the coach house, the extravagant gifts that used to arrive from India, and Anna. Not forgetting poor Anna.

Connie knows she must force herself to go back there now. Back to that dreadful night. That night when she awoke to the cries coming from the coach house; when she crept to the window and saw Father emerge from the top room carrying that mysterious bundle of rags. She remembers him coming up to the bedroom and standing there at the door, then coming across the room to check that she and Evie were asleep. When those dreadful sounds had started coming from under the window she had blocked her ears and tried to ignore them. She'd tried to blot them out. But it had been impossible to do that. How could she just go back to sleep after what she'd heard? She needed to find out. She needed to know.

She crept out of bed and pulled on her dressing gown. She made her way down the stairs. Still the sounds came; the sound of something sharp striking the earth. Thump, thump, thump. She crept across the hall, down the passage and through the kitchen, the tiles cold on her bare feet. She stood at the glass door shivering, and peered through into the conservatory. What she saw made her blood run cold.

Something inside her snapped at that moment. Something broke, and changed imperceptibly. She knows now that it was this moment that led her to rebel; *that it was then that she decided to help Anna.*

Connie spends a restless night, turning uncomfortably in her bed, sweat pouring from her body. Her dreams are inhabited by images of her father. He's walking down the coach house steps in the moonlight, the bundle in his arms. In her dream he stands at her door, here in her room at Fairlawns. She holds her breath, afraid that he will hear it, that any moment he will walk over to her bed, lift her covers and put his face close to hers to check she is asleep. Then she's watching him in the conservatory, his huge shadow dancing on the wall, lifting the pickaxe and bringing it down with a thud. Thud, thud, thud, the sound goes on all night.

In the morning, Connie feels dreadful.

'You want to take breakfast in the dining room today, Connie?' asks Erica.

She's about to refuse, but she remembers Tommy. Suddenly she wants to see his face again, remember how it had once been between them, feel the reassuring touch of his hand on her arm.

Tommy is already sitting at a table when Connie enters the dining room. There's an empty space beside him. He looks up from his meal, waves and motions for her to come and sit with him. There's a lively buzz of conversation as she enters the room, but as she makes her way across to where Tommy sits, she can sense a hush descending. Dozens of pairs of eyes are watching her, following her as she moves between the tables.

She settles herself down beside Tommy. He smiles and greets her, but there's something in his look, some sort of distress that hadn't been there yesterday.

'Tommy, is anything wrong?'

'We saw it on the local news, Connie.'

'News? What do you mean?' But that dreadful sick feeling comes back to the pit of her stomach. She can't meet his eyes.

'You must know what I'm talking about. The baby, Connie. At Cedar Hall. It was on the news this morning. On the television.'

'Oh!' She isn't prepared for this. She stares at the cereal in her bowl and nausea floods her mouth. She pushes the bowl aside.

'I was going to tell you about it,' she says. 'That's why I came.'

'Do you want to go somewhere quiet to talk? I've finished here.'

They make their laborious way along the passage to the day room. It's empty apart from a cleaner working at the far end. They sit in a pair of chairs beside the window. The ones they sat in yesterday.

'Do you want to tell me all about it?' he asks gently, his steady eyes looking into her own.

'The police came yesterday evening,' she says quietly. 'They said they'd found something. They said they'd found the bones of a baby under the conservatory. They wanted to know if I knew anything about it.'

'And do you?'

She shakes her head miserably, but she can't meet his gaze.

'Do they think it had something to do with your father?'

Connie nods.

'And you want to protect his memory? Is that it?'

'Of course.'

There's a long silence. Connie's eyes wander to the window and she looks across the damp garden. She watches one of the gardeners clearing fallen leaves from the grass. He rakes them into small piles, then brings a barrow and loads them in with a fork. He's very methodical, working his way up and down the large lawn in strips. Several minutes pass. She begins to wonder whether Tommy will ever say anything.

But at last he speaks.

'I wasn't going to mention this. The past is the past and I was going to let it lie. But it might help you to know this about your precious father.' He says those last two words bitterly and Connie looks at him sharply.

'I left Weirfield because your father forced me to leave. And the day I left was the day I lost my faith.'

'Tommy! Whatever do you mean?'

'When I first came back from the farm to work for him I misjudged him, Connie. I made some mistakes. My landlady in the town was ill. Do you remember, your father had forced me to take lodgings in town?' She nods. 'He said he needed the room above the garage, it was his private hideaway and I wasn't even to look up there. Anyway, the landlady was very kind to me. She knew I had no family and she really took me under her wing. When she got ill, the doctor said she needed plenty of fresh vegetables. I knew where I could find some of those – the orphanage garden – hadn't I worked like a slave in that garden all the years I was a lad? So, a couple of times before I went home, I took a couple of cabbages, some runner beans and some carrots. On the last occasion, as I came back past the garage, Ezra was waiting for me.

'He hit the roof, Connie. I'd seen him angry before, over things that happened in the orphanage, but this time was different. Boy, I've been to war and even then I didn't see such ugly, brutal anger! He got me up against the wall and said that pilfering was something he despised more than anything and that he was going to make me pay. He said he knew people in high places including the local police and he could make sure I felt the full force of the law. I threw myself on his mercy. I pleaded with him to give me another chance. I hadn't got anywhere else to go, you see. After a while he calmed down and I could see in his eyes he had a plan. He was thinking that he had one over on me.

'He had me over a barrel. Time went on. He made me pay for the vegetables several times over. Sometimes I got curious and I'd ask him questions. Once I thought I heard voices in his hideaway so I asked him about it, straight up. He flew into a rage again. Do you remember how his rages used to descend on him from nowhere, Connie? His face would darken, like the sky when a storm was coming, and you'd know his anger would soon burst from him, like thunder and lightning?'

Connie nods, her blood running cold at the memory.

'He told me to mind my own business, and said if I asked any more questions I'd be out on my ear so I tried to do that. I tried to mind my own business and not ask questions but every so often, I got so curious I had to mention things. Like who were the gentlemen I had to collect from the station for a meeting, like where did he get that silk waistcoat from? Things like that. My questions would send him crazy every time.

'Anyway, things went along like that, until something happened that meant he needed to shut me up. To get me right away from there.'

Connie stares at him, her face screwed up in a frown at the memories.

'Do you remember, Connie, around the time I left, that a young woman was found dead, floating in the Thames at Henley? The one with red hair?'

'Yes. Yes, I do remember.'

She thinks back to how she pored over the story in the local paper. She was young then herself, about the same age as the young woman who died. She remembers reading the newspaper report. *'Young woman suicide bid in the Thames'* screamed the headline. The report gave details of how her body had been found bloated and almost unrecognisable. The young woman had come from Manchester and had no known connection to Henley at all. Her death was a mystery.

Connie's heart had gone out to that poor young woman and she'd stared at the photograph for a long time, trying to imagine what dreadful circumstances had led the poor wretch to take her own life. She kept imagining how low she must have felt to have plunged herself into those swirling waters below the weir. For years afterwards, Connie couldn't walk past that weir on her trips to Henley without thinking of that young woman and her dreadful plight.

'Well, you remember she wasn't a local girl,' says Tommy. 'It emerged she came from up north, from a good family, but she'd come down to Henley for no apparent reason and thrown herself in the river and drowned herself. No one could work it out, and the police closed it all down pretty quickly and people forgot all about it.

'The fact is, Connie, that girl didn't drown herself in the river. No. She was dead well before that. She died at Cedar Hall and her body was dumped in the river.'

'Tommy, what on earth do you mean?' Connie's hand flies to her mouth. His words make her tremble but somehow they have the dreadful ring of truth about them.

'I came to work very early one day. I wanted to make an early start, because I was meeting you later, and I wanted to be able to get home and change. I didn't want your father suspecting anything, of course. I arrived before sunrise. I had a key to the garage and I unlocked it. When I walked inside and switched on the light, your father was in there. At first, I couldn't see what he was doing. The back door of the car was open and he was leaning inside, hauling something heavy onto the back seat. He turned as I switched on the light, and I saw straight away what he was doing. On the back seat was the body of a young woman. I could tell immediately she was dead. I can still remember her face to this day. She had beautiful red hair.

'I started to back away, but he came up close to me and grabbed me by the collar. He was strong, he nearly choked me.

'"Tommy Braithwaite, you didn't see this," he said.

'I stared at him. I knew what he was capable of. I knew what influence he had in the town. He had everyone from the policemen to the mayor to the doctor in his pocket so when he told me to leave, to never contact you again, I did what he said, Connie. I went back to my lodgings and I packed my bags with a lead weight in my heart. I enlisted – it was the only way I could get far away, the only way I could survive. I had nothing, and I wanted to get as far away from Ezra Burroughs as I could.

'But there was one order that I disobeyed. I *did* try to write to you, Connie. I wrote three letters. I tried to disguise my handwriting on the envelopes. Did you ever get them?'

She shakes her head. 'No, Tommy. Not one.'

'He must have found them and thrown them away. I had to send them to the house. I just hoped you would get to the post first. That was my biggest regret, Connie, believe me, leaving you behind, knowing you would be distraught and angry. That you'd end up hating me.'

'Never, Tommy. I never hated you.'

'Really?'

'I knew there must have been a good reason for you leaving. I always hoped you'd come back.'

'When the war ended and I came home I was a changed man. All those years in prison camps in the jungle, suffering starvation and disease had taken its toll. I was skin and bone. I got lodgings in London and found a job in a garage in the East End. I asked around and found out that Ezra Burroughs was still alive and well and living in Weirfield just as before. I knew that if I came back, he would carry out his threat. He wasn't a man to forgive and forget.

'I met a girl in the end, Nancy. She worked in the office in the garage. We started walking out together and one thing led to another. She was a lovely girl, Connie, but she was never like you. No one was like you.'

He reaches out and takes her hand. His hand feels bony and cold, but that doesn't matter. Just the touch of it is a comfort.

'So, you see, Connie,' he goes on, 'that's what your precious father was capable of under all his bluster and charm. He was a brutal, dangerous man. But I think you knew that all along really, didn't you?'

Chapter Twenty-Seven

Sarah

'We've completed our investigation, Mrs Jennings,' says Sergeant Coxon. He's standing in the corner of the kitchen at Cedar Hall, sipping a coffee. 'I'm afraid it's going to be very difficult to find anything out about the provenance of the bones,' he goes on. 'As I mentioned yesterday, our forensic team dated them to the early thirties. And as you know, Miss Burroughs claims to know nothing about it.'

She exchanges glances with Matt, who's sitting opposite her at the table. The police had asked for him to be there when they came to speak to Sarah.

'I'm afraid there's nothing else we can do at present,' the Sergeant goes on. 'With all the current crimes we're having to investigate, not to mention the cutbacks. We're short-staffed now at the station as it is. There's even talk of closing us down altogether.'

'So what will happen now?'

'We're going to have to close the file on the case, Mrs Jennings. I wanted to tell you in person.'

'Close the file?'

'I understand how you feel, but I'm sure you'll appreciate our position.'

He drains his coffee and puts his cap on. 'I'd best be on my way. If anything does happen to turn up on the case, I'll be sure to let you know.'

'What about the bones?' Sarah asks suddenly.

He pauses.

'The bones? What do you mean?'

'Well, the baby… the skeleton. What will happen to it?'

He turns and stares at her. 'In cases like this, remains are usually incinerated at the hospital.'

A shudder goes through Sarah. She thinks again about the baby. Who was its mother? What might have happened to her? What dreadful circumstances had led to these tiny bones being buried under the flagstones, lying there neglected and forgotten for decades?

'Won't there be a funeral?' she asks.

'If you like, we could release the remains to a funeral home. They'll be able to arrange a funeral for you.'

Sarah feels responsible somehow. 'I'll pay for the funeral,' she says suddenly.

'That's a very generous gesture, Mrs Jennings. If you'd like to pop round to the police station in the next couple of days, we'll arrange all the paperwork for you.'

After he's left the house and driven away, Sarah sits down and puts her head in her hands. She feels stunned. Matt's arms are around her shoulders.

'Are you OK?'

'I just can't believe how casual they are about it. How they can give up on it so soon? It's only been a few days.'

'Well, like he said, it's not a priority for them.'

She's thinking hard. 'I don't think I can just let it rest like that. It would feel odd to go on living here with that hanging over me.'

'But what can you do? If the police can't do anything…'

'I'm not sure. But there must be some way of finding out. I'm sure Connie is hiding something, but that she really wants to speak out. Something is stopping her. You know, Matt, I can't help thinking all this has some sort of connection to Dad and his past. It all happened in the early nineteen-thirties. I really want to get to the bottom of it for his sake too.'

Her mobile buzzes and her father's number shows on the screen. She answers quickly, surprised. He doesn't normally call at this time of day.

'Dad?'

'Sarah. Are you OK?'

'Of course, Dad. Are you? Has anything happened?'

'I've just been listening to the local news on the radio. There was something about Cedar Hall. You found some bones?'

'Oh, Dad! I'm sorry, I had no idea it would be on the radio. I should have warned you.'

'I thought you were a bit preoccupied when you came round yesterday evening. Was that what it was about?'

'Yes. I was trying to find a way of telling you. But in the end, I didn't have the courage. I'm so sorry.'

'What a dreadful thing to have happened. Are you all right? Should I come over?'

'No, I'm fine thanks. I've got someone with me.'

'Oh, I see. Who's that, Sarah?'

'Oh it's Matt from the bistro. I told you about helping out there, don't you remember?'

'Oh yes. Of course. Well, it's good that you have company. You know, they said on the news that the remains dated from my time at Cedar Hall.'

'Yes, that's right. That's what the police told me. I've no idea how the radio got the story.'

There's silence at the other end of the line.

'Are you still there, Dad?'

'You know, Sarah, there seem to be so many unanswered questions from that time. It seems so odd that there are virtually no records at all to do with the orphanage. I've drawn a blank everywhere I've looked – the parish records, the church, the internet. It feels strange that I haven't been able to find out anything. And now this tiny baby, buried under the floor… it must be connected somehow. I really wish I'd been able to find out more.'

'You could carry on trying, Dad,' she replies. 'It's early days yet. I could help you.'

There's another short silence, then he says in a quiet voice, 'I'm not sure how long there is left for me, Sarah.'

She catches her breath and tears prickle her eyes.

'Please don't talk like that, Dad. Shall I come over and see you, if you're feeling down?'

'I'll be fine. There's no need. It's just that I have the appointment with the consultant at the end of the week. He'll have the results of the tests they ran. He might want me to stay in…'

'Oh, Dad, perhaps the news won't be as bad as you're expecting. I'll be there with you, whatever he says.'

'I know, I know. I'm sorry to burden you.'

'It's no burden.'

'I'll let you get on. I'll see you this evening, then.'

'Poor Dad,' Sarah murmurs as she rings off. 'He's desperate to know more about his past. You know, Matt, there are so many mysteries surrounding the orphanage.'

'Why don't you go and talk to Miss Burroughs about it again?' asks Matt. 'She might talk to you once she's got over the shock of the police visiting.'

'You're right. Perhaps she felt intimidated. Maybe she'll talk to me now.'

Chapter Twenty-Eight

Connie

Anna's Diary
August 1st, 1933

Today, I got up and tried to carry on as normal. But Manju noticed something was wrong as soon as she saw me.

'Memsahib looks very sad today,' she said, concern brimming in her soft brown eyes. She had brought clean clothes fresh from the dhobi into my room to put away. I was sitting at the dressing table brushing my hair. How did she know? She is so perceptive. She seems to pick up on my moods even before I know them myself.

I ate little at breakfast and decided I couldn't face the club this morning. I kept picturing Donald strolling through the bazaar, appraising a young, fresh-faced Indian man, their eyes meeting.

At two o'clock, though, I was standing out on the veranda, ready and waiting with my sketchbook for Rajiv to appear round the bend in the road. I was determined not to give in to my sadness. I knew I needed to get out of the house. My sprits always lift when I see Rajiv pedalling towards me enthusiastically, his white robes flapping round his ankles, his broad smile displaying teeth stained red with betel nut.

But today, he didn't come. Instead, on the dot of two, I heard the sound of a car engine. After a few seconds a familiar vehicle nosed its way around the corner and approached the house. My heart did a nervous lurch: it was Charles Perry's car. It pulled up next to where I stood and Charles leaned out of the back window.

'Hop in, Anna. I'll take you for a ride.'

'I can't, I'm afraid. I'm waiting for my rickshaw-wallah to come. He's normally here by now.'

'He won't be coming today.'

'Oh? How do you know?'

'I saw him at the maidan. I asked him to stay away this afternoon. I paid him handsomely, so he won't lose out.'

I stared at him, blinking with astonishment. His imperiousness was astounding.

'I can't believe you did that,' *I said, my voice brittle.* 'You had no right.'

'I thought you might take it like that. But I had the best of intentions, Anna. I saw you coming out of the club yesterday with old Ma Smethurst. You looked very upset. I thought I would take you out and cheer you up.'

'I was looking forward to my rickshaw ride, actually. And what business is it of yours whether I'm upset, may I ask?'

He got out of the car and approached the veranda. He took off his hat and looked up at me.

'It is no business of mine, as you say, and you've every right to be annoyed with me. I just felt… I felt a certain empathy for you, that's all. You and I have a lot in common. I thought we could console each other when things get difficult, Anna.'

He was staring up at me with such a genuine look in his eyes and I couldn't help but soften a little. I relaxed and smiled at him.

'So, will you come out with me this afternoon?' he asked.

'Perhaps. Where were you thinking of?'

'There's an old abandoned summer palace beside a lake in the next valley. It's too far to go in a rickshaw. If you don't go in a motor car, you might never get to see it. And it's worth seeing, believe me.'

My interest was piqued. 'Abandoned palace? Is it derelict?'

'No, not derelict. It's just not used any more. The last maharajah used to visit in the summer season with his beloved maharani, but when she died, he stopped going there. It is still beautiful, though. It's just as he left it. As district officer, I have access to the key, if you'd like to look round. You can bring your sketchbook if you like.'

'All right, I'll come along,' I said, on an impulse, picking up my bag and going quickly down the steps towards the car before I could change my mind.

We had soon left the cantonment and the straggling outskirts of Kandaipur behind and were heading out on the long straight road towards the distant mountains. I stared out of the open window at the dreamy peaks ahead.

The road began to rise as we entered the foothills, and to wind upwards on switchback bends. But as soon as we were over the ridge it descended again and we had crossed the pass and were into the hills. Then we were travelling through a narrow rocky valley beside a fast-flowing river. I watched the rushing white water as it flowed over rocks, into whirlpools, over waterfalls. The road was bumpy here and driving through that desolate gorge seemed to take an age, but at last, after a few miles, the mountains became gentler and the valley opened out. Ahead of us lay a vast shimmering lake, its crystal-clear waters reflecting the craggy hills that surrounded it.

The road began to skirt the edge of the lake and soon I could see the outline of the palace at the far end. I caught my breath as we got closer and I could make out its Moorish domes and crenelated arches and spires, and closer still, I could see the detail of its elaborate masonry. It was built of honey-coloured stone and blended perfectly into its surroundings.

When we finally reached the palace, the driver pulled the car through some gates and into a cobbled courtyard. An old servant emerged from a gatehouse and, after exchanging smiles and greetings with the driver, handed him a bunch of keys and waved him through an archway into a further courtyard.

We left the car and driver there. Charles took the keys, led me across the courtyard to the entrance and unlocked some huge double doors. He beckoned me forward, up some stone steps and into the serene cool of the palace itself. We walked through the ground floor, a series of high-ceilinged rooms where the sun streamed through stained-glass windows throwing colourful patterns on the marble floors. There was not much furniture – just the odd oak chest or carved wooden bench. I followed Charles through the pillared echoing halls, entranced at what I saw. He showed me silk hangings of exquisite beauty, depicting myths and historical tales, and pointed out beautifully carved sculptures of elephants and gods that graced every corner and recess.

'It's beautiful,' I breathed. We had reached the other side of the building by now.

'Come out here,' Charles said, unlocking another door that led onto a stone terrace directly beside the lake. We wandered along beside the water that lapped at the low wall and I stared up at the building.

'Would you like to sit out here and sketch it?'

'I'd love that.'

'I'll leave you to it,' he said. 'I need to take a closer look at the building and have a word with the chowkidar. There have been some rumblings of trouble around these parts and I want to make sure none of it has come this way.' He left me alone and I began to plan my drawing. I sketched out the shapes of the distant mountains, the surface of the water, the shimmering reflections, a few distant dwellings on the other side and a couple of fishing boats out on the calm surface of the lake.

I sat alone on the blanket on the low wall and sketched for a long time. I was completely absorbed in the task and the picture came together quickly. When I had finished the drawing of the lake and mountains to my satisfaction, I turned round and began to sketch the palace. It was difficult from this angle, but I think I managed to convey the essence of the building. I must have been sketching solidly for well over an hour. When I got up to stretch my limbs, I noticed that the sky had started to darken in the west. I realised that the journey must have taken a good two hours, so it was probably around six o'clock. I looked around for Charles, beginning to feel a little anxious.

I closed the sketchbook, put it in my bag and wandered back into the palace. It was still and silent. A sudden chill went through me. I felt quite alone. Feeling a little anxious, I wandered back through the halls towards the main entrance, thinking he must be with the driver and the chowkidar in the lodge. But my attention was taken by a shaft of light flooding in through an open door in one of the side rooms. Perhaps Charles was through there? I walked towards it. Reaching the door, I saw that it opened out onto a courtyard. It was vast and surrounded on all sides by the inner walls of the palace. Windows and balconies looked over it on every side. The floor of the courtyard was paved with bright blue ceramic tiles and there were trees creating shade around the edge, surrounded by flower beds. In the very centre was an elegant pond with a bubbling fountain. I walked towards it. The sound of the lapping water was soothing to my jangling nerves.

Charles was clearly not there but I couldn't resist lingering and admiring the symmetry and beauty of the place, as the pink evening sun played on the pale stone walls. Birds and insects chattered in the trees.

Suddenly there was a thundering of feet from the palace roof and in a matter of seconds I was surrounded by dozens of monkeys. They pulled at my clothes, jumped around me, bared their teeth at me. I cried out as one leapt on my shoulders. The others pawed at me, looking up at me with pleading eyes, begging for food. I tried to push them off, but the one on my shoulders clung on, his claws digging into my face and neck. I was shouting now, 'Charles! Please! Help me!'

Other monkeys leapt up at me, scratching my arms and legs, leaving me with bleeding cuts.

Then Charles was there, shooing them away, clapping his hands. As quickly as they had arrived, the whole troop scattered and ran away, scurrying up drainpipes, jumping from window to balcony to return to their vantage point on the roof.

I felt Charles's arms around me. He pulled me to him, holding me close. I couldn't stop shaking. Tears were streaming down my face and I couldn't speak.

'Come on,' he said. 'Let's get you inside and clean up those wounds.' He picked up my bag. The contents had spilled out and the sketchbook had fallen on the ground. He examined it. The cover was torn and dirty, but the sketches inside were unharmed.

Charles guided me inside the cool of the building along a corridor and through some inner rooms that we hadn't seen on our way through. Deep in the interior of the palace was a room with sofas and low tables. He led me to a sofa of red velvet.

'This is the maharani's chamber. Sit down and rest. I'll get some salt water from the chowkidar.'

His footsteps echoed away, and I lay back on the cushions, still shaking. The room smelled of must and mothballs. I took a deep, shuddering breath, trying to calm my nerves. He quickly returned with a bowl of water, cloth, brandy and a couple of glasses.

'I think you'll need this after a shock like that,' he said, pouring us both a generous measure. He handed me a glass. 'Your hands are shaking,' he added, seeing the brandy in the glass trembling as I held it.

He put his glass down on the table and took up the cloth.

He sat down beside me and started dabbing at my cuts. At first the salt in the water made it sting and I gasped each time he touched me, but I got used to it. He was very gentle, stroking my skin, doing his best to ensure he didn't hurt me. I was silent as he bathed my wounds. I was concentrating on his breathing, his gentle hands.

'I think that's it,' he said finally, putting the bowl on the floor. 'Are you feeling any better?'

The brandy was coursing through my veins, warming my insides.

'Yes, I do feel a bit better now, thank you.'

'Have some more brandy. It's obviously doing you good,' he said, holding up the bottle. I held out my glass without thinking.

I watched him go to the far side of the room where some Tilley lamps stood on a table. He lit two and brought one over, placing it on the table in front of us.

I glanced at his face, its clean lines, warm and golden in the flickering light of the lamp. I realised how close he was sitting to me, that his arm was touching mine. Heat seemed to radiate from him. I tried to shift away, but he moved closer and put his arm around my shoulder. Then he turned my chin towards him and started kissing me. I tried to pull away at first, but after a few seconds I was kissing him back, abandoning myself to him. Soon he was unbuttoning my blouse and his hands were on my breasts. He pushed me back onto the sofa, carried on kissing me, moving his lips to my neck, down my body. I was reluctant at first, unresponsive, knowing it was wrong, that we were both married. That it shouldn't happen. But the brandy and the seductive atmosphere of that mysterious, romantic palace broke down my resistance.

'I've wanted you since the first time I saw you, Anna,' he murmured. 'I know you feel the same way. Tell me it's true.'

I stared into his eyes. Those words he'd said to me when he brought me home in his car had gone round and round in my head ever since that night. 'Anna, please don't fight it. Don't you feel the attraction between us? Why can't you admit it to yourself?' he'd said. I had not been able to banish them from my mind because I knew they were true.

'Yes, it's true,' I said. And in that moment, it was. In that moment, I threw caution to the wind. Why shouldn't I know what it's like, I thought, to have someone strong and attractive make love to me? Those painful fumblings with Donald on the train were all I had known, but I knew it could be different. I wanted to find out.

He was on top of me then, covering me with kisses, pulling off my clothes, pulling off his own clothes. I responded to him passionately, pulling him towards me, wrapping my legs around his back. Soon, we were moving together, moving as one, moving towards ecstasy together. And in that final moment of rapture I finally understood what it could be like.

All the way home in the car, Charles held my hand on the back seat. We didn't speak. My thoughts were all over the place, veering between guilt and soaring with joy at the memory of what had happened between us.

September 5th, 1933

Over a month has passed since my trip with Charles to the summer palace. He hasn't been in touch with me since that day. At first, I was restless and inconsolable, waiting for the sound of his car outside the front gate, for a bearer to bring a note from him, something. Anything would have done. But I watched in vain. Nothing came. After a few days, anger began to replace the hurt, and I began to feel ashamed and very foolish. I should have known what sort of man he was. Why did I let myself be drawn in by him, thinking it was something different, that I actually meant something to him? I hope the servants haven't noticed my anguish and guessed the reason. Ali remains unfathomable. I will just have to hope that they keep their silence when Donald comes home.

I have received a few letters from Donald.

His letters describe the barren mountains, the spartan conditions in the camp, the night patrols into the hills to seek out rebel Pashtuns. Despite his stiff language, through his words I can visualise the place if I close my eyes. I can visualise him too, sitting down in his bare room in the officers' mess to write. He will do it dutifully but thoroughly. Then he will seal up the letter and ask his bearer to take it to the post office. He will then put on his cap, check it is straight in the mirror, take up his cane and go down for drinks in the bar, putting me and the letter completely out of his mind until the next time.

October 5th, 1933

I hoped it wasn't true but I'm afraid that it is. Another three weeks have passed and still I haven't bled. My breasts are tender to the touch and I feel a new and strange heaviness in my legs and abdomen. This morning I couldn't face my breakfast and I had to rush down to the bathroom to bring up what little porridge I had eaten. When I came out of there, Manju was standing outside, watching me with fear and anxiety in her eyes.

What am I to do? I cannot pretend this baby is Donald's. There was only that one time on the train with him and that is far too long ago now. I dare not even go to the cantonment doctor, because I know an army wife's medical record is not confidential as far as her husband is concerned.

I have thought about doing a dreadful thing and ridding myself of this trouble. Manju discreetly told me about a woman in one of the villages in the mountains who can perform miracles like 'making babies disappear'. She was watching me carefully when she told me that. Neither of us had even acknowledged my predicament. Her words sent a chill right through me. I thought about it, but I quickly realised that I couldn't go through with it. I couldn't get rid of another human being, no matter how inconvenient and how inauspicious the circumstances of its conception.

There is only one thing I can do. I have resolved to go to Charles and ask him to help me. He's the only person I can turn to.

November 12th, 1933

This morning I spoke to Charles, but I feel even worse for having done so. I rang the club, found out the telephone number of Government House and called him at his office. He sounded surprised to hear my voice and a little annoyed that I'd called him at work. I told him I needed to see him urgently and he agreed.

He drove me to the Maybelle Hotel. We were ushered in through a rear entrance, avoiding the bar and the main restaurant. The bearer took us upstairs to a back room with glass doors that opened out onto a balcony overlooking the colourful exotic garden. A table for two was already set with linen, silver and cut glass.

I was relieved as I took my seat. Driving here, I'd imagined the worst: a sumptuous suite set out with a double bed, champagne on ice. I wouldn't have put it past him to take the opportunity to try again with me.

'I think we'll go native if you don't mind,' Charles said, examining the menu. 'They do a frightfully good Kashmiri rice and chicken here. I prefer to eat Indian in these establishments. Indian cooks always make such a hash of British food.'

I remained silent, not feeling much like eating anything.

'Champagne? We need to celebrate our reunion,' he said.

'No, thank you,' I said, going pale at the thought. 'I'll stick to water.'

He clicked his fingers and the bearer brought water for us both.

'Bring me an ale if you would, please,' he said.

When the man had gone, I blurted out that I was pregnant. His eyes widened and the colour drained from his face. He put his glass down.

'Are you quite sure?'

'Quite sure,' I whispered.

He was silent for a moment and I could see from his eyes that although he wasn't speaking, his mind was working quickly.

'Look, how do you know it's mine?'

I stared at the tablecloth, my cheeks burning.

'I'm quite sure, Charles. It has to be yours. Nothing of that nature happens between Donald and me. And in any case, he is away on the North West Frontier.'

'I thought as much,' he muttered.

We sat in silence as the bearer and two assistants brought our food, setting it out laboriously on the table, ladling rice and chicken onto our plates, refilling our glasses.

'There's simply no choice, Anna. You'll have to get rid of it,' he said once they'd gone. 'I can't afford any scandal.'

Tears sprang to my eyes at the brutality of his words.

'I won't do that, Charles.' I had already thought about this, and I wanted to convince him. 'I came here for your help, to ask you what to do, because I'm desperate. I've already decided that I can't do that. Perhaps… I know it sounds crazy, but perhaps I could go and live somewhere, up in the hills or something. Far away from here. I could have my baby and perhaps you could send me money to live on. It's the only thing I can think of.'

He blinked and I could see the anger on his face.

'You don't seem to realise my position here, Anna. Do you know who I am? What I do?'

'You're the District Officer, aren't you?'

'I'm much more than that. I've got a special role in peace negotiations with the Indian independence movement. I've been appointed for this district by the Viceroy as his eyes and ears on the ground. It's dangerous and sensitive work. I have to be seen to be exemplary in my conduct or I won't be trusted by either side to negotiate. I'd be seen as a security risk.'

'So why didn't you think of that before you seduced me?'

'I thought you would have more discretion, Anna. Really. We're both grown-ups. I had no idea you would let this happen. It's bad enough having a drunk for a wife, but people turn a blind eye to that because of her family connections. But this as well. If anyone found out, if you left Donald and people realised I was the father of your child, I'd be ruined. It would be the end of my career.'

He tucked his napkin into his shirt collar and started eating. The high emotion of the situation obviously hadn't dampened his appetite. I watched him devour his plateful of rice, but I could hardly touch mine. I wasn't sure exactly what sort of help I'd been looking for from Charles, but the conversation wasn't going as planned. In fact, the more I spoke to him, the more I realised how little I really knew him. How could I have let this vain, self-centred man anywhere near me, let alone make love to me?

'Aren't you eating?' he asked, pausing and noticing me.

'I can't.'

He finished his food, pushed his plate away and lit a cigarette.

'There is one solution,' he said, blowing smoke rings into the air. 'If you can get away to England, I know someone there who could help. He's done it for a number of chaps I know in the Indian civil service and in the army. Are you able to get away on home leave?'

'I suppose so. But what is this? I'm not getting rid of the baby, even in England, if that's what you mean.'

'No. This fellow offers a very discreet service. I'll write to him today, see what his terms are. He used to be a missionary and a preacher here in Kandaipur. In fact, he was once the minister at that abandoned church. Do you remember the story I told you?'

'Of course. Is it the one who left in a scandal? You never did tell me what that was all about. I don't like the sound of it, Charles.'

'I really don't see that you have much choice. He will help you. I'll have to pay, of course. But he's completely discreet.'

'But what does it involve? What will happen to my baby?'

'Rest assured, the baby will be well cared for, they'll take responsibility and you'll be able to return to your life here. You won't have to worry on that score. As I said, Burroughs has helped out a couple of chaps I know in the ICS who've found themselves in an equally embarrassing situation. It's all worked very smoothly. Before you know it, you'll be back home in Kandaipur as if nothing's happened.'

I've mulled over what he told me. I'm really not sure that I can go through with what was proposed. I'd already felt the presence of my baby. How will I possibly let go when the time comes?

November 13th, 1933

I waited for Charles outside his office today and as he came out of the building at lunchtime and walked towards his car, I went up to him. He looked none too pleased as his syce was holding the car door open for him and the sun was baking hot.

'Charles, I need to talk to you about what we discussed yesterday.'

He looked irritated, but having cast his eyes around to see if there was anyone about, he said, 'Hop in the car. I was going to the club, but we can go for a drive instead.'

I got in the back and he asked the driver to drive out of town to the nearby lake.

'What's the matter? I thought everything was sorted out yesterday. I've already begun preparations.'

'I don't think I can go through with it, Charles. I don't think I'll be able to give up my baby when the time comes.'

'But you agreed. It's all sorted out now, Anna. It's by far the best thing all round. I'm sure you'll see that if you give it some careful thought.'

'I don't think so, Charles. Perhaps I should just stay here in Kandaipur, let nature take its course. Explain things to Donald.'

'I don't know where you're getting these ridiculous ideas from. That would be a very dangerous thing to do and the best way to start a scandal.'

A vein pulsed in his neck and red was creeping into his face.

I fell silent. I felt so utterly abandoned and alone and as if all my choices were being snatched away from me. I felt a tear form in my eye and roll down my cheek. Instead of softening him, though, this seemed to harden Charles's resolve.

He turned towards me with a look of determination in his eyes.

'I know more about you than you think, Anna,' he said with quiet venom. 'I happen to know that your father has been staying at His Majesty's Pleasure for the past few years even though you've never breathed a word of it to me. I also know that he is soon to be considered for early release. Now, if you don't do as I say, I'll personally see to it that that doesn't happen. There are even ways of extending sentences if you've got the right influence. And believe me, I certainly have that.'

I stopped crying instantly. It was as if I'd been slapped hard across the face.

'Stop the car,' I said, shaking. 'I'll get out right here.'

'As you wish. But think about what I've said, Anna. I think you'll find I'm a man of my word.'

We were on the edge of town in a deserted area. The car sped away in a cloud of dust and I set off towards home. I'd walked for a good half-hour in the baking heat before a rickshaw came pedalling along beside me and I climbed gratefully into the seat. I felt drained and beaten. I could hardly think straight, but I knew Charles had the upper hand. I couldn't fight that. I came home and took a long bath, then went to lie on my bed.

I realise now that I have no choice. I could not bear my father to be in that place for a moment longer than he has to be. And perhaps Charles is right after all, even though I find it hard to accept. If I want to give my baby a chance at life perhaps it is the only thing I can do. It's impossible for me to look after a child either here or in England.

So, I find myself reconciled to Charles's plan. It will tear my heart out, I know, but I will have to go through with it.

February 5th, 1934

Manju has been looking at me with sorrowful, soulful eyes since I told her I was going to England.

'You will be careful, Memsahib,' she keeps repeating. I haven't told her why I'm going but I'm sure she suspects. 'You will come back to Kandaipur, won't you?' she has asked on a couple of occasions.

'Of course, Manju, please don't worry.' But nothing I say seems to console her.

I must stop writing this now and try to get some sleep.
I have a long day ahead of me tomorrow. In two days' time
I will be sailing away from this continent that I've grown
to love. How it has changed me. How much has happened
to me in those two short years since I arrived.

Tomorrow, I will put my trust in Charles's friend. In
Reverend Ezra Burroughs.

Connie puts down the diary, her scalp prickling as she sees Father's name written there in Anna's handwriting for the first time. She sits contemplating it, for a long time, images of her father vivid and fresh in her mind. Anna's story, the way she was used and deceived, has affected her deeply. She thinks of Charles and Donald; of how they used their power and influence to control Anna. Once again, she can't help comparing them to Father – how he controlled all those around him in a similar way, with tragic results. Now Connie understands Anna's sadness, that May night back in 1934, the desperation in her eyes, the pleas for help. Connie's hand strays to her filigree chain yet again. Thinking of that tear-stained face brings unwelcome feelings to her heart. There's pity there, but guilt too. Guilt that in some way, she too has failed Anna. And that she's failed the children too; the poor baby they found. There is no doubt in her mind now that the time has come to tell what she knows. Perhaps, in some small way, that might help to make up for her weakness in the past.

Chapter Twenty-Nine

Sarah

Sarah awakens to sunshine streaming in through the bay windows of her bedroom. The first rays of spring. Even in that half-conscious state between sleep and wakefulness she's aware that something happened last night to make her spirits sing. She feels it deep inside but for a split second, she can't place what it is. Then she rolls over and sees Matt lying there beside her, still asleep. A smile spreads across her face.

He'd come round to the house after he'd closed the restaurant yesterday evening. They'd shared a bottle of wine in front of the living room fire and had talked for hours. She'd been surprised when he started to speak about Rosie.

'You know, it's the first time I've talked about her properly to anyone,' he'd said.

'You don't have to carry on, if it doesn't feel right,' she'd said.

'No, I want to. It's been over two years, it's time.' He bent forward, staring into his glass, so that Sarah couldn't see his expression.

'There's this temptation when someone dies to put them on a pedestal, you know. To think that they were perfect, that they never did any wrong,' he began. 'I did that for a time. But Rosie wasn't perfect, far from it. She had a wild streak.'

He took a sip of wine and smiled, his eyes far away, remembering. As he went on, at times it felt to Sarah as if he was speaking to himself, as if he'd forgotten she was there.

'We met at school, you know. She was hugely popular. A magnet for friends – boys and girls alike. It was because she was a rebel. A daredevil. People wanted to be like her, only they knew she was unique. All the same they tried to copy her and follow her lead. But she had a dark side too. She had black moods, deep, deep anger. She didn't show that side of herself to everyone, not then at least, but she did to me. I wanted to protect her from herself – to help her, I suppose.

'We started dating when we were fourteen and fifteen. Child-hood sweethearts. It lasted all through school and college too. When we got married, we were crazy about each other. We could only afford a tiny studio flat, but it didn't matter to us as long as we were together.'

Sarah watches him closely, loving the warm way he's speaking about Rosie.

'She worked in a gift shop in Weirfield and I worked in a hotel in Henley. After a few years, the bistro came on the market and my dad lent us the money to buy it. It was a struggle. You know what it's like, Sarah. Difficult at the best of times. We pulled together, though. At first, anyway. But after a time I began to find I couldn't always rely on Rosie. Often she wouldn't turn up for shifts. She would sometimes get angry with customers and make a scene if things didn't go to plan. I began to suspect she was unfaithful to me too. That was devastating.'

He frowns and pauses for a while.

'How awful for you,' Sarah murmurs, watching the flames leap in the grate, feeling the warmth of Matt's body close to hers.

'When Simon came along, things got worse,' he went on, 'Rosie became severely depressed. Simon wasn't an easy baby and she found it hard to cope, right from the time he was born. It feels disloyal to say this, and I've never told anyone before, but it was almost as if she rejected him. She was so preoccupied with her own unhappiness that she had no room to nurture a child. She left most of the caring to me. I knew there was something terribly wrong with her. She was depressed and needed help. I pleaded with her to talk to the doctors about it, but she wouldn't hear of it. I didn't mind looking after Simon, but it worried and distressed me all the same.' Sarah reaches for his hand in the darkness and feels his gripping hers back as he goes on.

'Time went on. Years and years went by and Rosie's moods grew worse. She was virtually no help at all in the restaurant towards the end, and I had to hire in extra staff to replace her. But she would resent that too and make life difficult for them, so several people left. I tried to get her to go for help, but she was too proud to do that.

'"There's nothing wrong with me," she'd say. I knew she was ill, but I couldn't reach her. Then one day she disappeared. I thought she'd finally left me, like she was always threatening to – we'd been arguing a lot just before she went so I assumed she'd carried out her threat. I left it a couple of days, hoping she'd be in touch, but one day the police came to the restaurant. I'll never forget it. We had a full house and I was in the kitchen, up to my ears in it. They told me that a man walking his dog had found a body in the spinney next to the river. It was Rosie. She'd taken an overdose.'

Sarah's hand flew to her mouth. 'Oh, Matt! I'm so sorry. I had no idea she died like that.'

Matt had tears in his eyes. Sarah took his hand again and he gripped hers as he went on.

'It affected Simon really badly. He was supposed to be doing his A-levels but he couldn't face taking the exams. He's never been outgoing, and he didn't find school easy, but Rosie's death knocked him sideways. He lost all his confidence. He tried retakes the following year, but didn't do well at those. I gave him a job in the restaurant. I'm really trying to rebuild his self-esteem.'

'It must have been so hard for you,' Sarah said. 'For both of you.'

'Simon and I helped each other through it. Gradually, day by day, things began to improve. But in truth, it was only when you came along, Sarah, that I started to have moments where I could forget and actually begin to feel vaguely human again. Because of you, I'm feeling happiness for the first time since I can remember.'

Sarah slipped her arm around his shoulders and held him for a long time, feeling the rise and fall of his chest as he breathed. After a time, he turned to kiss her, tentative at first, but she found herself responding, drawing him closer. Soon, she was unbuttoning his shirt, running her hands over his chest, feeling the warmth and strength of his body against hers.

They made love there on the floor in front of the fire, with the light from the flames flickering on their bodies. To Sarah, as they moved together gently and naturally, it felt as honest and as familiar as coming home; as if they'd known one another for a lifetime, as if she already knew and loved all the contours of his body, and as if the movements they made together were as practised as if they'd been lovers since the beginning of time.

Now, she watches him sleeping in the pale light of the morning, and thinks about his words. About how he'd only begun to feel happiness again since she'd been in his life. She realises that the same is true for her. That it is only through him and through her work in the bistro that she has begun to get over the blow that Alex dealt her. She often goes hours now without even thinking of him, and she can even admit to herself to feeling her own glimmers of happiness, although her father's illness has cast a shadow over that.

At the thought of her father she gets up, kissing Matt's sleeping eyes. She pulls on her dressing gown and goes through to the bathroom.

She knows what she must do today. She owes it to her father to pursue the truth as far as she can.

She showers quickly and dresses in the bathroom. As she goes back to the bedroom, Matt is stirring. She sits down beside him and strokes his hair.

'Why are you up so early?' he asks, his voice bleary with sleep.

'I'm going round to Fairlawns this morning to see Connie.'

He puts his arms around her and pulls her to him. She resists, just a little. Is she ready for this? Last night was wonderful, but in the back of her mind lurks the fear of being hurt. She knows she must take this slowly.

'Well, good luck.' He props himself up on this elbows and kisses her. 'Let me know what happens. Shall I let myself out?'

'Yes. Just slam the back door behind you.'

She bends to kiss him again. 'Thank you for last night, Sarah,' he says, looking up into her eyes.

Chapter Thirty

Sarah

Sarah stops off at the florist on the High Street and buys a big bunch of white lilies for Connie. When she arrives at Fairlawns and asks to see her, the receptionist calls Matron.

'I'm not sure she'll want to see you, Mrs Jennings,' Matron tells her. 'She hasn't got over the shock of the other day yet.'

'I understand. That's partly why I called. I thought she might want to see a friendly face. If she'll see me, I'll try not to tire her.'

'Wait there. I'll go and have a word.'

Sarah waits in the reception area, pacing the floor. She is still glowing from her lovemaking with Matt. She feels alive for the first time in years. But she is plagued with sudden doubts about what she's doing now. What if Connie refuses to see her? And even if she does agree, what if she won't speak? But Matron is back in a matter of minutes, striding towards her, a smile on her face.

'She'll see you, Mrs Jennings. Go on through. But please don't stay too long. She isn't strong, you know.'

As Sarah enters, Connie looks tired and drawn. She's in her chair with a knitted blanket drawn up around her. Her face has a grey, pallid look that Sarah hasn't noticed before. But her eyes light up when she sees her.

'Oh, you've brought me flowers again. How thoughtful!'

'Shall I put them in water? I know what to do now.'

'If you don't mind. You have such a knack for arranging them.'

Sarah goes to the sink in the corner, takes a vase from the cupboard underneath and fills it with water.

'I'm sorry that you had such a shock last week,' she begins, turning to look at Connie. Connie remains silent, picking at her cardigan. Sarah starts to arrange the flowers on the table.

'It was such a shame that you told the police you didn't know anything about what we found in the conservatory.'

She glances at Connie, but Connie doesn't reply. Her bony fingers move up to her chain. The minutes pass. Sarah starts to think Connie is never going to speak when she looks up and bursts out, 'I wasn't going to tell *the police* anything. It's all so long ago now. No good can come of raking up the past.'

'That poor baby, Connie,' Sarah continues. 'The one who was buried. Don't you think you owe it to that baby to tell what you know? You do know something, don't you?'

Connie is shaking her head now, very slowly, and her eyes have filled with tears. She rubs them with the back of her hand.

'Perhaps, for that poor baby's sake, you'll tell *me* about what happened back then?'

Connie doesn't respond, so Sarah persists.

'I'm going to hold a funeral for the baby, Connie,' she says gently. 'Perhaps you could come along, if you're feeling well enough?'

Connie stares at her. 'No! No, I couldn't do that.'

Sarah leaves the vase of flowers on the table and goes to kneel on the floor in front of Connie's chair. She looks up at the old lady.

'You know, my own father was a foundling at the orphanage.'

Connie purses her lips and looks away.

'I mentioned it before, but you said you didn't remember. He's unwell, Connie. He really wants to know about the circumstances of his birth and I worry about him. So, I owe it to him to ask you, and you owe it to him too, to tell me what you know.'

Connie remains silent, fiddling endlessly with the chain around her neck. But Sarah senses that her words might have hit home. She leans forward and tries again.

'Please tell me what you know, Connie. My father has never forgiven his mother for abandoning him. He came back here to find out the truth, but he's drawn a complete blank. He's tried everything. He joined the local history society and looked into all the records he could find locally, including the church.' She pauses, watching Connie's face. Then she says as gently as she can, 'He even went to your house once, Connie. He spoke to someone… your sister, I think.'

Connie's eyes widen instantly, then her head goes down and Sarah can no longer see her expression. She goes on, 'She told him that there were no records in the house and that he shouldn't come back.'

Connie remains silent for a long time, her fingers still working on her necklace.

'You know,' Sarah continues, 'I found a couple of things in the old bureau that I can't make sense of. I was wondering if you might know anything about *them*?'

'What things? All my father's things went to the archives at Cartwrights. There shouldn't have been anything left.'

'There was a secret drawer under the bureau. Terry found it when we moved it to decorate.'

Connie is sitting up straight now, her back rigid. She's staring at Sarah. And more than ever before, Sarah is convinced that she does know something.

Sarah gets up from the floor and delves into her handbag. She takes out the sheaf of blank birth certificates and the ledger and hands them to Connie. Connie takes them and stares at them for a long time. She turns the pages of the ledger over and over, running her hand down the columns, puzzling over the entries.

Suddenly she looks up and her expression has changed. Her mouth is set in a determined pout and in her eyes gleams a look of defiance.

'I've learned some things,' she says, 'that have made me very angry with my father. I always tried to defend his memory, to remember the best side of him and to put everything else aside. I thought that was the right thing to do, but now I'm not so sure.'

Sarah sits down on the chair opposite Connie, her heart beating a little faster.

'It was so hard to live with my father, you know. There were so many rules to follow, and I was nothing like Mother, nothing like Evie at all. It was so difficult for me.'

'It must have been so hard for you,' Sarah says gently. 'You can tell me, you know.'

'I will in a moment. Before I begin, though, I want someone else to be here.'

'Of course. Is it Matron?'

'No, not Matron. It's another resident. His name is Tommy. We knew each other when we were young. He's the only person I've ever thought about telling these things to. I nearly did a few times, but I was too afraid of the consequences. I only wish I had done… but I wasn't strong enough. Maybe if I had, I never would have lost him.'

It takes the woman on reception a while to find Tommy. He's out strolling in the garden, getting some fresh air. When he enters Connie's room he looks flushed and healthy. Sarah notices the old light back in Connie's eyes when she looks at him.

'Sit down, Tommy,' says Connie. 'This is Sarah Jennings. She's the owner of Cedar Hall now. She's been asking about what she found in the conservatory and I'm going to tell her what I know. You deserve to know it too, Tommy. I wanted to tell you all those years ago. If only I'd had the courage…'

'I always knew there were things you were holding back,' he says. 'I thought you'd tell me in your own time, Connie, but in the end, you never got the chance.'

Tommy shakes Sarah's hand. 'I'm very pleased to meet you,' he says. His grip is strong and firm and his eyes steady.

Connie turns to Sarah. 'Tommy used to work for my father. He and I were close. But Father forced him to leave one day and we never saw each other again.'

'But why? Why did he have to leave?' asks Sarah.

Erica comes in with a tea tray and Sarah pours, passing cups to Connie and Tommy. Then she sits down and waits for Connie to begin.

Connie takes a deep breath.

'Have you ever been into the room above the coach house?' she asks Sarah.

Sarah nods, but a shiver runs through her at the thought of that filthy, abandoned room with the chilling atmosphere.

'That was my father's private room. He called it his hideaway. Father had the room done up for himself and he stopped Evie and me from ever going up there. Mother told us never to disturb him and never to question him about it. But one day something happened to pique my curiosity, and it's only now that I understand why. It was when Evie had started teaching in the schoolroom and I was still a pupil. I was coming back to the house alone after my lessons one day.'

Connie pauses and looks up at Tommy. Sarah can see the fear in her eyes, the fear and the dread that had dominated her life.

'I heard something,' she said. 'I was almost sure it was the sound of someone crying.'

Chapter Thirty-One

Connie

Connie didn't dare ask Father about the strange sounds she'd heard coming from the room above the garage that day. How could she risk provoking his anger by being so inquisitive? Hadn't he said over and over again that what went on in his hideaway was nobody's business but his own? Connie realised that she had to keep it to herself, and that she must do her best to forget about it.

A few days later, a foundling baby appeared on the doorstep of the orphanage. The housekeeper found the baby girl as she was unlocking the front door first thing one morning.

Connie saw the baby in the orphanage in the Moses basket reserved for newborns. It was tiny and could only have been a few days old. She stared down at the tiny wrinkled face, and the wide unblinking eyes staring up at her. Her heart twisted in pity for this scrap of humanity, abandoned to its fate, and for its mother too. What terrible circumstances had led her to take the decision to abandon her child? What must she have been feeling when she laid the bundle down on the step and walked away?

The baby was cared for in the orphanage among the others, but unlike the other babies, this one wasn't destined to stay at Cedar Hall for long. Father found her a home after a few months. He drove her himself, setting off with the Moses basket on the back seat of the Jaguar, along with bottles of milk for the journey.

Every few months another baby would appear on the steps. Though it was normal for new orphans to arrive, they were always brought to the orphanage by some official source; by Mr Walters the vicar from St Mary's, Doctor Peterson, or even a member of the local council, dressed in his finest suit. In those normal situations, Father would complete some paperwork and book them in as residents officially, but Connie could see he treated these foundling babies completely differently. He would take them himself for a private meeting with the local registrar – one of Father's inner circle, a man Connie had seen during smoke-filled meetings in her father's office.

It seemed odd to Connie that there was now a constant stream of foundling babies appearing on the steps of the orphanage, but Mother and Evie appeared to take it in their stride.

'Young girls in trouble must know we'll take care of those poor foundling babies and find homes for them,' Mother once said. 'Word must have got around that we can help.'

But there was something that didn't feel quite right about it to Connie. She wondered why her father chose not to get the authorities involved instead of finding these babies homes himself. But she knew she couldn't say anything, so she held her tongue. God forbid that she should even think to question Father about it.

Little by little, though, she started to see her father in a new light. She began to mull over some of the things she had accepted without question for years. She wondered again about those secretive meetings he had in his office. She also started to wonder for the first time in her life about his expensive tastes. It had never occurred to her before, she was so used to Father's extravagant ways, but once she began to think about it, it didn't seem to add up. And the more she thought about it, the stranger it seemed.

One day, everything changed.

Connie was bringing Father a cup of tea in his office. The door was slightly ajar and she was about to go in when she realised that he wasn't at his desk. Instead, he was kneeling down in front of the fireplace. The rug had been pulled back and a section of one of the floorboards had been removed and laid aside. At first, she thought he must have been mending something, but Father never mended anything. He would always call for one of the orphan boys to do that sort of thing. And there was something strange in his manner too, something furtive. Connie realised that he wasn't aware of her presence, so she just waited quietly behind the door. She watched as he put something under the floorboards, slotted the board back, covered it with the rug and stood up, dusting down his knees. She waited until he was seated at his desk, then went into the room with the tray as if she'd seen nothing.

When he was out at the orphanage the next day, she crept into the office and pulled back the rug. Her heart was in her mouth, anticipating someone discovering her. It was easy to lift up the loose board. There was a small metal box inside and to her surprise the lid opened easily. Inside were several letters addressed to her father. They were marked 'Private and Confidential'. Connie took one out and opened the envelope. She knew it was wrong and that God must be watching her, but her curiosity won out. She opened the letter and scanned it quickly.

The letter was from Joshua Cartwright, the solicitor, one of the frequent visitors at Father's meetings. It was very formal and was about some sort of service that Ezra had agreed to perform for one of Joshua's clients, who was apparently coming from India specially. It didn't say what exactly, but it discussed payment to Ezra in two tranches, the sum of five hundred pounds. At the end, the letter emphasised the importance of discretion and confidentiality in the matter. There was a silver key in there too, hidden under the rest of the letters in the bottom of the box.

Then Connie heard footsteps in the hall and shoved the letter back.

Connie would lie awake at night going over and over it in her mind. She would watch Father as he went about his daily business, wondering what was really going on. She knew about his missionary days in India. She knew he still had letters from people he'd known out there, gifts too. Only the previous week a box had arrived, containing some exquisite silk paintings. Connie wondered what kind of service Father could offer someone from India who was willing to pay five hundred pounds. It was such a huge sum.

Connie knew she couldn't ask Mother. It was out of the question. She tried to pluck up courage to talk to Evie about it, but she could never find the right words to broach the subject. Evie was so much like Mother: they both guarded Father fiercely, wouldn't brook any suggestion of criticism of him. Connie had the feeling she wouldn't understand, but she just had to talk about it to someone. In the end she began by asking Evie if she knew what Father did in his hideaway. Evie just stared at her with horrified eyes and shook her head.

'We mustn't speak of those things, Connie,' she said. 'That's Father's private business, as you well know. Please don't mention it to me again.'

But a few months later, something else happened. Connie had been watching the coach house carefully, and one rainy night, when she'd been lingering in the yard, she met the young woman on the coach house steps.

Her long dark hair was loose around her shoulders, her fringe, already wet, plastered to her forehead. Connie could see that she'd been crying and that her eyes were filled with fear.

'Who are you?' Connie managed to stammer.

'My name is Anna,' replied the girl. 'Anna Foster. Please don't tell him that you've seen me. I'm not supposed to come out of the room.'

Connie stared at her blankly. Why could this young woman possibly be staying up in the room, and for what earthly reason was she forbidden to come out?

'I'm not supposed to make a sound,' the young woman whispered, and as their eyes met, there was a sound from the room upstairs. It was unmistakeable. The sound of a tiny baby stirring in its sleep.

'Why are you here?' Connie asked, sitting down on the step and motioning the young woman to sit beside her. As Anna sat down, she suddenly started to cry. Her whole body was racked with great sobs. Connie put her arms around her slim shoulders and tried to comfort her. The sobbing went on for several minutes, but after a while, Anna began to speak.

'I came here to have my baby,' she said, in a faltering voice.

Connie was shocked, but the words had the dreadful ring of truth about them. All she could do was to stroke Anna's hand and shoulders, doing her best to comfort her. When Anna had finally stopped crying, she began to speak again.

'I can hardly bear to leave my baby behind, but it's the only thing I can do. The Reverend Burroughs has promised to find him a good home when he is six months old. He says that until then, he will be cared for in the orphanage.'

Again, she broke down, her shoulders shaking with her sobs.

'It will tear my heart out to leave, to go back to India without my baby. That's where I live, you see.'

'I'm so, so sorry,' Connie kept saying, squeezing Anna's hand. She felt helpless to comfort her. But Anna's tears gradually slowed and eventually she looked at Connie.

'You know, perhaps you could help me?'

Connie's scalp tingled at the thought. What did she mean?

'These last few days I've been watching you from the window. You've got a kind face. The first time I saw you it struck me that you might be the one to turn to for help. When I came out just now, I was feeling desperate. I was praying that you might be here. You're my last hope.'

'I'm not sure I can. What do you want me to do?'

'Perhaps you could write to me in India? You could keep an eye on my baby and let me know how he's getting on. Is he happy, is he growing strong, has he smiled yet? And when he goes away to his new home, you could let me know where he's gone to.'

Anna had dried her tears now and seemed cheered at this new idea. Connie was already terrified at the thought of disobeying Father in this way, even if what he had done was very wrong. If he were to find out! Just the thought of his anger made her mouth go dry.

Suddenly Anna was on her feet. She took Connie's hand and pulled her up the steps and into the room. Connie hadn't been inside for years and was shocked to see a bed in there and a cot beside it.

'Look!' Connie peered over the sides of the cot and there was a tiny baby, fast asleep. He was perfect in every way, his little face crumpled and his chin dimpled.

'You will help me, won't you?' Anna asked, her eyes pleading.

'Of course,' Connie said, melting at the sight of that tiny, helpless creature.

Anna scribbled her address on a piece of paper and handed it to Connie.

'Wait,' she said. 'There's something else.'

She went over to the writing table under the window and returned holding a little book bound in blue leather.

'It's my diary,' she said. 'Give this to him when the time is right.' She handed Connie the book. 'It might help him understand why I've done what I've done.'

A few days after Connie's night-time encounter with Anna, another foundling baby appeared on the steps of the orphanage. A baby boy this time. Now, Connie knew where all these 'foundlings' had been coming from. Of course, her father took him in, just as he had all the others.

The baby stayed in the orphanage for several months. He was a beautiful child, with dark, sparkling eyes and dimpled cheeks.

Connie was charmed by him in a way that was quite different from the way she'd felt about the other babies. She kept seeing his mother in those dancing eyes.

Over the next few weeks she sent Anna two letters. In them she told her all about the baby's daily routine, and about his development. How he started to smile, to grip people's fingers. As a precaution, Connie told Anna not to write back to her at Cedar Hall, worried that Father would intercept the letter. She asked her to write to Post Restante at the post office instead. A letter arrived within a month and she was stunned by the contents.

Dear Connie,

Thank you for writing to me about my baby's progress. I have been missing him so much, I am finding life unbearable without him. I was distraught for the whole journey home and hardly came out of my cabin, not being able to face the world.

I have only been back at home in Kandaipur a week, but I've decided to come straight back to England again to fetch him. It will mean defying my husband and living a life of poverty in England by myself, but I'm prepared to face that. I need you to respond to me and say you will help me. As soon as I get your letter, I will book my passage and will get the next P&O liner out of Bombay to Southampton. Please write to me, Connie. I know you owe me nothing, but I could tell in the short time we spoke that you are a good, kind person. I'll need you to take him out of the orphanage and bring him to Weirfield station to meet me when I arrive. I will take him straight away on the next train. I have it all planned out. Will you do that for me, Connie? Please think of the baby and how he needs his mother.

*

Connie's heart sank when she read those words. She stared at that letter for a long time. Writing to Anna to tell her of the baby's progress was one thing, but actively removing him from the orphanage and stealing him away was quite another. What would Father do to her if she did that? She couldn't even begin to imagine his anger. He would disown her. He would throw her out of the house and refuse to speak to her again. She would lose her family and her livelihood. Besides, she knew that her father was likely to be looking for a home for him already. None of the foundlings had ever stayed in the orphanage for more than six months. What if he took the baby to his new home while Anna was on her way back to England? Her journey would be pointless, and she would be left distraught.

Not being able to face the consequences, Connie hid Anna's letter away and tried to forget about it. But every time she saw the baby in the orphanage nursery, she caught another glimpse of his mother in those shining dark eyes. It tore her heart out to think that it was in her power to reunite them and yet she was doing nothing about it. How could she fail to fulfil a mother's wish to be with her child? At night, she would take the letter out and reread it.

A few weeks went past, and Connie knew that time was running out for Anna; if she didn't act soon, Father would find the baby a home and he would be whisked away.

She realised that this was her opportunity to do something worthwhile, and that she now had to face up to the reality of what her father was doing up in the hideaway. Now was her chance to stand up to him and against what he was doing.

One night, Connie was wide awake, Evie sound asleep in the bed across the room. She heard a noise coming from across the yard and the hairs on the back of her neck stood on end. It was happening again. There were cries coming from the coach house. She crept over to the window and saw that there were lights on in there. As she watched, she saw someone emerge from the side door. It was the unmistakeable figure of her father. As he came down the steps, she could see that he was carrying a bundle of rags. He crossed the garden and came into the house. After a few minutes Connie heard him coming up towards her room. She dashed back to bed, pretending she was asleep, although her heart was hammering against her ribs. She was terrified he would realise that she was awake.

But he left and went downstairs. After a few minutes she heard thumping sounds coming from the conservatory. They were sounds of digging, of a spade in earth. Connie was almost paralysed with fear, but she knew she had to find out what was going on. She crept downstairs and hid herself in the kitchen, watching through the glass door. She watched in silent horror as her father removed a couple of tiles and went on to dig a hole in the conservatory floor right in front of the door.

Connie was aghast by what she had seen, revolted and appalled. The next day, she could hardly face her father. She couldn't meet his eye. How could he have done such a dreadful thing in the middle of the night, then sit at breakfast munching toast and reading the morning paper as if nothing had happened? Watching him, she suddenly saw what a sham his life was. From that moment on, she began to despise him almost as much as she feared him.

After breakfast that day. she went up to her room and wrote to Anna to say that she would do as she asked, but Anna must come quickly or the baby might have already been taken to his new home. Anna wrote back by return to say she was coming on the next ship and that she would contact Connie as soon as she was in England.

Over the following weeks, Connie prepared herself for the repercussions of what she was about to do. She knew she would have to leave home when her father found out what she'd done. Through the classified ads, she found out about cheap lodgings in London and started to look for a job there. By this time, she was a qualified schoolteacher, just like Evie.

She also decided to practise what she would do when Anna arrived. She started taking her baby out in the pram for walks. Nobody minded that; some of the staff would take the babies out for fresh air in the afternoons. A couple of times she even went to the station to meet the London train. She stood on the platform as it puffed into the station, imagining Anna getting down from one of the carriages and running towards her.

But Anna never came. Weeks went by. Connie checked the liners arriving in Southampton from India in the newspaper, and after each one arrived, she expected a letter. She went to the post office every day to check. But there were no more letters.

Anna never wrote to Connie again.

One day, a month or so later, Connie went to the nursery and the baby was gone. She was devastated. If she had known, at least she could have slipped the diary into his belongings. When she asked Father where the baby had gone and who his new family were, he refused to tell her.

Chapter Thirty-Two

Connie

Now Connie picks up a blue book from her bedside cupboard.

'This is Anna's diary. I've kept it all these years.'

Then she fumbles at her neck and lifts the filigree pendant on the chain to show Sarah and Tommy. 'And this is the key. She gave it to me that night too, and I've worn it ever since.'

Connie takes a breath, wipes a tear from her eye with a trembling hand.

'I felt hopeless and weak after everything that happened then. I knew I should challenge my father about what he was doing but I never could pluck up the courage. I felt so alone, so powerless. It was as if I was a shell of a girl, creeping through my days like a ghost. I knew how weak I was, and I was ashamed, but paralysed at the same time. I couldn't do anything except pray. Two or three years later, Tommy here came into my life.'

Connie smiles at Tommy, who reaches out and takes her hand. Sarah smiles at the sudden intimacy and at the tender way they look at each other.

'I would sometimes bring Tommy a cup of tea in the garage and we used to talk—'

'It was more than that, Connie,' Tommie breaks in. 'We were sweethearts.'

Sarah notices a spot of colour appear on each of Connie's wrinkled cheeks. Her wet eyes twinkle with memories.

'Of course we were. We used to walk out together, didn't we?' says Connie. 'We used to spend as much time as we could in each other's company.'

'Our favourite stroll was along the riverbank,' Tommy chips in.

Connie pauses and she and Tommy exchange shy glances.

'I almost told you back then, Tommy,' Connie says, 'the things I've just told you and Sarah. I knew I could trust you. You were the first person I ever thought about telling. Each time we were together, I had it on the tip of my tongue, but I could never quite pluck up the courage to say the words. The moment never seemed right. And then you left. Suddenly. Without a word.'

'I was forced to go,' Tommy says bitterly, looking down. 'Forced by the Reverend Burroughs.'

He turns towards Sarah and, in a halting voice, tells her about discovering Ezra Burroughs with the body of a young woman on the back seat of the Jaguar.

Sarah feels the blood draining from her face.

'But that's dreadful,' she says. 'Do you think that Ezra Burroughs killed the young woman?'

Tommy shakes his head. 'I thought he might have done for a while, but even back then, I didn't actually believe that was what had happened. Knowing what I do now though, I think it was more likely that she died in childbirth, or perhaps she was in despair and killed herself up in that room. Perhaps something went very wrong and the Reverend Burroughs didn't know what to do. He had no medical training, just some experience in the field as a missionary.'

'I'm sure she must have died in childbirth,' says Connie. 'When I think back, I am almost certain that another foundling appeared shortly after the news about that young woman's death. I didn't associate them at the time because I didn't know that she had anything to do with Weirfield.'

'How many foundlings do you think there were altogether, Connie?' asks Sarah.

'I'm not sure. A few each year for several years. There was only a trickle during the war and it stopped completely a couple of years after that. Perhaps it was something to do with Indian independence – the law was tightened up and maybe Father thought he'd be running too much of a risk.'

Sarah looks from Connie to Tommy, at their lined faces, thinking about what they lost. She thinks about Anna too. Why ever didn't she return for her baby? Did she have a change of heart? Did she fall ill? Did someone stop her? There must be some explanation.

But there's one thing burning at the back of Sarah's mind. She knows she has to ask, she needs to know the answer, but she's afraid that it won't be what she wants to hear.

'Do you think that my father could be Anna's son?' she asks tentatively, breaking the silence.

Connie shakes her head.

'I don't think so. Didn't you say your father's birthday was September? I distinctly remember it being spring when Anna came. She came outside in a thin nightgown and although it was raining and she was shivering, it wasn't cold.'

'I asked you this before, but you weren't sure about it. Do you know if your father kept any records of the babies?'

'All the paperwork is in the archives at Cartwrights. I've never seen it. I've never wanted to see it.'

'That ledger I showed you earlier? The one with the numbers in columns. Do you have any idea what that means?'

Connie shakes her head again.

'Do you think it would be possible to go along to Cartwrights and look at your father's papers? I know it's a lot to ask, but perhaps there's a chance that we might be able to find out something about my father's mother from them.'

Connie is silent for a while. She closes her eyes and Sarah wonders if she has drifted off. She must be tired after the emotional effort of telling her story.

'Connie?'

Connie sits up, takes a sip of her tea. 'I've never looked at Father's papers because I was afraid of what I might find. After Tommy left, I gave up on life. I gave up even thinking about questioning Father about what was happening in the coach house and about the foundlings. I decided to accept it all, like Mother and Evie did. That's how I coped with it; by shutting down my doubts, by thinking about Father's good side.

'After he died, I tried my best to carry on with that. I didn't want to know anything about that sordid business, I wanted to close the chapter. That's why I had the study carpeted, so I wasn't tempted to look under the floorboards for the metal box of letters. I didn't want any reminders of what had happened. That's why I sealed up the cupboard with his presents from India inside. I had this feeling that it was wrong to throw them away altogether. I was still afraid of him, long after his death. It's why I never looked inside his bureau. I wanted to rewrite history, I suppose. To preserve the good side of Father and shut out the rest. But I can see now that this was wrong.' Connie pauses and takes a deep breath. Then she looks from Sarah to Tommy. 'I think I'm ready to look at Father's papers now. I'll ask Matron to call Peter Cartwright on Monday morning and make an appointment.'

'If you're sure?'

'Of course. I'm quite sure, I'm not going to protect him any more.'

Chapter Thirty-Three

Sarah

Before Sarah leaves Fairlawns, she asks Connie if she minds if she takes up the carpet in the study and looks for the box of letters under the floorboards.

'There might be some information in those letters that will help us in the search for information about my father's mother,' she says.

'If you think it will help,' says Connie. 'You know everything there is to know now. I don't have anything to hide.'

It's mid-afternoon when Sarah enters Cedar Hall. The sky outside is brooding and the rooms are dark and full of shadows. Connie's story has affected her so profoundly that she can feel the malevolent presence of Ezra in every room. She stands in the doorway to the dining room and pictures the Burroughs family sitting down and saying grace before eating a sparse breakfast. In the living room she can see them kneeling to pray before the fire. When she enters the study, she can almost smell cigar smoke and whisky on the air and hear the booming voices of Ezra's associates, laughing and joking.

She's not ready to tell her father that she's going to Cartwrights. She doesn't want to risk raising his hopes so close to the time he has to go into hospital. She's decided to keep it all to herself until she has some concrete news.

Sarah fetches the toolbox that Terry leaves at weekends and takes it into the study. She kneels in front of the fireplace and, placing the chisel under the edge of the carpet, prises out the nails that are holding it down, one by one. Soon, she has removed enough to be able to pull a large section of the carpet and underlay back. She scans the floorboards. There is one that is smaller than the rest and looks loose. She slips the edge of the chisel under it and prises it upwards. It comes out easily and she lays it aside.

She peers into the void and sure enough, lodged between the floor joists is a black metal box. She pulls it out and, just as Connie had found all those decades ago, it opens easily. It is packed with letters. As she takes the bundle out, there's a chink of metal. She peers into the box. There is a silver key there. She recalls Connie mentioning it. She picks it up and examines it, but there is no clue as to what it might be for. It is far too big for the lock of the metal box. She slips it into a zip-up section in her handbag, making a mental note to see if it fits any of the door locks in the house, although it appears rather small for that.

Then she turns to the pack of letters. She pulls one out, eases it out of its envelope and holds it up to the light with trembling fingers. Dated May 1933, it's from Joshua Cartwright to Ezra, and speaks about payment of five hundred pounds for 'the facility we discussed'. Joshua mentions that his client lives in India and urges that his client's name 'shall remain confidential throughout our correspondence'.

She places it back inside the envelope and takes out another letter. It's along the same lines, but dated a few months later, and this time there is no mention of India. She reads four or five more similar letters, all from Joshua Cartwright.

But there are some other letters in the box that are in different handwriting. She looks at one of the envelopes and sees that the stamps are Indian. This one is dated December 1933, and is from a Charles Perry. It asks about Ezra's 'discreet service' and mentions a friend who finds herself in a predicament and in need of his services.

There is a later letter from the same source, in which Charles Perry expresses sincere gratitude for Ezra's offer of help. It ends with the words:

I am also sending, under cover of this letter, a watch, as a token of my sincere gratitude to you for this service.

A chill of recognition runs through Sarah when she reads those words. She puts the letter down and hurries over to the shelves. She takes down the gold watch that she discovered when she opened up the cupboard. When she turns it over, sure enough there is the inscription: TO EZRA, WITH HEARTFELT THANKS, YOUR DEVOTED FRIEND, CHARLES PERRY.

She places the letters back inside the tin, and as she does so, she notices something about them. A number is scrawled on the corner of each envelope. Both the numbers on the envelopes from Charles Perry have the number five in a circle on them. Sarah stares at them, frowning. What can that mean? Perhaps the archives in Cartwrights will shed some light on it.

She glances at her watch. It's almost time to go over to her father's. She'd said she would go early today because he said he wanted to get a good night's sleep before his hospital appointment tomorrow. She goes through to the kitchen to make a cup of tea and her phone rings. Glancing at the screen, she sees that it is Judith Marshall. As she answers, she realises that she's hardly thought about Alex or the divorce for several days.

'I've got some news for you,' says Judith. 'Unless you've heard it from your husband already?'

'No, I haven't heard from him for weeks. What is it?'

'He's signed the divorce papers and he's finally agreed on a figure for him to buy you out of the business.'

'Thank goodness,' Sarah breathes. Finally, the ties with Alex will be cut. After she puts the phone down, she sits for a few minutes, letting it all sink in, examining her feelings.

She's been waiting for this moment for a long time, expecting it to be as if a huge weight has been lifted from her shoulders.

Oddly, it doesn't feel that way at all. Is it because soon she will no longer have any ties to the restaurant she poured so much love and energy into? Or is it because her focus has now shifted to Connie and her father? Without realising it, perhaps in her mind she's already moved on.

Chapter Thirty-Four

Sarah

Connie and Tommy are waiting in the reception area when Sarah arrives at Fairlawns. They're standing side by side and both look apprehensive. Tommy is wearing a battered three-piece suit and Connie is dressed in an old-fashioned brown coat and sturdy lace-up shoes. She is wearing a felt hat with a decorated band. Sarah is touched that they have made so much effort for their outing to the solicitors' office, but then it occurs to her that they might have dressed up for each other. How comfortable they look together, even though they have only recently met up again after almost seventy years apart.

Connie is able to walk now without her Zimmer frame, but leans heavily on Sarah's arm as she guides her to the car. They both choose to sit in the back. Sarah drives them the half-mile or so to Cartwrights and stops on the yellow line outside while she helps them out of the car.

Peter Cartwright meets them in reception. He looks shifty and ill at ease and Sarah knows it's because of the tension between him and Connie. Peter should have had Connie's best interests at heart. Trying to sell Cedar Hall to developers was the opposite of that. He seems suitably deferential towards Connie now as he helps her down a narrow flight of stairs from the reception area to the basement. Sarah and Tommy follow. It smells of damp and the mustiness of generations of forgotten paperwork.

Peter leads them along a passage and into a small room filled with filing cabinets.

'All your father's papers are here,' he says, pointing to two drawers. 'I've unlocked the drawers for you. There's also a deposit box stored separately, but I'm afraid the key to that has been lost. We could find a way of opening it, if needs be. It's there, on top of the cabinet.'

'There's no need for that for the moment, thank you, Peter,' says Connie and gives him a curt nod as if to dismiss him.

'All right. I'll leave you to it, then,' he says and he retreats. They hear his footsteps on the stairs.

'You look first, my dear,' Connie says to Sarah. 'Your eyes are sharper than mine.'

Sarah pulls open the top drawer of the filing cabinet and peers inside.

There's a pile of hardback notebooks in there and she takes them out one by one and scans them quickly before passing them to Connie. They all relate to the business of the orphanage: lists of household purchases, payments, bills, registers of children's names and dates of birth. In his work life, Ezra Burroughs was clearly a meticulous and careful administrator. Beneath the books there are piles of buff files held together by treasury tags, full of correspondence, which Sarah flicks through. She has a sinking feeling as she works through the piles. There is nothing here after all. This all relates to the day-to-day running of Cedar Hall.

Connie is looking at the books that Sarah passes to her, holding the writing close to her eyes and peering.

'Anything here? I'm finding it hard to see all of this.'

'I don't think so,' says Sarah, shutting the drawer. 'Let's look in the next drawer.'

More ledgers and files of registers, bills and accounts for Cedar Hall are piled inside the second drawer. Sarah goes through them one by one, her disappointment growing by the minute.

Connie is watching her.

'Nothing there?' she asks. 'Why don't you ask Peter to open the deposit box?'

'I don't think there's any need to call him. I wonder if this key might fit it. The one that was in the box under the floorboards. I brought it along just in case.'

Sarah takes the silver key out of her bag and tries it in the deposit box. It's a perfect fit.

The lid is stiff, but after a few attempts, it opens with a jerk.

There are two things inside the box – a brown leather-bound ledger with Ezra's handwriting on the front cover on a white label, stating 'Private and Confidential', and a large brown envelope.

Sarah holds her breath as she opens the envelope and reaches inside. There is a letter, with the address of another orphanage at the top. This one is in Reading and the letter is from the Superintendent there: Edward Bland. The date on this letter is much earlier than the others: 10 February 1916.

'Why don't you read it out?' asks Connie, leaning forward, her beady eyes on the letter. So, Sarah begins to read, but as she continues, her voice starts to falter as she realises the implications of what she is revealing.

Ezra,

I received your letter yesterday and I have given its contents considerable thought. You and I have been associates long enough for me to know that you mean what you say; that you are perfectly capable of carrying out your threat to report my minor financial indiscretions to the appropriate authorities. My reputation would be ruined and my family destitute if any of this were to come out.

I understand that you have an unusual request for me to fulfil in return for your silence. You would like me to send you two babies or young children for you to bring up as your own children — you and your wife being unable to conceive. There are two such children I have identified as suitable. Two little girls from different families. One is coming up to a *year old (Constance), and the other is three (Evelyn). Unlike many of the children here, they have no living relatives at all, and no one who takes an interest in either of them. It won't be difficult for me to say to the staff here that they are being transferred to another orphanage.*

I can bring them over to Cedar Hall at your convenience and I trust that this other matter will go no further.

Your faithful servant, Edward.

Sarah stops, feeling the colour draining from her face. She looks at Connie, who is staring at her, her brow furrowed, her eyes uncomprehending.

'It's unbelievable,' says Tommy, shaking his head slowly.

'I'm so sorry, Connie. That's shocking news,' Sarah says, kneeling in front of her, taking her hand. Connie shakes her head and is silent for a long time. She screws her eyes up and Sarah can see her mouth working as if she is trying not to cry. At last she speaks.

'It explains a great deal,' she says quietly. 'I always thought Evie and I were too different to be sisters. Not just physically, but our temperaments too. I understand why now.'

'It must be a dreadful shock,' says Sarah, squeezing her hand. Connie looks at her.

'To know that Father wasn't my flesh and blood? That's a relief at least…'

'You're very brave,' Sarah says. 'Would you like to go home now?' Connie shakes her head.

'We need to get to the bottom of all this,' she says, her eyes resolute. 'What's in that book? Why don't you open it up?'

'If you're quite sure…'

Sarah opens up the ledger. Inside, only a few of the pages are written on. The first column is narrow and contains numbers. Beside each number are written names. Sarah scans them and her heart stops when she sees 'King'. That's her father's surname and was her own name before she married Alex. It is beside the number five. Shock waves course through her, seeing it here in black and white. She thinks back to the letters she found in the deposit box under the floorboards. Number five was written on the letters from Charles Perry. Surely that meant they were connected?

'I think this has something to do with the foundlings,' she tells Connie and Tommy. 'All the envelopes in the box under the floorboards were marked with a number. And there are numbers here, in the first column. Look…' She shows the book to Connie, who peers through her glasses.

'But that doesn't really tell us anything, does it? Nothing about the foundlings themselves,' Connie says.

Footsteps sound on the stairs and Peter Cartwright's head appears round the door.

'How are you getting on? Need any assistance?'

'Peter, do you think there might be some other papers from my father anywhere? Letters? Accounts? Anything from the nineteen-thirties?' Connie asks, her voice a little frosty.

'All his archives are here, Miss Burroughs.'

'You're absolutely sure?'

'Unless you'd be interested in letters he wrote to my own grandfather, Joshua. Joshua kept all his letters from Ezra Burroughs in a special locked drawer. I looked through them once. It is almost as if he kept them for a purpose, for some sort of protection perhaps.'

'We'd love to see them. If you don't mind, of course,' says Sarah.

Peter leads them through a passageway into a room at the end of the cellar. This room is lined with locked wooden drawers with brass handles. Peter produces a bunch of keys and opens a corner drawer near the bottom. He lifts out a bunch of letters held together with pink ribbon.

'Take your pick,' he says.

The letters are all in a similar vein, about money and arrangements. They date from 1932 until 1940. They speak in euphemisms, never once alluding to birth, to babies or adoption. As Sarah reads through them, she begins to feel disappointed again. She is almost at the bottom of the pile when one letter catches her eye. This one doesn't speak in euphemisms, it tackles the subject head-on.

It is dated June 1934.

Dear Joshua,

I have to inform you that there has been a slight delay in delivery at my end. The last visitor was unsuccessful. It resulted in a fatality, I'm afraid. One I have dealt with appropriately. If your clients could wait a further two months or so, I expect a further visitor to my premises in early September.

Sarah reads the letter out loud to Connie and Tommy. Their eyes widen.

'The fatality must mean the baby,' Sarah says. 'The one he buried under the conservatory. Was there another foundling within another couple of months?'

Connie closes her eyes and thinks for a few moments. 'I think so, yes. Around the time that Anna's baby went. Shortly after that, there was another foundling. I'm almost sure.'

Then Sarah turns to the final letter in the drawer. This one speaks in even more explicit terms. She unfolds it and scans the words.

Dear Joshua,

Please inform your client that there is a discrepancy between the date they will see on the birth certificate and the actual date of birth. That is nothing to worry about. It is only a few months and as the baby grows older will not matter at all. It is done like that in order to ensure there is no public record of the correct date of birth, to prevent it from being traced back to the mother. Remember, she has paid for complete confidentiality. Your clients will understand this, I'm sure, as they also have paid for the confidential nature of this unique transaction.

'Look at this!' she says to Connie, passing her the letter.

Connie reads the letter slowly, holding it up close.

'So, what does that mean?' she asks.

'I think I know. Look at this.'

Sarah puts the letters down on the table and rummages in her bag. She has brought the book that she found in the hidden drawer under the bureau. She opens it up and looks at one of the pages, its column of single numbers beside what – she realises now – are dates. She runs her finger down the list to number five. She looks up at Connie, her eyes shining.

'I know what these are. These are dates. Look beside number five. There is one date – 5534 – and in the second column another date – 5934. I didn't realise they were dates before because he's left the full stops out to make it even more confusing.'

'So…' says Connie slowly.

'This is it, Connie,' Sarah says, her voice full of excitement. 'The first column is the real date of birth, the second one the one on the birth certificate. Like he says in the letter, the difference is to remove any trace of the birth back to the mother and back to his room above the coach house. So, if we look at the dates beside number five – which the other ledger says goes with "King" – it shows that my father was registered as having been born on the fifth of September 1934, but that his real date of birth was the fifth of May 1934.'

'May 1934,' murmurs Connie. 'The date that Anna came to Cedar Hall. So, your father is Anna's child.'

Sarah nods at her, but she can't speak. For a moment she is overcome with emotion.

'Would you do something for me, my dear?' Connie asks after a pause.

'Of course,' says Sarah, fumbling in her handbag for her handkerchief.

'Next time you see your father, would you give him Anna's diary?'

Chapter Thirty-Five

Sarah

As Sarah pulls up on the drive of her father's house, her mind is a jumble of emotions. She's brimming with excitement at the news that Anna Foster was her father's birth mother. But her joy is tinged with anxiety. How will he react to the news about Anna? Will it be too much for him this particular morning? He'll be ready for her to take him into hospital for his tests, feeling anxious and probably in a low mood. It might not be the right time for such momentous news, but how can she possibly keep it to herself? He's been waiting his whole life for this. He needs to know straight away.

She sees him wave from the kitchen window as she walks towards the house. Then he appears at the front door, dressed in his coat.

'Are you coming in?' he asks. 'I thought we'd be going straight off to the hospital. But if you want a coffee, there's time.'

'There's no need to make coffee. I've just had one,' she says, kissing him. 'But could we sit down for a few minutes? I came a bit early, I've got something to tell you.'

'Not bad news, I hope,' he says, frowning. 'Something to do with Alex?'

'No, Dad. It's nothing like that. Can we go through into the kitchen for a few minutes?'

'It all sounds very ominous. What's it all about?' he says, following her through and sitting down at the table.

Sarah sits down opposite him. Her heart thumping, she pulls the blue diary out of her bag.

'This is for you, Dad.'

He picks it up slowly and stares at the front cover.

'What's this? "Anna's Diary"?' he says, puzzled. 'Who's Anna, Sarah?'

Sarah leans forward and looks into his eyes.

'I think she was your mother, Dad.'

His eyes widen and colour rushes to his cheeks, 'My mother? You mean my real mother?'

'Yes, Dad. Your real mother.'

Chapter Thirty-Six

Sarah

The night train from Mumbai to Kandaipur rattles across the inky dark plain. Sarah twists and turns on the top bunk in the compartment, unable to get comfortable. She leans over the rail and looks at her father on the bunk below. He's sound asleep, his mouth open, snoring lightly. She smiles. How peaceful he looks.

The recent cancer treatment has been more successful than anyone could have hoped, his remission spurred on by his new desire to journey to India. 'I'd like to go over there and see where she lived, Sarah. Perhaps find her grave. Before I go.'

A week before they set off, they attended the funeral of the unnamed baby at the local crematorium. Sarah, Matt, Sarah's father, Connie and Tommy were the only people there.

Sarah read out a poem she'd found on the internet called 'Small Elegy', and Connie read a passage from the Bible. As Connie stepped forward to the podium, Sarah held her breath. Would Connie be able to go through with it? She'd been reluctant to come, but Tommy had insisted. She looked very frail, a tiny figure in a winter coat that looked a little too large for her withered frame, her face drowned by the rim of her felt hat. But when she turned and faced the small gathering, her face was composed and her eyes bright. She held her chin up and read in a clear strong voice; the voice of someone who had spent a lifetime delivering Bible readings. She sounded like someone who had finally been set free.

'Mark, Chapter 10, verse 13 to 16,' she announced. 'And they were bringing children to him, that he might touch them; and the disciples rebuked them. But when Jesus saw it he was indignant, and said to them, "Let the children come to me, do not hinder them; for to such belongs the Kingdom of God. Truly, I say to you, whoever does not receive the Kingdom of God like a child shall not enter it", and he took them in his arms and blessed them, laying his hands upon them.'

The next day, Matt had driven them to Heathrow. As they said goodbye beside the check-in desk, he'd held her close to him and said gently, 'Come back to me, Sarah, won't you?'

'Of course I will. You know that. Why wouldn't I?'

'You know, I have to pinch myself every time I look at you. I always worry that I might wake up and find out it was just a dream. If you don't come back, it *will* just have been a dream.'

'It's not a dream,' she'd said, kissing him.

'And you'll think about what I asked?'

'Of course I will.'

She savoured his loving words on the long, uncomfortable flight from Heathrow to Mumbai. Matt had asked her to marry him.

'I love you, Sarah. I want to be with you always. You don't have to say anything now, just think about it while you're away.'

She had thought about it constantly on the journey, but she'd also thought about Alex and the letter that had been waiting for her on the mat when she'd got home from visiting her father in hospital one day. With dread in her heart, she'd ripped it open.

Dear Sarah,

I feel I owe you some explanations now that the divorce has gone through. I don't want you to go on thinking that I cheated on you for the rest of your life. The fact was, I was paying Jemma because she was blackmailing me. She'd somehow found out about Jack investing in the business and threatened to go to the police if I didn't pay her off.

I've come clean with the police now, Sarah. I've told them everything — about Jack using the business to launder money and about the blackmail. I told them in return for my freedom. I know I was wrong and I made so many mistakes. Perhaps this is too much to ask, but I hope that one day you'll stop being angry with me and perhaps even begin to forgive me?

She'd poured herself a glass of wine and reread the letter again and again. She asked herself: if she'd known that Alex and Jemma weren't actually lovers, would she have walked out on him in the first place? It was impossible to say, but lying on her bunk on the train now, looking back on everything, she knows that she's glad she left him. The Alex she thought she knew and loved had disappeared a long time ago. She wonders when he changed. Gradually, imperceptibly over the years. It's taken everything that has happened over the past few months to reveal to her what he really is.

Still, sleep does not come, so Sarah takes up Anna's diary, turns to the final pages and begins to read by the meagre flickering light above her bunk.

Bombay, February 7th, 1934

I stood at the rail, absorbing the frenetic activity on the quayside as the SS Neuralia cast off from Victoria Dock. The deck shuddered beneath my feet from the vibrations of the great engines. The ship began to move, and the stretch of murky water between the grey stones of the dock wall and the white steel hull of the liner gradually widened. Smoke from the funnels mingled on the steamy air with the familiar smells of India: spices and cooking and drains.

Other passengers, jostling beside me at the rails, were waving and exchanging farewells with people on the docks.

I had no one to wave to on the quayside. I felt so alone, a world apart from all those noisy, friendly, normal people. To them I might have appeared self-possessed with my carefully applied lipstick, my linen suit and a solar topee shading my face. Inside I felt far from it. Although my eyes were dry, there was a dull ache in my heart.

I stayed there by the rails as the ship gathered speed along the seafront with a deafening blast of its horn, past the great arched edifice of the Gateway to India, and out across the bay towards the Arabian Sea. People were still waving their hankies and shouting. The docks became a blur against the backdrop of the city, its white colonial buildings crowding the seafront, lining the semicircle of the bay. Gradually, the buildings and then the hills behind the city melded into the misty blue of the Western Ghats.

The other passengers drifted away, to the bars and restaurants, or to their cabins. As the ship gradually put distance between itself and land I stood there alone, enjoying the cool sea breeze on my face after the sweltering heat of the docks, transfixed by the parting with the land I'd grown to love. The mountains and the whole land mass of India slowly became enveloped in a blue-grey mist, until it was just a smudge on the horizon, receding into a thin grey line. All there was to look at then were the twin furrows of white water left by the ship's propellers, and the seabirds wheeling and crying in its wake.

I kept reminding myself how short a time it was since I'd stood at an identical spot on another liner, sailing in the opposite direction. On that day, barely two years ago, I'd been entranced as I watched the coast of India and its blue mountains emerge from the haze, and the great city of Bombay come closer, revealing its detail to me minute by minute as my long voyage from England drew to a close. I'd had butterflies in my stomach, knowing I was about to discover a new exotic land; that I was on the brink of something truly wonderful.

How I'd changed from that naive, impressionable girl who'd stepped off that liner. I hardly recognised myself as the same person. And what a mess I'd made of things; an unutterable, stinking mess.

The words Aunt Nora had said to me during my first month on the subcontinent echoed in my mind. *You need to be very careful in India, Anna. You don't know its ways. Things often aren't what they might first seem here.'* I hadn't heeded what she said – I thought I knew better.

I fingered the letter in my pocket and resisted the urge to slip it out and read it. I knew its contents off by heart anyway. I'd read it so many times that the words in their flowing, flamboyant writing were etched on my mind, and the signature, Rev. Ezra Burroughs, sent a chill through me just thinking about it.

Once inside I bolted the door, sat down on an armchair, and finally gave way to the tears that had been threatening since I'd left Kandaipur by train three days earlier. The last few weeks had been a living nightmare. And the next phase of that nightmare was just about to begin.

I thought about Donald, far away on his military station on the North West Frontier, oblivious to everything I was going through. I'd written to tell him I was going home for a few weeks.

Donald's reply had arrived a few days later, written in his stiff, military handwriting. Like all his letters it was short and concise. As I read it, I had a clear picture of *him sitting at a table in his quarters in the officers' mess, in full uniform, his thinning hair neatly oiled, bending carefully to his task.*

How ironic then that I was embarking on this journey for him. I was doing it in order to preserve that shell of a marriage that we had constructed between us.

Sighing deeply, I took the letter from Ezra Burroughs out of my pocket and slipped it into the drawer beside the bed. Then I went over to the trunk that the porter had brought on board from the train, and opened the lid.

Manju had helped me pack the trunk. Her tear-stained face swam before my eyes now. She'd gripped my hand as we parted, and had said in a pleading voice, 'Please take great care, Memsahib. Come back very soon to Kandaipur. Please… for Manju.' It was the nearest she had got to saying that she understood why I was going, that she knew what I had done and what I was going to do.

On the top of the trunk lay a sumptuous smoking jacket wrapped carefully in tissue paper. I folded back the paper, ran my hand over the smooth cloth and sat back on my heels. It was of rich burgundy, of the finest quilted silk, made with exquisite skill by the Kandaipur tailor. He'd made it for a tall man, six foot one inches in height, forty-inch chest, broad-shouldered.

'He will expect a present or two from India, the Rev. Burroughs. A smoking jacket or something like that will probably do the trick,' I'd been told.

Looking at the jacket brought the events of the past few months back to me now, all too vividly. It was a physical reminder of everything that had happened. Lying there in its tissue paper, the luxurious garment seemed to rebuke me. I slammed down the lid of the trunk.

February 28th, 1934

The sea voyage from Bombay to Southampton is virtually at an end. I've hardly written in this little book since the day we embarked the SS Neuralia because I've been feeling so low and full of dread at what the coming weeks will bring.

Ezra Burroughs' letter said I should travel to Weirfield about a week before my due date. I need to write to him from Mother's and let him know when I'll arrive so he can arrange to collect me from the station. I don't think I'll be able to stand staying with Mother for the whole time, though. I've decided the best thing to do would be to book into a boarding house in a seaside town for the last month or so. Somewhere anonymous and a long way from Mother. I'm thinking of Torquay – it's easy to get there by train and I don't know a soul there.

There are only a couple of days left of this journey. We're almost at Gibraltar now, then it is only two days to Southampton. But that means crossing the Bay of Biscay. I remember the dreadful storms we had on the way out to India. The ship rolled and pitched in the most sickening way for hours on end. I had to retire to bed. I hope that doesn't happen on this voyage.

*

Sarah puts the diary down and wonders how long after this Anna was in Cedar Hall, sneaking down the coach house steps and coming face to face with Connie. Finally, the swaying motion of the train sends her off to sleep and she sleeps soundly until the steward wakes them for breakfast at seven o'clock.

At Kandaipur station Sarah helps her father off the train and they are immediately surrounded by a crowd of taxi drivers, touts and porters plying their trade.

'You want taxi?'

'You want hotel?'

'I take your bags. Very cheap price.'

'Where you go to? I show you nice place.'

Sarah strikes a bargain with one of the drivers, a portly man in a stained nylon safari suit. He has a kind face and promises to show them the best hotels in town.

'My name is Bharat,' he says as he guides them out through the din and clamour of the station entrance to a stately Ambassador taxi. He opens the back door of the car and with an elaborate gesture and bow invites them to sit on the scuffed leather seats.

'Do you know the Maybelle Hotel?' asks Sarah. She has read the name in Anna's diary. When they were at home her father had asked her to find it on the internet, but she had drawn a blank. She'd hoped that she'd be able to locate it once they arrived, so she hadn't booked anywhere to stay for this part of their trip.

'There are many, many beautiful hotels in Kandaipur,' says the taxi driver disapprovingly, wagging his head. 'I take you to Ananda Lodge instead. Very nice. Very clean place. Not expensive.'

'But do you know the Maybelle?' Sarah persisted. 'I don't mind paying extra if you'll take us there instead.'

'Maybelle is not called that any more. It is now called Mandaka Palace Hotel. OK, I take you there if you really want. But you might not like it. It's very old-fashioned hotel.' He pulls out of the station forecourt in the wrong gear, making the taxi shudder and jump. At the same time he winds down the window and spits a stream of betel-nut juice onto the road.

They drive along a shabby road of single-storey houses that leads towards the centre of town. The place has a run-down feel. The main street is crowded with ramshackle shops and businesses. People squat on pavements to do their cooking over open flames and the smell of food and spices drifts on the air. The road surface is full of potholes and the traffic proceeds at a crawl, with much blasting of horns and ringing of bells.

They pass a covered market, its once-grand pillars peeling and scabbed with age, its steps heavily stained with betel juice. Sarah realises with a jolt that this must be the bazaar where Anna first set eyes on Charles Perry.

The Maybelle Hotel has seen better days. They draw up onto a shabby drive. The once-grand building is in severe need of a lick of paint. The concrete pond in the centre of the drive is dry and filled with litter.

Inside the lobby, it feels a little better. The reception area is painted white with coloured floor tiles. It is high-ceilinged and airy, cooled by whirring overhead fans. The friendly young woman behind the desk assures them there are plenty of rooms available. They choose two adjoining rooms on the ground floor that open onto the garden. Bharat brings the luggage to the desk and stands beside it, waiting. Sarah pays him generously. He hovers around until they have finished checking in.

'Tomorrow, I take you out to see sights of area?' he asks eagerly. 'Many beautiful places to see here in Kandaipur and surrounding environs.' He smiles, revealing betel-stained teeth, and again wags his head from side to side as he speaks. 'Kandaipur is very quiet just now. Not many tourists about. Good time to see sights.'

Sarah glances enquiringly at her father, who shrugs and smiles. 'Why not?'

She clears her throat. 'There are a few things we're interested in seeing,' she says. 'Do you know the old British quarter, the cantonment?'

The driver raises his eyebrows. 'Of course. I know that area but there is nothing interesting to see there at all. It is very shabby. Only old buildings, some of them derelict. Overgrown gardens.'

'That's fine,' Sarah says firmly. 'We'd like to see it if you'll take us there. We're also interested in the British graveyard. Is there one in the town?'

'Of course. There is one. Like old cantonment quarter, it is quite overgrown now, but if you'd like to see it, I can take you there.'

'Excellent. Could we start around ten tomorrow then?'

The driver looks puzzled. 'You quite sure you don't want to see other places? What about wood-carving workshops? My brother owns one near here. Very interesting to see. Many cheap products to buy too.'

'No, thank you. At least not tomorrow anyway.'

'What about temples? Markets? I can take you to a palace in the hills. Thirty miles from here. Very beautiful. Former palace of maharajah. It is called summer palace.'

'The summer palace? Well, we'd love to see that. Perhaps the day after tomorrow?'

Bharat beams broadly, no doubt thinking how ridiculously easy it has been to secure their custom. Sarah doesn't mind about that. They are only here for a short while. There is not time for endless haggling and seeking out the best deal.

Like the rest of the hotel the rooms are a little shabby and old-fashioned, with heavy oak furniture and floral curtains and bedspreads. There is no air conditioning here, only ceiling fans. The bathroom in Sarah's room reminds her of the old one in Cedar Hall, with a huge bathtub stained with rust, and an old-fashioned lavatory with a high metal tank and chain that clanks and gurgles when it's pulled. But through patio doors she can see a beautiful lush garden, with palm trees, exotic shrubs and bright pink bougainvillea tumbling over the back wall.

That evening, they eat in the hotel dining room. They are the only guests but they are tired after their long journey and Sarah doesn't want to tire her father further by going out to eat. They are served by an elderly man dressed in a spotless white tunic. He has perfect manners and, to their surprise, speaks good English and is able to explain the menu to them. But the food is disappointing: greasy mutton curry with plain rice and cold vegetables. The old waiter sets it before them with such pride though, they don't have the heart to complain.

The next morning, the taxi crawls through the centre of town and out over the railway tracks and through some sparse suburbs, along a straight road where playing fields are laid out on one side and an army barracks on the other.

'Britishers built those barracks for British Indian Army,' says Bharat, nodding in their direction. 'Now they are used by Indian Army.'

They pass a parade ground, where a platoon of young soldiers stand to attention, being inspected by an officer strutting with a cane under his arm. Sarah thinks of Lieutenant Colonel Donald Foster. Perhaps this is the station where he once served. She wonders if he ever fulfilled his ambition to command the regiment.

The taxi takes a sharp turn left.

'This is old British area. Like I said, very run-down.'

'Do you know Dalhousie Road?' Sarah asks.

Bharat turns to her with a smile. 'Of course, madam. This is Dalhousie Road.'

The road surface is potholed here too and they proceed very slowly. Sarah and her father stare out at the crumbling bungalows, surrounded by either bare earth or overgrown gardens. Some are empty, but others appear to be inhabited by several families. Washing hangs on the balconies, people cook on open fires on the porches and children play in the front gardens.

'What a shame they haven't been maintained,' says her father.

'No one wants to live in these old places,' says Bharat. 'Inconvenient, damp. People prefer modern. Only very poor people live here now. Some of them are squatters.'

They reach the turning circle at the end of the road and there in front of them is a bungalow much larger than the rest. It is double-fronted and appears to have two wings at the back instead of one.

'That must be it,' her father says. 'I recognise it from the description in the diary. Could you stop please, Bharat?' There is suppressed excitement in his voice. 'I'd just like to have a quick look.'

The two of them get out, and stare at the rotting front gate. There it is, under the layers of mould on the top rung of the gate, a carved sign saying 'Connaught Lodge'.

'This is it,' her father says. They push back the fragile front gate and stare at the building before them. This one is boarded up and the garden so overgrown it is impossible to see where the lawn once might have been. There's mould growing on the outside walls and on the broken roof tiles. Weeds sprout from the gutter and along the front of the veranda in the cracks between the tiles.

'Be careful of snakes,' shouts Bharat and Sarah exchanges an exasperated glance with her father.

They go up the rickety front steps onto the wooden veranda. Several of the floorboards are missing, others soft with rot.

'This is where she used to sit,' says Sarah almost in a whisper. She glances at her father, who has tears in his eyes.

Sarah approaches the front door and peers through a crack between the boards.

There's not much light, but she can just about see into a big open room. A couple of dilapidated chairs stand in the middle of the room, and under the window an equally shabby chaise longue. They are covered with black dust. On one wall is a fireplace piled up with soot.

'Those must be her chairs,' her father says. 'Unless someone else had the place after them. It's hard to know.'

They return to the car, filled with thoughts of Anna and how she had once sat on that very veranda, staring out over the bare garden, eating her solitary breakfast, nursing her loneliness.

Sarah's father leans forward and speaks to Bharat.

'Do you think there is anyone in Kandaipur who remembers when the British were here?' he asks.

'I don't think so. I will ask around. It is a long time ago, though. Not many people that old. Now, where would you like to go next?'

'Do you know an old Baptist church a little way out of town?' Sarah asks. 'It is disused. Derelict for a long time, I think.'

He turns and smiles. 'Of course. I know this place. I take you there now.'

They drive out through more dusty suburbs, past streets of one-storey houses built of corrugated iron or wood, some on stilts along a riverbank. People stop what they are doing to stare as they pass. Bharat is right; hardly any tourists come to this town.

Once out on the plain the car picks up speed. Sarah leans out of the window to feel the cool wind in her hair and to see the view of the great mountains in the distance.

The church is a few miles out of town, along a narrow side road, past a couple of small settlements. They almost miss it, it is so overgrown, and all but hidden in a thicket of bamboo. Bharat pulls up in front of it and they get out.

Sarah crosses the road to get a better view. From this angle she can see that it is definitely the church in the painting that she first saw in Ezra Burroughs' study. The white paint is now obscured with moss and mould, part of the tower has fallen in and all the windows are broken.

'How sad that this place looks like this now,' she says.

'Do you know why it closed down?' her father asks Bharat.

'I hear stories,' he says. 'Many stories about the bad Englishman who used to run it.'

'What stories are those?'

'People say that he wanted money for everything. He forced the poor villagers he converted and who attended church to pay him money each week. A lot of money. He employed bad men to collect it from them. That is why he was sent back to England. After that, no one wanted to go to this church any more.'

'A sort of protection racket,' muses Sarah's father. 'No wonder the Baptists here had had enough of him!'

'Perhaps she sat here to draw the church?' Sarah suggests, noticing a low wall directly opposite.

'Yes, probably,' says her father, coming to stand next to her. 'You get a perfect view from over here.'

They sit for a while, remembering Anna, and although nothing is spoken aloud, the tears in her father's eyes say it all. She takes his hand, kisses him on the cheek.

They drive back into town, through the centre and out to the other side to the British graveyard. It's behind another church, but this one appears to be maintained and functioning. The graveyard itself is overgrown and neglected, just as Bharat had said, like so many things the British left behind in this town.

They start wandering between the headstones. The sun is high in the sky now and Sarah feels her shirt sticking to her body.

'Are you all right, Dad?' she asks, noticing him mopping his brow.

'I'm fine, thanks. I've got my hat.'

'You could always sit inside the church and I'll look round. I'll come and fetch you if I find anything.'

'No, it's all right. I want to look myself.'

Most of the graves are covered in creepers and moss. The grass between them is long. Sarah takes a stick and scrapes the moss from one of the gravestones. She reads the inscription out loud:

HERE LIES BERTHA MORGAN, BELOVED WIFE OF JOSEPH AND MOTHER TO TIMOTHY AND MARGARET. TAKEN FROM US TOO YOUNG, 9TH JANUARY 1926, AGED 35.

Next to Bertha are the graves of Timothy and Margaret, aged seven and nine. Sarah notices that they both died within a year of their mother.

'It's heartbreaking,' she whispers.

Many of the adults were young when they died too. Inscriptions like 'Taken from us suddenly by fever' are all too frequent.

'It was a dangerous place to live in those days,' says her father.

They go from grave to grave, peering at the epitaphs. Some of the graves have statues of angels or cherubs on top of them. Others are tall, decorated with elaborate stone crosses; yet others are inside full-sized crypts with metal doors.

They come to one with a statue of a lion standing on the top. The lion must have once been white but is now dark green with lichen and its once-proud nose is broken. Sarah's heart beats faster when she notices the engraving.

'Dad, look!' They peer at the headstone and read: CHARLES PERRY, DEVOTED PUBLIC SERVANT TO THE BRITISH CROWN AND WIDOWER OF ISOBEL. The date is 1955.

'That's your father, Dad,' says Sarah, staring at the grave. 'He must have stayed on after independence.'

Her father sits down on a pile of stones and puts his head in his hands. Sarah goes to him and puts her arms around him. She can feel his body shake as he sobs silently.

'It's overwhelming,' he says, his voice breaking. 'It's quite hard to take it all in.'

'Do you want me to carry on by myself?'

He nods his head. 'Just give me a moment.'

She leaves him and continues looking at the tombstones. There are no names she recognises from Anna's diary. She wonders what became of Mrs and Colonel Smethurst and the Napiers. Perhaps they went home to England after independence.

At last she finds it and her heart soars. She knows instinctively it's what she's been searching for. It's near the gate and she wonders how they can have walked past it without noticing it. It looks so different from the others.

This grave has no moss growing on it and someone has clipped the grass on top of it. The elegant but simple white marble stone is scrubbed clean and the gold letters have recently been painted. But most surprising of all, at the foot of the headstone is a bunch of fresh marigolds, arranged in a small glass vase.

The inscription on the gravestone is simple:

ANNA FOSTER, BELOVED WIFE OF DONALD, LT COL.
BORN BUCKINGHAMSHIRE MAY 7TH 1904,
DIED SUDDENLY OCTOBER 10TH 1934.

Chapter Thirty-Seven

Sarah

At the sight of the epitaph something catches in Sarah's throat and tears spring to her eyes.

'Dad, come here,' she calls urgently. 'It's here, Anna's grave. Come and look.'

He hurries to stand beside her. They hold hands and stare at the gleaming gold writing on the white marble.

'I can't believe it,' he says in an awed whisper. 'Look, she died in 1934. Only a few months after I was born.'

'That must explain it then,' Sarah says slowly.

'Explain what?'

'Why she didn't come back. Connie told me that she promised to, but that she never came. Connie waited for her for weeks, she couldn't understand it.'

'Why didn't you tell me that, Sarah?'

She turns to look into his eyes. She sees deep pain in them.

'I'm sorry, Dad, I didn't want to upset you, that's all. But now there's an explanation. She must have got ill and died quite soon after she got back to India. That's why she didn't come back to England.'

'So… she said she'd come back. For her baby? For me?'

'Yes. But she never made it.'

They're both silent for a while, thinking about Anna, dying so young and so far from her beloved baby. Sarah's father breaks the silence.

'Look… Look at the next grave.'

The grave to the right of Anna's is untended. The stone is green with mould from decades of monsoon rains. But despite that, Sarah can just make out the words carved into it: *LT COL DONALD FOSTER. BORN AUGUST 4TH 1884, DIED NOVEMBER 10TH 1936.*

'So, he died quite soon after Anna. And he never got to command the regiment after all. Poor Donald!'

'I wonder who looks after Anna's grave? It seems to be the only one in the whole churchyard that's cared for,' Sarah says.

'Perhaps someone can tell us. Shall we look inside the church? The vicar might be there.'

They wander in through the porch. How much like an English country church this is, thinks Sarah, only instead of the chill one normally gets on stepping in through a church door in England, here it is stiflingly hot and airless.

Inside is just like an English church with an altar, a pulpit, a covered font, rows of wooden pews. Sunlight streams in through the windows, lighting shafts of dust on the air.

Someone is sweeping the floor at the back of the church. It's an old man, bent with age. He glances at them shyly.

Sarah approaches him. 'Do you speak English?'

He shakes his head and looks as though he's about to scuttle away.

'I'll go and ask Bharat if he can help,' Sarah's father says and is back within seconds with the taxi driver.

'Could you ask this man if he knows who tends the grave beside the gate, please? The one with flowers on it?'

A stream of Hindi conversation passes between the two men. Then Bharat passes the sweeper a fifty-rupee note and turns to Sarah and her father.

'He says an old woman comes. She comes every Wednesday and every Saturday. She is very, very old indeed, but she never misses a day. He doesn't know where she lives, but she comes in a rickshaw. If you wait for her by the gate, she will probably appear in the next hour or so. She is bound to turn up then. He says she speaks good English.'

Sarah and her father go back to the taxi and sit there, hardly speaking, waiting breathlessly, waiting for the old woman to appear. Sure enough, forty minutes or so later, a rickshaw appears at the end of the road from the other direction and approaches the church. As it gets closer, Sarah can see that the passenger is an old woman. She wears a bright blue saree and her head is covered with a long pink scarf.

The rickshaw pulls up outside the gate and the rider, who himself looks fairly elderly, ambles round and helps the old woman down from the seat. She's carrying a shoulder bag over one arm and a bunch of marigolds in the other. She makes her way slowly through the gate and towards Anna's grave.

'Shall we go and talk to her now?' asks Sarah.

Her father shakes his head. 'Give her a little while.'

They wait another ten minutes or so, then Sarah gets out of the taxi.

'Are you coming, Dad?'

'You go first and explain why we're here. I'll come along in a moment.'

Sarah goes through the gate into the churchyard. The sun beats down on her back. The old woman is kneeling in front of the grave, clipping the grass with what look like tailor's shears.

'Excuse me,' Sarah says gently. The old woman looks up. Her face is heavily lined and she looks very frail, but when she sees Sarah approaching, her eyes light up and she smiles. Sarah notices the red tikka mark on her forehead and a gold ring through one side of her nose.

'Can I help you?' she asks.

'My name is Sarah Jennings. I believe that Anna Foster was my grandmother. I've come to Kandaipur with my father to see if we can find anything out about her. Did you know Anna?'

The old woman nods and gets to her feet slowly. She presses her hands together in a gesture of greeting.

'Namaste,' she says, bowing her head. 'I'm delighted to meet you. I never thought I would meet anyone related to her.'

'How did you know Anna, if you don't mind my asking?'

'She was my memsahib for two years,' the old woman says. 'My name is Manju.'

'Manju? Then you were her ayah when she first came to India. She wrote a lot about you in her diary.'

'Did she? Come close to me, madam. I need to see your face.'

Sarah moves closer and the old woman peers into her eyes, searching them with her own.

'Yes, I thought so. You have the look of her about you. Same dark hair. Same lovely eyes.'

'Really? Is that really true?'

'Yes, it is true. I thought that as soon as I saw you.'

'Do you think you could tell me about Anna? How she died, perhaps?'

'Of course. We should sit inside the church though. It is very hot out here.'

'I'll fetch my father.'

When Sarah's father reaches the church door, Manju takes his hand and smiles into his eyes.

'Anna's son. At last,' she says, her voice full of emotion.

Inside the church they sit on the front pew. Manju turns on a portable fan nearby and soon, the air starts to cool down.

'I have always tended her grave because I loved Mrs Foster. She was a beautiful, generous person and she was very kind to me,' she begins.

'What happened to Mrs Foster was a terrible thing…' Her face clouds over and she pauses, gathering her emotions, before going on. 'I knew she was leaving for England to have a baby and I tried to stop her from going, but she wouldn't listen to me, and when she came back, she was very sad. She had already decided to go back to England and fetch you.' She looks at Sarah's father.

'The night she was due to leave, she was waiting in the front room for Foster Sahib to come home. She had not yet told him of her plans. I could tell that she was afraid to tell him. Her face was pale and she was restless, walking to and fro, unable to sit still. He didn't come home until very late and I could see that he was drunk.' Again, the old lady pauses, dabs the corner of her eye with a handkerchief. She takes a deep breath before going on.

'I heard some shouting from the living room and I went and stood by the open door so I could hear what was said. I was so worried for Memsahib.'

'Foster Sahib was very angry. He said that the next day the General was coming to appoint a successor, and he wouldn't stand a chance without a wife by his side. He begged her to stay, but when she refused, he went up close to her.

'I was near enough to see real anger in his eyes, and when she told him what she had done, that she had had a child, and that it wasn't his, there was nothing any of us servants could do to stop him.

'I heard her head crack as she fell. She collapsed in front of the fireplace then, and he knelt down beside her, sobbing and crying, begging her to wake up, but she didn't move. I didn't dare approach him.

'I felt so sad for her baby – for you,' she says, looking at Sarah's father with deep regret, the tears in her eyes spilling over and rolling down her cheeks. 'But I didn't know where in England you were, and even if I had known, I couldn't have done anything.' She shakes her head and lets the tears fall.

Sarah glances at her father. He looks just as she feels. He is ashen-faced. They are both shaken, lost for words.

'I kept this. I often bring it with me when I tend Memsahib's grave. It helps me to feel close to her somehow. She was such a talented artist. Her personality is right there, in her pictures. I would like you to have it.'

She reaches into her bag and hands a battered sketchbook to Sarah's father. Sarah moves closer to him. The book is quite thick and has a red cardboard cover with a white panel in which is written, *Anna Baker. India, 1932.*

Sarah's father turns the pages slowly. The sketches are intricate and accurate, drawn with depth and great care. The first few are portraits of passengers on a liner, reclining in deckchairs or strolling along the deck. Each face or posture seems to convey something about the character of the subject. Then there is a study of the Gateway of India from Apollo Bunder and on the next page a sketch of a grand colonial house with pillars on both storeys.

'That must be Aunt Nora's house,' Sarah says. 'We drove past one that looks like that the other day in Mumbai, didn't we?'

There are many sketches of temples, Indian street scenes, grand British buildings in Kandaipur. There is also one of Anna's bungalow. After that, they come to a drawing of the derelict church. Sarah and her father exchange glances. It is unmistakeably Ezra's church, the one in the picture on Connie's wall; except in this one it is falling down, encroached on by undergrowth.

Then they come to a sketch of a shimmering lake surrounded by mountains, a couple of fishing boats on its smooth surface, followed by a drawing of an exotic palace, elaborately decorated and domed, its roofs glittering beneath a cloudless sky.

There are two more drawings left in the book. The first is of another English house, drawn from the rear. At first, Sarah doesn't recognise it and wonders why Anna drew it from this angle instead of from the front, and then she realises what it is.

'It's Cedar Hall, Dad. The back door and windows. And there's the conservatory at the side. She must have drawn it from the room above the coach house.'

'I think you're right. How extraordinary.'

The final drawing in the sketchbook takes their breath away. It's of a newborn baby swaddled in a knitted shawl, its face soft and puckered, a tuft of dark hair on its forehead, its eyes closed in a deep sleep.

'That's you, Dad,' says Sarah, a lump in her throat.

'It must be. I don't know what to say…' He looks at Sarah with tears in his eyes.

'And here is the photo of Anna Memsahib,' says Manju. 'I believe it was taken on her wedding day.' She dips into her bag again and hands them a small photograph. 'I carry this with me at all times.'

Sarah and her father stare at it in awe. The young woman who stares back at them is tall and slim. She's dressed in a figure-hugging white lace dress. Her dark hair is swept back off her face and into a loosely plaited bun in the nape of her neck. Her features are delicate and aquiline, with high cheekbones and full lips. Her soft dark eyes look straight at the camera. There is a sort of desperation in her expression, although she is smiling gently; she looks as if she's making a plea to the camera, a deep and moving plea for help.

When they finally say their goodbyes and heartfelt thanks to Manju, they promise to come back and visit her before they go home. They get back into the taxi. They sit in the back with the windows wide open and stare out at the rolling scenery. Occasionally, they glance at each other and smile.

As the taxi enters the foothills to the mountains and begins to climb, Sarah thinks about Matt. Something subtle has changed inside her now she's heard Anna's tragic story and seen her photograph. A page seems to have been turned in her own personal history, a missing piece of her jigsaw finally put in place. Perhaps that is what she was subconsciously waiting for? Perhaps that was what was stopping her from accepting Matt's love and the happiness a future with him would bring?

As the taxi crests the ridge and begins its descent down a narrow gorge she makes her decision. After a few miles, the mountains

ecome gentler and the valley begins to open out. Sarah leans out of
he window and sees ahead a vast shimmering lake, its crystal-clear
waters reflecting the craggy hills that surround it. As the road begins
to skirt the edge of the lake, she gets a glimpse of the outline of
he palace at the far end. She catches her breath. As they get closer,
he can make out its Moorish domes and crenelated arches and
pires; closer still, she can see the detail of its elaborate masonry.
he turns to her father with shining eyes and he takes her hand.

A Letter from Ann

I want to say a huge thank you for choosing to read *The Orphan House*. If you did enjoy it, and want to keep up to date with all my latest releases, just sign up at the following link. Your email address will never be shared and you can unsubscribe at any time.

www.bookouture.com/ann-bennett

I hope you loved *The Orphan House* and if you did, I would be very grateful if you could write a review. I'd love to hear what you think, and it makes such a difference helping new readers to discover one of my books for the first time.

I love hearing from my readers – you can get in touch on my Facebook page, through Twitter, Goodreads or my website.

Thanks,
Ann

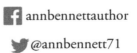 annbennettauthor

@annbennett71

Acknowledgements

I would like to thank my friend and writing buddy Siobhan Daiko for her enormous support and encouragement over the years; many others who've patiently read, reviewed and commented on my manuscripts, particularly Helen Judd; all my sisters, especially Mary, for her helpful comments over our lunches in Westminster.

I'd also like to thank my husband, Nick Rann, and our sons, Ollie, Will and Jamie, for putting up with me spending so much time at this task. Huge thanks to Jennifer Hunt at Bookouture for believing in this story, and of course, to everyone who has taken the time to read my books, review them or contact me with their thoughts. That's what's kept me going!